PRAISE FOR

THE JESSICA DARLING SERIES

"Comic and wise . . . Irresistible."

—*Miami Herald*

"Judy Blume meets Dorothy Parker."

—*The Wall Street Journal*

"McCafferty looks at teen travails with humor as well as heart."

—*People*

"A springboard for McCafferty's hilarious pop culture riffs . . . The series has won her a legion of fans, from teens and college students to twentysomethings, mothers, and the occasional grandmother."

—*The Star-Ledger*

"Witty, insightful, and a good read for anyone between the ages of 15–99."

—*Ottawa Sun*

"McCafferty's debut novel became a crossover hit, equally touching teenagers and adults nostalgic about their youth. . . . [A]n exhilarating and genuine take on teendom."

—*Boston Herald*

"Smart and accomplished enough to delight all readers. Jessica's an original, but her problems are universal, and McCafferty is formidably adept at channeling her self-deprecating, wise-guy voice. If you don't see yourself in Jessica Darling, you're not looking hard enough."

—*Chicago Tribune*

"Portrays teenaged life so accurately, you can forget about putting this one down."

—*Toronto Sun*

"It's Jessica, her wit and, especially, her utterly droll take on life, that draws readers (fans of the series include adult women as well as teens) into McCafferty's books. Entirely too smart for her own good, Jessica offers brilliant and cutting insights into the world of the adolescent about-to-be-a-woman."

—*Chicago Sun-Times*

"The snappy writing, au courant wordplay, and easy-to-relate-to plot turns will keep eager teens—and teens-at-heart—turning the pages."

—*Publishers Weekly*

"Surprisingly mature and witty . . . Should snag more than a few adult readers."

—*Kirkus Reviews*

"This genre at its best; it's literature full of life, unique voices, and unforgettable characters."

—*The Harvard Crimson*

"This charming series will appeal to both the young-adult crowd and women who like to look back and remember."

—New York *Daily News*

"Boy, do I wish Megan McCafferty had been writing books about high school when I was young and foolish and insecure. But even now, at my advanced age, I get a huge kick out of the bright, wickedly funny, and cheerfully off-color observations of Jessica Darling."

—*Miami Herald*

"Smart, tentative, and funny, Jessica is a likable and wry observer of the competitive, gossipy high-school world."

—*Booklist*

ALSO BY MEGAN McCAFFERTY

Sloppy Firsts

Second Helpings

Fourth Comings

Perfect Fifths

Bumped

Thumped

The Mall

CHARMED THIRDS

A Jessica Darling Novel

MEGAN McCAFFERTY

WEDNESDAY BOOKS
NEW YORK

Published in the United States by Wednesday Books, an imprint of St. Martin's Publishing Group

CHARMED THIRDS. Copyright © 2021 by Megan McCafferty. Foreword copyright © 2021 by Rebecca Serle. All rights reserved. Printed in the United States of America. For information, address St. Martin's Publishing Group, 120 Broadway, New York, NY 10271.

www.wednesdaybooks.com

Designed by Devan Norman

Library of Congress Cataloging-in-Publication Data

Names: McCafferty, Megan, author.
Title: Charmed thirds : a Jessica Darling novel / Megan McCafferty.
Description: First Wednesday Books edition. | New York : Wednesday Books, 2021. | Series: Jessica Darling ; 3 | Audience: Ages 13–18.
Identifiers: LCCN 2021015647 | ISBN 9781250781833 (trade paperback) | ISBN 9781250781840 (ebook)
Subjects: CYAC: Friendship–Fiction. | Universities and colleges—Fiction. | Dating (Social customs)—Fiction. | Internship programs—Fiction.
Classification: LCC PZ7.M47833742 Ch 2021 | DDC [Fic]—dc23
LC record available at https://lccn.loc.gov/2021015647

Our books may be purchased in bulk for promotional, educational, or business use. Please contact your local bookseller or the Macmillan Corporate and Premium Sales Department at 1-800-221-7945, extension 5442, or by email at MacmillanSpecialMarkets@macmillan.com.

First published in the United States in 2006 by Three Rivers Press, an imprint of the Crown Publishing Group, a division of Random House, Inc., New York.

First Wednesday Books Edition: 2021

10 9 8 7 6 5 4 3 2 1

FOR ALL THE FACES IN MY COLLEGE
PHOTO ALBUMS—
EVEN THE ONES I CAN'T REMEMBER,
BUT ESPECIALLY THOSE I COULDN'T
FORGET

foreword

Sloppy Firsts was published in 2001, barely a month shy of 9/11. Jessica Darling—a precocious, sexually curious, fast-talking teenage girl—spun into a world in turmoil. Schools the country over watched the towers fall, understanding that for many, for the first time, tragedy in life and country were unavoidable. A place that had felt so safe—America, *home*—changed practically overnight.

It's been twenty years, and today's teens face their own crisis of country. Progress, as we've seen, bends slowly, doubles back, barrels forward. Teens take up the fight. In many ways, they are on the front lines: the future belongs to them, to *you—yes, you—* after all.

So let's talk about Jessica, shall we? I first came to Ms. Darling my sophomore year of college. Like thousands before me, I was immediately taken with Jessica's voice. This overly average girl who was anything but. Like our queen Judy Blume, Megan McCafferty draws a young woman who is unafraid of her own sexuality. Who is curious, intrigued, and annoyed by the culture of high school. Who wants to be extraordinary, but who also understands and acknowledges her own singular existence. She is no more than a high school girl. And yet—what could possibly be more powerful?

Then there's Marcus Flutie. Jessica and Marcus, Marcus and Jessica. The most perfect teenage boyfriend of all time—and the biggest fuckup (I feel like I'm allowed to swear here). The stoner kid who needs Jessica's pee (literally), and who ends up being her greatest teacher and her greatest love. Throughout the five books, we get to see not only a real, true, deep, often tragic first love, but we also get to see the anatomy of a relationship. We get to question, along with Jessica, whether first love is forever love. And whether, in fact, love itself is enough. Marcus and Jessica's relationship is never trivial, and never trivialized. Not the way they speak to each other, not the pain they feel at sometimes being apart, not the way they have sex. It's part of the reason Jessica Darling continues to appeal to adults—some of us, now, on the better side of thirty. We could all learn a thing or two from the way these two love.

Throughout the course of *Sloppy Firsts*, *Second Helpings*, *Charmed Thirds*, *Fourth Comings*, and *Perfect Fifths*, we journey with Jessica Darling from fifteen to twenty-five. We watch the world change with her. She moves to New York, a city on the brink of rehabilitation. She tries to seek employment in a tough economic time. She gets a cell phone. Her world doesn't include Twitter or Instagram. There is no Uber, or Netflix, and yet—Jessica Darling is more relatable than ever. Why?

It's simple: the specific is the universal. The more immediately you can write a character's existence, mind, heart, life, the more universal it will feel to the reader. Because in order to inhabit the world, we first need to inhabit ourselves. When we meet Jessica, she is a teenage girl uncomfortable in her own skin. When we leave her, she's a young woman on the cusp of adulthood. Just like progress, the trajectory of Jessica's growth is not linear.

She is, arguably, the most lost of all when we see her in *Perfect Fifths*, the final book. But there is always the sense that the story the universe is telling—no matter how tangential the plot may get—ultimately does have meaning. That there is a humor and reason to why things unfold the way they do. That sometimes the moment when all hope is lost is the exact moment when your life begins to change.

Jessica Darling is a time capsule of her era—but she's also a timeless figure. A feminist, a leader, a daughter, a best friend. I have no doubt that in another two decades we will still be laughing and crying and swooning inside these pages. I'm jealous of everyone experiencing Jessica for the first time. Congratulations, Megan, on twenty years. And thank you, Jessica, for still being a friend. This thing is forever (whatever).

Love,
Rebecca Serle

freshman summer
june 2003

Dear Hope,

Whoever said that you can't go home again was wrong. You *can* go home again. Just don't be surprised when it totally sucks.

And so, I wait for the express bus to Pineville, New Jersey. To fake-and-bake salons and acrylic talons. To Confederate-flagged pickups. To DWI guys with suspended licenses pedaling their fat asses on tiny bicycles. To the cross-breeding of Pineys and bennies. To certain death by cerebral asphyxiation.

To home, bitter home.

I'm exhausted from dragging myself and two duffel bags down to 42nd Street. I took the subway, of course; it only *feels* like I trudged seventy-four blocks on foot. The first time I left Columbia's campus for the Port Authority bus terminal—almost six months ago, for winter break—I thought there would be a waiting area with a section of seats attached to TV sets bolted into the floor and I'd be able to pay a quarter for a sitcom or half a talk show. At this point, I'm so brain-dead and bored that I'd pay ten dollars for thirty minutes if Jerry Springer had guests who degraded themselves in an entertaining way. Could I be so self-centered as to blame the homeless for ruining this pleasure for the rest of us?

Is this an example of how New York City has made me as callous as Marcus fears I've become?

(A parenthetical anecdote to prove otherwise: Stubby is a homeless man who sings Motown songs on a patch of sidewalk near the gothic wrought iron gates separating the relentless bustle of 116th and Broadway from the relative calm of College Walk. He's short, as befits his name, and Black.

He could be twenty-five or seventy-five. He's always wearing some form of Columbia University apparel—shorts and a T-shirt in spring, a wool varsity-style jacket and sweatpants in winter—surely donated by someone affiliated with the school. He's there every day, clutching a grubby faux-Grecian WE ARE HAPPY TO SERVE YOU paper coffee cup, singing classic tunes like "My Girl," "I Can't Help Myself," and "Ain't Too Proud to Beg," the last of which is sung with a hint of irony. What once must have been a caramel-smooth tenor has been ravaged by misfortune. Everyone here knows Stubby; he's as much of a campus presence as the grand statue of Alma Mater on the steps of Low Library. I've never passed him without putting at least a nickel in his cup, usually more. But that's not the compassionate part. One day last winter, Stubby wasn't in his spot. A bit worrisome, sure, but I tried not to think about it because it was during midterms and I had five thousand pages of reading to catch up on. The next day, another absence. And then another. As his no-shows accumulated, I got more upset. Was Stubby dead? Had he frozen to death? ODed? I would've asked my friends if they'd seen him around, but they all seemed too preoccupied to panic about anything unrelated to academics. Finally, about a week later, on the morning of my Art Hum exam, Stubby was back in his spot. He looked and sounded the same as always: *R-E-S-P-E-C-T! Find out what it means to me!* I remember wanting to ask where he had disappeared to, but I decided to R-E-S-P-E-C-T his privacy. I popped five dollars in his cup that morning, which was a considerable percentage of my personal assets and therefore excuses me from any accusations that I'm just a spoiled Ivy Leaguer trying to pay off my liberal guilt. Then I took my exam and got an A.

See? I *do* care about people! I *am* compassionate about the plight of the homeless! I'm going to close parentheses now before the contents get any more self-serving.)

So far I've taken the NJ Transit #76 Shore Points Express for two reasons: holidays; and aid in nutritional or laundry-related emergencies, specifically, too little of one and too much of the other. On the laundry-related bus trips, I experienced the novelty of being the Port Authority passenger who no one wants to sit next to, as two duffels' worth of moldy clothes made me an even less desirable neighbor than the unlit cigar-chewing old-timer with the spooky glass eye who continually requested help with his *TV Guide* crossword puzzle.

As usual, I've allotted myself too much time for the type of mass-transit travel delays that only seem to occur when I'm not prepared for them. So with nothing else to do, I've spent money I can't afford to squander. I blew $3.80 on a speckled black-and-white composition notebook to match the dozen or so speckled black-and-white composition notebooks that I have exclusively used for my journals since, well…since you moved a thousand miles to Tennessee in tenth grade. I don't even know why I bought it though, since my old one still has ten blank pages, and I hope that seeing Marcus for the first time since mid-January won't provide more than ten pages of angst.

Speaking of, I promise you'll get more mail from me once Marcus and I are reunited. You've been very kind not to remind me that I haven't been sticking to our **Totally Guilt-Free Guidelines for Keeping in Touch.** Especially when you wrote monthly, called weekly, emailed/IMed daily, and *still* found time to emerge as one of the most promising visual artists in the history of the Rhode Island School of Design. (I know you hate hype, but those black-and-white portraits of "notable nobodies" from your "(Extra)Ordinary" photography project were so tragicomically brilliant—even as mere JPEGs via email.) I'll redeem myself over the next few months, you'll see. You escaped more than three years ago, but I still consider you an honorary member of Pineville High's Class of 2002 (a dubious honor, that). I'm sure you can't wait to hear all about the former classmates I'll try—and fail—to avoid all summer.

So, yes, I've been the hetero-female variation of pussy whipped. I wrote to Marcus so much this past year that it was hard to find time to write to you too. (And while I'm making excuses, I'll also mention how I actually had to apply myself for the first time in my academic career.) I'd like to apologize, but I won't, and not just because a lack of contrition provides the very foundation of the Guilt-Free Guidelines. You know me well enough to recognize that I'm in agony anyway because it's been a looooooooooooong time since I've enjoyed more than the—ahem!—figurative effects of my sexually spellbound condition...

Dickwhippedly yours,
J.

To: jdarling@columbia.edu
From: flutie_marcus@gakkai.edu
Date: May 31st, 2003
Subject: Poetry Spam #21

furious flutter

awakened hummingbird heart

hello hello love

—Original Message—

From: Joe Mailbiz [zihxziwkyg@mailbiz.com]
Sent: May 30th, 2003
To: flutie_marcus@gakkai.edu
Subject: hello objectify simmer tenement checklist

roadway hunk mat freudian mischievous buckboard love guber-
natorial snuggle cretin flatulent furbish quantity furious seven-
tieth controlled con tireless stereoscopy hummingbird lunch
mutineer fourth dialysis backlash concur triumphal percus-
sive allotting coxcomb desist copter aforesaid percent income
causation frilly incorporate awakened crosslink bleach apol-
lonian skullcap suspend betray ethel adjourn inhibition heart
consider fell pride compose foster dope inviolate flutter assuage
chock whale singlehanded sawtooth condescend sunshiny con-
note dehumidify prissy hello

the first

I keep rereading Marcus's latest haiku, printed out precisely for this purpose. How did he come up with Poetry Spam? Where did he get the idea to turn his junk email into poems? I marvel at his talent for revealing the hidden beauty in ordinary things.

I miss him and I know he misses me too.

There's nowhere to sit in the Port Authority unless you buy something. I got booted from Au Bon Pain because I stupidly disposed of my four-dollar shot glass of orange juice. The eagle-eyed garbage guard informed me that I was no longer allowed to occupy one of the umbrellaed tables. I left, dejected and dehydrated.

I'm now at Timothy's World Coffee, where there are no open indoor umbrellas to bring me bad luck. I'm sitting on a stool, breaking in my new journal, trying to take teeny-tiny sips from my overpriced bottle of Poland Spring water just so I can preserve my right to be here. I'm broke, and there aren't any water fountains for free, germ-ridden refills.

This is bad because I can chug gallons at a time. Accutane sucks every drop of moisture out of my body. I am one large flake of dandruff. The corners of my mouth are split open and bleeding, and I have to spread Carmex beyond my lip line, which makes me look like I've spent the morning sucking on a stick of butter. I hope that by the time I see Marcus my lips won't be so crusty/greasy.

Sahara skin and lips are just two of Accutane's side effects. According to the information booklet, I SHOULD BE ALERT FOR ANY OF THE FOLLOWING:

- DIARRHEA, RECTAL BLEEDING
- SEVERE HEADACHES
- NAUSEA, VOMITING
- CHANGES IN MOOD

Well, if suffering from diarrhea, rectal bleeding, severe headaches, nausea, and vomiting doesn't swing your mood in *some* direction, nothing will. Because my mood crests and crashes just fine on its own, I went on Accutane only at my mother's insistence. As a firm supporter of any and all advancements in the cosmetic sciences, she believes that not providing one's child with flawless skin is akin to child abuse. Accutane cured Len Levy, who was covered in pissed-off, purple pustules back in high school, so it should work for me. My acne isn't nearly as all over and angry as his was, but I have to agree with my mother when she points out how my complexion is never completely clear. I always seem to have one knotty cyst somewhere on my face, and when it goes away, another takes its place. One after the other after the other.

My daily dose of Accutane is the standard prescription for a person twice my weight. Three squishy yellow pills. This is my third cycle of the drug—the first two times didn't work—and I felt strangely proud when my doctor said that in twenty-five years of practicing dermatology, he had never seen such resilient zits. I'm a medical freak of nature.

I'd like to think that Marcus would call me unique.

Dr. Rosen also says my condition is stress related. No surprise there. Two weeks ago, I wrote four term papers and filled nine blue books over the course of five exams. In the midst of finals, I impulsively (and stupidly) chopped off my ponytail to get rid of my elastic band scalp-ache. The fix-it-up Supercut was supposed to give me a short geek-chic bob with bangs, kind of like Jordan in *Real Genius*. But with my hair's trademark flyaway frizziness, I look more like Mitch. The only upside to this coif-tastrophe is that in my state of scalp-ache-free concentration, I nailed a 3.85 GPA for the semester, which will make my parents happy, though only temporarily so. While my stellar grades help better my chances of postgraduation financial solvency, they do little to relieve my current money troubles. My parents give me minimal fiscal assistance because, in their own words, I made the choice to go into debt by selecting Columbia over my full scholarship to Boatwright University. I still stand by my choice, though less passionately now that I have a much better idea of how long it will take to pay Sallie Mae the $100,000 I'll owe for my BA by the time I graduate. Not to mention the cost of the MA and PhD I'll have to get if I want my undergraduate psychology degree to be worth anything at all. I've only got about half a semester's worth of my grandmother's inheritance left and zero summer moneymaking prospects because no well-paying employer is willing to hire me, train me, then let me leave for the entire month of July for my incredible, albeit totally unpaid internship at *True* magazine. During my salary-free servitude, I'll be staying in New York with my sister, Bethany (with whom I have nothing but DNA in common); her husband, G-Money (who has earned his nickname through gaining and losing millions on the stock market, yet still having enough spare scratch to buy into a local frozen custard and donut franchise in the hope of taking it national); and my niece, Marin (who is very cute, but has projectile-pooping issues), enduring yet another separation from a boyfriend I haven't seen or touched for six months, one who lives down the hall from a nudist Buddhist (Nuddhist?) named Butterfly who thinks clothing is oppressive and can't understand why people think nakedness always has to be sexual . . .

So. Stress? *Naaaaaaaaah.*

Sitting in the booth in front of me is a cutesy young couple still in the honeymoon phase of their relationship. Or they're lovers recently reunited. They're annoying to everyone who isn't them and haven't stopped pecking each other's faces since they sat down. Back and forth and back and forth across the booth, peck and peck. I prefer juicy tongues to these passionless kisses that are as dry as my needy lips.

I just tried Marcus on my cell. Topher, one of his "cottage-mates," told me he was out "cleansing." He told me this the way other roommates at other schools would say someone is out getting shit-faced. Marcus's world is so foreign to me that I can't help but feel that the person who inhabits it is a stranger. I love when I reach Marcus on the phone and as he says hello, I can hear the music he's listening to in the background. That music is the sound of him without me. How he surrounds himself when I'm not there, which is almost all the time.

And will be for three more years.

the seventh

'm sitting in the room that was my bedroom for the first eighteen years of my life. It's still called my room, but it really isn't my room anymore despite all the evidence to the contrary. The John Hughes movie posters are curling up at the corners yet are still mostly stuck to the bruise-colored walls. The plaques and trophies with my name inscribed in celebratory script still topple over one another on the shelves. And the framed mosaic of Hope and me—made by the artist herself and given to me on the day she moved, eighteen days before my sixteenth birthday—is still in its showcase spot over my bed. When packing for college, I intentionally left these things behind in Pineville, just so I could return to someplace that felt like home.

But after nine months at school, I'm seeing this room and its contents through a haze of psychological, if not actual, dust. It's like examining the artifacts found at an archaeological dig, where I can study the CD player on which Jessica Darling once listened to Morrissey, or the desk at which she once completed her college applications. The carpet on which she once failed to twist herself into impossible positions during her brief flirtation with yoga, or the skinny bed on which she once succeeded in twisting herself into the very quietest of possible sexual positions with her boyfriend while her parents sat downstairs on opposite sides of the Ultrasuede couch watching a Tom Hanks movie.

And yet, my dorm room, which was decorated in much the same way, isn't my room anymore either. I'm a refugee, one seeking asylum from my niece Marin's first birthday party.

Make that her *second* first birthday party. My parents insisted on throwing a soiree for Marin's "New Jersey friends." Bethany and G-Money failed to persuade any city folk to come out to our "house in the country," a seventies bi-level in a bi-level/split-level subdivision that my mom describes as possessing "a retro charm, with every modern amenity" when talking it up to her real estate associates. That means the architectural ugliness is redeemed only by new wood siding, extensive landscaping, and upgraded kitchen and baths.

But Jersey being Jersey, nothing could lure the New York City hip-ocracy that make up B&G's social circle, not even their offer to charter a luxury bus equipped with TVs for every seat, all tuned to Nick Jr. (They could afford such an extravagance now that they're conspicuously rich again, as five new Papa D's Donuts/Wally D's Sweet Treat Shoppe drive-throughs are already in the black. Not that they were ever *poor*, even after a dot-bomb comeuppance.) They ended up hosting a party last weekend for Marin's "New York friends," one dozen Benetton babies from Brooklyn's hippest family-friendly neighborhoods, all dressed in miniature versions of their parents' outfits. Girls: Lilly Pulitzer sundresses. Boys: seersucker suits worn "ironically" with tiny Che Guevara T-shirts. In her first year of life, Marin has somehow managed to acquire more friends than I have in nineteen.

Equally disturbing was Marin's insistence on having a Pinky

the Poodle theme party, inspired by her favorite television program. Not only has this sunshine-blond, deep-dimpled one-year-old developed a definite preference for one cartoon character over another, but she can clearly express her love by screeching, *"PEE! POO! PEE! POO!"* The thought of this picture-perfect child embarrassing her mommy with these seemingly scatological outbursts makes me weep fewer tears about my losing battle to improve my niece's intellectual fate.

In keeping with the theme, her grandparents (my parents) hired a neighborhood kid to dress up as the shopping- and shoes-obsessed canine. The costume can be best described as a fifty-pound fur ball. It's ninety-five degrees and chunky with humidity, so who can blame the kid for not showing up for this humiliation? And take one guess who's the only one who fits into this fuzzy pink prison. Suffice it to say that Pinky's trademark tap routine to her theme song ("I'm the Prettiest Quadruped!") was less inspired than usual. Try as I might, I just couldn't lift my weighty paws high enough.

"Do the kicks, Jessie—I mean Pinky!" my mother shouted from the sidelines. "One, two, three!"

"Boooooooooooooooooooooooo!" the ankle biters wailed as they pelted me with Jelly Bellies.

"No! No! No!" Bethany chastised the toddlers with a wag of her finger. "We are *not* unkind to animals!"

Oh, thank you, Bethany. Thank you.

Then she turned to me. "Come on, Pinky! Shake that tail of yours!" She twitched her juicy peach of an ass, almost obscenely perfect in a denim miniskirt. Often mistaken for Marin's au pair, my sister is the textbook definition of a MILF. If I had it in me to lift my hind leg, I would've pissed on her.

My father was the only one who seemed concerned for my health. "Take it easy on her," he said. "Jessie's not in the peak physical condition she used to be, back when she was a serious athlete." Christ. It's been two years since I gave up competitive running, and he still can't resist any opportunity to remind everyone of my deteriorating muscle mass. Of course, he himself was still spandexed and sweaty from a ninety-minute bike ride because dangerous weather is never a deterrent for one of his yellow-jersey jaunts around town.

And so, I wasn't driven to my room (which doesn't feel like my room) by the heckling or heat exhaustion or even anaphylactic shock from an allergy to synthetic poodle fur. I'm here because I had forgotten just how much I can simultaneously love and hate these people called my family. When I was at school, I kind of missed them. Not as actual people, but for their comfortable predictability. My dad always asks if I'm still wasting my time with my psychology major or if I get bored clocking seven-minute miles around Columbia's one-tenth-of-a-mile indoor track. My mom always asks if every girl at school dresses like a lesbian. Bethany always asks if I've gone to some invitation-only velvet-roped club. G-Money always ignores me because he's too busy coming up with new and creative ways to profit from the recession-proof futures market of American sugar addiction.

I've gotten so used to these and similar familial annoyances that I wouldn't know how to react if my family members didn't play their parts. Plus, I'm always more forgiving of their flaws when I'm still in the thrall of the hygienic and nutritional comforts of home. Here, I not only have unlimited access to a washer and dryer but a willing laundress who skillfully separates the darks from the whites and folds them up for me when they're finished. Here, the cabinets are stocked with genuine Cap'n Crunch—not the generic Colonel Crunchies bought by the ton at SaveCo. Here, the fridge overflows with Coke Classic.

But now that I've enjoyed a few weeks' worth of April freshness and a steady intake of vitamins and minerals, it's getting more difficult to overlook the tension created by what has been the most controversial subject in the household. Rather, it's a nontopic, one so taboo that it never gets brought up at all, as is customary in the Darling household.

Only once Marin had been scooped up by her doting Granny Darling and swept across to the other side of the yard did Bethany break the silence.

"I've been dying to ask you," Bethany said, flipping her golden hair, puckering and unpuckering her glossy lips. Sometimes I wonder if she realizes that she's flirting with her own sister. "Did you win the money?"

That's her way of asking if Marcus and I are still together. Only Bethany is brave enough to ask that which can't be asked. And even she waits until my mom is out of earshot and hides behind a euphemism referring to the money up for grabs in the Breakup Pool. Since I didn't document this (or anything else) for myself this year, I will explain the rules of said pool.

I was one of a few lucky first-years to score a sunny, spacious single in Furnald, which is arguably the most beautiful, most conveniently located dorm on campus. Built in 1913, it was renovated less than ten years ago, so it's both traditional (with its granite façade and soaring, crystal-chandeliered oak entry hall) and state-of-the-art (air-conditioned!). It's got views of the campus action on one side and of Broadway's hustle on the other. Furnald is also known as a bit of a party dorm, with each floor boasting an expansive lounge that lures even the most antisocial A-types away from their rooms with ample afternoon sunlight, cushy furniture, and free cable TV.

On my floor, there were fifteen first-years and ten sophomores. It was quickly discovered that most of the first-years on my floor were still involved in high school relationships. It wasn't difficult to figure out who the ten were, as they (okay, by "they" I really mean "we," but I hate to admit to this type of behavior) often began sentences with the phrase, "My boyfriend/girlfriend . . ." As in "My boyfriend loves Coldplay too!" or "My boyfriend has a sweater like that too!" or "My boyfriend eats and sleeps and excretes waste too!" Since no upperclassman would ever, ever, *ever* put a confining label like boyfriend or girlfriend on the person they were hooking up with on a semiregular basis, it was obvious that anyone making such a bold declaration of commitment was referring to a youthful union forged in the halls of their former high school.

The world-weary sophomores all looked at us with contempt. "You won't make it through fall break," they said. "And if you do, you're just doing it to prove us wrong."

Of course, we of the High School True Love Society were outraged. "We're different!" we all said. "We're not like the rest of them!"

Thus, the Breakup Pool was born. I can't remember who came up with it first, but F-Unit perfected it. F-Unit is a group of guys all enrolled in the Fu Foundation School of Engineering, who want to break the stereotype that all engineering students are nerds. Of course, F-Unit's bad boy engineers spend an inordinate amount of time on projects like the Breakup Pool because they don't have girlfriends themselves, which does little to thwart the nerd stereotype.

RULES OF THE BREAKUP POOL

1. Participants in the Breakup Pool are restricted to those residing on the fifth floor of Furnald during the 2002–2003 school year. Couples composed of a First-Year student and a High School Beloved (HSB) are referred to as Daters. Single First-Years and Sophomores participating in the Breakup Pool are referred to as Haters.

2. After paying a $25.00 entry fee, bettors are asked to predict which of the ten couples will last the longest, thereby winning the title of the Couple That Outlasted All Others and Showed the Haters Who Said That High School Relationships Don't Last.

3. Daters cannot bet on themselves. (A rule designed to prevent Daters who have grown to detest their insignificant other from sticking it out just for the cash.) However, any mercenary Dater doubtful of the strength of their own relationship can pay a $25.00 fee to bet on another couple's union outlasting theirs.

4. Daters in the Breakup Pool are asked to operate on the honor system, by which it is the Dater's responsibility to report any breakups or hookups with anyone other

than the HSB. (Second-person eyewitness testimony
will also suffice.) For the purposes of the Breakup Pool,
the term "hookup" refers to activities including, but not
limited to, kissing, oral and manual stimulation, intercourse, and any other physical activity that is generally
considered to be more than platonic.

5. If only one bettor puts money on the last couple standing, they win it all. Should more than one bettor choose
correctly, they split the take. In both cases, the Couple That Outlasted All Others and Showed the Haters
Who Said That High School Relationships Don't Last
doesn't win any money, but proudly wears said title.

6. If *no one* bets on the Couple That Outlasted All Others
and Showed the Haters Who Said That High School
Relationships Don't Last, the winning Dater keeps *all*
the cash, but only when their relationship makes it to
the end of the 2002–2003 school year. (Otherwise, all
bettors get their money back.) Likewise, if there is *more
than one* Dater still in the running at the end of the
spring semester, the money is split evenly among the
remaining couples. (These rules seemingly contradict
rules #3 and #5, but it is widely accepted that any Dater
desperate enough to stick with a detested insignificant
other for an entire year deserves a piece of the prize.)

Once the rules were established, F-Unit created odds using
ancillary data, such as geographical distance between Dater
and HSB and length of the relationship before separation. (They

wanted to include other variables that could help determine the probability that one would be led astray, but "hotness" and "horniness" were too difficult to quantify.) The odds wouldn't affect the payout but were devised merely to enhance the gaming experience.

Marcus was my first love and my first sex partner. I was his first love and his something-somethingth sex partner. We were together only two weeks before he left for California. I have done one tab of ecstasy and attend one of the most acclaimed universities in the world. He has smoked enough pot to be put in the High Times Hall of Fame and is attending Gakkai College, an unaccredited Buddhist school at which it is possible to major in chanting and purification. He was best friends with my best friend Hope's brother, Heath, whose heroin overdose was the tragic catalyst for her parents' sudden defection to Tennessee on the eve of Y2K. Our convoluted courtship was rife with his contradictions: He made out with his girlfriend but kept his eyes on me as I passed them in the hallway. He wrote seductive poetry but claimed he didn't want to sleep with me. He acted as Cyrano for his best friend, Len, telling him exactly what he should do and say to win me over, but shed a single tear when I obliged. He confessed that I was the woman who changed his life but chose to go as far away from me as he possibly could within the continental United States.

No wonder our odds were a hundred to one.

Yet, despite the promise of a full payout, no one bet on us. I thought they were all suckers. I was certain we would stay together. Marcus and I had been through so much that our lasting union seemed like the only logical reason for it all.

I wasn't tempted to stray. I mean, there were a few guys at

Columbia who were the geek cute kind of guy I go for. But—oh!—those bright-eyed, death-cab cuties, I didn't even get a chance to be dashbored by them all. Because they weren't just *my* type, they were *many* girls' types, which is why they were all married off before the end of orientation. But that was okay. I had the real thing. I had Marcus. And I tried not to worry about him and other girls, but it was kind of difficult to believe that someone with a carnal history as long and varied as his would be able to subsist on school-break sex fests alone. Especially when he told me about Butterfly, who just doesn't understand us silly girls who still live in the "textile world."

But all things considered, I didn't blame people for not putting their money on us. And I couldn't help but feel vindicated when Marcus and I were only one of two couples who made it through the academic year. That we split $375.00 with a couple set up by a professional matchmaker made the victory even sweeter.

I had just finished explaining this all to Bethany when my mother swooped in with Marin to "get in on the girl talk."

"What money?" my mom asked, briskly wiping her hands of nonexistent dirt. An aspiring GILF, she was dressed similarly to Bethany in her silk halter top and denim skirt, though she had the sense to lower the hemline by about six inches.

"Well, I doubt you'll be interested, because I was just telling Bethany how Marcus and I were one of only two couples on our floor to stay together all year."

Disgust would have dented her forehead; that is, if my mother hadn't recently Botoxed the spot between her brows. (I can't even comment on this latest vanity, so disturbing is it to me.) My mother must have learned a sudden-change-of-subject approach to Handling Your Daughter's Bad Boyfriend on a shrinky segment of *The View* or something, because the next thing she said was, "Jessie! Is Len back from Cornell? You should call him!"

My mother just can't let go of Len, who dumped me senior year—on Valentine's Day of all days—to be with Manda, Pineville's Official Revirginized Reformed Stealer of Boyfriends. (Really. It's in the brochures and everything. Okay, not really. But that's only because Pineville sucks too much to have a brochure.) Len and Manda have been together for more than a year and still claim they haven't had sex. They're very proud of their chastity, which is why it's common knowledge around here. Want to hear something people *don't* know? Earth? It really *is* flat! And the sun and planets revolve around it, not vice versa! I know this because a fleet of winged space monkeys just flew out of my butt and took me on an intergalactic tour of the cosmos! *Wheeeeeeeeeee!!!*

Needless to say, I think their celibacy is suspect.

"Scotty's also back in Pineville," my mom continued, her eyes straying toward the snack table on the opposite side of our swimming pool. She was clearly torn between her two favorite hobbies: playing Martha Stewart and torturing me. "He had a tough year, Jessie. He always liked you. You should call him! You could help him get through this difficult time."

Everyone knows Scotty spent the whole basketball season on the bench and quit the team shortly thereafter. Unlike Len and Manda, Scotty didn't go out of his way to broadcast this news. But his grotesque face puffery said everything anyone needed to know about his participation in the ritualistic alcohol abuse that inspires his fellow Lehigh University students to brag about their perennial top-five spot on *Playboy*'s ranking of biggest party schools. (This is an apocryphal honor because Hef has only published the list twice. In 1987, Lehigh wasn't mentioned at all, and in last year's rankings it was number twenty-three—far from the top five. I go out of my way to mention this because it makes their alcoholic pride all the more hilarious. Or sad. Depending on how you look at it.)

I doubt Scotty's fall from grace or inflated face negatively affects the onslaught of willing sex partners. Indeed, the mother of all gossipmongers still considers him "quite a catch." She has a sycophantic devotion to Scotty, who just happened to be my first boyfriend, if you can call him that when our entire relationship lasted for eleven days in eighth grade. It ended when he mistook my mouth as a repository for his saliva; you know, to avoid a global crisis should there be a worldwide shortage of this valuable natural resource in the future.

I will never quite understand what Scotty ever saw in me.

"Oh! And did I mention that Mrs. Milhokovich said Bridget will be back in a few days?"

I'm actually looking forward to seeing Bridget for the first time since winter break. But I'm worried too. She said she couldn't visit me at school during spring break because she was still recovering from the removal of what she calls "ugly marks," aka benign moles. She had been talking a lot about how cosmetic surgery is a fact of life in LA, and no more out of the ordinary than, say, brushing one's teeth. So I'm troubled by the possibility that the moles were just a front, and she now has the artificially pneumatic look favored by starving starlets and the horny casting directors who bang them.

"Oh! Grant said that Wally and his daughter are supposed to stop by later. Sara graduated with you, right, honey?"

Of course my mother knows that Sara graduated with me. It's just one of the asinine questions she asks as a means to launch into the meaningless conversations she holds so dear. But my mother may not know that Sara was caught trying to cheat on her Introduction to Fundamentals of Conceptual Finite Mathematics (a.k.a. Numbers for Dummies) exam by copying the formulas she had written on the inside label of her water bottle. She should have failed the class and been put on academic probation, but Sara's dad—the legendary Wally D'Abruzzi himself—promised to open a drive-through combo Papa D's Donuts/Wally D's Sweet Treat Shoppe on the Harrington campus and all was forgiven. I find it hilarious that Harrington prioritizes fast-food funding over an endowment for like, oh, I don't know, a *library* or something. And knowing Sara's love/hate relationship with hydrogenated fats, it's even funnier. Because G-Money and Sara's dad have made it their joint mission in life to take Papa D's Donuts and Wally D's Sweet Treat Shoppe national, I will bear unwilling witness to Sara's foibles for a very, very long time.

Thankfully, Sara was the last of my mother's name-dropping material. When she trotted out of earshot, Bethany leaned in conspiratorially.

"If you and Marcus are still together, why isn't he here?"

And that's when I decided I needed a break from the festivities and went to hide in my room.

Marcus is still in California, away from me for two more weeks so he can attend an elective "learning cluster" on the creative coexistence of nature and humanity.

You know what would be *really* creative? The coexistence of Marcus and his girlfriend. Me.

It's not entirely his fault. I'm the one who's leaving in July, not him. It's the promise of my internship at *True*, of doing something cool with one-third of my summer, that has made this very un-cool Marcus-free part of my summer bearable at all. Of course, the irony is that the internship itself will actually extend the Marcus-free part of my summer. Get it? It's an enigma, wrapped in a riddle, wrapped in a clusterfuck.

I can hear footsteps. It's probably my mom on her way upstairs to demand that I stick my hands back in my paws, put on my poo-dle head, and get out there to perform another tap—

MARCUS!

MARCUS IS HERE!!!!!!!!!!!!!!!!!!

the eighth

I have imagined my reunion with Marcus in many ways.

In the PG-13 version, I'm wearing something casually sexy, like the ME, YES, ME T-shirt Marcus gave me for graduation and a pair of shorts. In this daydream, I do not have a Supercuts trainee haircut; it's still long enough for a swingy ponytail. I'm lounging on my bed, writing in my journal about how much I miss him, when he sneaks up behind me. He grabs my journal and chucks it across the room. We kiss.

In the R-rated version, the setup is the same, except I'm wearing a tank top and a pair of bikini-cut skivvies. He says something like, "I need you right now," which doesn't sound all that sexy, but it's all in the sultry drawl of his delivery. My journal, chucked. My clothing, shucked. My body, (insert verb here).

In the X-rated version, there is no wardrobe or intelligible dialogue. The plot is best left to your (okay, *my*) prurient imagination.

As you can see, I like my daydreams to have an element of reality to them. (I even do my own nude scenes.) It makes them that much more interesting, like, *Oooooh, this could actually happen.* Which in this case it *almost* did. Except I never pictured a

G-rated version in which I was—from the neck down—dressed as a stuffed animal. (Although, for plushy-loving pervs, it could have been confused with the X-rated version.)

As always, Marcus had the perfect entrance line. He gently stroked my pink pelt (any plushy pervs who weren't already turned on are definitely wanking it now) and said, "My, how you've changed, Jessica." His surprise arrival proved that he hadn't changed at all. On the inside at least.

He definitely *looked* different since I'd last seen him. He gets so immersed in his studies that he forgets to eat, making him even leaner than he was before he left for school. He doesn't look gaunt and stricken; quite the opposite. The overall effect makes all that is Marcus even more so. His angular nose isn't merely dignified, but aristocratic. His eyes, more feral than feline. His cheekbones could slice through diamonds. He hasn't trimmed his hair since our goodbye, and it reminds me of fallen leaves, all burnt red and curling at the edges. His dusty jeans dipped down below his hips, and I could see the V-cut of his pelvis, pointing the way to happy territories below.

And he was wearing the summer version of the same outfit he was sporting the last time I saw him; that is, he'd removed the thermal from underneath his old COMINGHOME T-shirt. The iron-on letters I once wanted so desperately to stroke with my fingertips are faded beyond legibility and nearly translucent from so many sudsy tumbles through the washing machine. I once ached to touch those letters on his chest, to touch him. It was at the infamous high school Anti-Homecoming party at Sara's house, infamous not only because everyone who had ever attended Pineville High showed up for the beery lechery, but because it served as the backdrop for my first kiss with Len, not my first kiss with Marcus as it should have. (We wouldn't kiss until months later.) I compensated for that night's longing by wearing the COMINGHOME shirt after we made love for the first time, the second time, the third time. On those June nights, it smelled pungent yet sweet, like autumn decay. It still does.

Toward the end of last semester, I was dangerously close to running out of dining dollars, but I didn't want to replenish from my bank account because I was trying to save myself from financial ruin. So I went almost totally freegan: I limited my food budget to five dining dollars a day, and supplemented the rest of my meals with whatever I could get gratis at the various events thrown by any one of the bazillion campus organizations at Columbia. Bagels with Six Milks improv comedy group. Pizza with the Philolexian Society. Spicy chicken wings with Acción Boricua. No affiliation was too inappropriate for my hunger. (Actually, I did draw the line at the Columbia College Conservatives Club BBQ.) Sometimes the spread would already have been vultured by my fellow starving students by the time I got there, but most nights I'd be in for a feast. And no matter what was being served, it was always the most finger-licking deeeeeelicious meal I'd ever had in my life . . . not only because I needed it so badly, but because my nourishment was never guaranteed.

Seeing Marcus was like that. I wanted to devour him. Figuratively. Okay, more than a little bit literally too.

So my initial response was: "MARCUS!"

Followed by: "I hate my hair! It's okay if *you* hate my hair!"

And: "Get me out of this poodle suit!"

However, stripping off the Pinky the Poodle costume was not something that could be done spontaneously or (let's face it) erotically. So I just went with my canine instincts. I leapt off the bed with surprising agility for someone weighed down by fifty pounds of fur and pounced on top of Marcus. I howled as we tussled on the floor.

"AHWOOOOOOOOOOOOOOOOOOOOOOOO!"

"Happy to see me?"

"BOW-WOW-WOW YIPPIE YO YIPPIE YAY!"

"I'm happy to see you too. Happy anniversary!"

Our anniversary. He remembered that he had deflowered me one year ago. It's nice to know that mine stands out among all the many petals that had fallen before me.

I licked his laughing face.

"Down, girl, down!" he said, rolling out from under me.

"I'm just! So! So! So!"

Words failed me. I barked.

"Happy?" he offered.

"WOOF-WOOF! ARF-ARF!"

No surprise that all this commotion attracted the attention of my mother, even amid the deafening chaos of a one-year-old's birthday party.

"Jessie," I heard her shrill voice coming up the stairs, "what are you d—?" She stopped in my doorway mid-inquiry, stunned by the sight of her daughter dry-humping Marcus's leg.

"Oh," she grumbled, tugging at the bow at the back of her halter top as if it were a silken noose. "It's you."

Marcus hopped to his feet. "Hi, Mrs. Darling. It's nice to see you again."

Mom ignored him. "Jessie, we need you back downstairs. We want Pinky to bring out the birthday cake for Marin." She turned on her high heels and went out the door.

Marcus waited a beat before whispering, "Did your mom get some work done?" He froze his face into a startled Halloween mask. It would have been funny if it weren't so true.

"Botox," I replied. "She willingly injected a deadly toxin into her flesh."

"She looks permanently pissed off."

I patted his head with my paw. "No, honey," I said. "That's only her expression when she sees you."

Marcus was unfazed. "I've been hated by more fearsome moms," he said. "Besides, your dad is feeling me, so I can settle."

"My dad *tolerates* you," I said. "There's a difference."

"Well, we better get downstairs if we want our mediocre rapport to continue . . ."

But I wasn't ready to face my family yet. I kissed him. And he kissed me back in his liquid-lipped way I had missed. I don't mean that in the sense that it was wet and sloppy, but that our mouths melted away . . .

"Mmmmmmm," I murmured. "I don't want this to end."

"We have all summer," he said, nuzzling my furry shoulder.

"No, we don't," I corrected him. "We've only got half of June and just weekends in July. At least we've got August before we go back to school . . ."

"I just got here," he said, reaching out to stroke my cheek. "Why are you saying goodbye to me?"

He was right. I was already feeling nostalgia for this moment.

"I'm sorry," I replied. "Hello! Hello! Hello! Hello!"

"That's more like it," he said, lifting my furry helmet onto my head.

Hours later, before we shared a legitimate goodbye, he told me he liked my hair.

He's a liar.

But I love him for it.

the fifteenth

arcus has been home for a week.
AND WE HAVEN'T HAD SEX YET.

It's my hair. I just know it.

Let's look at the positives of this situation. If left up to our devilish devices, we could, conceivably, have sex all day long. But since we've been deprived of these pleasures, we've been forced to come up with more ways of spending our time. So in the past week alone we have: kayaked on Cedar Creek, hiked in Double Trouble Park, surfed (well, he did—he picked it up in California—I wiped out and nearly drowned), and done several other very physical activities that help sublimate our sexual urges.

It's not working.

Marcus is pure celibait. The longer we go without, the more difficult it is for me to stop myself from just ripping off his clothes. It's not my fault. I know from my Mind, Brain, and Behavior class that it's all biochemical. Blame the surge of serotonin in my ventral tegmentum! Curse the dopamine in my caudate nucleus!

Men are much more affected by visual stimuli, so it's not Marcus's fault that he doesn't want to have sex with someone sporting a cry-for-help haircut. Of course, he has assured me a bazillion times that my hair isn't the problem. It's a time and place problem. We are never totally alone.

In the past, this wasn't an issue. A lack of parental supervision is what allowed Marcus to lead his former life of drugging and promiscuity. (The opposite situation in my household explains why I was 99.44/100 pure until I turned eighteen.) Mrs. Flutie has always worked at a day care center, which is ironic and sad because it means she was too busy taking care of other children to keep watch over her own. And when he's not restoring historic vehicles, Mr. Flutie has always been out on land, air, and sea escapades. It's the elder Flutie's need for speed that has led to our sex-free predicament, as a broken leg suffered in a Jet Ski skirmish means he'll be couched for most of the summer.

Of course, there are other options. Like a motel room. We're both poor though, and I can't get over the sleaze factor. And I just know that we would bump into one or both of our parents in the parking lot just like it always happens in bad movies.

Or outside somewhere. But I have this irrational fear of insects crawling up inside places they should never be.

Or the Caddie. It's a '76 with a ginormous backseat designed for consequence-free couplings. But I don't have an autoerotic fixation, I guess. I simply can't let myself go in his car.

These are my hang-ups. Ultimately, our extended celibacy is mostly my fault.

It doesn't seem to faze Marcus. "We've got all summer," he said again tonight, after we had exhausted all the sweaty, partially clothed Cadillaction.

I was still breathing heavily and had trouble getting the words out. "How can you be so calm? Don't you want to have sex with me?"

He reared back, hitting his head on the fogged-up window, surprised by what, to me, was an obvious accusation. "Of course I do. But if this isn't the way you want to have sex with me, then I must accept that we aren't going to have sex. I have to let go of that desire."

"So you *don't* want to have sex with me!"

"I won't if you insist on keeping up this conversation!"

But he was smiling as he said it, and I obliged with a laugh, though right now I don't think it was that humorous.

the eighteenth

I n our relentless pursuit of things to do instead of having sex,
today Marcus and I visited an outdoor exhibition held at Al-
laire State Park by the New Jersey chapter of the Church of Creativity and Song. Their creed: "Finding spiritual enlightenment
through fine arts inspired by music." Um, okay.

With its forest of pine and oak trees, wildflower-tangled meadows, and cool, rushing waters of the Manasquan River, it would
be hard to find a freak show with a more lovely setting. Among
the more interesting installments were a series of pipe cleaner
depictions of Michael Jackson's noses through the years, lan-
yards (allegedly) made from locks of Jim Morrison's hair, and a
portrait of Bono painted entirely with breast milk. Yum. As we
passed from one zany stall to the next, I heard the strains of a
nasally Brooklyn vibrato, wringing every ounce of melodramatic
emotion from each syllable . . .

*"I've been up, down, tryin' to get the feeling again / All
around . . ."*

"Barry Manilow!" I shouted, running toward the music.

I have a soft spot for the Copacabana Man now, but it wasn't
always that way. For years I complained about my mother's embarrassing habit of blasting Barry on the stereo whenever she

did her down-and-dirtiest housework. But that was before Barry crooned with cheesy gusto at two key points in my relationship with Marcus: on our first nondate, when Marcus tauntingly nipped my lip instead of kissing it *(When will our eyes meet? / When can I touch yoooooouuu?)*, and later, at Gladdie's retirement home, when Marcus assured me that my failed relationship with Len was for the best, as it would help prepare me for the true love I deserved *(I'm ready to take a chance again / Ready to put my love on the line with yoooooouuu . . .)*.

Here was an entire tentful of decoupaged objects devoted to none other than the Showman of Our Time. Plant holders. Vases. Cutting boards. Tissue boxes. And . . . a toilet seat cover!

I grabbed it off the rickety folding table.

"I must have this!"

Barry was resplendent in an electric blue, bedazzled jumpsuit, unbuttoned to mid-chest. His head was thrown back, legs spread wide, arms outstretched, making a perfectly symmetrical X. A triumphant celebration of song by the man who writes them.

"I must have this," I repeated, trying to get Marcus's attention, which had wandered somewhere behind my shoulder.

"It's not for sale," wheezed an emphysemal voice from the back of the tent. It came from a lumpy-faced woman with cheap platinum extensions that looked more like pull cords on a windbreaker than genuine human hair. She was dressed in red stretch pants and a BARRY FANILOW T-shirt.

"Excuse me," I said, in my sweetest voice. "What's your name?"

"Lorna."

"Surely, Lorna, you can part with this one."

"Nope."

I groaned. "Then why do you have it on display?"

"To share my love for the Showman of Our Time," she said, taking a cancerous drag on her cigarette.

"Hey, Jessica," Marcus said, sidling up to me. "Why don't we get going?" There was a hint of urgency to his voice, one I'm unaccustomed to hearing. I thought I was embarrassing him.

"I'm not leaving without this toilet seat cover!" I shouted, clutching the most kick-ass, most absurd thing *ever*. "Name your price!"

"It's not for sale," Lorna and Marcus replied simultaneously.

And that's when it finally happened, the realization of my darkest fears about being Marcus's girlfriend. An inevitability that has been stalled for so long that I had fooled myself into thinking it would never come to pass.

"Holy fuck! It *is* you," exclaimed a scratchy female voice approaching the tent from behind me.

"Hey, Sierra," Marcus said, his dark eyes casting me an apologetic glance.

And with that look, one I'd never seen before, I knew: Sierra was one of the something-something girls Marcus had sexed before me.

If I had opened my mouth, it would have elicited a leonine roar, so completely overcome was I by primal, territorial jealousy. And it's not like she made a compelling nemesis. Sierra was shorter than I was, and scrawnier, with thinning hair that she pulled into a malnourished braid running down her back. The small, sporadic patches of skin *not* covered in freckles were as white as milk. She would probably object to this comparison, as she was clearly of the vegan variety in her cruelty-free plastic shoes, hemp shorts, and I THINK THEREFORE I'M RAW T-shirt.

"How the fuck are you?" Sierra asked.

"Oh, you know . . ." Marcus said vaguely.

Sierra burped. Loudly. And didn't excuse herself. Ack.

A top-heavy nymphomaniac with limited intellectual capabilities? Okay. That I could understand. But a vulgar raw-food freak? What had he seen in her?

Sierra launched into an expletive-riddled monologue about how much she loves Reed College and how she took his advice and has been putting her poetry to music and how she's been clean for three years now. Meanwhile, my insides threw furniture off balconies and crashed cars into trees and set buildings on fire.

"This is my girlfriend, Jessica," he said, pulling me closer and closer until I was actually in *front* of him, acting as a human shield.

"Well, fucking A," she said. "You're the girl Marcus is with now." She emphasized the word *now*. My anger burned hotter than the asphalt beneath my feet. But I felt oddly cold, like when you've got a 104-degree fever but can't stop shivering. I almost couldn't blame her for being blatantly unimpressed. After all, why should she think that he'd be more serious with me than with her? Than with any of them?

"We've been together for a year," Marcus said.

"Well, fuck me," she said, jumping up to playfully ruffle his hair.

And there was an excruciating fraction of a second in which I could feel Marcus physically shrink at her words, knowing that I would respond in the obvious way. I lunged at the opportunity, like a cornered animal.

"He already did," I spat before shaking off his arm and darting for the Caddie.

I would have loved to have made a dramatic getaway. To instinctively know how to hot-wire a car, or even better, for my female fury to fuel a paranormal event that would spontaneously turn on the ignition without a key. But, alas, I couldn't even open the door, and I burned my hand on the sizzling metal handle in my attempt.

"FUCK! FUCK! FUCK!"

"Are you okay?" asked Marcus, coming up behind me and reaching for my hand.

"I'm fine."

Marcus stretched out his white T-shirt with his fist and used it as a buffer between his skin and the hot handle, opening my door. He walked around the front of the car and did the same on his side, and adjusted the Holiday Inn towels meant to prevent our asses from blistering on the leather interior. He slid inside and cranked up the air-conditioning.

I was still standing, the rubber soles of my flip-flops melting and melding with the parking lot.

"Jessica," he sighed.

I got in the car and slammed the door so hard that the pink plastic flower tied to the radio antenna quivered as if in fear.

"Jessica," he said again, only this time with his hand on my knee. "I hope you understand . . ."

"Oh, I understand!" I said, with sarcastic venom. "I understand that we live in a very small town, and that you slept with a good percentage of the female population before you met me. And I understand that it was a statistical inevitability for us to bump into one of your former conquests. I understand that this is a consequence of dating someone like you . . ."

"Do you understand that she meant nothing to me? Do you understand that?"

Of course I understood that. This understanding is what makes it possible for me to be with Marcus at all. Outside of the awkward but necessary STD-clearance conversation we had prior to our first time, Marcus and I have barely acknowledged his industrious, illustrious sexual history. I accepted his past under the premise that he was a different person then. After all, he was largely under the influence of various mind-altering chemicals during his prime fuck years. (Ages thirteen to eighteen.) It was a necessary conceit for our survival.

But Sierra made Marcus's past seem all too present. He did it with her, he did it with all of them, and now he's doing it with me. Or *not* doing it with me. Which makes it even worse.

"Jessica?" he asked, squeezing my knee with calloused fingers.

"I understand," I said, arching away from him so I could rest my head on the window. "I just don't feel like talking right now."

And then he drove me home with nothing but the blast of the air conditioner to drown out the din of our silence.

the nineteenth

I blamed it all on physical logistics, but I now know why I'm turned off by the idea of sex in Marcus's car: It evokes all the girls I don't want to think about. The girls who were splayed and layed across the backseat. The girls before me. Girls like Sierra.

So now, I'm lying in this bed and I'm thinking this: I have had sex exactly four times. Three out of four occurred within the first two weeks of my sexual initiation on June 7, 2002. The fourth took place last New Year's Eve on the Columbia University campus, as the ball dropped from one year to the next.

Considering how I'm the anti–teen queen, it's ironic that I lost my virginity not only on prom night, but in a scenario straight out of the eighties teen movies I love so much, with Marcus, the reformed bad boy, boldly declaring his love in a song written for me, yes, me the Class Brainiac virgin, in front of the gaping mob otherwise known as the Pineville High Class of 2002. Prior to the act, I'd even made fun of the type of girl who fantasized about losing her virginity on an event night like her birthday, homecoming, or prom. I'm redeemed only because we never made it to the prom proper, and sped straight from a preparty to his bedroom, where he slowly lowered the zipper on my red dress and let it fall in a satiny whisper onto his floor. That night, Marcus loved me in ways worthy of overwrought adverbs—rapturously, deliciously—but most of all, tenderly. He took great care in making my first time as painless and passionate as possible, with a kiss for every sublime yearning that I didn't have the power to articulate.

I kept these details to myself when I called Hope to tell her that I lost my virginity. I was only peripherally aware at the time that this secret-keeping would intensify as my relationship with Marcus deepened. Women will always choose the man over the best friend. This is a sad but true fact of life, and it's only this certitude that makes me unashamed to admit it.

I have yet to get a reciprocal phone call from Hope because she still hasn't done it. Sometimes I admire her for holding out. But more often I pity her for not finding someone who makes the preservation of her virginity seem utterly pointless.

the twenty-second

Oh, thank God. Mr. Flutie got off the couch. And Marcus and I finally fucked.

Would you prefer a prettier phrase, like made sweet love? Well, that's not what we did. Marcus might argue that we're in love, so we're always making love—even when we're just plain ol'-fashioned fucking. Yes, even with my limited experience, I know there's a difference. And if you don't know what it is, well, I feel sorry for you.

Semantics aside, any sexual activity is a miracle considering the neutering effect of the run-in with Sierra. And the state of my hair. Not to mention that the Accutane is failing and I had a throbbing bubo on the tip of my nose. Buboes are the red, raging, open sores that marked the Black Death, my favorite of all the medieval plagues. When the bubo turned black, you were doomed (hence the name), and no one would dare come close to the infected corpse, not even for a burial. You were lucky if someone even bothered to throw a sheet over you.

I babbled about all this as Marcus recovered from coming because it was better than a conversation composed of apologies. (His for fucking Sierra, mine for retroactively punishing him for it.) He didn't react to my rambling, so I didn't think he was listening.

Or rather, I was hoping that he wasn't capable of listening after being laid so powerfully by the love of his life. But then he sat up in the twisted sheets and put his lips to my nose, lightly kissing my cyst.

"I'd bury you," he said.

I looked at him. In postcoital calm, his heavy-lidded eyes were even deeper, sleepier than usual. His arms and legs were so long that there seemed to be no end to them in the sheets. I crushed my body against his so intensely that I squashed his internal organs and he yelped in pain. I didn't want to injure him, but I couldn't help myself.

Why am I leaving him for a month? I'm insane! Insane!

the twenty-seventh

So I didn't write anything in my journal during the school year because Marcus was gone. And now I haven't written because he's here.

I prefer the latter excuse.

Similarly, I've been spending so much time with Marcus that I haven't hung out with anyone else. (And maybe I'm in hair-related hiding too.)

Today Bridget showed up in my bedroom all shrieky and annoyed. Even when she's pissed off, she radiates a golden aura that is soothing to the senses.

"Jess! I'm only, like, your oldest friend! Where have you been?"

She extended me the courtesy of not gawking at the brunette horror that protrudes in all directions from my scalp. I, of course, totally checked out her tits.

They looked the same to me, in all their perky, slightly bigger than B-cup splendor. I was so relieved that I gave her a huge hug, one that would not have been possible if her boobs had been upgraded to LA proportions. The rest of Bridget was as blond, blue-eyed, teeny-nosed, clear-skinned, and impossibly, if unimaginatively, pretty as ever. In a flirty, light-as-air floral sundress and flip-flops, she had perfected the sloppy-sunny-sexy style preferred by starlets-in-training, those whose greatest wish is not to win an Oscar but to be voted into the Winners' Circle by the Fashion Police in the pages of *US Weekly*.

"I'm so sorry that I haven't called you, Bridget!" And seeing her there, chewing on her ponytail, I felt genuinely bad about abandoning my only real girl friend in Pineville. "I've been spending as much time with Marcus as I can."

She spit out her ponytail. "I have a boyfriend I haven't seen in ages and I still made an effort to see you!"

She had too. She'd called and IMed me about a half-dozen times in the past few weeks. Whoopsie.

"Bridge, I'm sorry!" I dropped to my knees.

She waved me away. "Well, you can grovel for forgiveness on the way to graduation, which is *today*, in case you didn't remember." She sounded so much like my mother that it might prove the babies-switched-in-infancy theory that explains how Bridget wound up living across the street instead of in the household in which she truly belonged.

"Of course I remembered!"

"And *that's* how you chose to dress for the occasion?" she asked, thrusting a finger at the SIZE DOESN'T MATTER T-shirt I'd gotten for free during Safer Sex Awareness Week. (For the record, I don't know if size matters because Marcus is all I've had. But I can certainly say this: Size sure helps. Whew boy, does it help.) "Come on, Jess. Percy's my boyfriend, but he's your friend too!"

Percy's my boyfriend. When will that sound normal coming out of Bridget's mouth? Bridget and Percy make a ridiculously handsome couple, and yet I still have difficulty thinking of them as a unit. Part of me still remembers him as the prepubescent Black kid in my French class who lusted after me in a goofy Pepé-Le-Pew-like way. (Hence his private nickname, Pepé.) But that was more than three years, forty pounds, and six inches ago. (Six inches in *height*. Get your mind out of the SIZE DOESN'T MATTER gutter!)

"Give me two minutes," I said, heading toward my closet.

She gestured toward my head. "Should I even ask what, like, happened?"

"I cut it off during finals."

"It's not that bad," she said in a tone that implied the opposite.

"It's bad," I corrected her as I pulled on a tank top and a cargo skirt. "It keeps me awake at night."

"Everything keeps you awake at night," she said, riffling through my sock drawer. "Don't blame your hair."

Within seconds, she fashioned a headband out of a pair of fishnet stockings I'd bought but had never had the courage to wear, even in the city. "Use something like this to push your bangs off your face until they grow out. Whoever told you that bangs were good for your face should, like, have her cosmetology license revoked. It's too severe for you." She smoothed my hair with her fingers until she was pleased with what she saw. "Cute," she said finally.

I looked in the mirror. It wasn't quite cute, but it was a huge improvement.

"Thank you, Bridget."

"That's what friends are for," she said.

Some friends. Other friends are too busy with their own workloads to even notice my hair, let alone offer solutions for it.

My friends at school sometimes make my brain hurt. Sometimes it's fun to talk about hairstyles instead of, say, string theory. Not that we don't talk about crap too, because we do. But even when we're talking about crap, there's always someone with something to prove. There's this need to be an authority, and the more obscure the area of expertise, the better. I love my friend Jane, but when we're talking crap television, she claims that she can name the *Brady Bunch* episode before a single line of dialogue is uttered, based solely on the opening camera shot and entrance music. Or when we're talking crap music, she mentions how she's got the Sex Pistols' extremely rare cover of "Stayin' Alive" on vinyl. Jane is only trying to keep the conversation interesting—and most of the time she does—but it can still be very annoying. Being friends with Bridget is a relief because she lets me be shallow and there's nothing more to it than that.

It was a good time to be preoccupied with shallowness, since I would surely run in to people at graduation who hadn't seen me in a long time. As Bridget and I approached the sprawling, architectural mishmash of styles and materials comprising the Pineville High campus—the result of several additions built by the lowest bidder—my stomach cinched tighter than a straitjacket.

"It won't be that bad," Bridget said, pulling her old Jetta into a parking space between two colossal mud-covered pickup trucks.

"I know I'm going to see someone I don't want to see . . ."

Sure enough, we'd been out of the car for approximately five seconds before we were sonically assaulted by none other than Sara D'Abruzzi, daughter of my brother-in-law's business partner, Wally D, but better known as the slightly less skanky half of the Clueless Two. Thankfully, her counterpart, Manda, did not seem to be with her. (Perhaps she was busy battling the patriarchy in her own unique way, which seems to rely heavily on fellating other girls' boyfriends while not having sex with her own.) Manda's absence also meant that I would be spared from a bump-in with Len. I know that it's been more than a year, and I'm in love with Marcus and I didn't even like Len very much, but it still stings to think that he preferred that pseudofeminist hypocrite over me.

"Omigod!" Sara shrieked, swinging her Louis Vuitton X Murakami bag. "Bridget! You look so *quote* Hollywood *unquote*. And Jess, you look—omigod!—so *quote* New York *unquote*."

"And you look so *quote* Harrington *unquote*," we replied in unison, which is not something Bridget and I often do. Hope and me, yes. (That is, when Hope and I used to see each other, which afforded us the opportunity to say things simultaneously.) But Bridget and me, no. This is an indication of how it was the obvious thing, the *only* thing to say.

Sara looked exactly like a privileged princess attending a country club joke of a college should. Her hair was dyed an expensive blond (the kind Bridget and every Darling woman but me was born with) and chemically straightened into submission. Her skin was fake baked to the point that it was practically a racial slur. And she was the skinniest I'd ever seen her, which is not a compliment. Through all of her weight ups and downs, Sara hasn't realized that she actually looks better with some extra pounds softening up her beady-eyed, beak-nosed features.

Sara is not cute. And with this hack job haircut, I know cute from not cute.

She was wearing a sorority T-shirt with the season's ubiquitous Juicy miniskirt and überubiquitous Ugg boots, the latter being the best example of onomatopoeia that I can think of: Ugh.

"Your shirt's a joke, right?" I asked.

"What do you mean?" Sara asked, looking down at the pink and green Greek letters on her chest. "I'm proud to be in a sorority."

"But the letters," I began. "Omega mu gamma . . ." I trailed off, assuming she'd fill in the rest. She didn't. "O.M.G."

Still nothing. I offered a hint.

"Omigod!" I squealed.

"Omigod!" Sara's face exploded with excitement. "I never thought of that before. Wait until I tell my sisters!"

I found it difficult to believe that not one sister in the history of the sorority had put this together before. I suppose they're too busy taking topless pictures of themselves for collegehumor.com.

"Omigod!" Sara paused, pointing at her shirt as if to say, *Omigod! How funny is this? Omigod!* before continuing. "I'm on the CCR Ageless Body diet."

"CCR?" I asked. "Creedence Clearwater Revival?"

"Carb and Calorie Reduction," Bridget explained.

"Aren't all diets about carb and calorie reduction?" This is an area I know nothing about. I have never met a cheeseburger I didn't like, and, unfortunately, have the heart-attack-high cholesterol to prove it.

"It's not about the perfect body," Sara said. "It's about extending your life through dramatic reduction of food intake."

"It's big in LA," Bridget said.

"I'm sorry," I said. "The last time I checked, starvation killed people."

Sara ignored the dig. "So how *are* you?" she asked Bridget

in her most patronizing voice. "Are you still with Percy?" She turned to me. "Are you still with Marcus?"

We both gave her the answers she was looking for, which she would surely tack on to her gossip bulletin: Everything I Know About Everyone. And then for the next infinity or so, Bridget and I stood silently as Sara told us everything she knew about everyone. Not surprisingly, she had her own revisionist take on her cheating. ("Omigod! I totally did not cheat. The TA I was *quote* bang-a-langin' *unquote* told me I was allowed to bring notes to the exam!") Other highlights of the rundown were her confirmation of what I had already heard about Scotty ("Omigod! He's fat, but that doesn't stop him from *quote* bang-a-langin' *unquote* everything that moves!") and what I refused to believe about Len and Manda ("Omigod! They are totally not *quote* bang-a-langin' *unquote!*").

"Bang-a-langin'" is, apparently, her new and third-favorite phrase, one she probably picked up at Harrington. If you have to ask what her first- and second-favorite phrases are, you haven't been paying any attention at all.

When all the important issues had been covered and I was floating about a foot off the ground because of the mass exodus of brain cells from my cerebellum, Sara asked the new question. If you recall, the old question, asked by teachers, friends' parents, and grocery store checkout clerks alike, was "What school do you want to go to?" The new question is, of course, "How's school?"

Last winter break, when I inevitably collided with former classmates, I got used to answering the new question with a smile and an upbeat "It's awesome." And the inquisitor would beam and say, "Cool!" and move on, having no clue that I'd used a word that I always use when I never mean it.

I was inspired by Marcus, who would answer the new question with a note of genuine intellectual and spiritual enlightenment. ("Gakkai students and faculty are unified by our commitment to becoming global citizens.") I admired Bridget, who replied with lackluster candor. ("UCLA is okay, but I miss Percy.") I could relate to Len's somewhat disaffected pragmatism. ("Cornell is stressful. But. Um. Good for my career.") I was unmoved by Manda's claim of academic rigor. ("There's no way Columbia is *that* much harder than Rutgers. Puh-leeze!") I was unsurprised by the simple truths from Scotty. ("We party so hard at Lehigh!") And Sara. ("Omigod! We party so hard at Harrington!") Finally, I outright envied Hope, who could answer the new question with unbridled enthusiasm. ("I love RISD! It's changed my whole concept of creativity! Plus, there're a lot of really hot artsy guys.")

But for me, the truth has always been far more complicated than the boundaries of small talk permit, even when the listener is actually interested in hearing what I have to say, unlike Sara, who is only interested in her own adenoidal drone. If I had the time, and the right audience, I might explain that Columbia would be awesome if I were the type of person who could embrace awesomeness. But I'm not. I'm certainly happier than I was at Pineville, but it's hardly perfect. I've learned not to complain though, because it's obviously selfish and ridiculous to complain about attending one of the best educational institutions in the world.

However, less obvious is how selfish and ridiculous it is to complain about one of the worst educational institutions in, if not the world, then New Jersey, a.k.a. Pineville High School.

I found this out the hard way.

Early in the year, when everyone on my floor was still in the getting-to-know-you phase, a few of us had gathered in the lounge to play Who Hated High School the Most? Tanu hated high school because she was the only Indian girl in school. That's Southeast Asian Indian, not Native American Indian, which is why her nickname, "Tonto," was doubly cruel. William, one of the members of F-Unit, hated high school in Texas because he was the only pasty-faced punk in a school full of preppy cowboys. Jane hated high school because she got drunk at the wrong party as a freshman and was rumored to have fucked half the football team. It was a false accusation—she had blown *one* of them—yet she still spent the next three years hearing "Ride the Jane Train!"

So when it was my turn I said, "High school was torture after my best friend, Hope, moved away."

"I have no sympathy for you, Darling, Jessica," said William, pausing to tongue the ring in his bottom lip. "I know all about your so-called tortured past."

"You do?"

"I googled you."

"You googled me? Why?"

"I google everyone I meet," he said.

"That's neurotic," I said.

"That's *smart*," he responded. "We should all know about the company we keep. Of course, with you, Darling, Jessica, I had to get through about 150,000 porn sites first."

This is true. Go ahead and google me. And the result is what happens when you share a name with a porn star whose film credits include *Grand Theft Anal*, *Weapons of Ass Destruction*, and, of course, the celebrated *Booty Duty*, Parts One and Three. (Which of course begs the question: Was the script for part two not up to her high standards?)

"Eventually, I found local newspaper articles about how you were this big track star, and about your involvement in student council and all those other rah-rah activities for popular people."

"Did you find anything about how I hated all my popular friends because they were dumb and slutty?"

"So you *were* in the popular crowd," Tanu said accusingly.

"Well, sort of, but no, not really," I stammered. "I really hated them."

"But did anyone hate *you*?" asked William. "Did anyone throw garbage at *you* in the cafeteria?"

No matter how I tried to explain it, my high school years came off all wrong, in that they seemed all right. I was lusted after by the most popular meathead jock in our class. I had a boyfriend for several months, a hot one who was also smart enough to beat me out for valedictorian and get into Cornell. True, he dumped me, but it freed me up to be with my first real love, a former sex- and drug-addict genius who says I changed his life, one who wrote poetry and sang love songs . . .

"If you don't mind me saying," Jane said. "It sounds like you lived a goddamned charmed life to me."

Everyone else nodded in agreement.

"So shut up about it."

I admired Jane's bluntness. No wonder she became my best friend at school.

I've always known that my high school experience was only terrible because something inside me—my mucked-up brain chemistry, most likely—made me feel that way. So I was a bit surprised when being on the football field just one year after my own high school graduation made me strangely nostalgic for a time that I know is not worthy of such reverence.

The déjà vu really hit me when I saw Taryn Baker, stepsister of the former gay man of my dreams and current peer at Columbia University, Paul Parlipiano. I'd forgotten that Taryn was also graduating today.

"Heard any good gossip lately?" she asked.

Taryn had emailed me a few times last year, but I hadn't seen or talked to her since I graduated. So I barely recognized the voice, or the person who went with it. Gone was the mousy whisper, replaced by a Marlboro red pack rasp, and her hemophilic paleness served as an unnerving backdrop for a female fauxhawk that was tarlike both in color and texture. Now she's a pinup punkette just daring people to ignore her. But when I tutored her in math as a sophomore and junior, she was a fade-into-the-paint wallflower. Taryn was so easily missed that she was often witness to shady behavior, which she eventually put to her advantage. Inspired by my own critical editorials in the school newspaper, and fed up with her outsider status, she launched *Pinevile Low*, an anonymous email gossip rag devoted to the school's dirtiest hookups, breakups, and fuckups. No one was safe from her scrutiny—not even me. (To this day, she's the only one who knows that I once helped Marcus fake a drug test by peeing into an empty yogurt container.)

While revealing herself as the mystery muckraker didn't launch her into the Upper Crust, it did make her a bit of a hero among Pineville's most unappreciated subcultures. She had no problem persuading a band of misfit wordsmiths to join her on *The Seagull's Voice* staff, making the school paper *the* cool activity for the uncool. She'd even improved her grades to the point that she could get accepted by Loyola in New Orleans. I was proud to have served as her inspiration.

"Well, *you're* the eyes and ears around here," I replied. "What have you got for me?"

"Hm," she said, tapping a black fingernail against her chin. "What former Most Likely to Succeed has fallen on hard times and graced Pineville High with her superior Ivy League presence?"

"Har dee har har," I said. "Is Paul here?"

"Don't you know?" she replied. "He ditched PACO. He's in New Hampshire organizing meetups for Howard Dean."

I'd had several hello/goodbyes with Paul at Columbia, but little beyond it. His former group, People Against Conformity and Oppression, had a lot of campus protests this year—against the climate of racism and intolerance, the mistreatment of TAs, the lack of vegan entrées served in John Jay, and so on. I didn't get involved with those fights against injustice, but I did join Paul and millions of others across the globe in the all-time largest antiwar demonstration. This, of course, proved to be less successful than the campaign against the dining hall, which now serves wheatless, meatless soy-cheeze pizzas nightly.

Every time I saw Paul, he had a picket sign in one hand and Luis's hand in the other. Paul was never without this new boyfriend—who is Latino and muscular and painfully gorgeous.

Paul was my high school crush-to-end-all-crushes, so this was not easy for me to get used to, which is totally stupid because— HELLO, DOLLY!—he's gay. Anyway, Paul and I were always shouting promises to hang out across the campus, but never did. The point is, I had no idea that he had left the extremely unfocused PACO to channel his activist energies into something so specific.

Before I could express my surprise, Principal Masters's voice rumbled from the loudspeakers, reminding all graduates that they were needed in the auditorium at once.

"The evil one calls for the last time," Taryn said. "I'll send you my final issue of *The Seagull's Voice*."

"Sure," I said. "I'd love to see what you did."

"Our op-ed columnist was even better than you were," she bragged. "No offense."

And I assured her that none was taken. As an about-to-graduate senior in high school, Taryn's got hubris out the wazoo. And that's okay, because I was exactly like her just one year ago. I watched her and Percy and the rest of the Class of 2003 strut across the stage and giddily grab their diplomas out of Principal Masters's hand, and I envied them. I wanted their confidence, their excitement, and their anticipation of the next step. I think about my salutatory address last June, in which I told a football field full of people that I was happy being me, yes, me . . . and it makes me cringe. Where did I get off being so confident?

I didn't know anything about *anything*. And the only difference between then and now is this: I may know more than I used to, but my wisdom pales in comparison to that which I've yet to learn. I assume this is what Professor Samuel MacDougall—the instructor from the summer writing program I attended before my senior year—had in mind when he quoted Confucius in my letter of recommendation for Columbia: "Real knowledge is to know the extent of one's own ignorance."

Well, in that regard, I have surely exceeded my mentor's expectations.

the twenty-eighth

Tonight was our last night together before I take the two-and-a-half-hour trip to New York for my internship at *True*. Marcus and I thought about getting out and doing something that would inspire highly intellectual banter, but instead we stayed in and did some bang-a-langin'.

Sorry, I couldn't resist. Using Sara's word helps keep me in a state of ironic detachment about my life. It's where I often place myself when I'd rather not feel real.

"Maybe I shouldn't do this *True* thing after all," I said, tracing the thin lines that bracket his mouth like parentheses. "I don't know if I can handle living with Bethany and G-Money for a month."

"Think of all the quality time you'll get to spend with Marin," Marcus said.

"I've got two more summers to pad my résumé," I said. "And I'm not even sure I'm all that into publishing."

"That's the point of an internship, to find out if it's something that you'd like to do for a living," he said, pushing my bangs off my forehead with his fingertips. It was a gesture that was supposed to let me know that he didn't care about my hair, but it made me feel more self-conscious about it than ever.

"Stop," I complained, flicking his hand away from my face.

He rubbed his temples. "Stop pretending this has nothing to do with me."

Total body clench. "What do you mean?"

"You don't want to be the type of girl who doesn't do things because of her boyfriend. But I'm the only reason you don't want to go."

Marcus placed his hands on my shoulders and gently kneaded my defenses right out of me.

"You're right," I admitted. "I don't want to be that girl. I hate that girl. But I hate being away from you even more. So why don't I spend this summer with you? We've never been able to spend more than a few weeks together before being separated . . ."

Marcus lay placidly in the pillows, waiting for me to finish before asking, "Why do you want to do this internship?"

I thought about it for a moment. And then I told him.

True is the only magazine for women that is satirical and irreverent and funny about the types of things that I really think about. It's *Cosmo* with a brain cell. *Bust* without the in-your-face feminism. *The Onion* with ovaries. As a free publication only available on the coasts and nowhere in between, its marketing strategy reflects an inclusive yet elitist worldview that I can relate to.

True devotes each issue to a single topic. The first I ever saw was *True on Computers*. On the cover was a photo from the early sixties of a bunch of scientists with crew cuts in horn-rims and lab coats examining data on a floor-to-ceiling-sized machine. What sucked me in was an essay about the tyranny of IM, how it's not just the content of the message that's being scrutinized, but the message behind the message, and how responding too quickly or too slowly or too long or too short can destroy an otherwise solid relationship. There was a page of blog reviews, all composed of minutiae ("kings of leon are **sex.** i stuck my used tampon inside a sour patch kids wrapper and put it in my wastepaper basket because i'm too tired from slaving away at taco hell to get up off my futon and walk to the bathroom and flush it in the toilet. do you think the followills would love me any less? ;)") that are interesting only to the self-important writers who put them out there for the blogosphere in the hope that they will get noticed by and linked to other self-important blogs. Finally, there was a Q&A with a twenty-five-year-old guy named Duane who spends eight hours a day playing a MMORPG called ZooKwest. His avatar, a half-man, half-wolf warrior named AlphaLupis, is the most powerful in the Kingdom of Animals and has insane orgies with online groupies ("zoopies") of all sorts of half-and-half permutations of the species. In the "dead world" otherwise known as real life, he's an aspiring assistant manager at Kinko's.

Subsequent issues—*True on the 80s, True on Politics, True on TV*—were as perfect as the first. I read this magazine and wanted to be friends with all the editors because every issue was filled with the kind of snarky thoughts that fill my letters to Marcus and Hope, and my journals. I felt like they were writing for me, which, in turn, inspired me to write for them. When I saw an ad for interns in the back of the magazine, I wrote a fawning letter, enclosed clips from my Pineville High editorials, and hoped they wouldn't notice that I hadn't published a damn word at college.

When I finished talking, Marcus put his mouth in the bony valley of my clavicle.

Then he lifted his head and said, "You really want to do this."

"Yeah, I do."

"Then you should," he replied.

"But—"

"Go."

And so I will.

Dear Hope,

I'm waiting for Marcus to arrive in the Caddie. He's driving me to my sister's place. I've convinced her to let him stay over-night so we can add another eight hours to the whopping to-tal of twenty-three days we got to spend together before yet another separation.

Of course, this doesn't compare to the four months since I last saw you. But I've gotten used to not seeing you. So much so that when we said goodbye after your whirlwind forty-eight-hour trip to NYC last spring, I was comfortable with the idea of not seeing you again for a long time. Our reconnections feel more like continuations, as if our friendship has never suffered an interruption.

It should be the same with Marcus, but it's not. I don't think I'll ever get used to not seeing him. And when I do see him after a separation, I immediately get panicky about our next goodbye. I guess that's what happens when I get naked with someone. (I almost wrote "when *you* get naked with someone." "You" as in a collective you, a universal truth directed toward all of humanity. But this would be inaccurate, as Marcus got naked with something-something someones and has suffered no separation anxiety with them. But that's because they didn't matter and I do, right? RIGHT?)

I applied for the internship because I think *True* is a crack-up (as you could probably tell from all the articles I clipped and sent to you in lieu of actual letters) and to compensate for my lack of participation in any campus activities last year. Despite my misgivings about leaving Marcus, and my doubts about living with Bethany and G-Money for a month, I'm psyched about this internship. And excitement is something I rarely feel about anything. That, in itself, is, well, exciting.

One more thing: When you, meaning *you,* do finally choose that first and very lucky guy to have sex with, pick one that you don't have to say goodbye to. Pick one that will be there for you in mind *and* body. Because the alternative doesn't quite suck, but is definitely sucky.

He honked. He's here.

Woohooingly yours,

J.

freshman summer
july 2003

the first

Bethany and G-Money's new home is a five-thousand-square-foot granite-and-brick Romanesque revival mansion built in the late 1800s. My real estate mogul mother went into raptures upon her first walk-through and started speaking in tongues. "Parquetfloorscrownmoldingtiledfireplacegourmetkitchenbackyardpatiohighceilingssunliiiiiiiiiiiiiiight . . ." The House That Sugar Addiction Built would be a truly impressive domicile even if it weren't located on the promenade in Brooklyn Heights with breathtaking views of Manhattan. My sister and I don't have much in common, so I'm not sure if it says more about the allure of New York City or the repellant powers of Pineville that we've both ended up here.

"Don't get pregnant," Bethany said as she showed Marcus and me to the guest room. "Mom and Dad would kill me."

Kill *her*?

Bethany didn't have to worry about preserving the sanctity of my womb because I'm having my period and there's no way any impregnating activity would happen anyway. This sucked, but the alternative is far worse. When you're nineteen and totally not ready to be a baby mama, a period is never, ever a bad thing.

I couldn't sleep. I wasn't used to having a warm body in bed next to me, and I kept getting sweaty and overheated (not in the sexy way, but literally). And Bethany's sheets are just too smooth and I was sliding all over the mattress. And Marin was shrieking, "PEE! POO! PEE!" from her crib. And well, I guess I was nervous about starting my first real job. Well, as real as a job can be when the salary consists of a weekly MetroCard.

I guess I eventually fell asleep, because at 8:00 a.m. I shot up from the sheets, shocked by the alarm. Marcus slept right through it.

It didn't take me long to get ready. Since Bridget's makeover I'd never gone out without a headband. Today's was cut from the arm of an old T-shirt. I was going for a creative urban youth look: pleated mesh tennis skirt, shrunken denim blazer, pink-and-red-striped tissue T, Chucks. My mother would be horrified by my outfit but would be proud of my one nod to traditionalism: I was wearing a bra, though it was a totally unnecessary formality given my negative cup size.

Marcus was still in bed asleep when I leaned in to kiss him goodbye.

I'd never been in *True*'s editorial offices, located in the industrial wastelands of East Williamsburg. According to Bethany, this area is composed mostly of renovated lofts and studios filled with aspiring artists and musicians. It's pretty grungy now, but is already being touted as the *new* Williamsburg. I hope the hype isn't for real because you can't swing a trucker hat in the *old* Williamsburg without hitting an annoying unwashed hipster in a JESUS IS MY HOMEBOY T-shirt.

While I was in school, I rarely ventured below 110th Street. This is very sad, but true. A combination of too much work and too little money was partly to blame. But I think the biggest reason I rarely left Morningside Heights is because I was too overwhelmed by the everythingness of the city. Sometimes I'd wander the streets searching for my day's purpose. I'd stroll past the run-down café where the nutty aroma of coffee poured out of French doors flung open wide; past the gated park square nestled between uptown and downtown traffic where outdoor opera singers perfected their soaring laments for spare change; past the neighborhood's most unfortunate denizens and their sidewalk piles of woebegone wares—cowboy boots with scuffed toes and worn-down, triangular heels; record players with broken, duct-taped arms; out-of-print novels with pages as delicate as moths' wings . . . I'd walk all over the neighborhood, but no matter where I went, I always had this left-out feeling, like there was something better going on very nearby, if only I knew about it. I'd eventually just head back to my dorm, flagellating myself for having done nothing special with my time. I hoped that being an intern at *True* would give me insider's knowledge, if only for a month.

I had no trouble finding the HQ because the word *True* is graffitied all over the exposed brick wall on the side of the building. I got there at 10:02 a.m., paranoid about how those two minutes would negatively affect their first impression of me. It was irrelevant because no one was there.

For the first minute, I peeped around the office, calling out "Hello? Hello? Anyone here?" as if I were in a marooned-on-a-desert-island movie.

It didn't take long to conduct my search. The small room was divided into eight tangerine plastic cubicles. Like dorm rooms (except those inhabited by math majors because, as a rule, math majors do not decorate), the cubes were outfitted with objects reflecting the cheesy interests of their occupants: *Charles in Charge* bobblehead dolls, *Tiger Beat* pinups of the cast of *The Outsiders*, a limited-edition Handi-Capable Cabbage Patch Kid with leg braces, and so on. Though the kitsch dated mostly from the eighties, the overall aesthetics of the *True* office harkened back a few years earlier. Think a suburban basement circa 1976, with faux wood paneling on the walls, shag rugs and beanbag chairs in the color fondly known as vomit green and, appropriately, the orange hue of that sawdusty stuff used by elementary school janitors to soak up puke puddles.

I sat myself down on one of the suede dish chairs and waited.

At 10:03, I stayed cool, figuring that there was a reasonable explanation. The trains must be running slow.

At 10:10, I read the email I'd been sent, confirming that it did indeed instruct me to arrive at 10:00 a.m. on July 1.

At 10:13, I reread it.

At 10:15, I started to think that maybe everyone had taken an early Fourth of July holiday.

At 10:23, I convinced myself that I'd somehow wandered onto the wrong floor. So I went to each lower floor and asked the first person I saw where *True* magazine was located. They all said the fourth floor, which is where I came from, and where I returned to find that no one had arrived in my absence.

At 10:28, I re-reread my email.

At 10:37, I contemplated my options. I could try to call the phone numbers I'd used to call *True* in the past, but that didn't make any sense because I was the only one in the office who could pick up the phone when it rang. I could salvage my dignity and leave. Or I could stay put.

At 10:46, I was thoroughly convinced I was being Punk'd.

At 10:59, I decided that if no one showed up by 11:02, I would leave.

At 11:02, I stayed put, vowing to give them just ten more minutes.

At 11:14, I heard raucous conversation bouncing off the walls in the stairwell, punctuated by explosive bursts of laughter. Ten seconds later, the door burst open and Tyra Braun, *True*'s editrix, instantly recognizable from her editor's letter photo, swished through the door. She was accompanied by a pack of disheveled twentysomethings who wore the smoky-boozy-greasy perfume of those making the transition from the night before to the morning after with nary a break in between.

I tried very hard not to look like a tool who had been waiting more than an hour for their arrival.

"Holy guacamole!" she gasped. "You're the new intern!"

Tyra had such a winning way about her that I instantly wondered how I had gotten by in this world without ever using the phrase "Holy guacamole!" Her lexicon matched her outfit, which was prim and very 1950s: aqua silk ribbon-tie sleeveless blouse, black-and-white knee-length circle skirt, round-toe spectator pumps. Tyra's corny throwback expressions and love of all things ladylike somehow manage to make her even edgier than others of her ilk. With a jet-black pixie cut that very few people can pull off, surprise-wide eyes, and pink cheeks brightening up an otherwise alabaster complexion, Tyra is someone who my mother would say is "a striking girl, if she hadn't done that to her hair."

"How long have you been waiting for us?"

"Not long," I lied.

"Jeez Louise," she said, dramatically wiping her brow. "That's a relief!"

Tyra went on to explain that the *True* staff had all been out late the night before celebrating her thirtieth birthday at an unnamed Bulgarian disco ("And I do mean *disco*," Tyra said, and everyone cracked up, including me, for reasons I didn't understand) known for its apple-flavored hooch served out of wooden barrels with a ladle. From there, they went to an after-hours lounge known for its "Monday Morning Metal" karaoke contest. (Some guy named Smitty won with his stirring rendition of "Can You Take Me High Enough?" by Damn Yankees.) They had just returned from a dive diner in Greenpoint where they'd consumed enough French toast, pancakes, and hash browns to set the Atkins revolution back about a thousand years.

It was not exaggerating to say that they'd had more fun last night than I've had in my entire life.

Tyra quickly introduced me to the rest of the *True* staff. I would recap here except it happened so fast and I was so busy thinking about what I would say next that I can't remember any of their names, except for Hannah, but that's because she was the editorial assistant/intern coordinator who interviewed me over the phone. Hannah and the other five female staffers were dressed in various shades of totally cool. The one male was re-splendent in West Village flamboyance. They all went to their respective cubes to nurse their hangovers and pretend to work.

Tyra alone seemed unfazed by the lack of sleep.

"What's your name again?" she asked.

I told her.

"Hannah told me all about you! You're the one who worked on the boardwalk!" She clapped her hands. "Everyone! This is the one who worked on the boardwalk." The way she said it implied that she had discussed at length my credentials as Frozen

Confection Technician at Wally D's Sweet Treat Shoppe the summer before my junior year of high school. And their *oohs* and *ahhs* implied that they were duly impressed. I must have looked confused because Tyra quickly informed me why this expertise was so highly valued.

"Good golly!" she exclaimed. "Didn't Hannah tell you what this issue is all about? It's *True on New Jersey!*"

Apparently, the whole staff is filled with yorkles, people who never venture beyond Manhattan or the acceptably hip outer borough neighborhoods. They need me, according to Tyra, because I can share an *authentic* New Jersey point of view. And authenticity is what *True* is all about, albeit in a snarky, postmodern kind of way.

"Listen up, my chickadee," she said as she showed me to my cubicle. "I want your ideas. I want to hear from you what it means to be from the state that is the proverbial armpit of the nation. Brainstorm a bit and come back to my office after lunch."

So for the next two hours, I sat in my empty cube thinking about New Jersey.

Like how in kindergarten I was proud that our state was number one in population density until I found out what population density meant. Or how Kevin Smith is a brilliant ideas man but absolutely sucks at execution because all his movies look like they were filmed on a PlaySkool View-Master. Or how we host the Miss America pageant every year but our state's delegate hasn't worn the crown since 1984, and only then because the real winner, Vanessa Williams, Miss New York, had nude photos come out in *Penthouse* and was stripped of her title, so the first runner-up, Miss New Jersey, Suzette Charles (who was *also* Black, which was weird because Miss America never had a Black first runner-up before, let alone a Black winner) was required to take over for the disgraced Miss America and (according to my mom, who is an amateur Miss America historian) had only two weeks to prep for her appearance in the pageant and had really let herself go because it's not like she'd been making a lot of personal appearances as Miss New Jersey/First Runner-Up or anything so she had chunked up and looked not at all like a Miss America should when she crowned the winner for 1985 (who, incidentally, was a Mormon from Utah chosen by the judges to avoid another photo scandal) and it was very embarrassing for her and now hardly anyone remembers Suzette Charles, but Vanessa Williams is probably the most famous Miss America ever, which, to me, seemed like an apt metaphor of our state's inferior-to-New-York complex, but I hadn't really worked out all the allegorical details when Tyra emerged from her office with a bullhorn.

"Go home, chickadees!" she said, her voice painfully amplified, even for me, and I wasn't hungover. "I'm too tuckered out to work. I declare the day after my birthday an official holiday from now on."

Cheers erupted from around the room.

"Do you want my ideas?" I asked Tyra.

"Save them for tomorrow," she said as she skipped out the door.

That was good news. It gave me all night to come up with pitches worthy of the magazine I loved. I was almost kind of relieved that Marcus was gone, because I could just hole myself up in the bedroom and work. Imagine my shock when I returned to the brownstone to find him sitting on the Persian rug in the living room building a LEGO castle with Marin.

"Marcus! What are you still doing here?"

Marin crawled into Marcus's lap. "Bethany asked me to stay."

"You hung out with my sister all day?" I don't think *I've* ever hung out with my sister all day.

"Well, Marin was here too."

"PEE! POO!" Marin yelled with delight before burying her face in Marcus's shoulder.

Bethany entered the room with the phone to her ear, finishing up what was probably her tenth phone call of the day to G-Money. "Okay . . . okay . . . sure . . ." she said. "Okay . . . Will do! Sure . . . Okay . . . I love you!"

All of her phone conversations with her husband sound like this, and there were a lot of them. Since he was the co-owner of the Papa D's/Wally D's franchise, I didn't quite understand why he had to personally oversee the operations of each and every new location. Couldn't he hire some underling to do it for him? I said as much to him in our first and only conversation we've had since I've been here.

"Jessie," he responded with stoic condescension, "this isn't about opening up another store. It's about my commitment to brand penetration."

Then his Town Car honked outside and he was out the door, a blur of earth-toned khaki and Egyptian cotton. No goodbye. Not for me, not for Marin or Bethany. Not for anyone. I rolled my eyes then, much like I rolled my eyes when Bethany hung up the phone. Marcus shrugged. Marin demolished the castle with a karate chop.

"Hi-YA!"

"Jessie! Your boyfriend here is a natural with kids!"

I glanced at Marin, who was reaffirming this statement by

gleefully wrapping Pinky the Poodle's feather boa around Marcus's neck.

"He should be a manny! I'd hire him in a second!"

Marin danced in circles around him, screeching with approval. "Pretty!"

"Tell me," Marcus said, sensing my need for attention. "How was your day?"

I omitted the part about waiting around by myself for an hour and just cut straight to how cool and nice everyone was and how my opinion is highly valued because the next issue is *True on New Jersey.*

"So the whole time you're in New York, you have to think about home," he said.

"Yes," I said. "The irony does not escape me."

"It never does," he said.

"PEE! POO!" added Marin, still spinning around Marcus.

"Sooooo . . . Jessie," Bethany cooed. "I told Marcus that he is welcome to stay as long as he wants."

Marcus gave me an *Isn't-that-great?* grin.

I should have grinned back. Not only should I have been happy that at least one person supports our relationship, I should have been thrilled to spend more time with him. But I'd been looking forward to brainstorming ideas for Tyra. Plus, it was kind of disturbing to see him and Bethany so chummy. I don't get along with my sister, so Marcus certainly shouldn't be expected to.

I didn't notice that they were waiting for me to say something until I felt the weight of their eyes on me.

"Awesome," I said finally. "Awesome."

the fourth

Tyra thanked me for my ideas but didn't say anything else about them, which, I assume, means that she wasn't blown away by my insights as I had wished. I had particularly high hopes about a piece I'd pitched about the reclamation of the pejorative "guido." I supplemented my story idea with a "poem" (quotations necessary because it has no discernible rhyme or meter) written by the webmaster of jerseyguido.com:

FRIDAY NIGHT RALLY
by joey "the saint" santerello

You sit at your desk
Where you feel like a loser five days a week
It's 4:30
Living for Friday night
Living for the shore
Where you're always young and crazy
Even if you're old and lazy
Go out, go wild, just go!
Just a half hour of hell left
Until you can head for heaven

You wipe away a tear
Thinking about that first beer
PARTY LIKE A ROCK STAR!!!

Yesterday I was summoned to Tyra's office.

"What are you doing this weekend?" she asked.

"I'm spending it with my boyfriend," I said vaguely.

The ambiguity was twofold. First, the only real plans I had for the Fourth involved having lots of loud, uninhibited sex with my boyfriend. My period had ended, but I couldn't get freaky-deaky with Marin sleeping all goo-goo and innocent in the nursery next door. I didn't want to be responsible for scarring her subconscious. I planned on taking full advantage of the fact that BG&M were headed for the Hamptons for the holiday.

And second, I hoped that this answer was sufficiently specific that I didn't sound like a loser, yet noncommittal enough that maybe Tyra would give me an assignment for the magazine.

"You have a boyfriend?" She slapped her hands to her cheeks *Home Alone* style. "You don't strike me as the type to have a boyfriend."

"Uh." Did I strike her as the type more likely to have a *girlfriend*? DAMN THIS HAIR.

"You seem too independent to have a boyfriend," she said.

Oh.

"Well, Marcus isn't your typical boyfriend," I said.

"Well, have fun with him," she said.

Good advice. Since we've been in the city, we haven't had much fun. Together, that is. While I've been answering phones, opening mail, and fetching lattes, Marcus has been having a blast as Marin's unofficial manny. Every day I come home to hear about how they've had a grand old time with Bethany, skipping along the promenade, sharing sticky-sweet Popsicles and hours and hours of laughs. I shouldn't be surprised that Marcus has had such an effect on my sister and niece. He's charmed Bethany and Marin just like he won over my grandmother Gladdie. His charisma spans the generations.

But I was tired of vying for his attention. I wanted to be alone with him. So you can imagine how crushed I was last night by the familiar sight of Marin and Marcus on the living room rug and Bethany pacing the hardwood floors with the phone pressed to her ear.

"Okay . . . love you!" she chirped before hanging up.

"Bethany," I said. "Shouldn't you be on the road already? What about all that Hamptons traffic?"

"Grant has to launch a new store this weekend," Bethany said, "so we decided to stay here instead."

Right, I thought. More brand penetration, less Jessica penetration.

I know this is her house and she can come and go as she pleases. I know that I am the visitor here and that I should be grateful for her hospitality. But *my* turf was being violated. Or rather, *not* violated. And so, I asked Marcus to join me for a private tête-à-tête in the guest room.

"We'll have a barbecue on the roof," Marcus said. "It'll be cool. We can see the fireworks from there."

I made a face like I'd just taken a swig from a cesspool-flavored soda.

Marcus touched the space between my eyes. "You're getting a furrow right here from all your face-making."

"King Kong Kitchee Kitchee Ki Me Oh!" Marin shouted from the living room.

Marcus saw my bewildered look. "It's a song." He hummed a few bars of the simple ditty.

"How do you do it?"

"Do what?" he asked.

"How do you get down on her level?" I asked.

"Marin's a cool little kid . . ."

"I meant Bethany," I replied.

"Oh."

"But Marin too. How is it that you got along so well with my grandmother, and now Marin and Bethany?"

"It's not hard, Jessica." He shrugged.

It reminded me of when people used to ask me how I rocked the SAT. "It's not hard," I'd say. And they'd stare at me the way I was staring at Marcus at that moment, with slack-jawed incredulity.

"We're all people," he said simply. "It doesn't matter if you're two, thirty-two, or ninety-two. Everyone wants to be treated with respect. Everyone wants to feel like they matter in this world."

I sank onto the bed. His sincerity made me feel so soulless and mean.

"Your sister is not the banshee you make her out to be," he continued. "I think motherhood has mellowed her out."

There was evidence that this was true. For the first time in recent memory, my sister was talking like a normal person, no put-on faux-Euro accents or clipped, upper-class affectations.

"But is it so wrong for me to want to spend some time alone with you? I don't get how you and my sister are suddenly bestest buds."

"To tell you the truth, Jessica," he said, "I feel sorry for her."

"You feel sorry for her," I said in a mechanized, emotionless monotone. "You feel sorry for my gorgeous, rich sister with the adorable baby and a multimillion-dollar brownstone."

"Well, except for Marin, you should know that none of that stuff matters," he said. "Have you also noticed that she doesn't really have any friends? Or that her husband is on the phone more often than he is on the premises?"

"Well, sure . . ."

"Did you know that the reason Bethany doesn't have any help with Marin is because her husband refuses to pay for a nanny?"

"G-Money won't let her have a nanny?" I asked. "Bethany said she couldn't find reliable childcare."

"She's saving face," he said, lowering his voice. "Grant says that being a mom should be Bethany's full-time job."

"Why doesn't she just ignore him and hire a part-time babysitter to help her out?"

"Because he doesn't want her to," he whispered. "And Bethany doesn't do what Grant doesn't want her to do."

I always suspected that what brought Bethany and G-Money together were their symmetrical facial features, low body fat, and mutual appreciation of money. They were a perfectly shallow, simple pair. It was kind of a shock to discover that even their marriage had complications.

"That's so ridiculous," I said. "I would never tolerate that."

"I know you wouldn't," he said. "Which is why I love you. But not everyone is able to stand up for themselves. Not everyone is as independent as you are."

That was the second time that someone had referred to me as independent. Which was incredibly ironic, since I was feeling more clingy and dependent on Marcus than I had since we had gotten together.

"Why do you even put up with me?"

"I'm not putting up with you," he said softly. "I'm loving you."

This, of course, was supposed to make me feel better. Isn't this what we all want, someone who accepts us as we are? But it had the opposite effect. As Marcus enters the Enlightenment, I seem to recess further and further into the Dark Ages. And I don't know why.

"MMMMMMMMMMAHCUSSSSSSSSS!"

Marin was pounding the door with her tiny fist.

"Jessica . . ." Marcus began.

"MMMMMMMMMMAHCUSSSSSSSSS!"

"Well," I said. "Don't leave her waiting."

He opened the door and Marin rushed into his arms. "MMMMMMMMMMAHCUSSSSSSSSS!"

So today it was the four of us for the Fourth. One big happy family. Marcus was right; we could see the fireworks from the roof.

Whoop-de-freaking-do. I would have preferred them in the bedroom.

the sixth

Marcus drove back to Pineville tonight because his dad is still hobbling around and needs his help at the repair shop. Of our goodbyes, it was probably the least traumatic because I know I'm heading to Pineville next weekend.

It was worse for Marin, and Bethany by association. Marin literally clung to his leg and held on for dear life. She screamed, "MMMMMMMMMMAHCUSSSSSSSSS!" for what seemed like hours. She wailed for Marcus until her little body wore out and she could only continue with a plaintive whimper that, while a relief to the eardrums, was devastating in its sadness.

Clearly, my niece needs a father figure. The only reason I'm not totally freaking out about the impropriety of her current pick is the knowledge that Marcus won't be returning to the city any time soon. Marin will simply have to redirect her affections toward the mailman.

And if what Marcus says is true, I personally, privately, encourage Bethany to do the same.

the ninth

'm pretty much a glorified secretary at *True*. The staff hasn't really gone out of its way for me. They're all perfectly pleasant when they ask me to fix the copy machine or send a fax, but no one has asked me to hang out after work or anything. They're all busy in their cubes, and I'm busy in mine. They probably don't see the point in getting to know another intern when I'll be gone at the end of the month. It's more practical than personal, and my complete lack of paranoia in this regard is proof of how much I've matured since my days at Pineville High.

Today I overheard Tyra and Smitty talking about a fashion show/party where all the clothes are inspired by *Cops*, as in the TV show. Despite my new and mature attitude, I hope that maybe after some recent successes they'll have more of a reason to want to invite me along.

See, one of my more editorial, less administrative duties is to read through a bunch of New Jersey newspapers and clip any local news stories that the editors might be able to exploit for the issue. I'm also supposed to be on the lookout for any cultural events that *True* might want to cover. The other day, I cut out an item about Shanny Silverberg, a New Jersey native whose most notable achievements are in her bra. Okay. I'm not being fair.

She's also known for being Bruce Willis's barely legal girlfriend for a blink. Now all of twenty years old, she's trying to reinvent herself as—natch—a lingerie designer. It was the first item I'd clipped that caught Tyra's attention.

"Jeepers creepers!" Tyra squeaked. "Thank you!"

Tyra was an editorial assistant at *Mademoiselle* before it folded a few years ago. At the time, the editor in chief liked to host what she called "educational salons." During these mandatory gatherings, the staff was enlightened and entertained by one of the editor in chief's many close friends and associates. Tyra has co-opted this tradition for herself, only in the spirit of *True*.

Inspired by the clip I'd given her, today's guest of honor was none other than Shanny Silverberg, there to share her insights about bras and panties. This meeting clearly had been set up by Shanny's clueless publicist, who must not have known that *True* was infamous for exposing quasi celebrities as poseurs.

Shanny explained how women were focusing more on what they were wearing *under* their clothes than the clothes themselves. Thus, the of-the-moment, faux-antifashion fashion statement was to go out looking like you really didn't care what you looked like when you went out. Even better was looking like you rescued your clothes from a trash can. Then, when you brought a guy back to your bedroom, as women like Shanny frequently do, you'd pleasantly surprise him with your freak-nasty skivvies.

Shanny was evidently putting this antifashion theory into practice with her sartorial selections: a gaudy *Golden Girls* tunic worn over black ribbed leggings, accessorized with pink aviator sunglasses, piles of Mardi Gras beads, and suede lace-up fringed boots. The dressed-in-the-dark absurdity of the outfit was enhanced by the Balenciaga bag tossed carelessly on the floor at her feet.

Shanny hunched over in her chair as she talked, hiding her greatest inspirations—and her best assets. Without the benefit of a pro hair and makeup job, or megawatt illumination projected by a famous, millionaire boyfriend at her side, she looked waifish and wan. In between staffers' sincere-sounding questions ("Do guys think girls in tighty-whities are sexy?") she shot furtive glances at her publicist as if to say, "Are we done yet? Please. Are we done yet?"

Shanny didn't have anything more important or insightful or interesting to say than any of the other equally cute twentysomethings in the room. But Shanny had to perform these duties if she had any chance of getting the publicity she needed to be known as something more than celebrity arm candy, something more than a professional partygoer, something, *anything* fabulous that would keep the name **Shanny Silverberg** worthy of bold type. That desperate need for attention would be her undoing.

After the educational salon had ended, Tyra handed me a digital photo of Shanny that had been taken without her knowledge, from behind as she bent over to pick up her $2,500 handbag. The flimsy fabric of her leggings revealed a wedgie so deep Shanny could choke on it.

"Hit or Miss?" Tyra quizzed.

I had to make a split-second decision. I knew the right, the *only* answer would prove to Tyra whether I was *True* or not, because the Hit or Miss? page was the magazine's most infamous feature. It consisted of pictures of people whose appearances were deconstructed by the *True* editors, then labeled a Hit or a Miss. Such determinations were not subjective, nor were they as obvious as you might think.

At *True*, the ultimate goal is "gameness." Being game means that you're brave enough to do *anything*, whether or not that thing is traditionally considered cool. For example: If you weigh in at a deuce and a half and are rocking a pair of gold lamé bike shorts with a total disregard for proper foundation garments and "I'm fat but fuck you" confidence, *that* is game. A Hit. But if you are one of the bazillion skinny girls wearing a velour Juicy sweat suit that is *so* cool, *so* trendy, *so* of the moment, you're actually being *so* boring, *so* predictable, *so* passé, and, therefore, not game at all. A Miss.

Thus, being game is cool, but the reverse is usually untrue. By this maxim, anyone and anything is capable of achieving coolness, as long as you're game when you're doing it. When you live by someone else's definition of cool, you are, in fact, anything but. This is when it gets *really* complicated. By putting out the Hit or Miss? page, *True* is pushing its own idiosyncratic notion of coolness, which contradicts the very self-determinative premise of coolness from which Hits are made.

It's all very confusing, even for me, and I've put a lot of thought into this. Which is not game or a Hit or *True*.

Ergo, a stuck-in-your-throat wedgie could have been a Hit if Shanny had pulled it off as a marketing strategy—an intentional reminder of the lingerie she was shilling. But that wasn't the case.

"A Miss," I finally decided.

"And why?" Tyra asked.

"Shanny can only hope to have a thought as profound as her visible panty line."

Tyra smiled. "Well done," she said, patting me on the head.

Knowing that she would be ripped apart in next month's issue, I almost felt sorry for Shanny. Almost. Not enough to tell Marcus about it, anyway. I just knew he wouldn't approve. And I didn't want to feel bad about my big break.

the fourteenth

Last Thursday Tyra asked me if I had a fake ID.

"No," I replied.

A few minutes later I was visited by *True*'s art director, Smitty, a self-described "bitch" who makes the *Queer Eye* guys look butch.

"Hand over your license," he said, holding out a perfectly manicured hand.

"Why?" I asked.

His eyebrows hit the ceiling. "Why? You dare to ask me why? Don't ask why! Just do! Do!"

So I did.

The next day he returned it.

"Thanks," I said.

He stood there, tapping his foot impatiently. "Aren't you even going to look at it?"

I did. "It's my license," I said. "Thanks."

"D.O.B.," he said testily.

1-19-82.

A smile slithered across his face.

He handed over my real—1-19-84—ID. It was impossible to

tell them apart. Impressive, because the NJ license is not an easy one to dupe.

"I know, honey; I'm an *artiste*," he said.

Equipped with my new fake ID, I was sent on assignment for *True*: Go to a bar in midtown called Persuasions.

"The owners recognize how a surprising number of hedge-fund hotshots spent their formative years on the Jersey Shore, and long to recapture those days without having to resort to reverse bridge-and-tunneling," Tyra explained as she riffled through a stack of papers on her desk. "I think it might make an interesting story how tacky Jerseyness is spreading like a cancer, beyond the Jersey Shore, beyond Long Island, and into Manhattan."

"I could tie it in with the guido idea I pitched you," I said. "About how they're taking back the name . . ."

"Mmmm . . . what?" she replied, barely looking up.

She had no idea what I was talking about.

"Uh . . . nothing," I said, not wanting to remind her of my lackluster ideas.

This unexpected coup meant that I wouldn't be going home for the weekend to see Marcus.

"This is your first professional assignment," he said when I told him the news. "How can I be mad?"

I guess I wanted him to be a little bit mad.

"Besides," he said, "it's probably better anyway. My dad really needs my legs."

"I need your legs too," I said. "And your arms and your back and your . . ." And I stopped there because phone sex is something I have never quite mastered.

So it was settled. I would go to Persuasions. But I didn't want to go alone. Unfortunately, I didn't know who I could possibly persuade (heh) to come with me on such short notice. There were only three girls I could imagine asking. Hope was in Tennessee. Bridget was in Pineville. Jane was in Boston. A few of my second-tier friends were in the city doing internships of their own, most located in the well-paid financial district, but I didn't really feel like going with them.

"I'll go with you!" my sister offered, when I made the mistake of sharing my dilemma over the phone.

"But who will take care of Marin?" I asked. "You don't like babysitters . . ."

She sighed. "That's something that Marcus and I discussed."

"Something you and Marcus discussed," I said through clenched teeth. "Isn't that something you and your husband should discuss?"

Bethany pressed on, ignoring the slight against G-Money. "Children learn best by example. And Marin needs to learn that her mother has a life outside the home, so she will grow up to be more independent-minded—"

"Bethany," I interrupted, not wanting to hear any more of Marcus's words coming out of her mouth, "I'm just not sure Persuasions is appropriate for you . . ."

Actually, it was far more appropriate for her than it was for me. I needed a fake ID to get in. My sister, at eleven years my senior, hadn't been carded since grunge was a pop cultural force to be reckoned with.

"Oh, I get it!" she said. "Now that I'm a mom I'm not allowed to have any fun. Well, let me tell you something, missy, moms need to have fun too."

"I can't believe you used the word *missy*."

She gasped in horror. "See what happens when you talk to a one-year-old all day? PEE! POO! PEE! POO!"

"I surrender," I said with a deliberate whine that I hoped might change her mind.

"Whoopee!" she cheered. "I'll call the new sitter!"

Persuasions:

A Cheesy Slice of Jersey in the Heart of Manhattan

By Jessica Darling

Located on a particularly alcoholic stretch of midtown, Persuasions doesn't look like a bar in Manhattan. Modeled after craptastic clubs on the Jersey Shore, Persuasions is a haven for Wall Street meatheads who can't put their sunnin' and funnin' days behind them. (Oh, and girls who love them for their money.) Its unapologetic celebration of 1990s neon gave me a sense of neither-here-nor-there, jet-lagged disorientation.

At eleven years my senior, my sister, Bethany, was the perfect person to join me for an evening at Persuasions. It was a dead ringer for the Bamboo Bar, a club on the strip in Seaside Heights, New Jersey, that was the setting for the fateful Jägermeister-fueled introduction to her future husband back in the summer of 1993.

"Grant would love this place!" Bethany said.

She was so right in that assessment that I would not have been surprised to find my brother-in-law at the bar, buying kamikaze shots for a bunch of his old trader buddies.

"We aren't spending a single dollar on drinks," Bethany declared with the confidence of someone who has always relied on libations kindly proffered in the pursuit of pussy. So we set up shop near the bar: two babes in body-hugging black. In less than ten seconds, the first wave of wannabe lotharios launched their libidinous attack: seven beefy guys wearing their gel helmets, ribbed sweaters, and shiny pants with pride. Oh! I could taste the Miller Lite already.

After a few minutes of mind-numbing Dow Jonesian conversation and a refill or two of their own drinks, they, as a unit, asked us, as a unit, to dance. This did not surprise me, as I had been observing their fellow guidos' surround-and-conquer dance floor strategy. The women would dance amongst themselves in a tight circle, which was enveloped by a larger ring of guidos, creating a hump-and-bump huddle. We might have been able to overlook this unacceptable attempt at busting a move if one of these guidos had offered to buy our beers. But none of them did, so my sister and I declined. They quickly and indiscriminately moved on to the next cluster of women. And so it went with three more waves of cheapskates.

Finally, after fifteen minutes of thirst, I caved in and bought our own beers.

"To sisterhood!" Bethany sang, clinking our bottles together.

I didn't have time to decide whether her toast was cute, corny, or a bit of both because "Pump Up the Jam" suddenly erupted from the speakers. This, according to Bethany, is a universally understood Jersey Shore signal that something monumental is about to begin. The throbbing base reverberated through the floor—I was literally buzzing with anticipation. Sure enough, the MC hit the stage. He was in his late thirties, a year-round-tan kind of guy glistening in such a way that if I'd gotten close enough, I'm sure I could've confirmed that coconut-scented suntan oil oozed from his pores instead of sweat.

He announced that it was time for Persuasions' Third Annual Homemade Bikini Contest. Bethany and I giggled with girly glee: *A fashion show! What fun.* Yes, we naively assumed that sewing machines would be somehow involved in the creation of the contestants' swimwear. So I literally spewed my beer when Contestant #1, "Cricket," took the stage wearing spoonfuls of creamy cake frosting on her nipples and her preternaturally waxed pube region. I knew contests like this existed (how could I *not* with the proliferation of MTV Spring Break specials and Girls Gone Wild videos?), but I never thought I would be in the audience.

We weren't the only stunned ones. The guidos fell into a collective coma—as though their brains had to take a time-out to give their dicks the news: ATTENTION! NAKED CHICK AT TWELVE O'CLOCK. Once that communiqué had been delivered down below, they unleashed a horny hoot-and-holler uproar loud enough to drown out the music. Bethany and I just stood there with our mouths open, strangely fascinated by our unintentional entry into the world of misogyny as entertainment.

As this was no mere T&A competition, it was time for Q&A with Cricket. Question: How did you come up with the idea for your bikini?

Answer: Cricket just celebrated her twenty-first birthday. The cake inspired her.

Question: What do you do for a living?

Answer: Cricket is a "dancer" taking classes at a community college in New Jersey.

The initial shock had worn off, so I took a better look at Cricket. Her dark blond hair was done up in pigtails that went well with her surprisingly innocent face. She had invested in teardrop-shaped breast implants—which gave her a nice D-cup rack without the tacky beach-ball effect. She accessorized the frosting with red patent leather do-me shoes paired with lacy little-girl anklets. Despite her lack of education, she was very shrewd, this Cricket. She knew the guidos wouldn't be able to resist the whole good girl/bad girl thing. (Men love that saint/slut dichotomy, as evidenced by popular porn prototypes including, but not exclusive to, the naughty, naughty schoolgirl; the naughty, naughty librarian; and the naughty, naughty nurse.) She exited the stage to thunderous applause and chants of "Crick-et! Crick-et!"

Contestant #2 certainly had her work cut out for her. Sammi came out in a red Saran Wrap bikini, which looked downright nunlike after Cricket's Duncan Hines number. She too had a sweet face, and her XXX body seemed designed for use as a male masturbatory aid. Nothing jiggled unless it was supposed to. This point was clearly illustrated in the talent portion of the competition, when she flexed each breast one at a time like the greased-up male bodybuilders on ESPN2. Her DD cups made this no small feat. I was much impressed, because I have a better shot at telekinetic titty flexing than moving my A-minus boobs through pectoral muscle power alone.

Lia, the third contestant, was introduced. Her pointy hips and nonexistent breasts were easily covered with a sort of chain mail made out of interlocked safety pins. She had the emaciated look of a Fashion Week runway model, but the guidos weren't having it. "No cushion for the pushin'," declared one.

They barely clapped when she quickly exited the stage after an abbreviated Q&A session.

I was about to congratulate the guido next to me for not perpetuating the starvation aesthetic when I was silenced by Contestant #4, who came out wearing three dollops of whipped cream. Like Cricket and Sammi, Ginger Lynn had a tight ass and huge, synthetic hooters, though hers were of the beachball variety. Also, unlike the fresh-faced competition, Ginger Lynn had home-dyed, Kentucky fried hair, and an unfortunate schnozz. She knew she couldn't get away with the "I'm a nice girl who just happens to be naked" angle, so she resorted to skankier measures.

"So, Ginger Lynn, why don't you tell the audience what your favorite hobby is?"

She grabbed hold of the microphone.

"FUCKING!"

I expected the boys to go berserk, but her announcement was met with a humiliating lack of interest. I was starting to have a whole new respect for the male gender. First the skeleton rejection, now this. They saw through her thinly veiled attempts to win them over with the promise of an expert lay by a nymphomaniac, and I was proud of them. But then I heard the truth from the Jack Daniels–swilling guido to my right.

"I'd fuck her if she put a bag over her head."

Bethany clucked her tongue in disapproval. Apparently, sluts are acceptable. Ugly sluts, well, that's another story. I never thought I'd feel sorry for a self-described nympho with gravity-defying knockers—but I did.

While the panel of their "peers" (former homemade bikini queens by day and sex industry pros at night) voted, the MC reminded us what was in store for the Third Annual Home-made Bikini Queen. Namely, she would get to pose for the Girls of Persuasions Calendar. Cricket was by far the audience favorite—she had won over the guidos' hearts *and* private parts. Sammi, the tit-flexer, was definitely the underdog. The other two didn't stand a chance. But, much to our dismay, the audience votes didn't count. So when the MC announced that the winner was Lia—the sickeningly thin safety-pin girl—the audience gasped in disbelief.

For a moment, I hoped that the bimbos had a wicked sense of humor, since one of the prizes was dinner for two at a local steakhouse. But as I watched the barely clad judges hug and kiss and fawn all over the winner, I realized that wasn't the case. This skin-and-bones bod really was the envy of the all-female panel. Lia's crowning as the Third Annual Homemade Bikini Queen was a victory for binge-and-purgers everywhere . . . a realization that, appropriately, made me nauseous.

The outcome also left a sour taste in Bethany's mouth, but she was more reluctant to leave.

"I've got a babysitter!" she shouted. "I'm not ready to go home!"

I was. On the way out, we had to fight our way past the throng of guidos vying to buy Cricket her first consolation beer. Oh, *now* they had money to burn. I spotted the MC working his mojo on Sammi, well aware that Cricket was way out of his league. Lia, the undernourished queen, was still holding court with the porny panel of her peers. I had almost made it out the door when I was shoved by a steroidal elbow, which made me crash into the body in front of me. I said I was sorry even before I realized that I was apologizing to Ginger Lynn, the girl who less than a half hour ago had pulled out all the XXX stops—and failed.

Ginger Lynn looked at me with tired, blue-mascaraed eyes and said, "Hey, it's okay. We're both just trying to get out of this hellhole."

In cut-to-the-crotch Daisy Dukes, a tube top, and cow-boy boots, she was wearing considerably more than she had onstage—but it didn't help. Ginger Lynn was the unsophisti-cated type that this publication loves to mock, a Miss on the Hit or Miss? page of life.

But at that moment, I didn't want to make fun of her. I re-lated to her. I understood her. Ginger Lynn and I were both invisible in that bar, and united by our desire to get out of it. But one monumental difference was clear to me then, even if it wasn't to her.

Ginger Lynn would definitely be back.

the seventeenth

I knocked on Tyra's door to find out whether she would prefer an electronic or hard copy of my first draft.

"Mighty Aphrodite! I'm so thrilled to see you!"

I blushed with pride, honored that she was so excited to read my essay.

"You need to read this book," she shouted, thrusting a hot pink paperback into my hands. "For inspiration!"

And Tyra started going on and on about how the author was one of the brightest among a new breed of social satirists, and how the Park-Avenue-born-and-bred author had reinvented the submersion genre of journalism by going undercover at a po-dunk New Jersey high school to see what middle-class life was like there, and how the author had crafted a *Fast Times at Ridgemont High* for the MTV generation, and how the author had eviscer-ated suburban culture with her razor-sharp wit and wisdom, and how the author had surprised them because as a Manhattan heirhead she had no reason to do anything with her life besides go shopping and clubbing, and how the author was being pro-filed in the New Jersey issue because the unreleased film version of the book was already generating a lot of bad buzz and she wanted to relaunch herself as a social activist . . .

"Have you heard of the author?" Tyra asked. "Have you read the book already?"

What to say? What to say?

Do I tell her that yes, I have not only heard of the author, Hyacinth Anastasia Wallace, and the book, *Bubblegum Bimbos*, but I hung out with the author when she was hiding behind the name Hy and also, unintentionally, provided her with the title of her poorly written opus? Do I tell her that I have read this book already because the "fictional" high school the author trashes, located in the "fictional" town she trashes, is none other than the very real high school in the very real town I am from, and the "fictional" characters she trashes are all based not-so-loosely on very real people I know, and the "fictional" character Jenn Sweet is none other than yours truly?

This isn't something I brag about. It's something new friends only find out about me through a third party, usually a Pineville resident who is proud of being immortalized with an ISBN number. I'm too embarrassed about not living up to the high standards set by my supercool fictional self. Yes, I trash people privately in the pages of this journal. And yes, I get a schadenfreudian lift from reading about people being trashed in the pages of *True*. But I think the reason I'm incredibly uncomfortable with doing the public trashing myself is because I know firsthand what it's like to have my trust violated in that way.

Of course, if I had submitted my editorial "Miss Hyacinth Anastasia Wallace: Just Another Poseur" along with my internship application, Tyra would know this already. But I was down to my last copy and I was too lazy to go to Kinko's and I had other op-ed samples ready, so I sent it without. See how one innocent decision comes back to haunt me?

"Cinthia Wallace is writing a piece for us," Tyra said.

"She is?"

"Jiminy Cricket! Yes! She's studying sociology and political science at Harvard. And she's using what she's learned there, plus her innate investigative skills, to write an in-depth piece exploring the reclamation of the term 'guido' from a pejorative to a positive."

My mouth just hung open.

"What do you think of that?"

What do I think? I think I'm being ripped off, that's what! That was my idea! Mine!

Of course, I didn't actually say any of this.

"Holy horse hockey! What about your piece about Persuasions?"

My chin was getting a nasty case of rug burn. But I was still too shocked to speak. How could Tyra give away my idea right in front of me?

"Nothing about Persuasions was worth writing about?"

Still dazed by Tyra's news, I shook my head.

Tyra leaned back in her chair, studying my face. I concentrated on the cartoon sperm swimming on the poster above her desk: SAVE THE WIGGLEPUPPIES.

"I'm disappointed," she said.

Now I was really confused. If this is how she really felt, then why was Hy writing *my* essay? And it got even more baffling.

"When I read the editorials from your high school paper, I thought, Jeepers creepers. Here's someone who is onto the joke of her suburban New Jersey existence. Here is someone who is brave enough to expose the artifice of the culture that has made her what she is. Here, I thought, is someone *True!*"

I took this all in and thought, Are you kidding me? I have no idea when anyone around here is being real or ironic. Genuine or game. All or none of the above.

One thing I do know is this: If I were really *True*, I would have confronted Tyra about my connection to Hy and my stolen idea. But I didn't. So I guess I'm not.

the nineteenth

Today is Marcus's birthday. We had agreed that we would celebrate in the city.

Instead, I got a dizzying phone call.

"Come here," he said, without saying hello. This isn't unusual. He doesn't call much, but when he does it's because he has something very specific to tell me and can't wait for social conventions like hello.

"Marcus, what are you talking about? And why aren't you on your way?"

"Come here!" he said again, ignoring my question, his voice sunnier than the California sky.

"Marcus, I know it's your birthday, but *you* were supposed to come to *me*. So why do *I* have to come to *you*?"

"Why are you focusing on what *didn't* happen instead of what *can* happen next?"

"Why are you answering my question with a question?"

"It's a Buddhist thing," he said, keeping his tone light.

This is his half-joking stock response whenever Marcus talks about concepts too complicated to explain without sounding preachy. I felt a nauseous thud of emotion, one I don't like to admit to: annoyance.

"My dad is depressed about not being able to get around," Marcus continued. "And my birthday is more important to him than it is to me. So I feel like I should stay here."

"I'm sorry, Marcus. It's just that I'm dying of boredom and I can't wait to see you and I made special reservations at Czarina, this crazy Russian restaurant on Fifty-Second Street where the waiters are circus performers and they do insane acrobatic tricks as they serve your food and I don't understand why you just couldn't tell me that you weren't going to come . . ."

I stopped talking because I was sounding like a hysterical girlfriend and I did not want to be that girl.

"Am I your alternative to boredom?" he asked.

"Well, yes. I mean, no." Lately, talking to Marcus had felt more like a test than any of my actual end-of-semester exams. I never had the right answers. "I mean, I'm bored because I'm alone here and I don't have any money and it would be less boring if you were here with me . . ."

"Where are Bethany and Marin?"

"They met G-Money in the Hamptons," I said. "You know, I've been staying with Bethany for almost a month and I've only seen her husband three times. I think he's avoiding his wife. Or his *life*."

"Maybe they need to be separate to be together."

"How can you be both separate and together?" I asked. I was eager to hear the answer from the boyfriend I hadn't seen much of for the past year. I didn't want the stock answer either. "And don't tell me it's a Buddhist thing."

I could almost hear his mouth snapping shut. Without his joke to fall back on, Marcus changed the subject.

"What did you do today?"

I was feeling manic, pacing wildly around the perimeter of Bethany's guest room, a lap circuit almost as long as Columbia's indoor track.

"Today? What did I do today? I woke up around noon. I ate Cap'n Crunch right out of the box and washed it down with Coke. I looked through the paper and clipped articles that Tyra won't think are edgy or subversive or *True* enough. I watched *The Real World* for an episode or five, but turned it off when I realized that the soul-baring conversations on the show sounded alarmingly like the same soul-baring ones I'd had with my floormates at school. It made me feel like nothing I said or did was unique, that someone somewhere was thinking and doing and saying the same things I think and do and say. It's like when I'm at a party and I'm screaming along with everyone else to 'American Girl' or 'Paradise City' or 'Sweet Caroline' or whatever and it all feels so full and real and in the moment, and then I tell Hope about it later and she says, 'Oh yeah! We love those songs here too!' which means that my experience isn't unique to my group of friends, or even Columbia, but is part of a ubiquitous experience playing out at high volumes on campuses all around the country. And while I used to crave the comfort of knowing there were people out there like me, now I feel generic . . ."

"You are not generic," he said, interrupting my rant. "You are you. And I love you for wanting to make this day special for me."

Other guys would sooner have their balls served sunny-side up for breakfast than say the L-word. Marcus has never had this problem. I should have hopped on a bus to Pineville right then and there. But I just didn't have it in me, and I'm not quite sure why.

"Well, happy birthday then."

"We'll celebrate the next time we see each other. Okay, Jessica?"

"Sure."

About a half hour later, I received an email that reminded me that we still have August. In August, we will be face-to-face, flesh-to-flesh. In August, it will be easier.

It has to be.

To: jdarling@columbia.edu
From: flutie_marcus@gakkai.edu
Date: July 19th, 2003
Subject: Poetry Spam #22
chromosomal dance

oh, heavenly happenstance

rare creation, you

—Original Message—

From: Ruth Spotnik [ajfklajfldj@netgo.com]
Sent: July 18th, 2003
To: flutie_marcus@gakkai.edu

Subject: you degeneracy fleeing amperage oh

cranny tissue flintlock forum antacid thoroughgoing equal creation salesian annuity buena rare rote gourd mba cocktail bluebush cashier principle heavenly dean murder abovementioned manhole deft impoverish chronicle divorce plausible functional demo cove blessing discriminate meantime contradistinction winch cholesterol familiarly dance sawdust dungeon contrition obliterate gauge olfactory mona homebuild arcing acclimate coulomb cranberry droplet film deportee happenstance synod conjecture ambidextrous aviatrix polity neuralgia chromosomal

the twenty-first

This morning, Tyra threw another salon. Unlike the Shanny salon, which was rather unceremoniously held around the conference table in the very gray, very dingy, very unfabulous newsroom, today's took place in the dining room, located on another floor of the building and often used for wooing advertisers and other potential money donors. I assumed that the move meant that we were going to be treated to the insights of a legitimate dignitary.

And indeed, the smiling fiftysomething woman who greeted us certainly looked the part with her poufy, perfectly groomed hair, shiny lacquered nails, and Chanel suit. The guest of honor was Ms. Toni Sheridan, frequently quoted sexpert and author of *Land Any Man in Minutes (and Keep Him Forever!)*, among others. Ms. Sheridan had arrived at *True* to conduct one of her popular sex seminars, the likes of which she routinely gives for margarita-swilling Jersey Shore bachelorettes.

Ms. Sheridan began her presentation by asking us to select from a Birkin bag full of dildos.

Yes, dildos. As in mock cocks.

They came in myriad shapes (Huge Nads?), sizes (six-inch

"Executive"?), and skin tones (Light? Medium? Dark?). After much lose-lose-situation deliberation, I settled on a ten-inch Medium model with unobtrusive testes. Everyone else picked their penises with relish. (Meaning enthusiasm, not the condiment. Though I am sure that if given the opportunity to have their penises with relish, they would have—gamely—done so.) Then we gave them perma-hard-ons by attaching them to our plates via a suction cup base located under the balls. On my plate, mere moments before, I had put a fat-free muffin from the breakfast buffet, having incorrectly assumed that the place setting was for my dining pleasure.

"Now stroke and pull," Ms. Sheridan commanded. "Stroke and pull!"

"Hella, hella big fella!"

Tyra yanked on her twelve-inch Black Stallion with enthusiasm, her dainty pearl necklace thumping her chest with every thrust of her fist. Taking her lead, the rest of the *True* staffers stroked and pulled and stroked and pulled and stroked and pulled. Dressed almost identically in their own twinsets and pearls, silks and pastels, as ladylike as the editrix herself, they resembled an assembly line of horny Stepford automatons. The only one abstaining was Smitty, who instead waved his King Commando model in the air, admonishing Ms. Sheridan for thinking that she could teach him something about male pleasure that he didn't already know.

I was *so not cool* with performing a sex act in front of my peers. I go to college, an Ivy League institution of higher learning that prints its diplomas in Latin, for Christ's sake. There is only one thing more mortifying than practicing hand job techniques in front of your boss. And that is *watching* your boss lube up and jerk off. All in the name of what? Of journalism? Of science? Of saving face in front of a guest lecturer who charges $250 an hour?

Of being game?

I halfheartedly gave the dildo a quickie *one jerk, two jerks, three jerks*, to show I was a team player, but I wouldn't degrade myself by participating 100 percent. As I uncomfortably watched my coworkers rubbing their rubber phalluses, I started to worry: What if they mistook my inept manhandling as the technique I used behind closed doors? The scenario wasn't that far-fetched. I could just imagine them gossiping about how I clearly had no clue how to please my man . . .

My man.

My man, whom I hadn't seen all month because I was working here. But why? Why was I working here? Why was I doing this?

I was doing this because it was funny. I was doing this because I could handle it. I was doing this because it was *game*.

Right?

Recently there was a newspaper article about New Jersey high school football players accused of sodomizing freshmen with Popsicles until they melted. Within jock circles at this school, it was a fairly well-known hazing ritual. To be chosen as a Popsicle Player was a bizarre honor. It meant the upperclassmen saw you as one of the most promising athletes, who therefore needed to be put in his place. As I read the story, I found it unbelievable that someone would subject himself to such humiliation just for the sake of belonging.

But as I sat there, gripping my dildo, it didn't seem all that strange anymore. I had tried all month to be *True*. But it turns out that I don't have it in me. And never will.

"And now," Ms. Sheridan announced. "Oral techniques!"

Before I got up, before I grabbed my backpack and walked out the door, before I headed to the train station to get on the bus that is bringing me back to the place that I should have never left to begin with, I said, "I'm not giving head to get ahead."

I think it's the first truth I've told all month long.

Of course, no one responded. Their mouths were full.

I can't wait to tell Marcus this story in person. He'll be proud.

At least I hope he will be.

July 31st

Dear Hope,

Who knew that snarking could weigh so heavily on my psyche? And here I was, all this time, living with the grand illusion that *you* were the nice one.

Thank you for trying to make me feel better about my short and undistinguished journalism career. I see your point about how all experiences are learning experiences, therefore nothing is a total waste of time, etc. But the thing is, I doubt the staff has even noticed my departure, if they were aware of my presence at all.

I didn't do anything cool in the city because I was too poor. And I didn't bond with my sister and niece because I was too preoccupied by their fucked-up family dynamic. (Let's just say that after seeing the state of Bethany and G-Money's nonunion, it makes me wonder why gays are lobbying so hard for the right to marry.) So in spite of your wise assurances, I can't shake the feeling that this month could have been better spent.

Yes, this has much to do with Marcus. If I'd come away with a byline, or a recommendation, or a paid internship in the fall, I'd feel better. But it upsets me to think I willingly chose to spend time away from him and now have nothing to show for it but a fake ID. It's strange how a three-week separation from Marcus was somehow harder than not seeing him at all last semester. Maybe it's easier when he's in California and there's no chance of us getting together. When he's in New Jersey, being with him is always within the realm of possibility, so it's like, *Why aren't we?*

I miss you too.

Tragically, hiply yours,

J.

freshman summer
august 2003

the fifth

I haven't written for one reason: Reunion sex rocks.

Today was the first brilliantly sunny day since I've been home, so Marcus and I left his bedroom and took the ten-minute drive—past the sketchy motels and junky souvenir shops, the greasy fast-food drive-throughs and run-down bait and tackle shacks—to the beach. Tuesdays are generally good beach days because the weekend bennies are back in the boroughs and the cleanup crews have had a day to rid the sand of their cigarette butts, bottle caps, and used condoms.

It's been more than a week, but I'm still reeling from my *True* fiasco. For the first time in my life, I'm grateful that Pineville is so hicks-in-the-sticks. When the new issue of *True* comes out with Hy's-but-should-rightfully-be-my essay, I won't be confronted by my failure on the checkout line at the Super-Foodtown.

"I really thought that *True* would be cool," I said this afternoon. "I really thought I'd be happy there."

"That was your first mistake," Marcus replied as he drew circles around my belly button with his fingertip. I shivered with the recent memory of his tongue making the same round-and-round-and-round.

"How so?" I asked.

Then Marcus went into what he had learned in a seminar called "Miswanting: Unhappy with Having It All." Most people have no idea what will make us happy. So we go after something we *think* will make us happy and might be temporarily elated when we get it. Ultimately, we end up disappointed because the thing—whether it's, say, getting into Columbia or snagging a cool job at *True*—doesn't have the enduring, euphoric emotional payoff that we thought it would. So we set our sights on something else that we think will make us happy, only to repeat the cycle indefinitely until we die. The upside to this is that the same holds true for negative experiences. Something we think will kill us—say, a best friend moving a thousand miles away or a boyfriend choosing a college across the country—won't have the long-term devastation on our psyches that we think it will.

And by "we" I really mean "me," since this sums up my whole life.

"So how do we stop the cycle? How do we learn to accurately predict what will really make us happy?"

"Well, if I could answer that," Marcus said, "people would be praying to me."

He squinted because he faced the sun, but also because he was smiling. And right then, sitting cross-legged in the sand, with the sea and the sky serving as a backdrop, Marcus did look like a golden god. One this atheist would gladly bow down and worship. Which made me think.

"So everything we believe about happiness is wrong," I said.

He nodded.

"Everything?" I asked, when what I meant was, *Everything? Including you? Including me?*

And Marcus, being Marcus, knew what I really wanted to know, and answered my silent, more significant question. He held up his hand to shield the rays and looked me in the eyes.

"Almost."

the eighth

Jane is here for the weekend!

She called me yesterday, said she was arriving by bus today, and now she's here. I can finally prove to my parents that, yes, I do have friends at Columbia.

Despite the diversity of our campus, students of the same race, ethnicity, religion, sexual orientation, and gender (and so on) tend to stick together, often through campus organizations designed to define us through similarities with one another and differences with everyone else. Jane and I didn't form an official club, but as white, Anglo-Saxon, lapsed-Catholic heterosexual women, we made a perfect pair.

The similarities run even deeper. She too was a distance runner in high school who had no desire to run in college. She also came from a suburban wasteland close to (yet so far away from) a major city (Boston). She was an only child, and I felt like one because my sister was out of the house for most of my formative years. We had both been brutalized by the high school rumor mill, though her reputation ("Ride the Jane Train!") had been more damaged than my own.

In fact, Jane and I are so tight that one of the F-Unit nerds who dabbled in music snobbery gave us the nickname 2 Skinny

J's, inspired by an underground rap/rock group Jane and I had never heard of. Yet it was an appropriate nickname because of our similarly prepubescent builds. We often shared each other's jeans, cords, and T-shirts, and until I chopped off my hair, we both wore our brown hair in careless ponytails. No wonder we were constantly mistaken for each other. Hope and I were tight, of course, but we never inspired nicknames.

When I picked Jane up at the bus station, she clamped her hands above my ears and shook my head from side to side. "Your hair is growing wide before it grows long!"

I swung my leg around and kicked her in the butt.

"Hey! If I can't tell you the truth, who will?"

It's so ironic that someone so ruthlessly honest spent her whole summer lying for a living as an "undercover spokeswoman" for ALPHA-pups, a guerilla marketing firm. She was paid eight dollars an hour to loudly extol the virtues of new liquors in trendy bars. ("This Yellow Jacket cosmopolitan makes me want to dance all night!!!") Or she'd spritz on an experimental fragrance before flirting with weary but horny nine-to-fivers. ("This mesmerizing perfume makes me feel *sooooo* sexy.") She has no qualms about being so manipulative and mercenary, which is one significant difference between the two of us.

"Speaking of all things true, you *must* tell me about the internship!" she gushed as she stepped into the Volvo. "If you didn't have the best time ever, I will kill you."

"Uh, it was a job, J. Like any other job . . ." I said, keeping my eyes on the rearview mirror to avoid her scrutiny.

"Oh sure, just like any other job at the coolest, funniest magazine in the universe! Like any other job that a bazillion girls are dying to put on their résumé!"

When she put it like that, it almost made me jealous for the person lucky enough to snag that job, until I remembered that the person was me and that the job sucked.

"Well, it really wasn't that fun."

And then I explained how I was ignored all summer, and the only way to get attention from anyone was to be catty and snarky and, of course, game for anything and everything that Tyra deemed cool, which was a complicated classification, one that included giving a blow job to a suction-cupped dildo in front of a dozen people in the middle of the afternoon.

"You *what*? That's *hilarious*!" Jane cackled.

I tried explaining that it wasn't funny at all, that it was degrading and weird and uncomfortable and gave me an icky *uh-oh* feeling like you get warned about in antimolestation videos in elementary school.

"You walked out on them?" Jane slapped both hands on the dashboard in shock. "But you love that magazine! How can you suddenly decide that it's not you! It's funny! Ha-ha! Funny! Jokes! Remember jokes? Remember laughter?"

"Har-dee-har-har," I replied.

She popped in a CD mix that she had made for me. An Eminem/Depeche Mode mash-up burst from the speakers: "*It'd be so empty without me . . . I just can't get enough . . . I just can't get enough . . .*"

"So! When do I get to meet the famous Marcus Flutie?"

"Tomorrow." I smiled at the thought of it. "He's giving us 'girl time' tonight."

I've been looking forward to introducing Marcus to Jane, for educational purposes. Jane is a very together chick, and there is only one thing about her that I do not get at all: her boyfriend.

First of all, he's got a chin-warmer; you know, all bushy below the mouth but completely naked above it, a peculiar facial-hair fashion that has never worked on *anyone* in *any* period of history. And he'll wear the same thrift shop corduroy blazer every single day until the elbows rub down to a greasy sheen. He's undertall and underweight and would need to gain about fifty pounds before he'd look healthy enough to achieve heroin chic. Finally, his face always has that flared-nostril, openmouthed look of a person about to yawn.

But I'd forgive his physical flaws if his personality wasn't so beyond redemption. He's so godawful that I hate saying his name because it provokes a visceral puke-in-my-mouth repugnance, which is sad because it's the same as a certain cinematic hottie who has provided me with many a sexual daydream. Which means Jake (*bleeech!*) has all but ruined *Sixteen Candles* for me.

Need proof? There's the time he heaved a heavy sigh and hesitated for a few moments before joining us in the cab taking us to Roseland to see the Yeah Yeah Yeahs, because "New York City hasn't made a significant contribution to the music scene since the Ramones." At the club, he slouched in the corner, arms crossed and unsmiling, until Jane took him out of his (our) misery midway through the set.

Or the time a bunch of us went for Italian at Carmine's and Jake (*bleeech!*) got so bored with our conversation about all the antiwar protests on campus that he literally rested his head on the table like he was taking a nap. He only snapped to attention when Jane turned the conversation toward a topic he likes: himself.

Or the time I introduced myself.

I said, "Hey Jake! [*Bleeech!*] I'm so happy to finally meet you."

And he said, "Uh-huh." Then he turned his back on me, walked into Jane's room, and slammed the door in my stunned face.

As a self-appointed "Poli-Poetics" major at Brown, he wasn't around to foul us with his presence too often. But on these three occasions that I had the misfortune of sharing air with him, I couldn't understand why Jane would bother being *friends* with someone like him, let alone have sex with him. Jane is the reason for the existence of self-help books like *Why Smart Chicks Pick Total Dicks*. How she can be so observant when it comes to other people yet totally blind to her own errors is beyond me. She's always making excuses for his obvious flaws—He's really shy! He's not comfortable around new people! He's different when it's just the two of us!—all of which sound exactly like the types of things people say about puppies and babies when they misbehave. If Jake (*bleeech!*) made a steamer on the rug right in front of me, Jane would sheepishly shrug her shoulders and say, "He isn't potty trained yet!"

I'm Jane's closest friend at Columbia, but I know that if it came down to choosing him or me, I'd come out the loser. Which is why all I can do is smile as tightly as I possibly can to keep the words from screaming out of my mouth: *WHAT ARE YOU DOING WITH THIS ASSHOLE!!!*

So I'm excited to introduce Jane to Marcus.

"I can't wait," Jane said.

Neither could I.

the tenth

With Jane here for only three days, I wanted to make them memorable. She'd already been to Sleazeside during the *MTV Beach House* summer, so the boardwalk didn't hold the cheesy allure that it usually does for out-of-town guests. I wasn't sure how we'd pass the time, until Jane ripped a page out of our newspaper at breakfast.

"We *must* do this!" she said. "Won't it be a *riot*?"

I read the torn piece of paper.

"The Glam Slam Metal Jam?" I asked, not really knowing if she was serious or not.

"Poison! Warrant! Quiet Riot! Six hours of glam rock glory!"

For the record, I'm into the eighties, but I've never been a fan of the hair bands. But I didn't want to be a buzzkill.

"We've only got eight hours to get our outfits together!" she said.

"Outfits?"

"The only way to get in the glamming, slamming, metal jamming spirit is to dress the part, right?"

"Sure!" I replied, trying to match Jane's enthusiasm.

For inspiration, we consulted Bethany's high school yearbooks, as she very conveniently started high school in 1987. We marveled at the foot-high bangs and plastic earrings and saw that we had our work cut out for us. Because my sister's look back then was more Debbie Gibson than Lita Ford, we couldn't piece together an entire outfit from oldies-but-goodies from my parents' attic. However, there was one notable, notorious exception, one that my mother was all too thrilled to mention.

"You can finally wear the Jacket!" Mom exclaimed, pulling out a plastic dry-cleaning bag.

The Jacket, which cost $150 in 1987, was the most expensive piece of clothing my mother had ever bought Bethany. Made of white leather, The Jacket had huge padded shoulders and long fringe running across the chest and back. When Bethany begged for it in ninth grade, she was inspired by Sloane Peterson, Ferris Bueller's very cool girlfriend, who wore a similar jacket in the movie. But not two months after she got the Jacket, NJ's own JBJ (that's Jon Bon Jovi to those of you in the other forty-nine states) wore a black leather version in his seminal "Livin' on a Prayer" video. Instantly, her beloved jacket was sought after by Pineville High School's headbangingest students, and she just couldn't wear it anymore. My mother has kept it in the closet ever since, as a reminder of what a spoiled brat Bethany was back then.

"The Jacket that was going to make your sister happy for the rest of her life!" my mother said, still annoyed sixteen years later.

"Well, everything we know about happiness is wrong," I said.

"You can't really believe that," Jane said. "It's too depressing."

"It's true," Marcus said, entering the room and the conversation.

"Marcus!" shouted Jane as she charged toward him. "I feel like I know you already!"

"His reputation precedes him," my mother muttered, twisting her lips into more of a sneer than a smile as she retreated from my bedroom.

"So Marcus," Jane said, grabbing two fistfuls of white cotton T-shirt above each of his shoulders. "Guess where you're going tonight!"

"I'm going somewhere?" Marcus asked, sliding out of Jane's grip.

"The Glam Slam Metal Jam," I said, showing him the newspaper clipping.

"Really?" Marcus asked, smoothing the rumpled fabric at his neck. "You hate hair bands. And you hate nostalgia for hair bands even more."

And before I could answer, the phone rang. My mother yelled from downstairs.

"Jessie! It's Bridget!"

"And you say you aren't popular," Jane teased. "Tell Bridget she *must* come with us!"

"Hey, Bridget; I was going to call you," I said instead.

"That's, like, your motto for the summer," she said, not without reason.

"I know, I know," I said. "But I'm going to make it up to you big-time. How'd you two like to join me, Marcus, and my friend Jane from school at the Glam Slam Metal Jam tonight?"

Percy got on the line. "What's this about?"

I explained how it was a hairbandapalooza, and how they'd have to show up in all their glam rock glory or not at all.

"We're in," Percy said. "I'll drive."

"Cool," I said.

"*Au revoir,* Jess."

"*Au revoir,*" I replied with a pang of sadness, the way I always do whenever Percy and I speak French now, which is rare and never goes beyond *au revoir* or *bonjour* or the occasional *oui.* Long gone are our private conversations in a language no one else understood. Such intimacies are reserved for Bridget alone, as they should be. He got over his foolish, fervent crush on me and found someone so much better. And I'm happy for them. Really.

"So Bridget goes to school in California, like you," Jane said to Marcus. "And her boyfriend is going to school in New York, like you," she said to me.

"Yes," Marcus and I said simultaneously.

"Interesting," Jane said cryptically, shifting her attention back to Marcus.

"It's not interesting as much as it's inconvenient," I said.

"It is how it is," Marcus said.

"So!" Jane gushed, clasping Marcus's hand. "You *must* come shopping with us! Unless you've got some choice acid wash hiding in your closet."

"I'm gonna take a pass," he said, looking first at Jane and then at me.

I tried my best to mask my disappointment. I didn't want Jane to see that I thought our night would be ruined because of my boyfriend's absence.

"Why?" I asked, calmly. "Won't it be fun to hang out with Bridget and Percy?"

"I'm just not in the mood to play dress up."

And then we just kind of stood there for a few moments.

"Well, we *must* go if we want to find the right outfits at the consignment shop."

If I hadn't memorized every millimeter of Marcus's face, I

wouldn't have noticed the almost imperceptible wrinkling of his brow at the word *must*. He muttered his goodbyes and I followed him out the door.

"Hey," I said, reaching for his fingertips before he stuffed them in his pockets. "What's going on?"

"Nothing," he said. "I just don't feel like going, that's all."

"Okay," I said. "But I get the sense that something else is going on here."

"You hate hair bands."

"So?"

"This reminds me of one of your assignments for *True*," he said. "Proving how *game* you are."

"This is different," I said defensively. "Because Jane is my friend."

Marcus looked like he was about to say something, then stopped himself.

"What?" I asked.

"Nothing."

Of course it wasn't nothing. If I were to guess, whatever he was about to say had something to do with Jane's use of pushy imperatives.

Marcus thrust his hands inside his loose pockets. "Go have fun with your friend. I'll see you tomorrow."

It wasn't a fight. Not even close. But I felt conflicted because Marcus was obviously disappointed in me. But who was he to say why I was going?

As I watched Marcus drive away, Jane came from behind and swung her arm through mine.

"C'mon," she said. "We *must* get glammed, slammed, and metal jammed."

With a budget of twenty-five dollars, Jane and I set out for Good Stuff Cheap, a dumpy strip mall consignment shop that would never be confused for a vintage shop in the Village.

"This place is so crappy!" Jane exclaimed once we were inside, not caring who heard.

"It *is* Pineville," I said, covering my embarrassment with sarcasm.

"It's perfect. Just look at these!" Jane quickly slipped on a pair of white spandex bike shorts. They were so tight that I could see her unborn children.

"Perfect," I said, finally sort of meaning it.

I really started to cheer up when I unearthed peg-legged, acid-washed Sasson jeans with bows at the ankles. The jeans were an ideal match for the screaming pink push-up bikini top, over which I wore a perforated half-shirt.

"What do you think?" I asked, modeling my outfit for Jane.

"Bret Michaels would definitely have sex with you," she said appraisingly. "And he wouldn't even bother to learn your name."

At this point we were enjoying ourselves so much that I'd almost forgotten about what had happened with Marcus back at the house.

Almost.

We raced home and barely had enough time to tease our hair, not an easy feat with my current coif. (DAMN MY HAIR.) We smothered our eyes with black eyeliner and slapped on red, airbrushed press-on talons. We were ready to rock.

"Your friends better outdo themselves," Jane warned.

"Oh, don't worry. They've both got a flair for the theatrical." I went on to explain that Bridget is an aspiring actress, and that

Percy once dressed up in an authentic rhinestone jumpsuit for his talent show–winning performance as the Black Elvis.

I was right. They didn't disappoint. Bridget still managed to look gorgeous, even with roof-raising bangs, red-rinsed jean shorts, and an oversized shoulder-padded T-shirt. But Percy outdid us all. He was shirtless under a pleather vest covered in decorative metal grommets, and he had squeezed into jeans so tight that one wine cooler too many and they would surely explode off his body with a force that would rival the onstage pyrotechnics. The final, perfect touch? A platinum, curly wig in the Dee Snider tradition.

"It's an honor to meet you both!" Jane whooped.

"Likewise," Percy said, admiring her outfit. "The Glam Slam Metal Jam is probably the only place on earth where white spandex bike shorts will be the norm."

Percy, like the rest of us, assumed the majority of concertgoers would also show up in heavy metal drag.

Uh. Well. We were wrong.

As we drove around the parking lot looking for a parking space, it soon became clear that of eight thousand fans, only four were in costume. And they were us.

"We can't be the only people dressed like this!" Bridget said, horrified.

"We are! We are!" shouted Jane, thoroughly thrilled.

Most were dressed on the casually preppy side, like we *would've* looked had we not been wearing costumes. However, a minority *were* dressed in headbanger gear. But they, unlike us, *clearly dressed like that all the time.* Suddenly, an idea that started out as fun seemed anything but. We were scared to get out of the car, afraid that the authentic metalheads would be offended by our attire, interpreting our tongue-in-cheek tribute as a personal attack.

"Come on," Jane said, opening the cooler of beer that Percy and Bridget had packed before we left. "We *must* get drunk!"

And this time, I took her imperative to heart. Which is why the rest of the night is fuzzy. Once emboldened by a few cups of Miller Genuine Draft, we left the safety of our car. And to our utter amazement, the fans—Mötley Crüe and J.Crew alike—loved us. They high-fived us. They woooo-hooed us. They realized that we were out to *have* fun, not to poke fun. We were, in the words of the craptacular Poison song, out for "Nothin' but a Good Time." We had risked embarrassment by throwing ourselves hair-first into the spirit of heavy-metal excess, and it had paid off. Fans laughed at us, and we laughed with them. I've been to *better* shows, but I've never had more fun at one. Ever.

I wish that Marcus had joined us. He could have seen the difference between merely pretending to be game, as I had at *True,* and actually being game, as I was tonight. It's a distinction I couldn't explain before the fact, as I wasn't even too sure of it myself until now.

And I also could have avoided this conversation on the way home.

"So, Jess," Bridget said as she yanked off her press-on nails in the passenger side of Percy's hand-me-down Subaru station wagon. (I assure you that all jokes about this car and Percy and Bridget's nauseating domesticity have already been made.) "You never told us why Marcus didn't come."

"He said he didn't feel like dressing up," I replied.

"Isn't this the same person who came to school wearing a jacket and tie because he thought he needed to look like a goody-goody honor student?" Jane asked.

"Well, yeah," I replied.

"And didn't he for a while wear teenybopper T-shirts, like Britney Spears, on purpose?"

"He never wore Britney—" I began.

"I remember his Backstreet Boys shirts," Bridget piped in. "And he wore days of the week T-shirts too. Except on Tuesdays he wore a black shirt, in tribute to 9/11. And then there was THE GAME MASTER T-shirt. And the YOU, YES, YOU T-shirt . . ."

"Christ, Bridget," I snapped. "Who are you? *Sara*? Why have you paid so much attention to my boyfriend's wardrobe?"

"Well, J," Jane said. "Marcus *must* have wanted to be noticed. Isn't that why he dressed that way? It's kind of like his . . ."

"His what?" I asked.

"His shtick."

Bridget knew how much this remark would bother me and came to Marcus's—and indirectly, my—defense. "But he was wearing a plain white T-shirt when I saw him the other day."

"When I saw him too," Percy said.

"That's what he was wearing when I met him," Jane said. "It *must* be his new shtick."

"No, no, no," I protested. "He just doesn't want to be bothered with choosing an outfit . . ."

"Or maybe Marcus is sending a message by not sending a message at all."

It irritated me that Jane had declared herself an expert on my boyfriend and was passing judgment on his character after meeting him for all of two minutes. But it's hard to have a serious discussion when you're wearing acid wash and white leather, so I didn't say anything about it the rest of the way home.

"You're mad," Jane said later, as we stood side by side in my bathroom, rubbing off our makeup. The lipstick, the orange concealer, the red clown blush all came off easily with soap and water. The mascara was impenetrable and, evidently, permanent.

"I'm not mad," I said, scrubbing one eye roughly with a washcloth, as if it were the blackened bottom of a burnt pot. "I'm annoyed."

"At who?"

"At who?" I asked, incredulous. "At you!"

She dragged a brush through her crunchy hair, scattering Aqua Net shrapnel all over the countertop. "I was just making an observation about Marcus, one that *you* would totally make if he were anyone else's boyfriend."

Anyone's, I thought, but yours. Was I a bad friend because I couldn't be as candid with my observations? Then I rejected the question. There's a very good reason why I can't share her candor: Marcus might be shticky, but Jake (*bleeech!*) is . . . uh . . . dicky.

"Hey," she said, holding a cotton ball up to my eye. "I've got the right makeup remover for that. You *must* let me help you." And before I could protest, she very gingerly dabbed at my lashes until every last bit of artifice had vanished. I felt Jane's warm, licorice-spiced breath on my face and imagined that my own smelled of the same flavor of Altoids. Then I thought about how Hope and I would never do this for each other. We were not touchy-feely friends. I can think of three times that we've hugged: (1) the day her brother died, (2) the day she moved away, and (3) the day she surprised me on the football field at my high school graduation, our first reunion since hug #2.

Our friendship ran deeper than any demonstrative displays of affection.

"See?" Jane asked, holding up the blackened lump of cotton. "What would you do without me?"

"I don't know," I said truthfully.

And that's when I decided to forgive Jane for being a poor judge of boyfriend material. This doesn't make her a bad person. Just a very unfortunate one.

the eleventh

Jane made an important announcement on line for the bus back to Boston.

"J," she said. "I *must* tell you something."

"Okay," I said.

"You're my best friend in the world!"

She spread her arms wide and crushed me with a hug.

I categorize my friends, which is unnecessary because it's not like I've got so many that I need extensive record keeping to get a handle on them. But I've always referred to *Hope* as my best friend in the world. And when I've referred to other friends, I'd put a qualifier on it, like Marcus is my best friend *who has sex with me*. Or Bridget is my best friend *from childhood*.

Jane is my best friend *at Columbia*.

So I wasn't quite sure how to respond, until she pulled away from me and said, "Hey, J! Don't leave me hanging!"

And that's when I told her that she was my best friend in the world too.

Afterward, Marcus came over to my house. I sat on the diving board and dipped my toes into the deep end of our pool as he voluntarily skimmed the leaves off the top.

"Did you have fun with your friend?" he asked. As he

extended his arms, muscles popped up like surprises underneath his (white) T-shirt.

"We sort of got into a fight," I said.

"About what?" he asked, dumping the slimy brown clump into a garbage can.

"About you."

"Really?" he asked, but he didn't look surprised at all.

And then I told him everything she'd said about the shirts being his shtick and how it annoyed me because she made him sound so fake and calculating. I guess I was expecting Marcus to defend himself. I know I would have, if someone had said something like that about me. But he seemed unfazed by Jane's analysis and didn't stop skimming.

"So why *do* you wear the white T-shirts?" I asked. "Is it because anyone with ten bucks can buy a fake vintage ALABAMA: SO MANY RECIPES, SO FEW SQUIRRELS T-shirt from a sidewalk street vendor? Because what once might have been an authentically quirky find in a secondhand store has become manufactured for the masses, which makes it anything but funny? Because to combat this crass commercialization, a small but growing segment of the population has, like you, started making their own one-of-a-kind T-shirts? And the T-shirt makers have a lot of pressure on them to put a grand statement on their chests, or at least a really clever one, which is tough to do, so rather than get caught up in this walking billboard competition, you've decided to opt out and—"

"Jessica!" He rapped the skimmer against the patio to get my attention. Tiny droplets caught the sun, making miniature, split-second rainbows. "Sometimes a T-shirt is just a T-shirt."

Everything Marcus did was deep with meaning. There had to be more to it than that.

"Okay, Freud, but why the white ones? Why?"

He sighed. "My mom bought them for me."

I didn't say anything after that. Marcus kept dragging the net along the surface and didn't stop until the pool was clean and pure. Then, without any ceremony, he stripped off his controversial T-shirt and jumped in. The water splashed up and hit me in the face. I watched him swim underwater, his image ripply and distorted beneath the surface.

His head popped up. "Want to join me?"

"Nah," I said with a shiver. "It's too cold."

the sixteenth

I t didn't hit me right away. Not even when I saw my mom slumped at the breakfast bar in her pink bathrobe, her blond hair flat and matted, her face reluctantly showing its age.

"Hey, Mom," I ventured. "Are you feeling okay?" My mother *never* came downstairs in the morning until she was fully dressed, blown out, and made up.

She made a murmuring sound that was neither affirmative nor negative. It was a thoroughly indistinct sound, made by someone who didn't give a shit about the question that had been asked. She wasn't sipping her morning tea while simultaneously perusing the fall preview Pottery Barn catalog and talking to my sister on the phone, as was customary at this hour. She was just sitting there, staring at the splotchy granite countertop, an unreadable expression on her naked face.

"Mom?" I asked, with more urgency.

A few seconds passed before she swiveled her head and looked through me with dead-eyed, drug-induced zombification.

And then I remembered: Today would have been my brother's twenty-third birthday.

Matthew Michael Darling succumbed to SIDS at two weeks old. I'd say that he would have been three and a half years older than I am, but if he were still alive there would be no me. The Darlings wouldn't have wanted a third kid to mess up their picture-perfect family, a blond girl who looks like Mom and a brown-haired boy who looks like Dad. Not that I'm even sure he had brown hair, or any hair at all, because no one ever talks about him. I only know as much as I do from Bethany, who was seven years old at the time of his birth and death. Old enough to re-member that he briefly existed, but too young to know the details. And I can't bring myself to ask anyone else.

For the next two weeks, my mom and dad will mourn their way through the length of their son's brief life. My mom will pop emotion-numbing pills. My dad will get on his bike and ride and ride and ride in what I can only assume is a vain attempt to outrace Matthew's memory.

"Oh, Mom . . ." I wanted to say something that would let her know that I understood. But the truth is, I didn't understand. Matthew is such a nontopic of conversation that I don't have the vocabulary for speaking the language of senseless loss. So I said nothing else before grabbing a Coke and escaping upstairs.

Now I'm *really* dreading these last weeks at home. I can't wait to get back to school. When I saw him later that afternoon, Mar-cus picked up on my restlessness, though I didn't explain the deeper reasons for it.

"I know just what you need."

"What?"

"A road trip!" His eyes didn't merely dance. The greens of his irises do-si-doed with the browns, swirling, dipping, twirling in excitement.

"Road trip?"

"You know how you wanted us to hang out more with Percy and Bridget . . ."

He told me how spending so much time with his dad this summer, and hearing his tales about the open road, had given him a serious case of wanderlust.

"Why can't the four of us drive from New Jersey to California? Let's explore this great nation of ours. *From the mountains to the prairies!* From the *land where my fathers died* to the *land of the pilgrims' pride! From sea to shining sea!*" He sang the last parts, his hand patriotically thumping his chest.

I did not share his excitement. I was getting tired of everyone thinking they knew what was best for me all the time.

"How are Percy and I supposed to get back home?"

"Fly," he said, as if it were merely a matter of flapping my wings.

"Marcus, I didn't work all summer, remember? I've got no money. I'm barely keeping myself afloat . . ."

He dropped his hand to his side, sensing defeat. "I'm sure you can get a cheap flight on the internet. You don't start school for a few more weeks; you can be flexible."

Flexible was not how I felt. This was how I felt: My middle school science teacher once did a demonstration to illustrate how physical properties are transformed by outside forces. He stretched a large rubber band into a cat's cradle between his hands. Then he released the rubber band and dipped it into a beaker of liquid hydrogen. After a few seconds, he removed the rubber band and banged it against the lab table, and it shattered into a bazillion pieces.

"No, I can't," I said.

"Nothing is absolute," he said, his voice calm. His voice was always calm lately, the result of hours and hours of solitary reflection, he tells me. "Everything can change . . ."

Everything can change, I thought. Everything already had. Instead I said, "Why don't you just stay here and fly out when you had planned? Are you afraid to spend time with me?"

"Jessica . . ." The sound of his voice saying my name soothed me, and it's all I wanted to hear him say. Just my name, over and over and over again in his buttery baritone. I wanted my name to be his mantra, the word he meditated on, his tool for finding calm in the world.

But he kept on talking.

"I just asked you to drive three thousand miles with me. How would that make me afraid to see you?"

"You knew I probably wouldn't or couldn't do it."

"I thought you would say yes. We've talked about taking a cross-country trip ever since I decided to go to California."

"Yes, but I imagined us taking our time and taking a totally crazy, indirect route. We would camp out in the Grand Canyon. Hike in the Rocky Mountains. Swim in the Great Lakes. Try on wigs in Dollywood. Eat pretzels with the Amish. Whatever!"

"We can still do that . . ."

"And I imagined us being alone."

"I thought you'd enjoy spending time with Bridget and Percy," he said.

"I'd enjoy spending more time with you," I said. "Alone."

"You're implying that I'm somehow trying to upset you here, which is not my intention, Jessica. So we'll jettison Bridget and Percy. Does that make it a better proposition?"

"It makes it a better proposition, but still not a possible one."

"Jessica," Marcus repeated. And then he said some other stuff that I didn't really listen to because I was thinking about how Marcus is the only person who calls me Jessica. Everyone else calls me Jessie (my parents), Jess (anyone who knew me in high school), or J (anyone who met me in college). I was thinking about how if you say Jessica over and over again— jessicajessicajessica—it starts to sound like gajussgajussgajuss. And "gajuss" means nothing.

"What are you afraid of?" Marcus asked, breaking through my thoughts.

What am I afraid of? Why should I be afraid to spend uninter-rupted time with my boyfriend? Is it because more time means more opportunities for him to change his mind about me, like he does about everything else?

Or for me to change my mind about him . . . ?

"Jessica?"

"Nothing," I replied. "Nothing at all."

the eighteenth

So one happy couple is going on a cross-country adventure. But it isn't Marcus and me. And it isn't Percy and Bridget either.

It's Marcus and Bridget.

I am, apparently, the only one who sees anything sketchy about this. And my paranoia made me do something I'm not proud of. I went over to Bridget's house and interrogated her.

"So . . . uh . . . are you and Marcus going to stay in the same hotel room together?" I fished.

"Probably," she said. "It's cheaper."

"Are twin beds cheaper than a queen?"

"Jess, you're not serious, are you?" she asked. "Marcus is, like, totally not my type."

"Well, wiry Black guys weren't your type before you hooked up with Percy."

"Need I remind you how, like, upset I was when Manda slept with my boyfriend?"

I slumped to the pink carpet, beat down by it all. "I'm sorry, Bridget. I'm just . . ."

"Jealous," Bridget said, finishing my thought.

"I'm not jealous of you!" I protested weakly, not even bothering to get up off the floor. "You can't date someone with his history and get jealous all the time." I conveniently neglected to mention the Sierra episode. And also that I was a dirty liar.

Bridget set down the straightening iron she was about to put in her suitcase. "You're not jealous of *me*, but the chance to go with him."

And I responded by drawing my legs up to my chest and resting my head between my knees. She was right. By going on this trip—one that I turned down—Bridget would be spending more uninterrupted alone time with Marcus than I ever had.

What was wrong with me?

"Look, if it upsets you that much, I'll fly out to California. I wanted to drive so I could save money—I need new headshots—but if it's going to hurt you, I won't do it."

Girls want to hate Bridget because she's so goddamn gorgeous. Hell, I used to hate her for it. But she is the most trustworthy person I know. I attribute this to the fact that she wasn't always so stunning; I mean, she'd always been *cute*, but she didn't blossom into an eye-popping beauty until the summer before seventh grade, when the removal of orthodontia miraculously coincided with the addition of boobage. She had more than a decade to actually develop a soul, unlike girls who are born beautiful and never bother because they don't have to. But how do I reward her loyalty? By ignoring her. Doubting her. Accusing her of the worst.

"Bridget, I'm so sorry we didn't really hang out this summer," I said.

She twirled a strand of hair around her finger. "I know you were busy with Marcus and your big-time magazine job and everything," she said.

And for some inexplicable reason, I heard the rumble in my head and felt the burn in my throat that serves as a warning that I'm about to cry.

"It's okay," Bridget said.

"No," I croaked. "It's not."

She rushed to my side and threw her arm around me. "Look, Jess," she said. "As long as my mom lives across the street from your parents, we will be friends."

Bridget always smells like a day at the beach, not unlike the coconut-scented palm tree deodorizer hanging from Marcus's rearview mirror. She'll fit right in.

"One bad summer can't change everything," she said with confidence. I sighed and repeated her words back at her.

"One bad summer can't change everything . . ."

Never before have I needed Bridget to be so right.

the twenty-first

I haven't seen much of Marcus in the last three days. He's been packing and mapping. I've been doing a lot of melodramatic moping. This is something I do: avoidance. I did the same thing right before Hope moved. I didn't spend time with her because I knew she'd be gone soon anyway. Then after she left, I regretted the last talks, the last jokes, the last cries we missed out on.

"Are you okay?" Marcus asked as he put his battered guitar case in the backseat of the Caddie.

"I'm fine," I said, kicking the SEXY GRANDPA bumper sticker, a faded relic from the previous owner.

"Are you sure?" he said, reaching for my hand.

He was really asking me about last night. We'd gotten together at his house for a carefree farewell fuck that was anything but. It was intense. Too intense, actually. I cried as I came. And then I couldn't stop.

"I'm just sad that you're leaving," I said, stroking his calloused fingertips. "I feel like we hardly had any time together this summer. There were always all these other things in the way."

To his credit, Marcus didn't mention how I effectively chose not to take this trip. In fact, he didn't say anything. Instead, he glanced over at Bridget and Percy, who were swing dancing to music only they could hear. They too wouldn't see each other for months, yet didn't seem all that traumatized by it.

"There will always be other things," Marcus said quietly. "That's life."

I thought about how I've never danced with Marcus. Anywhere. Ever.

Marcus asked Bridget if she was ready to go.

"Woo-hoo!" Bridget whooped. "Let's hit the road!"

"I love you, Jessica," Marcus said.

"I know," I replied.

My eyes were dry as I watched the Caddie round the corner and drive out of sight.

Percy suggested that we cheer ourselves up over coffee and high carbs at Helga's Diner. I didn't have the energy to tell him that this wasn't the best cheer-upper locale, as it was the first place Marcus and I ever went together in public. A nondate, I called it, because I couldn't bring myself to acknowledge that what was happening between Marcus and me was genuine. We were spotted there by the Clueless Crew, who made salacious accusations that it would take another year and a half to make good on. On that first night, the furthest we got was Marcus's gentle nibble on my bottom lip.

To this day, I still wonder whether that lip nip counts as our first kiss.

And now, as back on the nondate night, I walked through Helga's front doors and straight in to the innermost circle of high school hell: Manda, Len, Scotty, and an anonymous girl were clustered by the cash register. I had nearly made it through the summer without seeing or being seen by them. This is why I don't like to leave the safety of my bedroom. Or Marcus's. To bump into them today of all days was just . . . so . . . *me.*

Percy, of course, was unfazed.

"It's like a high school reunion here tonight!"

And Manda, whose breasts are larger and realer than any on display in the Homemade Bikini Contest, said, "Jess! It's *soooo* great to see you! Where's Marcus? We wanted to hang out with you guys all summer! You're still together, right? Right?! Wait, are *you* two together?!"

Len shuffled his feet and said, "Um."

The giant Thanksgiving Day parade balloon affixed to Scotty's neck said, "Mutherfucker."

And I said, "JESUS CHRIST! HAVEN'T YOU PEOPLE EVOLVED AT ALL?"

Actually, I didn't. I did what I always do in situations like this. I made the kind of polite small talk that I hate, just to get it over with as quickly as possible. So I very calmly explained that no, Percy and I weren't a couple because I was still with Marcus and he was still with Bridget and that we had just said goodbye to them because they were driving to California in the Caddie.

Then Manda, who has never met another girl's boyfriend she didn't blow, said, "Wow, you must really trust them."

And Len looked up through his overgrown bangs and apologetically said, "Um."

And Scotty asked, "Is Bridget still smokin' hot?"

And the whole thing was so excruciating that I wanted to grab the mini-spoon out of the complimentary mint dish and stab myself in the eyes.

Fortunately, they were on the way out. The fearsome foursome hadn't arrived together, but had simultaneously arrived at the cash register to pay their respective checks. Now they were all considering heading out to the Bamboo Bar for happy hour.

"For old times' sake," Manda said, which was a strange thing to say considering the old times included Len cheating on me with Manda, Manda cheating on Scotty with Len, and Scotty suggesting that we get back at both of them by banging each other.

"I think we'll pass on the Boo," Percy said, saving me.

"Your loss," said the helium-headed beast. "Twenty-five-cent drafts."

"We have to get together before we go back to school," Manda said, hugging me as tightly as one can with elephantine tits. "Oh, and your hair looks *soooo* cute, by the way."

My hair. DAMMIT.

Len held out his hand all formal-like and said, "Um. It was really good to see you, Jess."

I shook it and said, "You too, Len."

And I sort of meant it, though it would have been nice to talk to him solo and find out about his first year at Cornell. But such opportunities aren't afforded to the Ex-Girlfriend Who Has Moved On. What Len lost in points for his questionable choice in companionship, he made up for in his choice of attire—a totally sincere Cornell T-shirt. This makes him the only other college-aged male besides Marcus who hasn't succumbed to the tyranny of the ironic T-shirt. To make my point, Scotty was wearing the worst of its kind: the fake *homemade* ironic T-shirt, the likes of which are often seen on the Ryan Seacrests of the world. This particular version was Astroturf green and silk-screened with the name of a nonexistent fitness club, but the print was faded and reversed to create the *illusion* of being worn inside out, a lazy trick confirmed by the location of the 95 percent cotton, 5 percent Lycra tag sewn on the *inside* of the shirt, rubbing up against Scotty's neck, and not on the *outside* of the shirt, which is where it would be if it were truly being worn inside out. But the hallmark of this fake homemade ironic T-shirt was the iron-on-like letters spelling MOST ATHLETIC across Scotty's double-barreled chest, as if he had come up with the fashion innovation all by himself. *Gee, this secondhand shirt is really cool. But it would be really, really cool if I turned it inside out, and applied some iron-on irony. I'm gonna heat up the good ol' Proctor Silex right now!* And furthermore, this isn't even a smart choice for an ironic T-shirt because Scotty was indeed voted MOST ATHLETIC in our yearbook superlatives, which just goes to show you how irony has become so misused, abused, and confused in these early years of the twenty-first century.

Okay, let's just get this out of the way: The reason I'm so annoyed by the pervasiveness of the fake homemade ironic T-shirt is that they ruin the purity of Marcus's genuine homemade ironic T-shirts of yore. There, I said it.

By the time Percy and I sat down at our table, I was thoroughly exhausted. I didn't feel like talking anymore, so while Percy went on and on about how amped he was about starting at NYU, I pretended to take great care in picking songs from the mini jukebox in our booth. And I was doing pretty well with not thinking about Marcus and the long stretch of highway ahead until later in the meal, when, in between mouthfuls of cheese fries, Percy asked, "Isn't it funny how Marcus and Bridget are both in California, and you and I are both in New York?"

"Yeah," I replied. "It's a laugh riot. I'm in stitches. My gut, it's busting."

"Seriously, maybe Manda is on to something," he said.

"How so?"

"Maybe we're in the wrong relationships," he said, laughing.

He meant it as a joke. And I even admired how secure he was in his love for Bridget to make it at all. But again, as before, my relationship with Marcus wasn't something I found humorous in any way.

And now, as I'm lying alone in my own bed, I keep thinking about writhing against him last night, naked and vulnerable. Even after we'd both risen and fallen, peaked and plummeted, even after Marcus was physically shrinking from inside me, I couldn't stop clutching, crying, trying. Trying to pull him deeper, deeper, deeper within.

Trying to make him more a part of me than I am myself.

sophomore winter
december 2003

Dear Hope,

I'm on the bus home for winter break. Consider this letter a Christmas miracle. I apologize for being so distant last semester. You've heard my excuses before and I don't know what else I can say, except maybe this:

Flash back ten years to Christmas 1993, and my first TV appearance in the Pineville Elementary School winter concert. This was during my short-lived career as a clarinet player, and I actually had a solo in the *Beauty and the Beast* part of the Disney medley. The show was only broadcast on the local cable station, but my family captured this legendary moment on video. It wasn't my performance that was so noteworthy—oh no!—but the appearance of my very first pimple. Not a bashful blemish, the scarlet starlet on my chin had so much personality that it practically upstaged me. My family dubbed our act "Notso & Friend," my solo made into a duet.

Throughout adolescence, other humiliations followed, including the First Day of School Furuncle, the Maid-of-Honor Nodule, and the Senior Portrait Pustule. My dermatologist prescribed an array of antibiotics and topical treatments, including a sulfur-based ointment that smelled like rotten eggs and gave my skin an Oompa Loompa hue. As each one failed to work, I learned to adapt to my acne. Like you'd mix paints on a palette, I taught myself to combine half a dozen shades of foundation to achieve the perfect camouflaging color. But no matter how much makeup I used or how often I reapplied it, my zits would inevitably shine through, being the attention-starved abscesses that they were (and still are).

And finally, after nearly a decade, I was prescribed Accutane.

On the back of each Accutane pill compartment there's a tiny drawing of a woman who appears to be at least eighteen months pregnant. A red JUST SAY NO diagonal slashes her distended belly. When I punch through the perforations to get to the pills, the little oval pictures come off in my hand. The pregnant-lady petals always end up on the carpet, often surrounding my bed. An offering to the goddess of anti-fertility. As if such measures were necessary. It's Dr. Rosen's duty to ask whether I'm using birth control, and I assume asking me about my sex life must be the highlight of a day primarily occupied by lancing boils. I disappoint him every month: "My method is abstinence." The next time I see him, I hope to give him a thrill. "CONDOMS! I USE CONDOMS!"

The red JUST SAY NO warning is what I thought about when I sat in a stall three months ago, searching for any sign of my period on the toilet paper. It soothed me as I stood barefoot on the cold, damp bathroom tiles on a late September morning, waiting for the white stick to give me a sign: plus or minus. Positive or negative. Yes or no. I braced myself on the sink, forehead pressed to the mirror, my breath fogging up my frightened reflection. I told myself, "I have to get rid of it. I have no choice." But I knew that even if I wasn't on Accutane and the baby was twenty-digits perfect, I would've come to the same reluctant conclusion.

When I finally got my period, inexplicably twenty-seven days late, I had already ignored as many messages from Marcus. This wasn't something I wanted to talk about over the phone or email. I was tired of telling him everything in absentia.

You too. Which is why you're getting this letter now. And for that, and all of my other unspoken secrets, I'm sorry. So, so, so sorry.

Repentantly yours,

J.

To: jdarling@columbia.edu
From: flutie_marcus@gakkai.edu
Date: December 11th, 2003
Subject: Poetry Spam #32

coastal quarantine

inoculate, isolate

secret soul disease

—Original Message—

From: Pinky Webguy [mailto:AXQOI@mailbx.com]
Sent: December 10th, 2003
To: flutie_marcus@gakkai.edu

Subject: chevrolet quarantine marjoram fuzzy sprocket Pocono

stairway cognition isolate imprudent tantalum denotation pipe-line stomp analogy playwright durable centimeter wizard aristo-crat inoculate rhododendron testicle asthma torpid ascendant cherry bunt silicone transmittable tool downcast lacy sallow im-itable swathe wreck stadium bohemia secret educable soul ac-robat morphology demystify bolshevik wyoming auburn pagan fear showmen ban editorial escapee harmful zone self hetero-dyne hitler synchrotron polytechnic ahoy attack disease convul-sive soak broody basilar coastal prickle rio cogent recriminatory brazil ridge defunct exclaim

the seventeenth

A h, there's no place like home for the hellidays . . .

"MERRY CHRISTMAS!!!" might seem like an improvement over my mother's usual first-glance, still-on-the-doorstep greetings (usually a recrimination or an accusation about my appearance). But in truth, her seasonal cheer was an affront to my humbuggy sensibilities. As was the house in general, which smelled like pine needles and cinnamon sticks and was all aglow in the tasteful, unblinking little white lights my mother favors. Surround-sound carolers contributed to the merriment. Fa-la-la-la-la-la-blah-blah-blah-*bleeech*.

Mom grabbed me by the arm. "Let me show you your present!"

I was surprised that she hadn't commented on my wardrobe (third-day-in-a-row jeans, ratty black thermal), epidermal land mines (mostly clear), or hair (finally! finally! finally! long enough to twist into a sloppy topknot). I interpreted her haste as a sincere desire to spread joy to the world, one malcontent at a time. She guided me down the hall and then stood for a moment outside my room, blocking me from entering. And then, with a dramatic sweep of her arm, she opened the door.

"Ta-da!"

Ta-da! My room was gone! Gone! My mosaic from Hope, my snapshots of Marcus, my movie posters, my books, my CDs, my everything . . . GONE!

"Mom! What the hell happened to my room?!"

I guess it could have been worse. It *could* have looked like the results of one of those not-even-third-rate *Trading Spaces* rip-offs, with, like, seaweed stapled to the walls. It was all very tasteful. Very . . . beige. Natural wicker furniture, a polished wood floor covered with a sand-colored sisal rug, photographs of beach scenes on the creamy walls. It could be a hotel room, a room for anyone.

"Isn't it beautiful?" she said, pulling me inside. "It looks so much more spacious and sunny without all your stuff strewn about."

"*My* stuff! Where is all my stuff!"

"Why are you upset? You were always complaining about how babyish your room was. You even tried to paint over the wallpaper, remember? I thought I'd surprise you with a makeover!"

She was showing a little too much enthusiasm. I tapped my sneaker in defiance.

"Don't get all huffy with me, Jessie," she said, sounding a bit huffy herself. "I redid Bethany's room too."

"Now I'm really confused," I said.

Then my mom went on to explain that she needed to redo our rooms as practice for what she hopes will be her new career as a professional stager.

"A what?"

My mother brightened. "A stager is real estate professional slash design specialist who sees the hidden potential in spaces and makes superficial yet strategic cosmetic enhancements to let the true personality of a property shine."

"And people *pay* you for this?" I asked skeptically.

"Yes!" She was very proud of herself.

"Why would anyone put more money into a house they want to sell?"

"This is not designing for living, it's designing *for leaving*." My mother draped her arm around me apologetically, feeling sorry for this daughter of hers who was *so* in the dark about *the* most obvious truths. "My work creates a faster sale and more money for the seller. Sometimes it's simply a rearrangement of furniture and a removal of clutter. But some rooms are in such disarray that they require a total overhaul."

"Like mine," I said dryly.

"Yes!" She was too excited to notice that I was insulted. "I've reinvented it as a guest room, inspired by the casual elegance of a Caribbean resort. But for your sister's room, I wanted to try my hand at something entirely different . . ."

She crossed in front of me to open the door, leaving me in a fog of perfume. Nothing could have prepared me for what was inside: a burst of blue. Baby blue, to be specific.

She had reimagined Bethany's room as a baby boy's room.

My mother started talking very, very fast, her excitement now bordering on mania. And psychosis. "It was my intention to do a baby girl's room, which would be practical because of Marin, but then when I was shopping for bumper sets I saw this adorable one with the blue choo-choos and I thought, This is how I want to transform this room! So I just went with it."

I looked around the room, at the Dr. Seuss books on the blue shelves next to the teddy bear sitting in the blue rocking chair across from the blue diaper stacker on the blue changing table under the blue choo-choo mobile . . . and I couldn't help but wonder how much this fake nursery looked like the real nursery in which the older brother I never met was discovered blue in his crib . . .

I thought maybe this was a cry for help. That by doing something so drastic, so over the top, she was begging for a long overdue discussion of that which is never discussed.

"And Marin can still sleep here," my mom breezily continued, unaware of my discomfort. "She's surrounded by a pink and sparkly feminine aesthetic at home, so I don't think that sleeping in a blue room a few times a month will—how should I put this?—make her more masculine, now, do you?"

This was the creepiest thing I've ever seen. And there was only one way to escape.

"Mooooom! WHERE! IS! MY! STUFF!"

"Jessica Lynn Darling, don't get so testy," Mom said testily. It worked.

"First of all, anything in this room was left behind when you went to school. If these things were so important to your well-being, why didn't you take them with you?"

I was so freaked out that I wasn't even thinking in English anymore. I was thinking in some made-up language unknown to the longest-tenured professor in Columbia's Linguistics department. I couldn't form a single word, let alone a sentence that could express how supremely horrified I was. My mother misinterpreted my silence.

"See?" my mother said, fluffing her bangs in the choo-choo mirror. "You know I'm right."

"Just tell me where my stuff is," I said when the powers of speech had returned.

"Stored in the basement," she replied. "In a properly labeled container."

I went into the cellar and found the large bin she was referring to: JESSIE'S JUNK.

And so, for the next few hours, I sat on the floor of the dim, dank basement, sorting through my junk. The mosaic picture of me and Hope brought a drizzle of tears to my eyes. The ME, YES, ME T-shirt that Marcus gave me to wear for my graduation speech created a steady rainfall. But the "Fall" poem, proof of how far we've come, all the way to being *"naked / without shame / in Paradise . . ."* Well, this brought on a torrential thunderstorm of tears. I might still be drowning downstairs if my dad hadn't come to get me with his corny Christmas cheer.

"Ho ho ho, Notso!"

I wish I could get high on frankincense or buzzed on myrrh, just to get me through these next few days until Marcus comes home. His last poetry spam told me what I'd suspected all along: He knew a heavy workload wasn't to blame for my lack of communication last semester. It was something else, something big I was too afraid to tell him, something he knew existed simply because he knows me so well. Something I will tell him when I see him. I swear.

the twenty-fourth

I wasn't the only one anxiously awaiting Marcus's arrival at my parents' house.

"MMMMMMMMMMAHCUSSSSSSSS!" shouted Marin as she careened into my knees.

"She associates you with Marcus," Bethany explained, setting out a tray of Papa D's Holidaze Donuts, which, to my knowledge, were the same as their regular variety, only coated in red, white, and green sprinkles. "Where is he, by the way?"

"On his way. He'll be here very soon." I stroked Marin's curls to console her. Her fair hair is the same color mine was before it darkened with age and temperament to its current bitter chocolate hue. Sometimes this gives me hope: The blond bond is broken! On more jaded days it makes me grieve for her future, which will be more dun than sun.

"YAY! YAY! YAY!" Marin whooped as she bounded toward the Christmas tree.

"She's more excited about Marcus than Santa Claus," I observed.

"So how are things between you two?" Bethany asked.

"Well, you know, this is Santa's really busy time of year . . ."

"I meant Marcus," she said, clarifying the obvious. "You haven't talked about him in ages."

I wanted to point out how she'd scarcely mentioned her husband in the past six months and she was *married* to him. But bringing him up would have created a Christmas crisis. G-Money believes no American of any color, class, or creed should ever be deprived of the opportunity to go into a diabetic coma. So if an atheist gets a craving for a king-sized cone of eggnog custard with a side order of Holidaze donuts at 2 a.m. on Christmas morning, *someone* has to keep the Shoppe open to serve him, and that person is G-Money. I'm sure if you asked him—not that I have—G-Money would tell you that he's doing it all for his wife and child. But haven't those priorities gotten a bit out of whack when loyalty to the brand seems to come before everything else, *including* your wife and child?

"You're not having problems, are you?" my mother asked, pinching stray sprinkles off the poinsettia print tablecloth.

Now that Marcus has been endorsed by Bethany, my mother is less hostile about our relationship. This proves the indestructibility of their blond bond.

"No," I said. "It was a tough semester, that's all."

"How tough could it have been?" my dad asked, the bells on his corny Santa hat jangling. "You got four As and a B-plus."

"That B-plus is really going to ruin your record," my mom said mockingly.

"I don't know if Bethany could find four As and a B-plus on all her report cards, ever," my dad said.

My sister gasped in offense. "I made the dean's list my last semester in school!"

"Was that the semester you got an A in step aerobics?" Dad asked.

My sister huffed herself out of the room. As she's gotten older, Bethany has grown less tolerant of her role as the Hot but Dumb One. Guess what that makes me?

I shouldn't complain about my status. After all, I just completed my third semester at one of the most selective institutions of higher learning in the world (and I have used up almost all of Gladdie's inheritance for the privilege of doing so). I have read Socrates, Plato, Aristotle, Machiavelli, and Nietzsche. I have listened to Josquin des Prez, Monteverdi, Bach, Handel, Mozart, Haydn, Beethoven, Verdi, Wagner, Schoenberg, and Stravinsky. I've analyzed works by Raphael, Michelangelo, Brueghel, Bernini, Rembrandt, Goya, Monet, Picasso, Wright, Le Corbusier, Pollock, and Warhol.

La-di-da.

See, you'll forgive me for all this name-dropping when I confess that I don't remember a damn thing about them. Okay, that's not entirely true. I remember Pollock paint splatters and discordant Stravinsky noise and Machiavelli's primitive political methods, you know, the stuff of *Jeopardy!* Daily Doubles. But my knowledge really doesn't go much beyond that. If I have a photographic memory, it's a shitting Polaroid camera that self-destructs after producing a single, flawless picture that fades to nothing almost immediately after first viewing.

I was like this in high school too—I was only as smart as my last exam—but I thought that maybe it was because my brain was in feast or famine mode. I'd stuff it with info for tests, but because it would be deprived of any sustenance on a day-to-day basis, it would get used up and forgotten. I was hoping it would get better at Columbia; that through Columbia's "legacy of cross-disciplinary scholarship," I'd be "compelled to analyze and ponder thinkers from the past" so that I could "better contemplate and influence the future." (Uh, like it says in the brochure.) However, I can barely remember anything from Contemporary Civilizations, a class I aced less than two weeks ago. Yet I can recite every line of dialogue from *The Breakfast Club*. Other Columbians have room for this kind of arcane knowledge *and* the stuff their parents are paying for.

One could argue that it isn't any school's role to make you smarter per se, but better educated, because intelligence is innate. If that's the case—you're smart or you aren't—I know I *am*. But that old get-laid aphorism is totally true: Tell smart girls how hot they are, and hot girls how smart they are. I used to be okay with being well above average in intelligence, and just average in looks because I was still above average—a 3.0—for the total package. But after three semesters at Columbia, I now know there are plenty of girls out there who are A-pluses in looks *and* intelligence. (And they surely exist in California too.) I already know Marcus loves me for my mind, so I think I'd get more out of him telling me that he loves me for my ass.

This is what I was thinking about when the doorbell rang.

My dad answered it, and there he was. Marcus Flutie. Marcus Flutie standing in the foyer underneath the mistletoe, as stretched out as his white T-shirt, as skinny as the thin wales of his corduroy pants. Standing as he had stood so many times before. Marcus Flutie, my boyfriend. More than that. My love.

And yet, he still seemed as ineffable to me as he did back when I'd see him with Hope's brother, when I knew nothing about him other than that he was just another one of Heath's dirty, dangerous, druggie friends. No matter how close I get to Marcus, I will never know exactly who he is. And the only reason that didn't send me screaming back up the stairs was the certainty that he will never know me either.

Marcus didn't say anything when he saw me, only pointed upward to the beribboned sprig of greenery hanging above his head. I floated over to him. I opened my lips to say something. *Hey*, maybe. *Merry Christmas*, or *I missed you*.

It should have been *I'm sorry*.

But he pressed his mouth over mine and sent these and all words back where they came from. My apologies would wait.

the twenty-fifth

I get why people have kids, besides the whole propagation of the species thing. Kids give you license to do dorky things and have fun while doing them.

Before Marin, Christmas had kind of devolved into this depressing festival-forced holly jollity. YOU WILL HAVE A VERY MERRY CHRISTMAS, GODDAMMIT. There were all these holiday traditions that simply *had* to be followed, even though they had lost all their meaning. For example, in the Darling household we don't put on any Christmas music until the day after Thanksgiving. And the annual inaugural record is Johnny Mathis's first Christmas album, the one where he's wearing the red jacket in the snow, not to be confused with his many follow-up Christmas albums, all of which have synthesized instruments and suck. And the first playing of Johnny Mathis has to be the original record, as in vinyl, not a CD, because it has certain scratches that make the record skip in predictable spots that would be missed by key members of the Darling household. And so, we have kept a turntable in the house for this once-a-year event, just so we can all hear Johnny stutter the last line in "White Christmas."

"*Annnd maaaay aaall yoour Christmases . . . ses . . . ses . . . ses . . . ses . . .*"

Until my mother laughs and says, "Spit it out, Johnny!" and bumps the needle so he can finish the line.

"*. . . be white.*"

This *has* to happen every year. Just like the tree always has to be draped in freshly strung cranberries even though it's a long and tedious and finger-stinging process. Just like we always have to bake Gladdie's butter cookies, even though they always come out tasting like oily tongue depressors.

But this year was different. There was a genuine excitement about waking up this morning because there was a wee one among us who sincerely believed that something magical had occurred while we slept. Think about the very concept of Santa for a second: A fat senior citizen in a tacky red suit flies around in a sleigh pulled by magic reindeer, delivering gifts for all the good little boys and girls in the world in just one night. It's absurd. Yet kids totally buy it. Totally. And in small children, that pure, untainted faith is a beautiful thing. In grown adults, however, I find it disturbing. After all, how different is Santa from Jesus and Buddha and Allah and so on? But that's an easy comparison for an atheist to make.

Anyway, I didn't want to spoil Marin's fun with my misanthropy. So I got all hopped up on candy canes and hot chocolate and threw myself into the Christmas cornballiness. And thus, I found myself wearing a jingle-bell reindeer-horn headband, entertaining my niece with very loud, very atonal versions of yuletide classics. Marcus accompanied me on guitar.

"YAAAAAAAAAAAAAAY!" cheered Marin with delight after I tore through "Good King Wenceslas."

"Now, this next number contains a very important life lesson, Marin, about being true to yourself, even when everyone around you is putting you down."

She blinked her huge blue eyes in bewilderment.

"It's a little song about the culture of conformity, and how easily individuals can be victimized by groupthink and . . ."

"ING! ING! ING!" Marin's word for "sing."

And so I cut short the life lesson and positively shredded "Rudolph the Red-Nosed Reindeer." Despite my very punk rock performance, Marin lost interest before we even got to the middle eight and drifted over to her Pinky the Poodle Playhouse. I kept singing until my performance went down in "HIS-TOR-Y."

Then Marcus said, "Rudolph Revisited: A Red-Nosed Nerd's Revenge."

When I heard him say the title of the high school editorial I wrote three years ago, an editorial that I'm sure has been forgotten by everyone else who read it, I was reminded of just how much HIS-TOR-Y we have together.

Marcus deserves to know the truth, but isn't demanding it from me. He's content to just be, which is very Zen of him. Besides, we were so full of sincere holiday cheer that I didn't want to spoil the mood.

Tomorrow. I will tell him tomorrow.

We had made gifts for each other because we were sickened by our culture's conspicuous consumption and MORE MORE MORE materialism. And also because we're poor. Marcus is friends with a silversmith at school—yes, a silversmith—who taught him how to make a ring out of a quarter. He somehow soldered a message for me in teeny script: *My thoughts create my world.* It only fit the middle finger of my right hand.

"I love this," I said, making the obscene hand gesture necessary to model it for him. "I'll think of you every time I tell someone to fuck off."

"Who's the last person you told to fuck off?" Marcus asked.

"You." A laugh struggled its way out of my throat. "New Year's Eve 2000–2001."

Before he could comment on this historical low point, I grabbed him by the red and green nubs of wool sticking out from around his neck. It was supposed to be a scarf. I tried knitting it last semester but didn't get very far.

"It's *almost* long enough to be an ascot," I apologized.

"I love it," he said. "I love you."

We kissed with sticky peppermint mouths.

Then Marin ran back over, showing us how she had taken the Virgin Mary out of the Nativity set and given her a makeover.

"PEE! POO!" Marin can say "Pinky the Poodle" but prefers the scatological shorthand because it makes her very immature aunt Jessie laugh. And I laughed even harder when I saw that Jesus's mama had red Magic Marker "makeup" smeared across her face, and Pinky's bikini and feather boa over her robes. Mary looked like she'd fit in at Persuasions.

"Nothing is sacred," Marcus said.

And I silently agreed.

the thirtieth

Marcus isn't here. He'll be back tomorrow to ring in the New Year with me.

Marcus is in Maine visiting his brother, Hugo, whom I have never met. All I know about him is that he's twenty-two, never went to college, works in construction, and lives in a log cabin on a lake in a salt-of-the-earth Ashton and Demi arrangement with a woman named Charlotte who is twenty years older than he is and has two teenage sons from a previous marriage and ekes out a living making pottery that she sells in a tent pitched on the side of the road. Marcus has never offered to take me with him to meet them. I've been his girlfriend for almost a year and a half now, so I considered it beneath me to ask to be brought along. Or maybe I felt like I didn't deserve to ask. At any rate, I didn't. Which is why he's in Bangor and I'm here.

Percy is also away until tomorrow. He's visiting assorted aunts, uncles, and cousins in Chicago. Bridget felt too guilty to leave her mom alone during the holidays and declined when he asked her to go. (She now regrets that decision since her mom is always working overtime at the Oceanfront Tavern because she gets paid double to cover for servers or hostesses or bartenders who— ahem!—take time off to spend with family.) So Bridget and I have been hanging out with each other because we hate everyone else in town.

The weather sucks. It's not cold enough to snow, but still soggy and gray—like hugging wet construction paper. Bridget and I have stayed indoors, mostly at my house because she fully appreciates all of my mom's manufactured holiday cheer. A single, working mom, Mrs. Milhokovich doesn't have any time for it. When we were ten, my mother was shocked—SHOCKED!—to discover that since the divorce, Mrs. M. didn't even bother trimming the tree anymore; she just stored it in the basement fully decorated, and dragged it back out as-is every third weekend in December. Since then, my mom has encouraged Bridget to spend as much time with our family over the holidays as she wants.

"You know that *Bubblegum Bimbos* is supposed to come out in a few weeks, right?" she asked on the day of her boyfriend's departure.

"How can I forget when you forwarded me a bazillion articles from *Ain't It Cool News*?"

I'm not looking forward to seeing the film version of Hy's book. Bridget needs to see it because she auditioned for a role and was justifiably miffed when she wasn't considered "seasoned" enough to play the "Gidget Popovich" role inspired by . . . herself.

"To give a totally honest review, I need to be schooled in the art of the teen movie. You know, for, like, a base of comparison."

And so, for the past five days, Bridget and I have seen every eighties teen movie in my DVD collection. The Best of the Genre (*Sixteen Candles, Fast Times at Ridgemont High, Real Genius*), the T&A Romps (*Private School, Porky's*), the Stupid Supernatural Comedies (*Teen Wolf, Weird Science*), the Brat Pack Dramadies (*The Breakfast Club, St. Elmo's Fire*), the Dark

Social Commentaries (*Less Than Zero, River's Edge*), and—of course—the Against All Odds Romances (*Say Anything, Pretty in Pink, Some Kind of Wonderful*).

"You know what's, like, totally annoying about these movies?"

I shrugged, picked up the remote, and shut off the DVD player.

"All these couples are, like, supposedly so into each other but all they do the whole movie is talk about how they're such opposites and how it's so cruel that their friends and family just can't accept their love and how tough it is for their romance to survive and *wah-wah-wah-wah.*"

"Hm."

"Percy and I have had a lot of tough stuff to deal with and you don't hear us *wah-wah-wahing* about it all the time."

Tough stuff. I was interested in hearing about this.

"Like what?"

She plopped herself down in my old beanbag chair that I had rescued from the basement.

"Well, even though his parents accept me, and my parents accept him, like, the whole world isn't so ready to deal with, like, interracial relationships."

"You get a lot of shit for dating someone Black?"

"No!" Her blue eyes bulged. "Just the opposite!"

"Really?"

Then she went on to say that since Percy started at NYU he's been hassled by women of color for choosing a white girl-friend—a blond Barbie-doll-gorgeous white girlfriend, no less—over one of them.

"Wow," I said, surprised by Bridget's intensity. "How does Percy feel about all this?"

Bridget's smile returned to her perfect face. "He says he's never let race determine his friendships and relationships, so why start now?"

She sighed, squashed down into the beanbag, and closed her eyes. "And, like, the long-distance thing makes this even harder."

"Uh-huh" was all I could say.

"It's so hard to find the line between, like, missing him enough and living your life, you know?"

My mouth soured with the metallic taste of blood. I hadn't realized that I'd been gnawing on my upper lip that hard.

"Like, *logically*, I know it makes sense for Percy and me to just break up now and just live our separate lives and not have to worry about missing each other all the time. But when I think about that, I get sick. Physically sick. Like I seriously throw up. I need to be with him, even if I can't, like, be *with* him."

I shivered.

"Why am I telling you this?" she asked, her face flushed with the rush of emotion. "You know all about it! You miss Marcus as much as I miss Percy!"

I nodded convincingly, pressing a tissue to my lip.

"You know he never stopped talking about you, like, the entire three thousand miles to California . . ."

"I know," I said, my eyes dropping. "You've told me." Bridget went out of her way to remind me time and again, just so there was no doubt in my mind that nothing had happened between them.

"I mean, it was, like, really, really sweet but, like, really, really annoying too," she went on, half-joking. "There's only so much gushing you can listen to. About how you were the most dynamic, the most interesting person he'd ever met. About how he loved your way with words, your ability to laugh at yourself. How you always managed to keep him guessing. How the sexiest thing about you is that you have no idea just how sexy you are. And on and on and on and on . . ."

I knew this was all true. And yet, it bothered me now, as it bothered me then: Why did I have to hear these things through a third party? Why hadn't Marcus ever said any of these things to me?

Is it because I never asked?

"It's just so hard to be in love sometimes," Bridget said. "Maybe we can find some inspiration in this next film, *Better Off Dead*."

Bridget giggled, but I didn't.

"That's a joke," she said, looking me over with concern. "Are you okay?"

No, I wasn't okay. Now *I* was the one who felt sick. I looked at myself in the mirror and my skin was like chlorophyll.

"Yeah," I said. "I just miss Marcus, like you said."

She patted my head sympathetically, much like I had with Marin when she was upset by his absence. "He'll be back tomorrow."

Yes, tomorrow.

As Bridget popped in the DVD, I took off my ring and read its inscription: *My thoughts create my world.*

What about my actions? What about those?

the thirty-first

Marcus returned today. And with him, a sky so bright and blue I had to squint.

"Let's go for a walk," he said, grabbing my hand and pulling me off my parents' doorstep. "I still need to thaw out!"

He breathed in deep and hummed happily on the exhale. Then he started talking. Marcus had a lot to talk about. I did too, but I let him go first. As if it made a difference.

Proving that they are their father's sons, Hugo and Marcus bonded through adventure. In three days they managed to go skiing (cross-country and downhill), ice fishing, and dogsledding, and do several other activities with "snow" as the prefix, including, but not limited to, -boarding, -mobiling, and -shoeing. In the middle of an anecdote about almost running over a moose during one of these pursuits, he paused long enough for me to pose my question.

"Marcus, why didn't you ask me to go with you?"

"I had no idea you'd be interested."

"Of course I'm interested in meeting your brother," I said. "I'm your girlfriend. I feel like I should know your flesh and blood as well as you know mine."

He rubbed his hands through his bed-heady red knots. "I'm sorry, Jessica. I guess I'm not well versed in boyfriend-girlfriend protocol. I forget that you're this person I'm supposed to introduce to my brother. I just see you as you."

I was about to ask him what exactly he saw, so I could hear for myself all those things he had so willingly confessed to Bridget. But we were both stopped dead in our tracks by an unexpected sight.

"Our park!"

"They changed it!"

"They changed *everything*!"

The Park That Time Forgot was no longer. Gone were the swings, slide, and sandbox of my youth. All were replaced by a plastic FUNTASTIC PLAY CENTRE.

This was a cosmic joke. The Park That Time Forgot was the Fifth Wonder of Pineville. Wonders one through four—the wine-bottle-shaped cement eyesore known as the Champagne of Propane, the VW bus on the roof of Augie's Auto Parts, the purple dinosaur statue in front of the carpet store, and the hot-dog-shaped truck known as Der Wunder Weiner—have all been immortalized in the pages of the *Weird N.J.* coffee-table books. The Park That Time Forgot was the only wonder that had been kept our little secret, which was fitting as the most significant stop on the tour.

Three years ago this very night, it was the setting for the infamous "Fuck you!" New Year's Eve. On the Park That Time Forgot's rusty merry-go-round, Marcus confessed that he had eavesdropped on my angsty conversations with Hope while getting high with her brother. That he had used our mutual angst as a devirginization tactic, just to see if he could bed the school's biggest goody-goody. That his dirty intentions were purified as he'd gotten to know me.

Until this revelation, I had been ready to sleep with him. But I wasn't ready for the truth, so I told him to fuck himself. It was such a devastating blow—for him to hear it, for me to mean it— that it would take us another year and a half to overcome.

And come together.

Only to return here, to be torn apart.

"I hate this!" I yelled, kicking the purple kiddie climbing wall that had replaced the dinged-up merry-go-round.

"The old one wasn't very safe," he said, skimming his hand along the curves of a twisty slide. "I wouldn't want Marin playing on any of that old equipment anyway."

"You're missing the point!" I screamed. "This was our park! And it's gone! Gone!"

Marcus took a step back. "What's going on with you? Are you all right?"

No, I wasn't all right. I was wrong. Wrong, wrong, wrong, wrong.

And that's when I ruined everything with a whisper.

"What?" he asked. Though from the stricken tone of his voice, I knew he had heard my words above the breeze.

"I cheated on you."

And then, as quickly as I could, I told him everything I should have told him over the phone, months ago. How I thought I was pregnant and how it terrified me, not only because I wasn't ready to be pregnant, but because I didn't feel ready to be in the kind of relationship in which a pregnancy would be a significant mistake, a love that was already so deep that it wouldn't be easy to just forget and get back to normal. And how this fear had something to do with why I fooled around with this other guy, but I wasn't exactly sure how, but we didn't have sex and it really, really didn't mean anything . . .

Marcus held up his hands in capitulation. "Enough."

"But you should know everything . . ." I said.

"I know everything I need to know." His voice was flat.

"Oh God, I'm so sorry," I said, searching his face for a sign, any sign as to what he was really thinking. "I should have told you sooner."

"You told me when you were ready to tell me."

He didn't seem traumatized by my revelation. He seemed almost totally unaffected, as if I had confessed to breathing: *I did it, Marcus! I inhaled and I exhaled!*

"Do you hate me?"

He took my hand. "I don't hate you."

"Really?"

"I could never hate you. There's no good in hating you."

He stroked the middle-finger ring gently before letting go and walking back toward my house, the park of our past receding into the background. I followed. And for about a minute, I reveled in my relief. *Marcus doesn't hate me! I'm so lucky to have such an understanding boyfriend. He knows that everyone makes mistakes and that I'm no exception. He's a better person than I am, because if he ever told me that he had kissed Butterfly, I would totally lose it because I can't deal with the idea of him being attracted to anyone who isn't me, even for one regrettable moment . . .*

How can he be so okay with this?

I started to get mad that he wasn't mad.

"Uh, Marcus?"

"Yes?"

"You don't hate me?"

"No."

Pause.

"You're *really* not mad?"

He sighed. "I didn't say that."

"Okay. Then what are you?"

He didn't say anything. Instead, he stopped and sat down on a curb only a few blocks away from my house. He was hunched over, hugging his legs, and he seemed so much smaller than I know he is. I sat down next to him and hesitantly took him in. He smelled like the dying embers of a bonfire. I waited for him to say something.

He didn't.

And he didn't.

And he still didn't.

Finally, after what seemed like a silence as endless as the universe itself, I couldn't take it anymore.

"Marcus? Why aren't you saying anything?"

He shifted in my direction, and I heard every inch of his body rubbing against the concrete.

"I was trying to find the right words. And I can't. So I'd rather say nothing right now."

"Nothing? I do what I did and you have nothing to say? You don't care enough about our relationship to say anything at all?"

He got up and walked to the Caddie parked in the driveway. All without a word.

"I can't believe you have nothing to say," I mumbled as he put the key in the door and slid into the driver's seat. He fastened his seat belt, put the key into the ignition, turned it on.

The door was still open.

"You're not listening," he said, finally.

I looked into his eyes and saw that they were shiny with tears.

"Most people talk when they have nothing to say," he said. "I'm not talking because I have too much to say. None of which I'd want you to hear."

Then he shut the door, backed the car out, and drove far away from me.

Dear Hope,

Four years ago on this date, you moved to Tennessee.

Three years ago on this date, Marcus confessed that he only befriended me so he could have sex with me, and I told him to go fuck himself.

Two years ago on this date, I did ecstasy with Scotty, almost lost my virginity to Len, and wished out loud that Marcus was the one I was (almost) having sex with.

One year ago on this date, Marcus visited me in New York for the sole purpose of leaving a party early so we could have sex in my skinny college bed.

I can't help but wonder if any of this would have happened if you had stayed. I used to tell myself not to think about it, and just accept my past as it was because there was nothing I could do to change it now. I told myself, and others, that I was happy with how I'd ended up and that's all that mattered. But that was just naïveté talking. It's really easy to convince yourself that you're just so goddamn *evolved* when you don't have a clue. Because the truth is, I'm not all that happy with who I've been these past few months, and I'm not quite sure where I went wrong, or whether there's a resolution strict enough to fix me.

Commemoratively yours,

J.

sophomore winter
january 2004

the fifth

I was flattened on the floor in shame.

"You cheated."

Bridget was sprawled out on my bland beige bedspread, staring at the ceiling, still reeling from my news. She'd come by to tell me that the release date for *Bubblegum Bimbos* had been pushed back yet again, which meant that its suck-ass, straight-to-video future was practically guaranteed. Compared with my cover story, her gossip was like the teeny sidebar hidden in the back of a magazine next to the horoscopes.

"Jess, you *cheated*."

"I know."

"I don't like cheaters," she said gravely. "I was so hurt when I found out that Burke had cheated with Manda."

"I know."

"And you were so upset when Len cheated with Manda . . ."

"I *know*."

"What's wrong with everyone?" she asked. "Why does everyone cheat?"

"*Everyone* doesn't cheat . . ."

"I just don't get it," she continued, ignoring me.

"What don't you get?"

She puffed up her cheeks, then blew all the air out in agitation. "Let's say a girl is attracted to someone who has a girlfriend. And then the guy with the girlfriend decides, like, *What the hell? We're not married, we're just hanging out. I can hook up with this other girl if I want to.* It seems obvious to me that any self-respecting girl would realize that the guy's decision to cheat on his girlfriend would make him an undesirable person to hook up with, right?" She paused for a moment to give this profound inquiry its due gravitas. "And the guy who wants to cheat should be turned off by any girl who is so willing to hook up with someone else's boyfriend. Being so, like, *morally bankrupt* should cancel out all the attractive qualities that tempt you to cheat."

I pressed my forehead into the scratchy sisal rug, branding red pockmarks into my flesh.

"The cheater's paradox makes perfect sense, Bridget. Really. But humans are irrational creatures, especially when it comes to matters of the heart."

It's true. Studies have shown that people convince themselves that they're acting rationally when making major decisions— where to go to college, what to major in, who to kiss or not to kiss—when they're really acting on unconscious impulses. The human brain simply can't handle all the complexities that life offers, so emotions kick in and end up making the call. And when that call blows, people don't understand why.

And when I say people, well . . . you *know* who I mean.

"You and your research," Bridget said dismissively. "You're getting so . . . *clinical.*"

She sat up and shook her head. Tsk-tsk. I rolled over on the rug and read the bumps on my forehead like Braille. Here's what they spelled out: YOU FUCKED UP.

"Have you talked to Marcus?"

"No."

"Are you, like, officially broken up?"

"I don't know."

I've decided not to force a confrontation with Marcus, leaving it up to him to contact me. The uncertainty is torture, and I deserve each excruciating second of silence.

"I never thought you guys would end like this," she said.

"How did you think we'd end?"

Bridget twisted her hair into a bun on top of her head.

"I didn't," she said, letting go. Golden waves spilled over her shoulders.

That was not what I wanted her to say. I would have preferred it if she had seen our demise as inevitable. She must have picked up on this.

"But if I did, like, *hypothetically* think about it," she said, "I would have thought that he would've been the one to cheat, you know, because of his history as a male slut and all."

This also did not make me feel better. And I think Bridget saw what she was up against and gave up on trying.

"This is just so not like you, Jess," she said. "Who's the guy? How did it happen?"

I sighed. And then I told her the whole sick, sordid story.

Since Columbia University went coed in 1983 there has been a glacial relationship between the women of Columbia College and the women of Barnard College, the women-only school located right across Broadway. It has everything to do with the scarcity of single Columbia men. Between the two campuses, guys are outnumbered roughly two to one, which makes for very heavy competition on the hookup front. Columbia women claim that the Barnard women are (1) preoccupied with appearances, (2) dumb, and (3) slutty. (That is, the ones who aren't stereotyped as man-hating lesbians, making them a versatile group, indeed.) Columbia women generally concede that this combination makes Barnard women irresistible to Columbia men. The Barnard women claim that they are indeed (1) cuter and more stylish than the Columbia women, but are (2) equally smart and (3) more liberated and confident in their sexual power, all vehemently unslutty explanations for their attractiveness to Columbia men.

I got into this debate with my suitemate William, the F-Unit punk who helped create the Breakup Pool.

"Not that I care, because I already have a boyfriend, but I think it's pathetic that guys don't hit on me because I go to Columbia," I said. "They know I'd be more of a challenge than a Barnard girl."

"You've got it all wrong," William said. "Guys don't hit on you because you give off an unavailable vibe."

"I don't broadcast to total strangers in a bar that I've got a boyfriend," I said. "How would they know?"

"It's your whole demeanor," he said. "Everything about you says, 'Don't even think about it.'"

This was an unnerving moment of truth. I mean, *I* know how much people annoy me, but was it so obvious to others? I was worried that William might be right, but I wasn't ready to back down.

"Oh yeah? Let's see what happens when I wear a Barnard T-shirt at the West End tomorrow night."

We saw this as an anthropological experiment. Would men find me more attractive simply because I was wearing a Barnard T-shirt? Or would I be as off-putting as ever? So I hung out at the bar on a Thursday night in my baby pink Barnard teeny T. And much to my simultaneous delight (to be right) and disgust (to be right about something so sexist and gross), several guys tried to get me very, very drunk.

After I'd been flirting for about two hours, William approached me at the bar. Even through beer goggles, he looked the same as he always did to me: pale and wan and wearing a Misfits T-shirt and more black eyeliner than I did.

"Ha! Look how drunk I am! Being a Barnard girl pays off after all!"

"You're very fetching in that T-shirt," William replied.

"See? It's even having a pheromonal effect on you. Men cannot resist the arousing powers of the Barnard T-shirt!"

"Actually, it's not the T-shirt . . ."

And then, surrounded by dozens of beer-swilling witnesses, he leaned in and kissed me. And as much as I was expecting another boy's mouth to feel and taste strange, it didn't.

So I kissed him back.

At this point in the story Bridget asked the obvious.

"Did you sleep with him?"

"No!"

She placed her hands on her hips defiantly, knowing there was more to it than that.

"We . . . uh . . . *did* go back to his room and we . . . uh . . . hooked up . . ."

"Hooked up," Bridget said dryly, knowing full well that its unspecific, open-to-interpretation definition makes it a very popular term in situations like this.

"Right," I said breezily. "Then I fell asleep."

"Passed out," Bridget corrected, most accurately.

"Same difference!"

I neglected to mention the part about hurling into his wastepaper basket before I passed out. I'm a puker. It's not an attractive quality. Though in this case it was good, putting a damper on the mood and guaranteeing that William wouldn't take any illegal, licentious liberties with me while I was out cold. Not that I think he would, but you can never be too careful. Date rapists in real life aren't as obviously simian and sinister as they are in made-for-TV movies.

"So what's up with you and this guy now?"

"Nothing," I said. "It was a onetime thing. And it got hostile between us after it happened."

"Hostile? How?"

My words were strangled by disgrace.

"What?"

"Christ. I can't even say it . . ."

"What?" Bridget said, grabbing my arm and pumping it up and down. "What?"

"He's a GOPunk!"

"A what?" she asked.

"A Republican!"

Bridget's face clouded with bafflement. "A *punk* Republican?"

"We call him Mini Dub."

"Why? Because he's got a small penis?"

"No," I said. Though in my brief handling of it, I did notice his penis was on the petite side. But I hadn't thought of that connotation simply because I had tried not to think about his penis at all, because when I did, it nauseated me. "It's short for Mini Dubya."

"*Ohhhhhh*," Bridget said, nodding her head.

"I felt like I was promoting tolerance by putting our political differences aside. We would spar with each other on the issues and it was all in fun. To tell you the truth, I kind of admired William in a strange way because his conservative politics were extremely unpopular with most punks, and his punk appearance scared most conservatives. He caught shit from all sides, and he *still* didn't change to please anyone."

"But . . . ?"

"But kissing him? That crossed some kind of ideological line that I just shouldn't have crossed. Just thinking about it makes me want to rip out my tongue and scrub it with sandpaper!"

"It would serve you right," Bridget said firmly.

"Well, he must have felt the same way about kissing me because he started turning purple whenever we crossed paths."

"Red and blue make purple," Bridget pointed out.

I groaned and buried my head into the rug.

"Why did you do it?"

"I don't know," I replied without lifting my head up off the floor.

"You, Miss Psychology Major at Columbia, have had some time to obsess over every little detail of this huge, probably relationship-ending event, and overanalyze it the way you overanalyze everything, and you're telling me that you don't even have the slightest idea why you did it?"

I shrugged.

And that's when Bridget lost patience with me and said I should spend time alone until I made some sense of the totally insensible thing I had done.

Bridget was right about one thing, as she usually is. I had tried applying my newfound knowledge to come up with an answer to her question. A considerable aspect of social psychology is trying to figure out what internal and external cues influence people to act the way they do. Suffice it to say, I've provided myself with my own case study. Because all actions have numerous motivating factors, any single explanation for my misdeed would be an overgeneralization. And so . . .

A COLLECTION OF THEORIES TRYING TO EXPLAIN WHY I KISSED A REPUBLICAN AND FUCKED UP MY RELATIONSHIP WITH MARCUS

- **The Deindividuation Theory:** I felt anonymous in the bar mob, wearing my Barnard T-shirt disguise, so I kissed a Republican.
- **The Conformity Theory:** I was the only one in my suite who hadn't broken up with or cheated on my high school boyfriend, so I kissed a Republican.
- **The Passive-Aggressive Theory:** I was bothered by Marcus's extensive sexual history and wanted to even things up a little, so I kissed a Republican.

- **The Aversive Event Theory:** I was still reeling from my pregnancy scare, which made my relationship with Marcus feel too intense to handle, so I kissed a Republican.

- **The Cultural Force Theory:** I have been taught by repeated viewings of *The Real World* that hooking up with someone who isn't my boyfriend is a de facto component of any long-distance relationship, so I kissed a Republican.

- **The Proximity Theory:** I was here and Marcus was three thousand miles away, so I kissed a Republican.

- **The Cognitive Dissonance Theory:** I missed Marcus, and I didn't want to miss him so much anymore, so I kissed a Republican.

- **The Biological Pull Theory:** I recognized that with his good genes and Ivy League education, William could be a better provider for future offspring, so I kissed a Republican.

- **The Bipartisan Theory:** I want liberals and conservatives to work together for the best of this great nation of ours, so I kissed a Republican.

- **The Immunoglobulin Theory:** I was run-down and sniffly, and sexual activity helps boost microbe-fighting antibodies, so I kissed a Republican.

- **The Sensory Deprivation Theory:** I hadn't had any physical contact with the opposite sex for three months, making me desperately crave such contact, so I kissed a Republican.

- **The Childhood Attachment Theory:** I learned from

my parents that people who love me will do so uncon-
ditionally, even when I fuck up, so I kissed a Republican.

- **The Psychosocial Theory:** I am in the identity versus
role confusion stage of development, during which it
is perfectly normal to want to try out a skanky persona, so I kissed a Republican.

- **The Reciprocal Influence Theory:** I flirted with William, making him want to kiss me; in turn, he flirted
with me, making me want to kiss him, so I kissed a
Republican.

- **The Social-Cognitive Theory:** I was flattered by William's superficial compliment about my hotness, so I
kissed a Republican.

- **The Freudian Theory:** I subconsciously want to have
sex with my father—a retrocon—so I kissed a Republican.

- **The Situational Theory:** I was drunk off my ass, so I
kissed a Republican.

- **The Humanistic Theory:** I have a history of doing
things I otherwise wouldn't do when under the influence of mind-altering chemicals, so I kissed a Republican.

- **The Dispositional Theory:** I'm a malcontent by nature and wanted to fuck things up for myself, so I
kissed a Republican.

- **The Rational-Emotive Theory:** I'm young! I'm not
married!! I've got a city full of people and possibilities
to explore!!! The world won't stop turning if I cheat
on Marcus!!!! So I kissed a Republican.

None of my analysis has resulted in a theory that rings true. The closest I've come is this:

- **The Fight-or-Flight Theory:** I was aroused by the danger of the forbidden, of getting caught, and I wanted to take that exhilarating risk, like taking a leap off a soaring, breathtaking cliff, so I kissed a Republican.

And the only reason this one feels right is because every bone in my body aches from just recently smash-landing into the depths of the darkest crevasse.

the eighth

15 DOWN: BIGMOUTH STRIKES AGAIN

The media has been on Britney Spears's case for "ruining the sanctity of marriage" with her whirlwind wedding/annulment weekend, but I think matrimonial monogamy is a seriously flawed concept. Roughly half of married couples split up. Those odds suck. Think of it this way: Would you buy a car if you knew there was a fifty percent chance it would blow up somewhere on the road of life? I think not.

"But what about the fifty percent who do stay together?" you ask. "What about them?"

Well, they should probably break up too. Exhibit A: my parents.

My parents have been married for thirty-two years. They are the exact opposite of Bethany and G-Money. They're always in the same house, but never speak directly to each other. They talk *around* each other, and almost always through other people. I never really noticed this before, but since I'm trapped in the house with nothing else to do, I've had ample opportunities to observe my parents' dysfunctions up close and personal.

Like this morning, when I was brooding over coffee and the

New York Times crossword puzzle. I wasn't *really* doing it. I was just filling in spaces with titles of songs by the Smiths and Morrissey as a solo artist. I wasn't even checking to see if I had the right number of letters. When 7 **DOWN** came up short, I just added three exclamation points to SUEDEHEAD. When 13 **ACROSS** proved too long, I let THE LAST OF THE INTERNATIONAL PLAYBOYS dangle off the edge of the puzzle.

My mom breezed in with a handful of swatches in a variety of plaids.

"Do you know when your father plans to take down the Christmas tree?"

And I said, "Uh, no."

16 ACROSS: GIRLFRIEND IN A COMA

And she said, "Well, he needs to take it down today if he wants to put it out on the curb for recycling tomorrow."

And I said, "Okay."

And she said, "He's going to come back and track mud all over the floor."

And I said, "Probably."

And she left, leaving a mist of Chanel No. 5 in her wake.

5 DOWN: OUR FRANK

Not two minutes later, my father came in, still wearing his bike helmet, smearing muddy footprints all over the floor.

"Have you seen your mother?"

"Yeah," I said. "She wants you to put out the Christmas tree."

"It doesn't need to go out until tomorrow," he said. "Did she buy my deodorant?"

"I don't know," I said. "But she did say something about how you track mud all over the floor, so you should probably clean it up."

He shot a derisive look at the floor before grabbing a paper towel and rubbing the dirt into the ceramic tile.

"If you see her, tell her I need my deodorant. She never remembers to buy my deodorant."

And then he went into his office and shut the door.

41 ACROSS: HOW SOON IS NOW?

Later, in two separate incidents, my mother congratulated herself for knowing that my father would muddy up the floor, and my father congratulated himself for knowing that my mother would forget to buy his deodorant. This is what thirty-two years of marriage gets you: the utter satisfaction of predicting *precisely* how your life mate will annoy the hell out of you.

I can't imagine that they were *always* this way with each other, bickering about recycled Christmas trees and Right Guard—and through a proxy, no less. They should be arguing about more important things, like how it was completely certifiable of my mother to design a bedroom for the dead baby boy she never got to see grow up, or how it was almost equally certifiable that my dad *didn't even know she had done it* until I showed it to him, because he's off riding his bikes for hours and then holes himself up in his office "working" whenever he's home.

I'm sure that in their youth they felt as passionate toward each other as Marcus and I do. (Did? What tense are we in?)

So my point is this: Whether on the way to the altar or after, all relationships are doomed.

And yet . . .

3 ACROSS: PANIC

46 DOWN: GIRL AFRAID

10 ACROSS: WILL NEVER MARRY

40 ACROSS: WHAT DIFFERENCE DOES IT MAKE?

17 DOWN: LAST NIGHT I DREAMT THAT SOMEBODY LOVED ME

47 ACROSS: NOW MY HEART IS FULL

34 ACROSS: THERE IS A LIGHT THAT NEVER GOES OUT

8 DOWN: THE MORE YOU IGNORE ME, THE CLOSER I GET

12 DOWN: THIS CHARMING MAN

2 ACROSS: THE BOY WITH THE THORN IN HIS SIDE

6 ACROSS: FOUND, FOUND, FOUND

22 ACROSS: DISAPPOINTED

9 DOWN: HEAVEN KNOWS I'M MISERABLE NOW

1 DOWN: PLEASE, PLEASE, PLEASE, LET ME GET WHAT I WANT

the fifteenth

A FINAL CONVERSATION

Me: I wasn't sure if I'd see you before I left.

Marcus: I wouldn't let you go without saying goodbye.

Me: When I didn't hear from you, I thought the worst.

Marcus: I needed time away to think.

Me: I'm so sorry, Marcus. You have no idea . . .

Marcus: You did what you wanted to do.

Me: But I didn't really . . .

Marcus: Part of you must have, or you wouldn't have done it.

Me: But . . .

Marcus: I didn't come here to make you feel bad about what happened.

Me: You're breaking up with me.

Marcus: I'm not breaking up with you.

Me: You're not?

Marcus: No.

Me: But . . .

Marcus: Please.

Me: Okay.

Marcus: We didn't talk much last semester. And now that I know it was because you thought you were pregnant, and were worried that it would change our relationship, as it ineluctably would, I don't blame you for your distance.

Me: But . . .

Marcus: The Buddhists believe that desiring begets suffering. That every pleasure itself consists of a continual striving that ends as soon as it's reached. I've spent my whole life craving something. Attention. The next high. Girls in general. Then one girl in particular.

Me: Me?

Marcus: Yes, you. But none of it has helped me feel truly at peace. Not even my love for you, which is as pure and real and true as anything I've ever known.

Me: But what does this have to do with . . . ?

Marcus: I was at unrest because I knew, deep down, that love, though a beautiful beginning, isn't enough. It's the practice of honoring and caring for another that's noble, not the emotion of love itself. The emotion is the easy part.

Me: . . .

Marcus: But how could I honor the responsibilities that come with being in a genuine love relationship? The sort of responsibilities your pregnancy scare brought to the fore for you. How could I try to understand your needs if I'm still a mystery to myself?

Me: . . .

Marcus: Throughout the period when I wasn't talking to you, I found that I could go days without talking to anyone. And I realized that when I didn't talk, I became a much better listener, both when it came to other people and myself.

Me: . . .

Marcus: And so I've decided to embark on a silent meditation.

Me: A silent meditation? Marcus? What?

Marcus: It's not that complicated, Jessica. I'm just going to shut up for a while.

Me: Are you not talking to me or not talking to everyone?

Marcus: Everyone. Including you.

Me: Starting when? For how long?

Marcus: Tonight. After we say goodbye.

Me: For how long?

Marcus: I don't know yet. I don't want to put a limit on it before I even begin.

Me: Do you have an idea?

Marcus: At least a month. Or two. Maybe more.

Me: Is this because of what I told you the other night?

Marcus: Maybe. Yes. No. Neither. Both.

Me: Well, that certainly clears things up.

Marcus: See what I mean? Words make a mess of things.

Me: So do actions . . .

Marcus: Yes, they do too.

Me: I really didn't mean to hurt you . . .

Marcus: There's something else. I've volun-teered for Gakkai's World Without Web project. The concept is quite simple, really: to dis-connect with the internet and reconnect with real life. I'll be offline once classes start on January 20.

Me: So I can't talk to you or email you.

Marcus: We can write letters . . .

Me: I don't want to write letters! I'm already tired of writing letters to Hope. Now I have to write to you too?

Marcus: Then don't.

Me: Why don't you just break up with me?

Marcus: Because breaking up with you sounds so permanent.

Me: How can you be with someone when you don't see or hear from that person for months at a time? How is that a relationship?

Marcus: Our relationship is what we let it be.

Me: I am so sick of your Buddhist wisdom! It's bumper-sticker wisdom! T-shirt wisdom! My thoughts create my world. I'm so tired of being scrutinized through your goddamn third eye.

Marcus: I'm sorry you feel that way.

Me: You've changed.

Marcus: Maybe I have. I don't expect you to understand why this is so important to me. Just the idea of it helps me feel more centered and focused. For the first time in my life, I see a future where I won't need anything—T-shirts, getting high, having sex—to define who I am.

Me: You won't need me either.

[Pause.]

Marcus: I still love you, Jessica.

Me: I . . .

Marcus: . . . ?

Me: Nothing. I . . . nothing. It's my turn to shut my mouth.

[I take off the middle-finger ring and thrust it at Marcus. He takes it and puts it in his pocket. We go our separate, silent ways.]

THE END

sophomore summer
june 2004

Dear Hope,

You haven't been the only one to point out how my impatience with the human race might get in the way of my job as a shrink. I have to learn how to be a better listener. I'm usually too busy planning what I'll say next to focus on the person I'm supposed to be listening to. I would argue that this is because most people are boring, but my faculty adviser says that's a pretty narcissistic point of view.

So that's why I'm working for Columbia's Storytelling Project this summer. It's an interdisciplinary study of historical narratives. Basically, I'm being paid to sit in the park all summer with a sign that says TELL ME A STORY. When a freak takes the bait, I videotape them telling me whatever they want to tell me. Among other things, the psychology department will review the tapes to analyze the storytellers' gestures and facial expressions to see if there is a "universal unspoken language." I'm just psyched that my fellowship covers my room and board for the summer and I didn't have to move in with Bethany again. Or go home. I don't know which would be worse.

Of course, none of this is as exciting as a summer in France studying at l'École des Beaux-Arts de Saint-Étienne. *Les voyages forment la jeunesse, non?* The way I see it, this experience will not only improve your own global outlook, but it might even boost our entire nation's approval ratings abroad. I mean, if there's anyone who can improve the Gallic opinion of Americans, it's you. Maybe you'll realize that the French have every right to believe that we are a nation of idiotic imperialist pigs, chuck your US passport, and become an expatriate.

Speaking of ugly Americans, when you consider how much I dislike most people and how I cringe at small talk, you can see why this will be the hardest six dollars an hour I am ever likely to earn.

Empathetically yours,
J.

the second

I was rereading the postcard that I received in the mailbox today, the second of its kind. I've pinned these messages to the wall of my otherwise unadorned dorm room. I haven't had time to unpack my stuff for the summer, yet I've had ample opportunity to obsess over his minimalist missives. It's a matter of priorities, you see.

This is somewhat healthier than my other hobby: Google stalking. This is something everyone does but no one owns up to because it's just so pathetic. And yet, I can't stop. Every night before I go to sleep, I plug "Marcus Flutie" into the browser and pray that a new result will pop up. Unlike "Jessica Darling," "Marcus Flutie" is alone in the Googleverse, and is therefore easy to track down, or would be, that is, if there were anything to track. (Note to anyone who wants to Google stalk me: Use the advanced option and remove the word *anal* from your search.) He's got five listings, and three of them refer to his participation on Gakkai's Frisbee Golf Intramurals Squad. Another is from the Gakkai College's campus newspaper, the *Mahayana Weekly*, in a story about some baby fowl that were ducknapped from a petting zoo. ("All unhappiness stems from desire," says Marcus Flutie, twenty, a first-year student. "These thieves must be miserable.") And finally, the last listing, the most telling and most frustrating, the one I often fixate on for hours at a time, is from a mercifully short-lived blog called freetobeme.com written by none other than Butterfly the Nuddhist. A simple caption ("The infamous Marcus Flutie. ZZZZZZZ. 2-18-03.") beneath a blurry, too-close photo of Marcus's face, un-self-consciously crumpled up in a deep, deep slumber. Such a little thing, this photo, this caption, and yet it alone has inspired so many sleepless nights of tortured inquiry. (Why is he the infamous Marcus Flutie? I know why he's notorious around Pineville, but what had he done at Gakkai to earn such a distinction? Or was Butterfly being glib? And why was Butterfly there while he was sleeping? Had she just woken up herself? Had they been sleeping on that couch together . . . ? Etc., etc., etc.) I'm lucky that there are so few paths to search, otherwise I could find myself in an endless labyrinth of links, all yielding more questions than answers. As it is, I find myself poring over these same five listings, over and over and over again until I feel dirty and ashamed, as if I'd spent the whole night jacking off to porn, which, in a way, this has become for me. And yet I can't stop doing it. I compulsively type his name, hoping for a new connection to something, anything related to "Marcus Flutie" because even the most inane tidbit of information would be more than I already have.

Which, I know, will never be enough.

I imagine that I wouldn't be driven to such desperate measures if Marcus had written me letters like he said he would. Instead, he wrote postcards. The first was an old-fashioned black-and-white picture of a medical eye chart, postmarked February 22 from Nuevo Viejo, California:

Jessica—
I
—Marcus

That's it.

Was it a roman numeral one, to signify the first in a series? Or a lowercase *L* to stand for . . . oh, any number of words that start with *L* like in that "La La La" song sung by Bert and Ernie? Lightbulb? Lemon drop? Linoleum?

Or . . . love?

Nope. It's none of these. Because it's a capital *I*, as indicated by the homonymal hint on the front of the card. By "I" was he referring to himself, as the writer of the card? Or was I to read it aloud, so the message refers to the first person "I" as in me?

All this conjecture, you see, is exactly what he, being the Game Master, wants.

Today's postcard is a color photograph of the sky illuminated by stars, postmarked May 31 from Nuevo Viejo, California. The message was more straightforward, yet still indecipherable.

Jessica—
WISH
—Marcus

I WISH, I WISH, I WISH . . . You know those magic photos that look like a blobby nothing, then you stare at it until your eyes cross and suddenly a dinosaur or whatever pops up and reveals itself and you can't believe you didn't see it right away? That's how I felt when I read this word, instantly realizing that these weren't one-word messages Marcus was sending me, but part of a larger message that he wanted to reveal bit by bit over time.

I WISH . . .

I WISH I KNEW WHAT THE HELL HE WANTED.

"He wants me to know that he's thinking of me, but he doesn't want me to know *what* he's thinking." I was sounding more and more like someone you'd cross the street to avoid. Meanwhile, my friend Dexy was rummaging through the piles of un-put-away clothes on my floor, humming a tune as inscrutable as Marcus's postcards. She was in a key that Philip Glass wouldn't even think to invent, like Q minor.

"Am I supposed to use these as mantras for Buddhist meditation or something?"

Dexy held a note. F bumpy.

"At least I know he's out there somewhere."

Dexy stopped humming and started singing. "*Somewhere out there, beneath the pale moonlight!*"

Dexy has lyrics for every occasion. She is a very enthusiastic singer. This is unfortunate because she is also a very terrible singer, which, coming from me, is saying a lot about her lack of musicianship. So, so, *so* painful are the sounds that assault us from the depths of musical hell, which, apparently, has a studio located directly inside Dexy's voice box. She makes ears bleed, and yet she just loves to sing, and so she sings loudly and often and one day hopes to be good enough to make the bad singers montage on *American Idol*. She was rejected by every a cappella group on campus from the badly punned Uptown Vocal to the even worsely punned Clefhangers. But there were no hard feelings. Dexy is an a cappella groupie and sleeps with tenors and basses and those who percuss. Unless spelling bee bitches exist, this makes her the geekiest kind of groupie one can possibly be.

"Wanna go to Tom's for a black-and-white?" Dexy asked, uninspired by my collection of T-shirts and jeans. This chocolate and vanilla shake is the magical elixir, the cure for any problem, be it a bombed exam or the endless aftershocks of a nonbreakup breakup. It must be nice to be such a blithe spirit.

"We can't," I said, glancing at my watch. "We have the hall meeting." Dexy and I were lucky enough to be assigned rooms on the same floor for the summer, and we were supposed to meet with the RA.

Dexy buzzed a loud, wet raspberry in my direction. "There's plenty of time!"

Dexy is unmoved by such pedestrian concerns as punctuality. She's always late because she's always cramming *just one more thing* into a life with a staggering surfeit of places to go and people to see. That I am one of those people still surprises me. I was just one in a classroom full of students fulfilling their course requirement with a biology class, and I'm not sure what inspired her to sit next to me. For my part, I was kind of looking for a new best friend at school after Jane proved to be less than sympathetic, I daresay enthusiastic, about the nonbreakup breakup.

"He's so pretentious, J," Jane had said when I told her about Marcus's departure. "And so self-absorbed! He couldn't have been less interested in getting to know me."

When she was unable to see that she had just effectively and unintentionally described her own heinous boyfriend, I realized I didn't have it in me to pretend I was her best friend anymore. I cowardly used "stress" (academic stress, work stress, breakup stress, terrorist stress, fill-in-the-blank stress) as a convenient, catchall excuse for not hanging out. It didn't take long—only a few weeks—before Jane finally gave up and moved on, which pretty much proves how tenuous our friendship was in the first place.

Dexy, on the other hand, lent a supportive, albeit tone-deaf ear. "Breakups are the new relationships," she said.

"Uh . . . really?" I had no idea what she was talking about.

"Yes! Consider it an opportunity to discover yourself! To celebrate your newfound freedom!"

And while I didn't go wild in Single de Mayo revelry, being around Dexy couldn't help but lift my spirits. While most students—myself included—throw on jeans and a T-shirt that challenge the widely held parental notion that there is *always* a clear demarcation between clean and dirty, Dexy wears what can only be described as costumes. For her, *every* day is sort of like the Glam Slam Metal Jam. For example, today she's feeling European, so she's wearing black capri pants, a sleeveless striped boatneck sweater, and ballet flats. There's a beret perched atop a black bobbed wig (hiding her dirty-blond hair), and her French-manicured fingers clutch a long, lacquered cigarette holder (filled with a candy cancer stick because she doesn't smoke).

Some people I know think she tries too hard. I mean, the costumes. The singing. The name. (Which is on her birth certificate. Her parents really liked the song "Come On Eileen" by Dexy's Midnight Runners.) The drama of her life can be a bit much. But she's so positive, so fun that it requires more energy to resist her charms than it does to just give in to them. Unlike Jane, who made me feel guilty when I *didn't* go along, there's no pressure from Dexy. She reminds me a lot of Hope, only without the talent or the personal tragedies that give Hope more depth.

Dexy's taking an art history class because she couldn't imagine spending the summer with her family in Pennsylvania. I don't know much about her family, only that her parents are still together and that she has a brother who is a junior in high school. She calls them all "hopelessly unoriginal," although, in her parents' defense, they must have once possessed a sense of whimsy if they named their daughter after a one-hit wonder about trying to get laid.

"Really, J," Dexy said today. "Put the past behind you."

"I know," I said, still gripping the postcard.

"Don't stop thinking about tomorrow . . . Yesterday's gone! Yesterday's gone!"

"Please! Not Fleetwood Mac! If I promise to stop obsessing, do you promise to stop singing and come to the hall meeting with me?"

She took a drag on her candy cigarette. "Dah-ling!"

Thus compromised, we went. And that's when I discovered that it wasn't going to be so easy to put the past behind me. Because standing in the middle of the lounge was none other than William the Kissing Republican introducing himself as our RA for the summer. Ack.

"Well, if it isn't Darling, Jessica," he said, tapping a finger on his alphabetized list. He's mastered the presidential cocky squint/smirk combo, and he didn't hesitate to toss one my way.

"We should have gone to Tom's," Dexy whispered.

So we sat through the meeting as Mini Dub dictated the hall rules and regulations for the summer term in that cowpunk twang of his. This authority role is one he relishes, one that brings out his most irritating quality, which is his inability to acknowledge any alternative points of view. And that's when I decided that post-hookup shame was not to blame for my avoidance of William. No. I just can't stand looking at his smug mug. As the F-Unit mastermind of the Breakup Pool, William is just pleased as can be with his role in my nonbreakup breakup with Marcus. I knew I'd have to try to wipe that smirk off his face if there was any hope of me surviving on his floor for the next three months. So after the meeting was over, I approached him to broker some sort of truce.

"So . . ." he said, oozing smarm. "How can I help you, Darling, Jessica?"

"You can stop calling me that," I snapped. "Can we talk?"

"Have you made an appointment?"

I glared.

"Okay, let's talk," he said, unlocking, then opening the door to his room. I followed, then shut the door behind me.

"Isn't there some kind of rule against RAs hooking up with their advisees?"

"You're reaching, J," he said. "I wasn't your RA when it happened."

"Well, uh, okay," I said, defeated. "But isn't there a *retroactive* rule?"

"No."

And then there was an awkward pause. A pause in which I had time to observe various Columbia College Conservative Club flyers (*Go up 116th and Broadway . . . and turn right*), a "Don't Mess with Texas" poster, and a framed 8 × 10 of his parents shaking hands with Bush 43 and the First Lady . . .

"Did you say something?" he asked.

"No, I just gagged."

"What happened between us was no big deal," he said. "Unless it was a big deal for *you*." Then he broke out one of his twisted smiles.

"Wipe that look off your face!"

"What look?"

"That . . . *presidential* look!"

"Four. More. Years," he replied, just to piss me off.

"Oh yes," I said. "Four more years of war, unemployment, environmental destruction, soaring deficits, attacks on civil liberties . . ."

"You've been brainwashed by the liberal media."

"ARRRRRGH! I didn't come here to debate politics with you!"

"That's the problem with you Democrats. You refuse to reach across the aisle in the spirit of bipartisan cooperation."

My head was about to launch off my neck and blast into outer space. 10 . . . 9 . . . 8 . . . I counted down slowly. 7 . . . 6 . . . 5 . . . I'd miss my head, you know, when it was orbiting the earth as a tiny, lip-glossed satellite. 4 . . . 3 . . . 2 . . .

Fortunately, William got back to business. "J, everything's cool with me if it's cool with you," he said. "You'll be treated no differently than any of my other advisees. Is that what you want to hear?"

"Well, yes," I said, relaxing.

"This is my job, J," he said. "I take my responsibilities very seriously."

"Okay."

"Besides," he said. "It's not like we slept together."

"Right!" I said, making my way to the door.

"And we were both under the influence."

"Exactly!"

"We weren't thinking properly," he said.

"Not at all!"

"Do you really think I would've hit on you if I'd been sober?" he asked, shutting the door in my face.

1 . . .

BLASTOFF!

the seventh

Being romantically unfettered is such a swell thing. See, if I were still with Marcus, I wouldn't be able to entertain and enjoy guilt-free sexual fantasies about my hot grad student partner in the Storytelling Project. If I were with Marcus, such an act would feel like a betrayal. But I can daydream without remorse because I am totally single. If only the same could be said for my hot grad student partner. He's married. With three kids, all five and under. Yikes.

But I'm not the other woman in my fantasies. I've conveniently made them adultery-free by getting rid of the wife and kids. I don't kill her off, of course, because any dead wife takes on a mythical perfection, and that is especially true of mommies smote down in the prime of youth. Perfection is something that I simply can't live up to, even in my own sexual fantasies.

No, in the sexual fantasies I've been having about my hot grad student partner (whose name, Bastian, I will now use if only to stop objectifying him with pornographic anonymity), his wife and kids are disposed of via a recent divorce, one sought by Bastian because his wife has become a mirthless harpy, a sexless shrew, since the babies came along. She gets full custody of the whole brood and moves to a remote village in Antarctica, befitting her chilly nature. And he, whose only relations have been of the one-handed variety, is primed and ready for the fresh-faced coed . . .

"So where should we go at it?" asked Bastian.

"Anywhere you want me," I murmured, dreamily.

"Pardon?"

"Anywhere," I said.

"Why don't we start in a familiar place, so we are not nervous our first time?"

I have to remind myself that this is real, and not part of the daydream. He's talking about the Storytelling Project. Not sex.

"Yes, nonthreatening environs," I said, like a moron, bringing me back to reality.

"*Está bien.*"

Oh, did I mention that he's Spanish, as in from Spain, and that he occasionally slips into his native tongue? (Add your own sexual innuendo here. It's just too easy for me. Really.) He's from Madrid but has lived here for more than a decade, long enough to master English, but without flattening his Castilian quirks. Who knew a lispy accent could be so manly? So damn sexy? I hear those "ths" clinging to his tongue and go loco.

We headed down Amsterdam on foot, past the dusty ninety-nine-cent stores, the sketchy storefront lawyers, the anonymous delis. He was carrying a camcorder and a sandwich board that said TELL US A STORY. I was carrying the fold-up beach chairs we will be sitting in, side by side, all summer long.

I cannot believe I'm getting paid to spend a long, hot season with this man. He is a man, not a boy. Not a guy. And Bastian's not my normal geek-cute type either. He's too experienced, his dark eyes bruised by a chronic weariness I've yet to know.

His nose and mouth are so delicate they're almost feminine, yet his visage is rendered rough and untouchable by a five o'clock shadow no matter what time it is. Bastian usually lets his thick, shoulder-length black hair hang loose. But when it gets too sticky, he occasionally ties it back in what I guess would technically be a ponytail, which sounds really nasty when I call it that, but in truth, that's what it is, and on him it's not nasty at all. He wears his jeans tighter than American guys; lower too, and almost always with gauzy shirts in pale swirly patterns that become translucent when the sun hits them in just the right way. And if the rays persist and the temperatures rise, a private, peppery scent radiates from his deepest skin, and I get dizzy with . . . what? Lust?

Yes, lust.

Why not? Hetero, homo, bi, and ambiguous—everyone in the program wants to fuck him. I could feel envious eyes on me when the Storytelling Project supervisors paired up the undergrad fellows with their grad school mentors. Jessica and Bastian. Bastian and Jessica. All summer long. *Dios mio.*

"Here?"

He stopped between 110th and 111th Streets, right in front of the red-and-white-striped awning of the Hungarian Pastry Shop. This is the "teensy little nothing of a pastry shop" where I had my momentous meeting with Paul Parlipiano, the one that convinced me that Columbia was the school for me. I had no idea at the time that it was a Morningside Heights institution, that dozens of poor students linger inside for hours, making the most of the only free refills in upper Manhattan, and as such, it would have been freakier if I *hadn't* bumped into Paul at the shop. If he weren't toiling at Kerry's campaign HQ (Paul, via email, told me that he quickly shifted allegiances after Dean's "I

Have a Scream!" debacle), I'm certain I would have seen him
there today.

I didn't even realize that I was babbling about all this to
Bastian until he held up a finger and said, calmly, *"Callate, por
favor."*

Shut up. Please.

"I am sure you have many interesting stories to tell," he said,
setting up the sign. "But we are being paid to listen to others, yes?"

I nodded, vowing not to say anything else until spoken to. It
didn't take long.

We were approached by a bent old man wearing a straw
fedora, white Bermuda shorts, a sky-blue polyester short-sleeved
shirt, black dress socks, and white orthopedic sandals. He read
each word slowly, deliberately.

"Tell . . . us . . . a . . . story." He raised a hefty, overgrown eyebrow. "Why should I tell you hippies anything?"

I wanted to crack up, but Bastian's stoic composure made me
reconsider.

"Because everyone has a story to tell," I said.

"Hooey!" the old man barked.

"We define ourselves by the stories we tell others," Bastian
added. "It is a revolutionary take on history, in terms of who is
making it and who has the power to document it."

"Hippie hooey!" he yelled as he hobbled away.

This time Bastian and I couldn't help but laugh.

"This is going to be difficult," Bastian said.

And it was. New Yorkers are very wary, an instinct that has always been necessary for survival, now more than ever. Hardly anyone believed us when we explained that we were sponsored by the
university and that their stories would be archived for educational

purposes only. Yet over the next few hours we did attract a few yakkers, most of whom fell into one of the following categories:

1. **People Who Wanted to Pick Fights with Us** ("Why the hell should I talk to you? Are you crazy people?")

2. **People Who Wanted to Prove They Were Smarter Than We Were** ("What's so revolutionary about your project when oral historical narratives predate Homer?")

3. **People Who Wanted to Get on Camera Because They Thought We Were Taping a Reality Show** ("Is this network or cable? Can my agent look over this release before I sign it?")

4. **People Who Wanted to Know How We Got the Book Deal They Were Convinced We Had Even Though We Told Them We Weren't Writing a Book** ("Who's your agent? I've got a novel that's *Harry Potter* meets *The Da Vinci Code*.")

5. **People Who Wanted to Mock Us Because They Thought We Were Scientologists** ("Hey! Where's my free copy of *Dianetics*? Can you introduce me to Tom Cruise?")

6. **People Who Wanted to Have Sex with One or Both of Us** ("I'll tell you a story you'll never forget. I'll tell it *all night long*, know what I'm saying?")

And throughout our shift, Bastian maintained a purely professional demeanor. I, on the other hand, barely heard a thing because I was too busy imagining what my hot, married grad student partner would look like naked.

If I ever do become a shrink, I'll have to open a very specialized practice, one that only caters to the emotional needs of women and extremely homely men.

the sixteenth

Dexy is as tireless as she is exhausting. Every morning she asks the same question, and today was no different.

"Where are you and your Spanish boyfriend headed today?"

"Dexy, I'm supposed to talk to strangers, not my best friend."

"Come on! I've got a ton of stories! I want to be immortalized in Columbia's archives!"

"Isn't it enough to be immortalized on television?" I asked, intentionally changing the subject.

"Yeah, I guess," she said, adjusting a long platinum blond wig. "Today I'm getting set up with a mechanic who, according to the producers, loves 'hot rods and cold Bud.'"

"Sounds like a winner," I replied.

"It'll make good TV," she said.

Dexy scores extra cash by appearing on any one of a number of cheesy-ass dating shows that are taped around the city. These are the late-night cable staples that make *The Bachelor* look like high art: *Blind Date, ElimiDate, EX-treme Dating*, etc., etc., etc. She's become such a fixture on these shows that she's relied on her talent for clever costuming so the producers won't catch on to her repeat casting. She's not looking for love, just easy money.

"If you tell me where you are today, I can swing by and introduce you to him . . ."

"Out!" I shout, literally pushing her through the door.

I can do my best to prevent Dexy from stalking me for camera time. But I can't stop random run-ins with the most unfortunate acquaintances. Since the first day Bastian and I have gone out of our way to encamp far from campus—from the Lower East Side to Washington Heights—to avoid seeing the same faces. Unfortunately, the steps of the Brooklyn Public Library weren't far enough.

"Well, well," Mini Dub said this afternoon, as he approached our sign. "If it isn't Darling, Jessica."

"Stop calling me that."

"You two are acquainted?" Bastian asked.

Neither William nor I acknowledged the question.

"I should have known that you would be participating in this waste of money," William said. "Oh, I mean this important interdisciplinary yadda yadda yadda." He opened and shut his hands like two squawking mouths. William was one of many engineering students who thought the money spent on the Storytelling Project should have been put toward what they refer to as the "real sciences."

"What are you doing in this zip code?"

"It just so happens," William said, "that I'm meeting a friend."

"Another date from the facebook?"

"The facebook," he said, clutching his hand to his stomach, pretending to laugh. "That's rich." If you closed your eyes and listened to William, he would sound just like any popped-collar yuppie meanie played by James Spader in the eighties. But then you'd open your eyes and see this person with the powdery-faced,

black-cloaked Bauhaus look of the living dead. When combined
with a GOP=NRA=USA T-shirt, it is an especially unsettling aesthetic, indeed.

"What is the facebook?" Bastian asked.

"An online dating service for college students," I answered.

"*Networking* service," William corrected. "It provides users
with connections of both the platonic and romantic varieties."

"I think it is sad that even flirting is now done by computer,"
Bastian said. "So much of courtship is the unspoken."

"So true," I said, with a serious nod.

William flicked his tongue stud at me. "That must be why
your profile is missing from the site."

He was right, my profile was missing. The reason I was hes-
itant to join the facebook (or CNet or myspace or any similar
site for that matter) is because I didn't want to be poked all day
long by people asking me to be their "friend." I didn't want any
friends in quotation marks. And I certainly didn't want to get
all huffy and hurt when that same "friend" snubbed me a week
later by terminating our "friendship." It seemed to me that too
many people joined these sites to collect "friends" and improve
their social capital in a way that didn't require them to leave their
dorm rooms, like Dexy, who had "friends" that she'd never even
met listed on the facebook. (Then again, she has been equally
adept at turning electronic pokes into, uh, literal ones.) And yet,
despite my skepticism, I was open-minded about the possibility of
signing up.

That is, until I recently checked out Hope Weaver's profile.

Hope Weaver was a flame-haired, alabaster stunner wearing
a brilliant smile and an off-the-shoulder sweatshirt dipping dangerously down to her elbow. Hope Weaver belonged to more

than a dozen nonsensical-sounding groups including "Super Totally Awesome Chicks & Dudes," "Mary-Kate Is Better Than Ashley," "Gnomes Are Great," and "I Hate the Word Panties." Her wall was filled with cryptic messages from names I'd never heard her mention. And no wonder—Hope Weaver had 491 "friends," through whom she was connected to 4,236 other college students across the country. Looking at the evidence of her life without me at RISD, and now in France, I felt like I wasn't Hope Weaver's friend at all. With or without quotation marks.

"I guess you don't need electronic intervention like the rest of us," William continued. "But we all can't be like you, Darling, Jessica. Juggling two, three guys at once."

Bastian sat up in his beach chair. "Really?"

"No," I said.

"Oh, don't be modest," William said, enjoying my discomfort. "You want to hear a story? I've got a story . . ."

"You can't tell a story about me!" I said, instantly knowing what he was up to.

"Why can't I?" he asked. "It says *tell us a story*. There's no qualifiers on it saying *tell us a story, but it can't be about Jessica Darling*."

I pleaded with Bastian. "I don't really see how this is helpful."

Bastian looked at William, then returned his eyes to me. "He is right. He can tell whatever story it is he wants to tell."

"*Gracias, amigo*," William said.

And so, for the next, oh, I don't know, bazillion years or so, William told, in excruciating detail, the story about how we had come up with the Barnard T-shirt bet and how he was relieved when he was wrong and I was right because it meant that guys had bought me many drinks and that I had gotten drunk enough to let down my defenses and finally act on the sexual tension that had been building between us and stop being so sanctimonious about the purity of my relationship with my long-distance boyfriend, whom I only spoke of with worshipful reverence when it sounded like this guy was as flawed as every other guy, if not more, and how it was so like me as a typically needy, love-hungry girly girl to blame William for the subsequent breakup between me and the long-distance boyfriend when I really should have been looking inward, and so much more that I can't bring myself to write it down because it's just so disturbing that this asshole has a better understanding of my weaknesses than I do.

"Well," he said when he was finished. "I'm sure that this story will prove to be relevant for many future generations of naïve college girls."

"Don't you have one of those girls waiting for you?" Bastian asked, as I had lost my will to live, let alone speak.

"Oh, right," he said. And with a swagger, he was off.

"So is his story true?" Bastian asked.

"What did his face say?"

Bastian, it should be noted, is writing a dissertation titled "Facial Metacommunications: How Microexpressions Influence Interpersonal Perceptions." (English is not his first language, but *all* dissertation titles sound like this.) A large part of it is devoted to the tiny, involuntary facial movements that reveal people's true emotions. Most people can't detect them because they flash past in a blink, but Bastian can.

"He did not seem to be lying," he admitted. "But I did not want to believe it."

"Well, believe it," I said. "Because it's true."

Bastian laughed. He has a very loud laugh for someone so soft-spoken. His laugh bounces off walls and almost seems to echo, as if he's filling up all the world's open empty spaces with his joy.

"You, *bella*," he said, "have very bad taste in men."

the twenty-ninth

I t's said that there are eight million stories in the naked city. Well, it's not true. By my count, there are exactly nine. They can be categorized as such:

1. Urban legends involving cockroaches and/or other vermin and the unlikely human orifices in which they decide to seek shelter and/or reproduce

2. Intoxication tales involving the breakdown of crucial bodily functions

3. Family sagas that seek to explain why the narrator is in therapy

4. Wistful childhood nostalgia for a time when life wasn't so damn complicated

5. Sexual hyperbole

6. 9/11/01

7. Eulogies (unrelated to #6)

8. Character sketches of crazy New Yorkers

9. Romances with crazy New Yorkers gone horribly, horribly wrong

I'm not saying other stories don't exist, it just seems that these are the types of stories that people care to share with others. The truly fascinating thing about New Yorkers, or, I suppose, humans in general, is that we assume that we are far more interesting than we really are. Why we think total strangers want to hear about the mundane minutiae of our small world, or banal observations about the big world, is beyond me. I guess it's the same compulsive creative impulse shared by bloggers and, to a lesser degree, diarists like myself.

I'm barely two weeks into this gig and bored out of my mind because most people just have no idea how to tell a captivating story. And I disagree with my adviser, who has said that my boredom stems from raging narcissism. I mean, I keep *waiting* for the teller to get to the good part, or the unexpected plot twist, and more often than not it never comes. Inside, I'm dying to ask more questions, to dig a little deeper, but we're not allowed to influence the storytellers in any way. And so, I find myself embellishing these tales inside my head, just to make them more interesting: "I'm banging this girl and she had a heart-shaped birthmark on her ass . . . *which means she's my long-lost twin sister!*"

Bastian is an extremely sensitive soul, so it's no wonder he has picked up on my disinterest. He's tried to keep me engaged by quizzing me on speakers' microexpressions. He's trying to teach me to see what he sees.

"Did you see how he tugged the corners of his lips down with his triangularis, then raised his chin by flexing his mentalis?"

"Uh, no."

"Then he contracted his zygomatic major in a classic smile, just for a split second?"

"No."

"He wanted us to think that he was sad when talking about the death of his stepfather, but actually he is quite happy about it."

"Really," I said, more of a statement than a question.

"Oh, yes," he said. "Words lie. I see the truth."

Wouldn't this be useful if Marcus were here? I thought. I could have Bastian read his thoughts without him having to say a single word. And then I hated myself for thinking about him at all.

At that moment, Bastian gently stroked my wrinkled brow with the very tips of his fingers, as if to wipe away my concerns. I too could be heard without saying a word.

"Don't worry, *bella*."

I felt comforted, knowing that someone, anyone, was paying attention.

I reached up to touch this man's hand. I let it hover over his for a moment, still unsure if this is what I wanted to do.

I did.

I pressed my hand against his. His fingers twisted into mine and I was surprised by how soft they were. We let them fall, entwined.

And I wondered, Is this a story I haven't already heard?

the thirtieth

Dexy is a madcap beauty right out of a screwball comedy—with emphasis on the "screw" part. Have I mentioned that Dexy is kind of a slut? Well, uh, she is. But she's also my new best friend at school since I kicked Jane to the curb. And I guess it's okay for me to say this about her because she'd happily tell you herself. Through Dexy, I've learned that prolifically promiscuous free spirits are incapable of embarrassment.

"So I'm blowing the Phishhead I met at the final show," Dexy said tonight at Mama Mexico. "And not two seconds into it it's like . . ." She grotesquely contorted her features into what I now instantly recognize as her imitation of the male "cum face." She then broke into what I now know is her favorite "cum song."

"*Ooo eee ooo ah ah ting tang walla walla bing bang!*"

As someone who's only kissed five guys, dry-humped four, jerked off three, gone down on two, and had sex with one, I often find myself asking questions that someone of her ilk might be able to answer.

"So Dexy," I said, shoveling a chip into guacamole. "Would you ever have sex with a married man?"

"This wouldn't have anything to do with your Spanish boyfriend, would it?" Her eyebrows did the hula. She affected a country twang. *"Tell me a lie, say you're not a married man . . ."*

"Shhhhhhh!" I said, thrusting a chip into her open mouth. "Someone who knows him might overhear."

"Don't worry," she said, spitting tortilla across the table. "The more openly and loudly you talk about something, the less interested people are in hearing it." She dramatically lowered her voice. "It's when you start whispering and acting all sneaky that people try to eavesdrop."

I doubted her logic.

"So what do you think?" I asked. "What would you do if you were me?"

"Okay." Her overloaded fork suspended in midair. "Am I *me*, but you on the outside? Or am I really you?"

"Uh . . . what?!"

"Because if I'm really me on the inside, but you on the outside so that everyone thinks I'm you, then I as you would fuck him, because that's something *I* would do." She loudly chugged her beer, then went on. "But if I were you as *you*, then there would be no difference between the you as you we know in reality and hypothetical me as you, in which case I wouldn't sleep with him because that's not something you as you would do."

I took a moment to process this.

"So you're saying that sleeping with a married man is something you would do, but not something I would do?"

Here's the insane thing about that quote: At the time, I said this defensively, as if an attack had been made on *my* character.

Dexy heaved a labored, bored-with-the-world sigh. "What if I told you that I've already had sex with a married man?"

I dropped my burrito. "You did not!"

"*Would I lie to you?*" she sang. "*Would I lie to you, honey?*"

"When?"

"Last winter, when I did that community theater thing. When I was in the chorus for *Joseph and the Amazing Technicolor Dreamcoat.*"

I nodded, remembering how shocked I was that anyone had cast her in a show that people would pay money to see.

"I screwed the director, who, shockingly, was both straight and married."

Well, that explained how she got the part.

"So how did it happen?"

"He said I needed more vocal coaching, so we started spending extra rehearsal time together. And then he started griping about how his wife didn't understand him and how they didn't have sex anymore and how he missed being with someone so young and with so much fire inside and, well, you know it doesn't take much to woo me, so it was like, 'Okay, let's do it!' So we did."

She took a huge bite out of her chimichanga, and greasy cheese oozed down her chin.

"Bastian complains about his wife too," I said. "When we first started working together, he insisted that we do very little talking to each other and focus all our energies on listening. But lately, he fills the time in between subjects with stories about how his wife is just a mommy now and doesn't want to talk about art or philosophy or politics or anything important, which is just so bizarre because this is exactly how I pictured it in my fantasies."

"Of course it is," Dexy said, holding up a sour-cream-covered finger. "They've all got the 'my wife doesn't understand me' rap. Every single one of them."

"I know," I said. "I've done my research." I'd googled every women's magazine article on the subject of adultery. "Did it feel weird to do it? To know you were responsible for destroying the marriage vows?"

Dexy snorted. "Since when have you become such a traditionalist?"

"I'm not," I said. "It's just . . ."

"Look, I did the guy because he was hot as hell and I knew he would worship my young, nubile body." She ran her hands over her own breasts for emphasis, leaving oily, R-rated prints behind on her geometric-print shift dress. "It was the ultimate fling because I knew he would never leave his wife, no matter how much he said he couldn't stand her. It was fun. And then it was over."

"I'm not so sure that I could be so . . ." I wanted to say slutty. But she *was* my best friend. And there's a big difference between thinking it and saying it directly to someone's face. Even if she said it about herself all the time. "Cavalier."

"I doubt you would, Dah-ling," she said, patting my head with her moist hand. "You're still freaking out over hooking up with Mini Dub, which wasn't even sex and happened almost a year ago! I love you, but you're a bit too tightly wound for adultery." She balled up her dirty napkin and threw it on her plate as if to say, *And that's the end of that.*

I didn't say much on the walk back to the dorm because I was so irritated. Why should Dexy be so carefree, so guilt-free about her life, while I agonized over the tiniest transgressions? She said and did whatever she wanted and never suffered any negative repercussions. When I said or did something unexpected, or even thought about saying or doing something unexpected, it always seemed to come back to haunt me. There isn't a television set large enough to house all my psychological poltergeists.

Case in point: When I got to the dorm, there was something in my mailbox. Dexy noticed it too and knew what it was.

"It's a sign, J! A sign!" She shimmied in her go-go boots, she was so excited.

I was more cautious. I slowly stuck my key in the lock and pulled it out, picture up. On it, a photo of the earth from outer space, beneath which were the words: *Nuestro mundo*.

I flipped it over. It was postmarked Nuevo Viejo, California, on June 20. It read:

> *Jessica—*
> OUR
> *—Marcus*

I . . . WISH . . . OUR . . .

Sitting there, postcard in my hands, I made a wish of my own: Stop, Marcus. Go, Jessica.

sophomore summer
july 2004

July 4th

Dear Hope,

Let me be the first to wish you an early Happy Bastille Day! Your last letter was so vivid that I almost felt like I was atop the Eiffel Tower with you, looking down on the famed City of Lights.

But, alas, I was not.

As for my own European adventures, I'm heeding your advice and backing off Bastian for a while. So I'm in Pineville at the moment, just in time for the cicada invasion. Millions of these buzzing, red-beady-eyed insects have waited underground for seventeen years before crawling up through the earth to see the light of the sun for the first time. The lucky ones go vertical to shed their shells—climbing trees, telephone poles, pant legs—before mating and propagating. The unlucky ones get squashed by bike tires, lawn mowers, and toddlers' tiny feet, never getting the chance to fulfill their instinctual urges. Pineville vibrates with their ominous presence, yet surrounding towns are totally unaffected. I'm not one to quote the Good Book, but these invaders do have biblical implications. Believe me, you're much better off on the other side of the ocean.

Apocalyptically yours,
J.

July 4th

Dearest Marcus,

Happy Independence Day! Are you enjoying your freedom?

Me, not so much.

I'm writing because I'm thinking about you. I'm thinking about you because of the postcards, which is what you want, isn't it? I've waited this long to write you about them, which is pretty miraculous for me because I rarely show restraint when I should. I won't even ask you what you're trying to tell me because I know you won't reveal your secrets until you're good and ready, whenever that may be.

And so, I'll reveal mine.

I'm thinking about the first time we ever spoke. I was leaving the Pineville High professional counselor's office, having just convinced that desperately bubbly woman that the LIFE SUCKS, THEN YOU DIE graffiti on my book cover wasn't a death wish, no, but the name of an indie funk band with a hit called "Tongue-Kissing Cousins." You were on the other side of the door, listening to my lies, slouching in a plastic chair with your legs spread wide, waiting for yet another disciplinary meeting with the principal for some serious transgression that I imagine involved underage drugging or sexing or both, which would explain why you seemed so tranquil in a narcotic and/or postcoital way. Not that I would've even known what either was, being sixteen years old, with only a few half-finished beers and one sloppy kiss to my credit. Before I could flee—Oh! How I wanted to run away from you!—you called out to me, "Hey, Tongue-Kissing Cousin..." in that undisturbed way of yours, eyes half-shut as if you'd already seen most of what the world had to show you. You called me a natural con artist and asked me what other secrets I was hiding. I didn't answer because I already knew, in some deep, primal way, what furtive truth you were referring to:

That I was destined to fall in love with you.

I'm thinking about a lot of moments like that. There's not enough paper and ink for them all. But I'm also thinking about how annoyed I was last Fourth of July when Bethany and Marin horned in on what I had envisioned as a very amorous holiday weekend.

If only I could be so annoyed right now.

Marin loved you. She may not be able to put her stubby little finger on what's missing—MMMAAAHHHCUUUUUUSSS!—but she feels your absence. She doesn't say your name, but her bottom lip curls in disappointment when I show up at Grandma and Grandpa's house alone. It's a good thing she and Bethany didn't show up for the Darling family BBQ, because I don't think I could have handled that pout today. But no worries. From what I've learned about babies and long-term memory in Child Development, it will only take a few more months before thoughts of you vanish completely. She's a lucky, lucky girl.

I'm still thinking about you. Yes. You. (Sorry. I couldn't resist this reference to our brief, beautiful halcyon days.) I think about you all the time, even when I'm contemplating having an affair with a married Spaniard. ("Nuestro mundo." You couldn't have possibly known about the Spaniard before you sent that postcard, and yet...)

So.

How are you? I shouldn't care, but I still do. I just wanted you to know that. I'm still curious about everything I don't know about you. Buddhists see this unknowing as a positive aspect of long-term romantic love. It creates surprises and serves as an antidote to any boredom that sets in. The trouble is, most people don't make an effort to stay interested in their lovers, and mistakenly seek excitement elsewhere...

Irony: The only reason I know this is because I took a standing-room-only Buddhism lecture last semester. A pathetic too-little-too-late attempt to understand you better.

I got an A.

You believe in the economy of words. That's a lesson I could have stood to learn from you, obviously, judging by this letter. One lesson of many, actually. If you had let me.

Love,
Jessica

the fifth

When I stepped off the bus from New York City yesterday, I was convinced Pineville was the nexus for Armageddon.

"It's the end of the world!" I shouted.

"It's not a plague of locusts," my dad shouted above the buzzing din. "They're the Brood X cicadas, the ones that only come out every seventeen years."

"They're frightening!" I screamed, ducking a whirring insect that had nearly flown right into my head.

"You should have heard them a few weeks ago at their peak," my dad said, brushing one off the door handle of his car. "It was like a bunch of motorcycles revving their engines in the trees. They're supposed to be gone by the end of June, but they just keep coming. They're loud, but harmless. You'll get used to the buzzing. It gets to be like white noise after a while."

My mother, of course, had a different opinion.

"They're driving me crazy!" she said, swatting at them with her beige Coach handbag.

"How can you tell?" my dad asked. "Between your menopause craziness and your turning fifty craziness and everything else?"

"Forty-eight!" my mom cried.

Dad groaned. "Have you forgotten *who* you're lying to?"

I was surprised by my father's comments, not by the cruelty, but because this was the closest I had heard my parents come to a direct conversation in a year.

"They've ruined the holiday!" my mother said, ignoring my father. "Bethany said she wouldn't dream of bringing Marin here when she heard the noise over the phone. I wanted to throw one last big barbecue, but who can enjoy themselves with this racket? I guess it will have to wait until Labor Day . . ."

"What do you mean one last big barbecue?" I asked.

Mom looked guilty. Dad kept his eyes on the road.

"Go ahead, Helen," my dad said. "Tell her the news."

Mom rearranged her features into her patented "Isn't it delightful?!" face.

"I sold the house!" she said.

"What?"

"We're moving!"

I looked at my dad for confirmation.

"Is this true?" I asked.

"Apparently so," my dad replied with a weighted-down weariness that I was getting more and more accustomed to hearing.

For the rest of the ride home from the bus station, my mom prattled on about how she hadn't intended on selling the house but she'd held an open house for other Realtors to show off the rooms she had staged in the hopes of drumming up interest in her fledgling business and one of the Realtors mentioned that she had a couple who were looking for a house in the area exactly like this one, they even had a little infant boy and they would likely pay top dollar for the house if all the furnishings were included and then she heard that Pineville had zoned prime property for new townhomes and when she heard what they were selling for she was stunned and knew she had to get in on it especially with interest rates on the rise . . .

"So, Mom," I cut in. "When do you have to be out of the house?"

"The unit should be finished in September, so we're in the old house all summer, which is truly a shame because it would be so wonderful to enjoy the summer on the water, but I suppose we have years of enjoyment ahead of us . . ." And she was off again.

All of this information before even pulling into the driveway was just too much to process. Upon laying eyes on 12 Forest Drive—with its blue siding, black shutters, verdant sod, blooming azaleas, red door, brass DARLING knocker—I couldn't help but hear Dexy screeching a sentimental ditty in my ear.

"Our house . . . is a very, very, very fine house . . ."

I went straight up to my fake beige-on-beige-on-beige room and wrote Marcus a letter. Then Hope. And when I was finished, I collapsed in bed, half wishing that I might sleep as soundly as a cicada. A deep slumber to get me through the next seventeen years.

I got seventeen hours instead.

the tenth

Why am I still here?

I was only supposed to stay here for the holiday week-end. But as Sunday turned into Monday, I just couldn't bring my-self to get back on the bus. Back to Bastian. And whatever would happen the next time we were alone together.

And so I found myself feigning a scratchy throat, phoning in a fake diagnosis of mononucleosis to the Storytelling Project coordinator. After all, how many opportunities does one have to watch the apocalypse up close?

My mother accosted me as soon as I hung up.

"Did I hear that you have *mono*?" she interrogated. "Isn't that the kissing disease? What sort of people have you been kissing?"

I rolled my eyes. "Mom, that's so 1950s," I said. "These days you should be happy if that's all I've got."

Her dark roots jumped up in hair-raising alarm. "Why? Do you have something else? Something worse? Oh my God, are you pregnant?"

I find it somewhat amusing that my mother only thinks I'm pregnant at times when it would be physically impossible for me to be so.

"Not unless sperm have found a way to travel telepathically."

She screwed up her face in the way she does when she has no idea what I'm talking about. It takes a lot of effort, as the botulism has rendered most of the muscles in her face useless.

"Then do you have a medical condition that I should know about?"

"I'm just not feeling well," I said truthfully. "The city stresses me out. I just need some quality time here at home to rest and relax."

She liked this argument, I could tell. She liked the idea of her home as a safe haven, so I continued.

"Especially since this is the last summer I'll ever get to spend in the place that created so many cherished memories . . ."

So that was three days ago. And I'm still here.

"Don't you have a job to return to?" my mom asked today while I was on the couch aimlessly channel surfing.

I was about to tell her that they were doing just fine without me when I saw a familiar face on the screen, sitting across from Oprah, chatting about his bestseller.

"Mom! That's my writing instructor from SPECIAL!"

"Oh?" she asked with a mix of curiosity and contempt. "The one who convinced you to turn down your full scholarship to Boatwright?" She focused on the screen anyway, since anyone talking to Oprah was worth a closer look, even in a repeat.

It is not hyperbolic to say that Samuel MacDougall altered the whole direction of my life. If not for his encouragement, and his letter of recommendation, I would not be at Columbia. Period. He was my writing instructor two summers ago at the Summer Pre-College Enrichment Curriculum in Artistic Learning but has since gone on to literary fame and fortune. He was on *Oprah* to promote his latest novel, *Acting Out*, a tragicomic tour de force set in Manhattan bathhouses during the late seventies and early eighties, when AIDS was largely unknown and commonly referred to as "gay cancer." I know it sounds depressing, but it's actually pretty damn funny too. Like life.

"I almost read his book, you know," my mom said.

"Well, almost doesn't count."

"The premise was so depressing. AIDS! Who wants to read about that?"

"Enough people to put it on the *New York Times* bestseller list!" I snapped back.

"You know," she said after watching him chat with Oprah for a minute or two. "Even though his book was all about being gay, he isn't so limp-wristed about it. That's the best kind of gay."

I cringed, as I often do when I hear my mom embarrass herself without knowing it, even if it's only in front of her own daughter. And what's worse is she felt the need to continue.

"Why do gays have to be so flamboyant all the time? It's just so off-putting."

I am so often stunned by my mom's ignorance that remarks like that should fail to shock me anymore. But they do. With nauseating regularity. Here's the Pineville paradox: When I'm at school in the city, I don't feel particularly worldly or wise. It's only when I come back home that I remember exactly why I left.

"So the best kind of gay is when you're gay but don't look or act *too* gay," I said, in need of clarification.

"Right," she said, picking up the West Elm catalog. "Like that gay boy from Pineville who goes to Columbia . . ."

"Paul," I said. "Paul Parlipiano." My mom still had no idea that throughout high school I had moistened many pairs of panties fantasizing about Paul Parlipiano.

"Now, he's gay but he doesn't go around advertising it to people."

"Why should he," I gasped, breathless with exasperation, "when news of his sexual orientation spread around town faster than you can say 'homo'?"

"Jessie!" my mom sniped. "Don't use that word. It's offensive." And then she reached for the clicker and switched to HGTV.

My mom's comments reminded me of how clueless I was before I went to college. My mother's parents wouldn't pay for her to go to college, which I'm sure might account for her ambivalence toward funding my education. She, unlike me, wasn't so inclined to pay her own way, for which I can't blame her because it totally sucks. But what's stopping her from educating herself now? Why can't she watch PBS instead of HGTV? See *Fahrenheit 9-11* instead of *The Notebook*? Listen to NPR instead of Lite FM? Why can't she pick up a newspaper? Or read a book in hardcover or, hell, in paperback? I'd even settle for a real magazine for Christ's sake, one that doesn't feature suede couches on its front cover, accept American Express, and come with an 800 number.

These are the choices my mother makes and they all say, I CHOOSE IGNORANCE.

Would I be the same if I had never left?

Which, again, begs the question: Why the hell am I still here?

the fifteenth

"A ren't you supposed to be somewhere else?"

Bridget spotted me all sprawled out on the front lawn this afternoon, cooling down. My parents were both out of the house, so I thought I could go for a five-mile run without being pressured to put my not-so-sick ass back on a bus to the Port Authority.

"Aren't you supposed to be in New York?"

"I'm convalescing," I said. "Cough, cough."

Bridget looked me over in my shorts, tank top, and running shoes. "It would be easier to believe you if you hadn't, like, just run a marathon," she said. Her face got serious. "What happened?"

"What do you mean, 'What happened?'" I replied, shooing away a cicada that had landed on my leg.

"You always fake an illness when you can't deal."

I didn't bother to argue. Bridget has known me my entire life. She has seen my hypochondria after disappointments including, but not limited to, forgetting to bring in an item for show-and-tell in kindergarten; losing the spelling bee ("Vogue." V-O-A-G? How could I?) in third grade; standing against the gymnasium wall, forlornly waiting for a boy to ask me to slow dance in seventh grade; finding out about Hope moving away in sophomore year;

sucking at the spring track sectionals in junior year; and being cheated on by Len Levy in senior year. If she was bold enough to call out my bullshit, then the least I could do was own up to it when she did.

"I'm just, I don't know, confused about . . ." I hesitated. "Stuff."

I almost told her about Bastian. But she was so appalled by my hookup with William, I couldn't imagine how she would react to the possibility of me sleeping with a married man.

"I've got some, like, really exciting news!"

I pulled my legs up to my chest. "If it's about Hy's movie, I really don't want to hear about it right now . . ."

"No, no, no," she said. "That's, like, all caught up in distribution problems. This news is about me."

"Okay."

"I got in to NYU!" she said, clapping her hands to congratulate herself. "I'm transferring in the fall!"

I sat up. "Really? I thought things were going well for you out in LA."

"I hate LA," she said, sticking out her tongue. "There's no better place than LA for making an aspiring actress give up and become, like, a truck driver."

"It's that bad?"

"There are hardly any *real* parts anymore, for shows with scripts," she said. "I have producers coming up to me all the time and telling me that I'd be just fabulous for all these crappy reality shows, but I'm like, no way. You have to be delusional if you think that eating, like, snake testicles in a string bikini is going to lead to an Academy Award."

"Snakes have testicles?"

This gave her pause.

"I don't think so, but you get the idea. Anyway, girls at school tell me I'm crazy to turn down these offers, because they'd do anything to get on TV. But the people on those shows always seem so, like, seriously desperate and starved for attention."

"Or poor," I said, thinking about Dexy.

"Whatever," she said, casually flicking a cicada off her pink polo shirt. "Anyway, LA kind of sucks, and Percy is in New York, so it just seems like, duh, I should be in New York too."

I opened my mouth to say something, then shut it tight.

"I know what you're thinking, Jess," she said, plopping herself down on the grass next to me. "That I hate LA *because* of Percy."

She was right. That was exactly what I was thinking.

"Sure, it would be easier to tolerate it if he were there with me. But the truth is, I hated it on its own. I'm just happy that the solution to my hating-LA problem also happens to solve my missing-Percy problem."

I hated myself for my skepticism, because I knew it had nothing to do with Bridget and Percy and everything to do with Marcus and me. What if I had transferred to Berkeley? Would we still be—?

"So let's go out!" she said, thankfully interrupting a thought that I didn't want to finish. "Percy and I will take you out!"

Everyone always thinks that getting me out of hiding and back into the world will do me some good. This, of course, makes no sense, when it's the world that makes me *want* to go into hiding. But remarkably I said, "Okay."

Partying in general exhausts me. But I've come to the conclusion that partying at college exhausts me, like, *existentially* even more than parties in high school. High school parties exhausted me because I always felt like I was the only thinking person in a room mostly full of dummies obliterating precious IQ points with every gulp of whatever booze they managed to steal out of their parents' liquor cabinets. College parties are exhausting in a diametrically opposite way. They are full of smart, funny people who are all used to being the smartest, funniest person in the room, so they spend the whole party talking over one another, overlapping and overtaking the conversation to prove that they are the smartest, funniest person in the room, if not the entire planet.

I figured that hitting a bar with Bridget and Percy wouldn't be such a burden on my brain, which is how I found myself in Seaside Heights, New Jersey, at a bar called Tiki Tiki Tonga. Triple T, as it's known, is a bar that's got sand on the floor, leering tribal masks on the walls, and wooden torches topped with swirling disco lights. It's a jungle jumble of Club Med and the Rainforest Café.

Obviously, the décor isn't the main attraction. Every season there's one bar on the Sleazeside strip that quickly establishes itself for its lax attitude about fake IDs and therefore becomes the favorite hangout for underage drinkers until the ABC busts up the party. This year, it's Triple T. Pineville High has no need to throw a reunion: Its graduating class of '02 could be found there in near-perfect attendance because most of us have yet to turn twenty-one.

No surprise, then, that we'd barely gotten past the bouncer before we saw none other than Sara and Scotty heading our way. She was still unnaturally brown and skinny, and in a yellow-and-red-striped tube dress, I'll be goddiggitydamned if she didn't look exactly, *exactly* like a Slim Jim. Sara had trouble making her way through the crowd, so Scotty was putting his pounds to good use by acting as her own personal offensive line, with emphasis on *offensive*. He wore a T-shirt bearing a message that might have explained what he was doing in her company: LIFE IS SHORT. GO UGLY EARLY.

"I'm *so* outta here," I said.

"Come on," Bridget said. "We've already blown fifteen bucks just to get in the door."

"I need a strong drink."

"A bottle of Grey Goose and a straw?" Percy suggested, on his way to the bar.

"OMIGOD!!!"

I shot Percy a look that said, *Make that a double.*

Sara was saying something, but I couldn't hear her over the tribal drums beating through the sound system. I nodded and smiled, hoping it would placate her. But that wasn't the desired reaction to whatever she had said, so she repeated it at a volume that would have otherwise seemed impossible through sheer vocal power alone.

"HOW ARE YOU HOLDING UP???!!!"

Percy and Bridget returned with my drink. It was antifreeze green and garnished with a gummy red-eyed frog clinging to a sugarcane straw. I took a sip and six teeth rotted out of my head. I didn't see how such a sweet concoction could possibly get me drunk enough to endure the rest of this conversation. The tribal drums did drop to a more survivable level as I slurped it down, though.

"Take it easy," Bridget warned.

"Yeah," Percy said. "They don't call it the Frogfucker for nothing."

"What?" I asked, smacking my lips.

"TWO OF THOSE AND YOU'LL *QUOTE* FUCK A FROG *UNQUOTE.*"

Scotty, who had been quiet up to this point said, "Go ahead, Jess, live it up. Drink it down."

Bridget punched his meaty arm. "You are so obvious."

"What?"

"You still want Jess so bad you can't stand it."

I expected him to deny it. So he surprised me when he fessed up.

"We're all adults here, aren't we? Sure, I'd tap that ass," he said, as if he would be doing my ass a favor. "What's the big fucking deal?"

In high school, a comment like this would have sent shock waves through the entire Pineville High community, from the Upper Crusters down to the miscellaneous Bottom Dwellers Unworthy of Names. But college has a way of democratizing bad behavior. No one really cares what anyone else does, just as long as you don't lose control. There was a guy on our hall last year who everyone knew was a major cokehead. But he could tell a good joke and had a 4.0 GPA, so no one was really bothered by it. He seemed like he had his shit together. But if he had barged into my room and begged to snort lines off my bare titties—okay, it would've been time to get the RA involved. Another good example would be Dexy, whose sluttiness would have been an impediment to our friendship in the past. But as long as she isn't hosting an orgy in our shared bathroom, it's like *whatever.*

The point is, after Scotty spoke we all looked at one another like, "What *is* the big fucking deal?"

And in a flash, I had a vision. I saw myself finishing one Frogfucker, then a second, and a third, until I'd consumed twice the volume necessary to engage in sexual activity with a tree-hopping amphibian. And in that state, I would get on the dance floor and start grinding into Scotty until he dragged me across the sand by my hair and out of the bar and into the back of his pickup truck, where I'd ride him so hard he'd have to replace his shock absorbers.

I was a free woman. He was an unmarried man. No big fucking deal. Right?

Sara took my mind off this disgusting track.

"AS I WAS SAYING BEFORE. IF *MY* BOYFRIEND JOINED A CULT IN THE MIDDLE OF THE DESERT, I'D BE DEVASTATED . . ."

"Who did that?" Bridget asked.

"MARCUS. RIGHT, JESS?"

"It's not a cult. He's at a school run by Buddhists . . ."

"ARE YOU SURE? I HEARD SOMETHING ABOUT HIM *QUOTE* GETTING NAKED AND DANCING AROUND A FIRE WITH A BUNCH OF GUYS *UNQUOTE* . . ."

"I heard that shit too," Scotty said, nodding. "Gay shit."

"From who?" I asked.

Scotty shrugged. "Don't remember," he said, checking out a chick in a cheerleader miniskirt. "Gay shit like that just has a way of getting around."

"I HEARD IT FROM MANDA, WHO HEARD IT FROM LEN."

"Well, they're both wrong," I replied.

"WHATEV." And then she yanked up the top of her dress, which had been dangerously close to a nipple slippage.

"So," Scotty said lasciviously, resting his hand on my ass. "Do I have a shot?"

I should thank Sara for reminding me that when it comes to my past, everything is still very much a big fucking deal.

"Unfortunately for you, Scotty," I said, removing his hand, "they don't serve a drink called the Idiotfucker."

This cracked everyone up, and Scotty surprised me by laughing harder than anyone else.

"They do have the Idiotfucker," Percy said sagely. "But it's better known as Natty Light."

And then we all surprised ourselves by laughing our way through another round. If you didn't know any better, you just might have thought we were all the bestest of friends.

the twenty-eighth

The cicadas are gone and I'm still here.

Why the hell am I still here?

This is what I was thinking tonight as I swung on the hammock in the backyard. The only light came from swirls of tiny fireflies switching themselves on and off and on again.

"Jessie!" my mom's voice called. "Is that you out there?"

She flicked on the floodlights, blinding me, the world, with the obnoxious glow of a bazillion artificial suns.

"Come inside," she said. "We need to talk."

I knew better than to resist. And with the lights on, the yard had lost its appeal anyway, so I pushed myself out of the hammock and followed her inside.

Mom was sitting at the kitchen table. My father was actually sitting next to her. This was not a good sign for me.

"Your father and I are concerned about your disappointing work ethic," she said.

"What? I've been busting my ass at school!" It was true. I had never studied harder in my life.

"I'm not talking about your classes," she continued.

"We're very proud of your grades," my dad added.

"*Very*," my mom said emphatically. "But I'm referring to how you complain about not getting enough money from us, and yet you don't find it necessary to hold up your end of the financial bargain. This is your second summer of unemployment!"

"I had the internship last summer! For my résumé!"

"What about now?"

"I haven't been feeling well," I replied meekly.

"You were fine enough to go running this morning," my dad argued.

"I thought the fresh air would do me good," I replied.

"You were fine enough to go out with your friends."

"Studies have proven that an active social life boosts the immune system."

"Is that so?" my mom asked with a moderate, passing interest. "Well, at any rate, it seems like you feel like you don't need to make any of your own money, when we *warned* you when you picked Columbia that you would have to contribute to its costs."

"I worked all last month," I said lamely.

"But what about this month? You left your job, which was bad enough. But then you didn't even bother finding a new one at home," she said.

"I'm going back to my job at school . . ." My energy was waning by the second.

"When?"

"Uh . . . soon?"

My parents made a sound that I can only describe as *harrumphing*, a word I have never used before that describes the noise perfectly.

"You need to start earning money as soon as you can," my mother said. "Because once we take on the new mortgage, we won't be able to help you anymore."

I rattled my head, unsure I'd heard correctly.

"What do you mean?" I asked.

"No more handouts."

"But I'm almost out of Gladdie's money. And I've already got a full course load *and* work study *and* student loans . . ."

"Which is why your laziness for the past two summers has been so upsetting to us," my mother interrupted.

"How can you do this to me? For a house?"

"We're doing it *for* you, honey," my mom said. "Waterfront property will only increase in value over the years. It's your inheritance!"

"But I need the money now, Mom," I said. "Not thirty years from now when you're . . ."

"Dead," my dad said bluntly.

I turned my attention to him, as the saner of the two. "Dad? Are you for this?"

He rubbed the top of his head like a worry stone. "*You* made this choice," he said. "*You* chose Columbia over a full scholarship to Boatwright. *You* chose to accept certain financial responsibilities . . ."

I usually zoned out when my parents launched into this particular spiel, but this time every *you* hit like a bullet to the chest. Was I being selfish and lazy? Was I taking them for granted? Despite my bitching, my parents *had* been throwing a few thousand bones my way each semester. It wasn't enough to forgo student loans or work study, but it did take the edge off. But that's all irrelevant now that I'm right back on the edge, staring into the fiscal abyss.

"*You* have been lucky to benefit from our assistance up to this point . . ."

"Stop," I whimpered, resting my forehead on the kitchen table. "Just stop. I can't take any more."

Having run out of ways to ruin my life for the time being,
my parents left the room. I looked down at the pile of mail on
the table. Sticking out from underneath the AmEx bill and the
Restoration Hardware catalog was a beat-up but unopened envelope. It was the letter I sent to Marcus at Gakkai at the beginning of the month.

The post office had helpfully stamped an explanation across
the front:

ADDRESSEE UNKNOWN. RETURN TO SENDER.

the twenty-ninth

'd decided that I couldn't hide anymore.

"Come in, come in," Mrs. Flutie said, waving me inside her home. Every time I see Marcus's mom, I am struck by her commanding height, as she has the self-effacing demeanor of someone half her size.

"I wasn't expecting to come," I said, "but . . ."

My eyes flitted around their modest living room, searching for a sign. Everything I saw was useless: plaid couch, blue wall-to-wall carpet, brick fireplace . . .

"Oh, dear," Mrs. Flutie said, her six-foot frame slumping. "He's not here. Did you think he was here?"

"Uh, not really but . . ." I didn't finish.

As she bustled out of the room, she gestured toward an over-stuffed chintz armchair for me to sit in. The chair would have been wholly unremarkable if it weren't for the fact that I'd sat on it once already—or rather, Marcus sat on it last summer while I straddled his naked lap until I brought myself to a writhing, roaring orgasm.

My crotch blushed.

I opted for the couch. When Mrs. Flutie returned, she was

holding a glass of pink lemonade. Mr. Flutie followed her in a wheelchair.

"Hey, kiddo!" Mr. Flutie bellowed as he rolled toward me. "I was about to shoot over to the park for some basketball but when the wife told me you were here, I thought, Hell, I can shoot on over there later."

"My god!" I gasped. "What happened?"

"What? This?" he asks, pointing to the steel cage contraption keeping his knee together. "Ahhhh, it's nothing. Let's talk about you and my son. That's why you're here, right?"

Mrs. Flutie gently tapped him on the shoulder. "Kid gloves," Mrs. Flutie urged him. "Treat her with kid gloves."

"Well," I said. "It's just. Uh . . ."

Whenever I see Marcus's parents together, I get momentarily distracted. I can't help but look at them and think, Wow. So you're the ones responsible for bringing Marcus into the world.

"Go on," Mrs. Flutie said. She has a truly comforting manner. I bet she talks many a toddler out of tantrums at the day-care center.

I took a deep breath, bracing myself for my second parental face-off in as many days. The house smelled like burnt cedar. Like Marcus.

"I haven't seen or talked to Marcus since Christmas and I know he hasn't talked to anyone because of the silent meditation thing but then again maybe he's not even doing that anymore I have no idea maybe he is talking again and just not talking to me I don't know and I thought well even if he isn't *here* exactly you would know where he is because I sent him a letter to his school address because that's where the last postcard came from, oh, he's been sending me these cryptic one-word postcards post-marked from California, so I mailed my letter there but it got re-turned so now I don't know where he is and I guess I would just really like to see him and talk to him because I miss him even if he isn't my boyfriend anymore I just want him in my life and I'm so embarrassed to be telling you all this."

Mr. and Mrs. Flutie exchanged pained looks. About which part of my confession, I wasn't sure.

"So. Uh. That's why I'm here."

"You mean he didn't write you about Pure Springs?" Mr. Flutie asked.

"Pure—what?"

Mr. Flutie whistled through his teeth.

"Pure Springs," Mrs. Flutie said. "Where Marcus will be for the next two years."

"He's not at Gakkai?"

"Nope," Mr. Flutie said. "He's near Death Valley, on the California-Nevada border."

"Death Valley," I repeated, just to make sure I had heard cor-rectly.

"Yup!" Mr. Flutie beamed with pride.

So maybe Sara was onto something after all.

"Okay," I said calmly. "What exactly do they study there in the middle of the desert?"

"That is a more difficult question," Mrs. Flutie said, tugging at the drawstring on her sweatpants.

And so, for the next few minutes, Mrs. Flutie told me every-thing Marcus couldn't. Or, rather, could but chose not to.

Pure Springs College was founded in 1915 by an oddball named Thaddeus Fox, a Harvard-educated steel magnate who thought that the traditional model for education bred "slow-witted, morally questionable dullards." So he set up the Pure Springs College campus smack dab in the middle of one of the most inhospitable places on the planet. Each year, a new class of fifteen young men (and only men) "with keen minds and unsullied hearts" who have grown disillusioned with traditional schools and "wish to pursue wisdom in its purest form" are admitted to the college after subjecting themselves to a rigorous application process that includes writing no fewer than ten separate essays answering questions on topics as varied as gravitational lensing and the semiotics of the Teletubbies. What makes this school like none other is that it is run completely by the student body. The Pure Springers are in charge of all the school's administrative duties, including admissions and the hiring and firing of faculty. Tuition is free, and the students support themselves by working on a cattle ranch.

"So there's no one in charge," I said.

"They're *all* in charge," Mr. Flutie said.

"I don't get it," I said.

"Each kid has a job that keeps the place up and running," Mr. Flutie said. "Rancher, butcher, mechanic, cook, and so on."

"So what is Marcus's role?" I asked.

"He has two," Mrs. Flutie said. "He's junior farmer and librarian."

I imagined Marcus in overalls and a straw hat. Pitchfork in one hand, *A Portrait of the Artist as a Young Man* in the other.

"I know what you're thinking: that it's a cult, or worse, one of those boot camps for troubled kids where some poor child winds up dead from dehydration," Mrs. Flutie said. "We thought the same thing."

"*You* thought the same thing," Mr. Flutie interrupted. "I thought it sounded like the greatest place on earth."

Mrs. Flutie put her hand on his unmangled knee. "As crazy as it sounds, this place has molded the minds of some of the best and the brightest. Nobel Prize winners, politicians—"

"That newscaster's son, whatshisname . . ." Mr. Flutie interrupted.

"Billionaire businessmen, novelists—"

"You know, that guy on that show . . ."

"Once we found out more about it, we knew it was the kind of place that could unlock Marcus's potential."

I was still skeptical. "I still don't see how with all that freedom and testosterone it doesn't turn into *Lord of the Flies*. And add a keg . . ."

"Well, we don't worry about that because there are only two strictly enforced rules, and the first is no drugs or alcohol," Mrs. Flutie said. "You can understand why we found that one appealing."

"And the second?"

A pause. And in the silence, I could hear every clock-tick of time passing me by. Tick tock. Tick tock. Tick tock.

"Total isolation," Mrs. Flutie said finally. She folded her hands in her lap, a gesture of acceptance.

"Meaning?"

"If he leaves, he can't come back," Mr. Flutie said. "And no one can visit."

"I know this must be very upsetting to you, Jessica. We felt the same way."

"*You* felt the same way," Mr. Flutie said. "I thought it was just the thing to get his head screwed on right."

"I wish . . ." I began, not knowing exactly how I wanted to finish that sentence. I didn't realize that I had started crying until I felt the warm rivulets coursing down my cheeks.

Mrs. Flutie therapeutically squeezed my shoulder. Her voice got deeper, more serious.

"Jessica, words cannot express just how much we loved seeing Marcus develop such a positive relationship with you."

"You were the best of the lot," Mr. Flutie said, obviously unaware of how being referred to in that manner might be a tad upsetting to me.

"Marcus was a troubled spirit long before you entered the picture."

"'Troubled spirit,'" Mr. Flutie grumbled. "Pain in the ass is more like it."

"Surely you can understand why Marcus might need to put Pineville behind him," Mrs. Flutie said. "There are a lot of bad influences around here. People from his past who don't understand that he's trying to live a life of sobriety. People who don't understand that he isn't interested in reliving his youthful foibles."

I thought about that girl Sierra, the one we bumped into at the park last summer, and how Marcus practically crawled out of his own skin trying to escape. I had been too upset to care about his discomfort.

She continued. "There were only two reasons why he ever returned to Pineville. His love for us, and his love for you."

"And we told him to get the hell outta Dodge!" Mr. Flutie shouted.

I stared at the chair on which we had once made love.

"And I . . . wasn't enough," I said softly.

Mrs. Flutie let go of my shoulder and lifted my chin with her hand so we could see eye to eye.

"I'm telling you this because I like you so much, Jessica," she said with a sad smile. "I'm telling you this as a parent who loves her sons more than life itself."

Mr. Flutie stayed strangely still and quiet.

"You need to let Marcus go and move on," she said. "You are not the source of his problems. And he shouldn't be the source of yours."

She said some more stuff after that, but it was all just different versions of the same message. One that I needed to hear, I guess. One that I would have heard months ago, if I had bothered to listen.

the thirtieth

When I called to tell Bastian that I'd be returning to the city today, he insisted on meeting me at the bus station. My heart swelled when I saw him waiting for me under the neon blue Hudson News sign, and nearly burst when he pressed his lips to one of my cheeks, then the other, as is customary in his country. His hair hung loose, and it seductively caressed my neck when he leaned in, and again as he pulled back.

"Is it safe, kissing you?" Bastian asked.

"Uh . . ." I hadn't expected us to pick up our adulterous banter right where we had left off.

"It is the kissing disease, the mononucleosis, correct?"

"Oh, right," I said, suddenly remembering my lie. "Yes, it is. But I'm not contagious anymore." I wondered if my face would give me away.

"That is good," he said with his bruised eyes as much as his succulent mouth.

Bastian threw my duffel bag over his shoulder and carried it all the way through the winding subterranean tunnels until we reached the stale-aired platform for the 1/9 line. As the train pounded through the tunnel like a drum corps one thousand strong, he turned to me and said, "*Bella*, tell me your story."

And from 42nd to 116th, we crowded together, side by side in corner seats of the icy, nearly empty train, shoulders and knees occasionally crashing into one another for no reason at all other than that we wanted them to. Over the furious roar of the air conditioner, I obliged his request. As Bastian listened, and afterward, he kept it professional. A total gentleman. Which I know he knows is exactly what he needs to be if he wants to sleep with me. My story proves that when it comes to Marcus, there is no simple beginning, middle, or end.

MY STORY

The first time I was ever aware of Marcus Flutie was in eighth grade at my best friend Hope's house. Hope had a brother, Heath, who was four years older than we were and who hung out with a bunch of unsavory characters, including Marcus. Marcus was a year older than Hope and me but in our grade because he was held back early on for mysterious reasons, reasons I could have probably asked him about later but didn't. Just like I could have asked him to translate the Chinese character tattoo wrapped around his bicep, but never bothered to because there was always something else to talk about. Though with respect to the latter, I suspect that another reason I didn't ask was because I was afraid to hear the answer, to discover that it was the name of one of the many girls he'd had before me. Or even worse, that it was a bit of nothing branded on his arm, an in-joke that seemed like a good idea at the time, that is, under the influence of mind-bending chemicals, but made less sense in sobriety. But what I really mean to say here is that

Marcus and I didn't talk about certain things because we were too busy having long, rambling, restless conversations about other things, like microbes on Mars or *American Idol*.

Marcus was the kid in their delinquent crew. They called him Krispy Kreme because he was always blunted, or in other words, "burnt to a crisp." And also because in our school, having sex with girls was called "getting donuts," the donut being a crude reference to female genitalia, of course. By the tender age of thirteen, Marcus had already honed his stonah lovah man persona, as my friend Bridget puts it. He's never had a problem getting girls to fall for him.

I remember seeing Marcus hanging around Heath and his drug buddies, and he made me nervous because he was in our grade and yet seemed so much more experienced, which he was in every way. He never so much as blinked at Hope and me, and yet I found out from him later that he was paying more attention than I could have ever imagined, eavesdropping on our conversations through the thin wall that separated the siblings' bedrooms.

Then Heath died of a heroin overdose and everything changed. Hope's parents decided that she needed a change of scenery and moved a thousand miles away to her grandmother's huge farmhouse in a tiny town in Tennessee. I was bereft. She was the only person who made Pineville tolerable, and I was left to stagger through the rest of my high school years stunned and alone. That is, until Marcus made his move.

The first time he spoke to me was outside our school counselor's office, where we'd been sent for separate juvenile infractions. I used to think that Marcus approached me in his sexy, serpentine way because he was bored and needed a challenge. Like, "Hey, can I use what I know to get in the goody-goody's pants?" He confessed as much to me one New Year's Eve when I had finally decided to indeed give up my virginity to him. But we didn't sleep together that night, and it was another year and a half before we did.

As the years have gone by, I've been startled by a revelation that a younger, callow Jessica wasn't capable of making: Marcus had lost someone too. Heath was a friend to him as much as Hope was to me, after all. And Heath was gone forever. Perhaps, unbeknownst even to himself, Marcus wanted to get close to me as a way of remembering someone he cared about. Marcus was just another wandering soul, like me, missing his friend and trying to find solace in another.

And I hope he found it for a while.

But this isn't the story I meant to tell. The one I was thinking of is this:

The first time I became aware of Marcus Flutie, he was showing off in Hope's kitchen, trying to juggle a raw egg, a bowling pin, and a squeaky toy in the shape of a T-bone steak that belonged to the family dog, Dalí. I don't know if he was high or uncoordinated or both, but after one or two successful hand-to-hand tosses, the egg was sent flying through the air and landed with a smash on the floor. I remember watching this heavy-lidded, wild-haired boy stand there with his guilty hands thrust deep in his pockets. He didn't move as Hope knelt on the linoleum with a paper towel and cleaned up his mess.

I remember glaring at Marcus Flutie and thinking, *You are trouble.*

July 31st

Dear Hope,

Wow. The photos you sent truly capture your joie de vivre. (I wish I could have turned a more interesting phrase *en français,* but I'm having a hard enough time thinking in English lately.) Everything about France—the art, the food, the wine, the men—sounds awesome.

So you'll forgive me (again) for another suck-ass letter. My life isn't nearly as interesting as yours is right now, and all I really wanted to do here was thank you for sharing it with me.

Appreciatively yours,
J.

July 31st

Dear Marcus,

I wrote you a letter last month that never reached you. It's better that it didn't because I wrote about a lot of things that you don't need to know about.

I got your current address from your parents, so I know this one will arrive as it should.

The thing is, now that I know you'll get this, I'm not sure what to say. I don't know how to end. This letter, or anything.

My apologies,
Jessica

sophomore summer
august 2004

the sixth

t's you!"

We both sounded surprised, though I had better reason to be. G-Money was merely reacting to the unexpected sight of his sister-in-law on his front doorstep. I was not only reacting to the unexpected sight of G-Money at the brownstone at all, but a G-Money who was easily thirty pounds heavier than the last time I saw him, six months ago. Atkins be damned! Papa D's Donuts/Wally D's Sweet Treat Shoppe franchise must have a huge profit margin because it's obvious that G-Money's gorging himself on the goods. In a white Wally D's Sweet Treat Shoppe polo shirt straining at the seams, my formerly fit brother-in-law has become a doughy, creamy personification of the very junk foods he shills.

"Bethany and Marin are at the park up the street," he said. "You can meet them there."

Fortunately, G-Money and I don't really talk to each other so what could have been an awkward silence wasn't really all that awkward.

"Goodbye," he said, shutting the door.

As I walked to the park, I thought about what a waste G-Money was. I mean, he was obviously smart. Smart enough to generate tons of dough. (Ha. In more ways than one.) But I would actually respect him if he used his brain for something other than making money and clogging arteries. Can his chosen vocation really give him a sense of purpose in life? Or is lacking a sense of purpose a fair trade-off for a summer house in the Hamptons, a plasma TV, and a 2005 BMW SUV? Meanwhile, I'm poor *and* I lack purpose.

I followed G-Money's directions and easily found Bethany and Marin. Being the culture chameleon that she is, the former looked like all the other young, hip, and hipless Brooklyn moms, from her head scarf down to her flip-flops. Thankfully, the latter showed her individuality as the only child on the playground wearing flowered rubber galoshes, a Spider-Man T-shirt, a pink sparkly tutu, a foam rubber Statue of Liberty crown, and a plastic sheath for a sword, only without the weapon. It looked like something Dexy would wear if she were in a "rejuvenile" mood. I was shocked that Bethany would let her progeny out in public in such an ensemble.

"Auntie J! Auntie J!" Marin gushed when she saw me. I think she's finally forgiven me for the nonbreakup breakup. I scooped her up and sniffed her hair. It smelled like muddy strawberries.

"What's shakin', bacon?"

"Marin," she said, all huffy. "Not bacon."

"Okeydokey, artichokey," I said.

"Auntie J!" she cried with exasperation. "Marin! Not ach-i-okie!"

She knows I know this. It's all part of our game. Marin has a good sense of humor, one that I hope G-Money and Bethany don't bore right out of her.

"I play now!" she said. "Ta-ta!" She blew me a kiss before galloping off to the sandbox.

I joined my smiling sister on the shady park bench.

"She's a real character," I said.

"She chose the outfit," Bethany sighed. "'Let them dress themselves to express themselves' the books say. Of course, my child is the only one who looks like a bag lady."

"I'll be looking like that soon enough," I said.

"What's your crisis now?"

"You know they bought this new house, right?" I asked.

"Yes," she replied. "Mom told me."

"Did she tell you the part about where I'll have to drop out of college and become one of those homeless people who rattles a can and carries a cardboard sign that says NEED MONEY FOR BOOZE, DRUGS, AND HOOKERS?"

"I'm not sure that would be the most effective way to penetrate the market," Bethany said, obviously having learned the lingo from her husband. "And what would you need hookers for anyway?"

Believe me when I say that these comments were made without a trace of irony.

"I'm being hyperbolic," I said.

"Hyper—what?"

"Forget it," I said, watching Marin shake her little fist at a red-haired boy a head taller than she was.

Bethany jumped up. "Marin! Listen to Mommy! Stop that! Play nice!" Bethany turned to me. "She thinks she's the queen of the playground and can boss the other kids around." She sat back down. "You're overreacting."

"Easy for you to say. You already graduated from college."

That my parents paid for my sister's Stockton State College education (the best five and a half years of her life!) yet won't fund my Ivy League degree is a cruel, cruel joke. Okay. Maybe I'm not being fair. Stockton cost about $8,000 annually—roughly one quarter the price of a year at Columbia. And her degree really has done her good. After all, you can't hang out at the park with your kid and shop for coordinating head scarves and flip-flops (or whatever else Bethany does to fill the endless expanse of nonworking days) without a college education.

Oh, that's right. *You totally can.*

"You should be happy for them," Bethany said. "They've got this amazing new home. Mom's new business is thriving . . ."

"Really?" I asked.

"Yeah, Darling Designs for Leaving is booked through the end of the year. You didn't know?"

I shook my head.

"How could you stay with them for a whole month and not know?"

"We don't talk much."

"Maybe you should talk to them more," she said. "Maybe you'd get along with them better if you did."

"I doubt it."

"Why?"

"Every time I talk to them they have something shitty to tell me."

"Marin! Listen to Mommy!" Bethany yelled, jumping up. "We don't hit with shovels!"

Marin froze in mid-swing, then dropped her weapon.

"Mom's a savvy businesswoman?" I asked. "That's so weird."

"Why is it weird?"

"Well, the real estate thing always seemed more of, like, a hobby than a career. I know she was good at it and all, but it was hard to take her seriously because I've always thought of her as you know, just a mom . . ."

Bethany's oceanic eyes turned dark and stormy. "Just a mom?!"

"You know what I mean . . ."

A never-before-seen vein popped out of my sister's forehead.

"*Just a mom*. That's your problem, Jessie. You don't have a clue just how many sacrifices Mom made for us. She stayed home to raise us. And as someone who is making the same decision, I can tell you that playing with a baby all day gets pretty boring."

She furtively looked around to make sure no one had heard her. Then she pulled a pair of oversized aviator sunglasses out of her Prada diaper bag, as if to disguise herself for the rest of her diatribe.

"Yes, you heard me. I love Marin, but there are only so many tea parties I can sit through before I want to scream. I'm sure Mom felt the same way, but she did it for the same reason I'm doing it: She didn't want anyone else taking care of her daughters. She only went into real estate part-time when you were too busy with after-school activities to be considered a latchkey kid. Did you ever think that maybe she wanted a career all those years she was home with us? That after thirty years, she's tired of being *just a mom*? That they're not paying for Columbia—a school they were against because it's so expensive and you didn't get a scholarship—because they're finally giving you the freedom you've begged for since you were three years old? That maybe, just maybe, she bought the house of her dreams because she's tired of putting her dreams aside for a daughter who never seems to appreciate it?"

Stunned. I was positively stunned by my sister's speech. And not just because (a) the only time I'd seen her this worked up was when MAC discontinued her favorite lipstick color and (b) she sounded exactly like my mother. No, I was mostly shocked because I was certain that she was 100 percent right. Even now, this realization doesn't make me any happier about my poverty, but at least I can sort of understand it. Sort of, but not quite.

"And while you've got me on a roll, I'll tell you this: I think you're upset about something else."

"Oh really?" I asked, scraping paint off the park bench with my fingernail as a distraction because this was getting too intense.

"You're upset that Marcus is at gay cowboy camp."

Bethany can say this with a straight face because she has no sense of humor.

"Marcus is not at gay cowboy camp! It's . . ." I tried coming up with a better way of explaining Pure Springs, but words failed me. I changed tacks. "Wait, how did you know about this?"

"From your friend."

"What friend?"

"Wally D's daughter. The tan skinny one."

"Sara?"

She nodded. "We saw her at the Papa D's/Wally D's opening on the Point Pleasant boardwalk," she said. "She flunked out of school . . ."

"Sara flunked out of school?!"

"Marin! Listen! We do not dump buckets of sand on people!"

Bethany yelled to a very triumphant-looking Marin. She turned back to me. "Yes, she's out of school, so her dad gave her a store."

Of course he did. Papa D to the rescue. Normally I would've made fun of this. But truth be told, I was kind of jealous that my parents weren't so carefree with their cash.

"Funny how Sara neglected to mention this while slandering my boyfriend at Tiki Tiki Tonga."

For the first time throughout this whole conversation, Bethany turned and gave me her full attention. "Your *boyfriend?*"

"My *ex*-boyfriend," I said, as I tried to dig out the paint that had gotten under my first fingernail with a second fingernail on the opposite hand. This worked in removing the blue schmutz from the first fingernail, but only at the expense of transplanting it to the second fingernail. I couldn't see how this pattern could correct itself. It was hopeless.

"Listen!" Bethany snapped. I was looking down, so I was expecting her to chastise Marin for more unlawful sandbox behavior. "*LISTEN!*" she repeated even more sternly. I was surprised when I looked up and saw her blue eyes targeted right at me, glasses off. "I think *he's* what's really bothering you. You're not over him yet. And you're never going to be happy until you are. Are there any prospects?"

In quick succession, Mini Dub, Scotty, and Bastian popped into my head—the last three men (well, two boys, one man) to show any interest in me. I lingered on Bastian's image before providing Bethany with a simple answer. "No."

"Well, you have to go out and make that no into a—" Bethany sprang up again. "NO! NO! NO!" She ran toward Marin, who had lifted her Spider-Man T-shirt to flash the ankle-biting crowd. Girls Gone Wild: The Sandbox Edition. I know from my Children at Risk class that this is perfectly normal behavior. Marin won't necessarily end up modeling a Cool Whip bikini eighteen years from now.

Anyway, on the long subway ride back to campus, I thought about Bethany's inadvertent advice and how easy it would be for me to take. I don't think there's anyone better than I am at turning a simple no into a NO! NO! NO!

the tenth

Tonight I let Dexy convince me to attend a Democratic fundraiser downtown.

"You've been talking about how you want to be more politically active!" she said, waving a flyer in my face. "Here's your chance!"

"I don't have two hundred and fifty dollars to get in the door," I said.

"You don't need it!" Dexy said, speaking even faster than usual. "I've got two tickets already. Remember that guy I shagged last week?"

I didn't—it was impossible to keep track—but I nodded anyway.

"Well, I was supposed to go with him, but he got Yankees tickets so he's going to the game instead."

I should mention that the event was being thrown by Beautiful People Against Bush, one of the tongue-in-cheek-yet-totally-serious political action committees that have popped up around town now that bashing Republicans has become fashionable. Don't get me wrong. I think it's great that my 18-to-24 demo is getting involved in the upcoming election, but too many of these events seem to be less about the Democratic Party and more about the *party* party. I mean, swilling "blue state" martinis

(2½ oz. vodka, ¼ oz. blue curaçao) isn't exactly comparable to standing in front of a tank in Tiananmen Square. And knowing what you know about me and social events in general, you can see why I was reluctant to go.

"Come on, J! Let's go! It's free! It's for democracy!"

Then she broke into song.

"Well I'm proud to be an American . . ."

"Okay! I'll go if you stop singing!"

Her voice is a violation of the Geneva Convention, I swear.

And so, while Dexy effortlessly assumed the guise of a young urban politically active hipster (low-rise Rock & Republic jeans, THE ONLY BUSH I TRUST IS MY OWN tank top), I agonized over my inability to so mindlessly do the same. There's always so much pressure to have the right look in this city, especially in the downtown cobblestone territories, and I never feel like I get it right. After more time than I'd like to admit, I borrowed silver kitten-heeled flip-flops from Dexy to go with a cutoff denim miniskirt and the Jacksons' Victory Tour '84 T-shirt that I've had since high school, which I thought could be interpreted as a political message, only one that wasn't so in-your-face obvious.

As we stepped into the elevator, we had a bipartisan clash with Mini Dub.

"What are you ladies doing tonight?"

"Meeting Democratic hotties!" Dexy chirped.

"Be careful," Mini Dub warned, with a smirk and a twitch of his eyebrow ring. "It's no coincidence that the Democratic symbol is the jackass."

And then the doors shut, leaving his snickering visage behind. This was a good thing because the only comeback that had popped into my head was, "Well, uh, *you're* the jackass!" which really wasn't very good. I hated getting faced like that, especially by a fascist.

Dexy crooned. *"Forbidden love . . ."*

"Oh please," I said, wincing. "There's a better chance of me hooking up with Saddam himself."

"You won't have to!" she gushed, wrapping her arms around me. "There are a ton of hottie liberals! Enough to get your mind off the Gay Cowboy!"

We had recently started referring to Marcus as the Gay Cowboy. Humor, Dexy assures me, is a helpful way to get over someone. That, and having sex with someone else. This was her mandate for tonight. One of us would surely fulfill our duty, but I doubted it would be me.

The Beautiful People Against Bush party was held at Moonshine, an upscale lounge designed to look like an old-fashioned speakeasy, complete with lack of signage marking the entrance. The only indication that a hipster haven was on the other side of the nondescript wooden doors was the wall of bouncers keeping the desperately underdressed on the wrong side of the velvet ropes. It's in the Meatpacking District, which is a misnomer now that boozing has replaced butchering as its industry of choice. (Insert meat/meet market joke here.) Moonshine is the type of place that I've read about on Page Six, the type of place frequented by the staff of *True*, the type of place that normally wouldn't let the likes of me squeak past the bouncers. But tonight I had the golden $250 ticket. And quite honestly, I'm not sure how I felt about that.

But democracy is alive and well, as long as there's an open bar. The place was packed with young, artfully dressed-down creative types who were drinking heavily and talking loudly over the music.

"What did I tell you? Hotties!" Dexy's pupils dilated with what I've come to know as her I'm-gonna-get-laid look. "Let's circulate!"

And then she crashed her way through the crowd too quickly and expertly for me to keep up. But it was okay because it wasn't long before I found more interesting company. The deejay was spinning REM's "It's the End of the World as We Know It (And I Feel Fine)" when I heard a male voice over my shoulder ask, "Have you ever noticed how people pretend to know all the words to this song?"

On cue, the crowd shouted, "LEONARD BERNSTEIN!" then quieted down to a murmur for the tongue-twistier lyrics.

I turned around to confirm that the person who had made this astute observation was a very familiar Democratic hottie in a form-fitting I LIKED BUSH BETTER WHEN HE WAS A SMACKHEAD T-shirt.

"If I didn't know any better, I'd think you were hitting on me!" I said, laughing.

"It's a good thing that you know better now," Paul Parlipiano replied.

"So where's your boyfriend?" I asked.

Paul's face actually brightened when he said, "We broke up."

"Oh! I'm so sorry!"

"I'm not," he said, grinning. "We had different priorities. He wanted to go clubbing. I wanted to overthrow a corrupt administration."

"Oh."

"He accused me of being more devoted to the DNC than I was to him. And you know what?" he asked, pausing to sip his martini. "He was right!"

If someone had told me four years ago that I would be tipping back martinis at a Democratic fundraiser in a tragically hip Manhattan zip code with the out-and-proud Paul Parlipiano, my high school crush-to-end-all-crushes, gay man of my dreams and obsessive object of horniness, I would have bent over to launch those winged space monkeys out of my butt.

Elvis Costello wailed, asking what was so funny about peace, love, and understanding.

"*I ask myself: Is all hope lost? / Is there only pain and hatred and misery?*"

"You probably don't know this," he said. "But you really turned my head around."

"Really? How?" I couldn't imagine how I'd possibly influenced him.

"Remember when you came to that PACO meeting, before you got into Columbia?"

Remember? How could I forget? I wasn't interested in becoming one of the People Against Conformity and Oppression. I only went because I had this sick fantasy about becoming Paul's wingwoman. I lasted about five minutes before I pissed everyone off by pointing out that by protesting everything, they accomplished nothing. Paul saw the same events in a different light.

"You made a solid point about PACO, about how we had no focus. We scattered our energies on too many causes. You helped me realize that voting is the most effective form of protest. We have to focus on elections and getting leaders in office who can help us with the causes that are so important to making the world a better place."

"You know," I said, feeling brave, "you had a significant effect on me too. If it weren't for you, I wouldn't have applied to Columbia. I wouldn't be here right now."

He clasped his hands together and brought them up to his lips. "It's interesting, isn't it?"

"What is?" I asked.

"We hardly know each other, and yet have made a big difference in each other's lives."

"It's kind of cool," I replied.

"The power to change is very cool," he said.

And we both drank to that.

"You inspired my stepsister Taryn too," he said. "Your high school editorials made her want to be the writer she's become."

"Oh?" I asked. "She's a writer?"

"You haven't read her political blog?"

"Uh . . ." I stammered. "I'm not really into blogs . . ."

"You haven't heard of Punkwonker?"

I shrugged apologetically.

"It gets 250,000 hits a day! She's even been asked to cover the conventions! I'm so proud of her . . ."

A quarter million hits a day??? Wha—? *I'm* the one who's supposed to use my way with words to right the world's wrongs. Taryn Baker is fulfilling *my* destiny. It was such a visceral, vicious irony that I needed to steady myself against the wall, accidentally ripping down a *Fermez la Bush* poster in the process. I used to be down on bloggers, thinking that they're just as bad as public masturbators. But there's something to be said for believing in your convictions so completely and confidently that you put them out there for *anyone* to see. I'm so unconvinced by my own opinions that I can't even bring myself to reread what I write in this notebook.

Paul didn't notice my near-fainting spell because he was already in the midst of one of his typically long-winded speeches. I couldn't really hear much over Public Enemy's "Fight the Power" but I watched his lips and nodded whenever I made out a distinct word or phrase.

"Activism has replaced apathy . . ."

(Nod.)

"Crossroads in American history . . ."

(Nod.)

"I want you to meet someone . . ."

(Nod.)

And before I knew what was happening, I was being led by the hand to be introduced to the woman who, according to Paul, had made the night possible.

"This," Paul said proudly, as we approached a petite woman with perfect posture and jet-black hair cropped in expensive, face-framing chunks, "is Cinthia Wallace."

Well, I'll be goddiggitydamned. They say politics make strange bedfellows, but I couldn't imagine a more unpredictable threesome than Paul Parlipiano, Miss Hyacinth Anastasia Wallace, and me.

She floated toward me on the gossamer wings of her red-white-and-blue cashmere cobweb poncho.

"Hey there, Jess." Her smile was more dazzling than the diamond chandelier earrings shooting off fireworks under the lights.

"Hi, Hy," I said. "Uh, I mean, Cinthia. Small world."

Hy embraced me warmly.

"But I wouldn't want to paint it," I added, backing out of her arms.

"Huh?" said Hy and Paul.

"Uh," I replied. "My grandmother Gladdie used to say that. Uh, because the world is small, but it's still pretty big."

I can always be counted on to say something corny at the precise moment it's required of me to assume an above-it-all air.

"My mother says that if the world seems small, it's because *your* world is small."

Hy's mother, it should be noted, is a Pulitzer Prize–winning poet.

"Did you know that Hy wrote a book about Pineville High School?" Paul asked. "How wild is that?"

What? How could *Paul* not have known?

Then I remembered: When the news hit, I was only a junior, still gasping from the social stranglehold Pineville High had on me. Paul was about to start at Columbia, about to come out of the closet, about to embark on his new identity as a social activist. He had already put petty Pineville life behind him. Basically, Paul has been so busy acting globally that he's had no time for thinking locally.

Hy clenched her jaw, not in anger, but as if to prepare herself for whatever I might say in response. Her book, as embarrassing as it was when it first came out, had little effect on my life now. How could I still harbor a grudge all these years later?

"I know," I said, finally. "It was pretty good too."

Hy groaned. "No, it wasn't. They should have a law against seventeen-year-olds publishing novels. It was just so . . . uninformed."

When she said that, I suddenly realized that Hy had dropped the round-the-way-girl dialect immortalized in her novel and was talking in plain English. I had never had a conversation with this person before.

"Would you want *your* thoughts at seventeen read by the world?"

I shook my head as I recalled the journal from my own seventeenth year, the one I shredded because I didn't want *anyone* to read it, myself included.

"I'm lucky Miramax is tanking," she said. "The film will never get released."

"Was it that bad?" I asked.

Hy held her nose. "A stinker."

Bridget will be so disappointed that she'll never get to see it.

"The irony is," she said, "now that I have something important to write about, publishers don't want anything to do with me! I pitched a book about inspiring political activism in young adults, and the editors were all, like, 'Will you pose naked, draped in an American flag for the cover?'" She shrugged in that fatigued way that beautiful women do when they are only wanted for their bodies, not their minds. Bridget shrugs like this a lot.

"So how's Columbia?" she asked.

"Awesome," I replied, like I always do.

And then she told me that she'd love to talk to me more but as the founder of Beautiful People Against Bush and the organizer of the party, she was expected to mingle. As the collegiate cochair, Paul was obliged to do the same. I was sure they were blowing me off. But then Hy squeezed my hand in an unexpected, sincere way.

"I really hope our paths cross again, Jess."

"You know, they almost crossed once before," I said.

"I'm sure they have. But when?"

"We almost overlapped at *True*."

"Really? I never knew you worked there."

I sheepishly looked at the floor. "I never wrote anything."

Hy laughed. "Neither did I! Tyra wanted me to do this piece

about guido culture that was just so derivative of my badly written book. I turned her down."

"Hm," was all I could say. I thought the idea had been swiped from me. Hy thought the idea had been swiped from her book. Considering the important issues people like Taryn tackle daily, the world is a better place without either version—hers or mine.

"Anyway, I hope our paths legitimately cross again soon."

"Me too," said Paul.

I really believed them. But not enough for me to go out of my way to stay in touch. It's better this way, leaving things open-ended. Because if I actually did email Hy or Paul and they ignored me, I would know that tonight was a fake after all, and I'd rather not think that.

I left the party not too long after that conversation, after I caught Dexy slipping out the door arm in arm with a masked man in a blue satin cape emblazoned with a huge rhinestone donkey. I'd find out later that he's known in downtown circles as Democracy Man. But at the time, I thought about what Mini Dub had said about the jackass and how he was more right than I would ever admit to his face.

the thirteenth

Bastian and I could see the commotion from several blocks away. A crowd was gathered in front of the entrance to the dorm, and several police cars were parked in the street. An ambulance was pulling away slowly, without its siren wailing. As we got closer, I noted that most of the students were touching their faces in some way—hands rubbing foreheads, hands covering eyes, hands clasped over mouths as if in prayer—all gestures of shock, of disbelief. Everyone was speaking in hushed tones.

"Something bad must have happened," I said to Bastian.

"*Muy malo*," he said, too concerned for English.

I approached a Japanese girl in pigtails, platform boots, and a Little Bo Peep pinafore. Her Gothic Lolita ensemble gave a surreal edge to an already strange scene.

"What's going on?"

"Some guy was found dead in his room," she said.

I must admit that when I first heard this news, I was comforted that it wasn't a terrorist thing. Some guy was found dead, I thought to myself. What a relief.

"Who was it?" Bastian asked. "Was it a suicide?"

She shook her head. "I don't know," she said. "They won't tell us anything."

"I heard it was someone on the fourth floor," said a curly-haired guy wearing a business suit and a yarmulke.

"Oh my God!" I cried, instinctively bringing my own hands to my cheeks. "That's my floor!"

"J!" I heard a hysterical scream. "*Jaaaaaaaayyyyyyyyy!*"

I turned toward the voice and saw Dexy barreling through the crowd. Her stricken face looked all wrong with her outfit, a chipper, pastel swing dress.

"It's Mini Dub!" she gasped. "William!"

And that, so they tell me, is when I passed out.

When I came to, I was lying on the sidewalk, the new subject of the crowd's attentions. I caught bits and pieces of their commentary as I tried to open my eyes.

"Is she his girl?"

"Dunno . . ."

"We can check the facebook . . ."

"Aw, shit. Homeboy's dead but the facebook lives on."

"That's fucked up."

It was all very fucked up. And as I got the facts, it proved to be even more so.

He didn't attend the mandatory meeting for all RAs about "racialization" last night, didn't show up for class today or pick up his paycheck. But when he didn't bring brownies to the Columbia College Conservatives Club (Anti) Affirmative Action bake sale this afternoon, his friends got worried. They contacted the head RA, who keyed into William's room and found him on the floor, unresponsive.

Dead.

There was no bloody razor blade. No noose made out of a bedsheet. No drugs or any other evidence of a suicide situation or "foul play," as the police put it. The preliminary medical examination has ruled his death to be from natural causes. According to the Dean of Student Affairs, William last swiped into the dorm on Thursday afternoon after his lab. Dexy and I might have been the last people to see William alive, outside the elevator. So he'd probably been lying there, dead and undiscovered, through the night and into the day. In retrospect, I probably should have noticed the absence of his annoyance.

But I didn't. Not at all.

The CCCC wants to have a candlelight memorial on the steps of Low Library. F-Unit is talking about dedicating a study carrel in the engineering library in his honor. Dozens of his facebook "friends" have designed online shrines. Grief counselors have descended on the dorm, and on our floor in particular.

"If you want to talk . . ." they say.

I don't. I really don't have anything to say. Because after the shock of my fainting spell, the most surprising thing to me has been how little I feel about William's death at all.

the sixteenth

Dexy is mourning enough for the both of us. She's been in full Jackie O. funeral regalia, widow's veil and all, ever since it happened.

"I don't know how you're managing," Dexy said over coffee at Tom's, in the grave tone she has adopted of late.

"Dexy, we weren't that close," I said, stirring in my sugar. "I know it's not in good form to speak ill of the dead and all, but the truth is, he really got on my nerves."

"But you hooked up with him!"

"And I've regretted it ever since!"

"But you hooked up with him and now he's *dead*," she said, stating the obvious.

"You make it sound like I killed him," I said. "Like he died of a heart attack while we were having sex, like a billionaire geezer in a bad movie."

"But *still*," Dexy intoned. "No guy I've ever hooked up with is dead."

I wanted to point out that there was no way she could possibly know this, as cataloging her sexual conquests would require the invention of complex bioinformatic databases by some of the world's top statisticians. Fortunately, some of them teach here at this very university, so maybe we could get them on it.

"We should have gone to his funeral," she said.

"It was in Texas!"

"I feel bad about it," she said, her eyes wet with tears.

"That's exactly why I want to be cremated," I said. "I don't want a funeral, and I definitely don't want to be buried in a cemetery because I don't want anyone feeling guilty about not visiting my grave."

Those last words triggered something in my brain that impelled me to look at my watch, which, in turn, provoked a succession of matter-of-fact observations: *Today is August 16. It would have been Matthew's twenty-fourth birthday but it's not, because he—like William—is dead. Right now my parents are in Pineville mourning Matthew. And I am here.*

I neglected to share this with Dexy, who had begun singing somberly, horribly.

"It seems to me you lived your life like a candle in the wind . . ."

As I listened to Dexy, it dawned on me that she didn't know I was in Pineville last month until I called her, and I'd already been there for more than a week. I could have just as easily been dead in my room from natural causes, but she was too busy to worry.

"Your candle burned out long before your legend ever did . . ."

Even though she's my closest friend at school right now, I've accepted that I'll never be able to rely on Dexy. Which makes me wonder: How long would it take for someone to find me? And who would that someone be? Who would miss me enough to come looking for me?

And what does it mean when the only people who come to mind—Hope and Marcus—are the two people I am least likely to see, for reasons that are entirely of my own doing?

the twentieth

William's death has really been a buzzkill on the adulterous banter. Bastian, like everyone else, is making way more out of my relationship with William than is deserved, so he's keeping a respectful distance. The more I insist I'm fine, the more he insists I'm hiding my grief.

"What does my face say?" I asked today.

He inspected my features.

"It says that you are trying too hard to look relaxed."

"Aha!" I cried, pointing an accusatory finger. "I'm *always* trying too hard to look relaxed. That's my natural state. Which just proves that I'm fine."

"You are . . ." He paused to choose his words carefully. "Complicated."

I tried not to get too turned off by the fact that the only other person who has described me in that same way was my mother.

When I got back to the dorm, I found a note on my door from Dexy: CRISIS!!! This wasn't unusual. She was often leaving one-word cries for help on my door. HELP!!! YIKES!!! AGONY!!! DRAMA!!! None of which ever lived up to the exclamation points.

"Bastian called me complicated," I said, breezing through

her door. "You know who else calls me complicated? My mom. Maybe it's just me, but I don't think a potential lover should remind me of my mom. And if you start singing Avril Lavigne, our friendship is over . . ."

It wasn't until I was in her room that I noticed something was odd: Dexy was crouched on the corner of her stripped bed, wearing gray yoga pants and a T-shirt, her hair in an unkempt ponytail. It was the most unassuming, un-Dexy-like outfit I'd ever seen on her. And the walls—usually strung up with Christmas lights and strings of beads and feather boas and other spangled, glittering personifications of Dexy herself—were bare. And then there were the lumpy garbage bags on the floor, stuffed with what I could only assume was the aforementioned wall décor and the contents of her now empty closets.

"Dexy, what's going on?"

"I have to leave," she said in a childlike voice. Her face was as red and raw as a skinned tomato. She was rocking back and forth and back and forth. With each swing of her body, the bed squeaked as if in pain.

"What?!" I asked as I sat next to her on the flimsy mattress.

"This whole Mini Dub thing has really . . . freaked me out," she said, her eyes wild.

I was willing to put up with all her Jackie O. bullshit. I knew I had to tolerate some over-the-top overtures if I wanted to be friends with someone like Dexy. After all, her exuberance is a considerable part of her appeal because it's so lacking in myself. But I'd had it. This was taking the grief a bit too far.

"Dexy!" I yelled, grabbing her by the shoulders. "Enough with all the death drama!"

She lazily turned to look at me, almost as an afterthought.

"There's a lot you don't know about me," she said in a hollow voice.

And that's when I learned everything I should have already known about someone I called a friend.

Dexy is bipolar, clinically so, and not in that casual way that people (like me) use to describe moody people (also like me). I knew Dexy has been taking meds for years—far beyond the usual Prozac and Ritalin, Strattera and Concerta—stuff I've never heard of, and I'm a psychology major. But it didn't seem like a huge deal. Sure, she popped more pills in a day than I have in my entire life, but a dependency on pharmaceuticals is hardly uncommon around here. In fact, I'd always had a perverse sense of pride in knowing I was one of the few people at school who didn't medicate my chronic blues, choosing to feel sad and real rather than happy and fake. And when Dexy popped a few extra Adderall to zoom through midterms and finals, I didn't blink. I don't know if it's the jaded influence of New York, of Columbia, or of college in general, but as I've said before, behaviors that would have been troubling in high school pass as normal now. I mean, I used to be really worried about my chronic insomnia. But here, no one thinks twice about not going to sleep until the sky whispers a purple-pink hint of a sunrise.

So I listened while Dexy taught me the difference between a few harmless personality quirks and mania. When I was sixteen, I was saddened when Hope moved away, but I never seriously considered suicide. When Dexy was sixteen, she was saddened when her first boyfriend dumped her, so she washed down a bottle of sleeping pills with vodka. She passed out, puked it up, and was put into a psychiatric hospital for three months. When she came out, she channeled her excess energy into creating characters and costumes, a different persona she could pretend to be every day because it was easier than being herself. She learned to always keep busy, so she would never be quiet enough to listen to her own dark thoughts. She put on a good front. And the prescriptions, combined with regular appointments with a psychologist, had kept her fairly stabilized throughout the remainder of her high school years. Enough to convince her parents to let her go to Columbia, only a short train ride away. And she had thrived here, which she attributes to being intellectually stimulated for the first time in her life.

But William's death changed that.

She admitted that the widowlike mourning was a pose, one that helped her think of William as a character and not a genuine person. But then the reality of his death set in and she got wrapped up in a heavy mantle of sadness.

"He *died*, J," she said. "He was alive, and now he's dead. Who's to say that the same can't happen to me tomorrow?"

"It won't . . ."

"You don't know that," she said with finality. "And the only way to solve the problem about uncertain death is to put matters into my own hands. Suicide started making a lot of sense again . . ."

"This is all happening so fast," I cut in, breathless with tears. "You were fine . . ."

She smiled wanly. "That's why it's called bipolar."

"Why didn't you tell me this before?" I asked. "I would've looked out for you . . ."

"You *were* looking out for me, J." She rested her head on my shoulder. "As much as I'd allow it."

That's what all love comes down to, doesn't it? We help others only as much as they let us.

Fortunately, Dexy had the presence of mind to help herself. She called her shrink, who called her parents, who were already on their way from their home in Bucks County when I arrived. I sat with her until they showed up and they were exactly like Dexy had described—two polite, nondescript people as plain as Dexy was ostentatious. In the waiting hours, I encouraged her to sing every song that popped into her head as loudly as she wanted to.

And I'd never heard such a beautiful noise.

the twenty-ninth

The whole city has been paralyzed by the stampede of elephants and those who protest them, a.k.a. the Republican National Convention. Any strange public behavior can be interpreted by the police as red alert terrorist activity, so we've been advised to temporarily suspend the Storytelling Project until the GOP is G-O-N-E. This is absolutely absurd. I would go off on fascism masquerading as national security but out of respect for William, I'll stop myself.

Besides, I've got something more important to write about.

Because today was the last day of the Storytelling Project for the summer until it resumes a few weeks into the fall semester, Bastian and I commemorated the occasion by returning to our very first spot: the corner of 110th and Amsterdam. About two hours into our final shift, we were revisited by one of our most colorful characters.

"You hippies came back!" gurgled the old man, still in his fedora. "Lights, camera, action! I've got a doozy of a story for you!"

What brought on this change of heart, I'll never know. But this unlikely source provided us with the most poignant story I've ever heard, in or out of the Storytelling Project. I wish I could tell it the way he did, and I almost kept the tape for myself, but I thought the Project would suffer for my selfishness. So here's my version of the story, with as few embellishments as possible.

HENRY'S STORY

When Henry McGlinchy was a young boy growing up in the 1920s, he had a huge crush on a silent movie actress named Lulu Livingstone. A delicate wisp of a girl, Lulu was every black-caped villain's favorite victim in the Westerns Henry loved. She was a raven-haired lovely, prized for her delicate, heart-shaped mouth and swanlike neck, rhapsodized over for her flawless porcelain skin and pleasing bosom. But despite her many virtues, it was Lulu's eyes that drew Henry in, eyes that sparkled with hope and wonder even when she was tied to a train track or barreling toward a cliff in a runaway stagecoach.

Henry was so smitten with Lulu he was inspired to write a letter professing his undying love in the way that only six-year-old boys can: *Your verry prety. I love you.* He sent it to the address he found in the back of his mother's *Photoplay* magazine, c/o Columbia Pictures, hoping against hope that he would hear from his beloved. Every day little Henry ran to meet the mailman, eager to see if today was the day that his affections had been returned. Days turned into weeks, weeks into months, until one day, nearly a year after he had sent his epistle, his mailbox vigil was rewarded with a jumbo envelope with a return address from Hollywood, California. Young Henry tore open the envelope faster than any birthday present he'd ever gotten. Inside was an 8 × 10 glossy photo of Lulu's gorgeous face, and a personal message signed in large, looping letters in genuine ink: *Dearest Henry*, it said. *You're the gnat's whistle! Love, Lulu.*

Henry, now all of seven years old, treasured this photo more than anything else, more than his trick yo-yo, his Lionel train set, his Babe Ruth baseball card. He pinned it to the wall above his bed. Every night, he knelt on the floor and spoke to her like he was supposed to be speaking to God. "I love you, Lulu" were, for a long time, the last words he whispered before falling asleep.

Years passed and both Henry and Lulu grew older. Lulu's Hollywood career was curtailed by the emergence of the talkies, as they cruelly exposed that she had a rather strident, nasally voice that was unpleasing to the ears. Her popularity quickly waned, and by the mid-1930s, she could no longer be found onscreen or in the pages of any magazines.

Henry wasn't so fickle. In fact, Lulu's absence only made his ardor grow stronger. Her picture stayed on his wall all throughout his childhood and adolescence. It became a sort of curio among his family and friends, a relic from a bygone era, a conversation piece. But to Henry, it meant so much more. It meant hope and wonder. And so, it was one of the few personal items he took with him when he was deployed to the South Pacific during World War II. Other guys could have their Betty Grables and Rita Hayworths—for Henry, it was all about Lulu Livingstone. And he took the photo with him to New York City when he enrolled at Columbia University, courtesy of the GI bill. And it was with him even when he met, married, and moved in with Barnard College student Edna Goldblatt. Edna, a sturdy, wide-hipped blonde who looked nothing like Lulu, made light of her husband's adoration, and even had

the old 8 × 10 framed. Throughout their fifty-seven-year marriage, until her death from ovarian cancer at age seventy-nine,
Edna cheekily referred to the woman in the photo as her husband's "girlfriend."

After Edna's death, Henry had no desire to stay in their
sprawling house on Long Island. So he moved into an assisted-
living community in Morningside Heights near his oldest
daughter, who happened to be a professor at his alma mater.
There, as one of the healthier, more mobile men in the community, Henry kept his own room and a number of fawning
old biddies at bay. In that apartment, among numerous photos
of his adored wife, four children, eleven grandchildren, and
two great-grandchildren, was that old 8 × 10 glossy of Lulu Livingstone. It was badly faded after all these years, the message
only legible to those who already knew what it said. But Henry
gave it a special place away from all the rest, on the kitchenette
counter next to his heart pills.

One day, about a month into his new residence, Henry
didn't make it to breakfast. Or lunch. Or dinner. Concerned,
one of the on-call nurses, Dora, came by his room to see
if he was okay, or more specifically, still alive. Henry was still
indeed breathing, feeling fine, but had decided to make his
meals for himself that day because he wasn't in the mood to
fend off the advances of the lusty ladies in the dining room.
On the way out of his apartment, Dora spotted the picture of
Lulu on the counter and stopped in her tracks. She'd seen this
photo before in one of the other residents' rooms. Had Henry,
she asked, ever met a woman named Lucille Greene?

Her hair was brittle and white. Her skin was mottled with
spots. Her bosom had shrunk, her neck hung loose. Her lips

were concealed by an oxygen mask. But her eyes, oh, her eyes were unchanged, still radiant with hope and wonder, despite being confined to the bed.

Just one look and Henry knew that this old woman was Lulu Livingstone.

For the next two months, Henry visited Lulu every day. He wheeled her around the halls, cut up her food, changed the channels, read books, played music, kept silent company while she slept. But most important, he entertained her with stories about his life. After a few weeks, Henry felt brave enough to show her the cherished photo and Lulu blushed with coy embarrassment over his devotion. It was that afternoon he also mustered the courage to say, "I love you, Lulu," as he had so many times before, alone in the dark. But this was the first time those worshipped lips responded in kind. "And I love you, Henry."

They talked of marriage, but only in the abstract way one talks about things that will never come to fruition. They both knew what would come next, but never talked about it, choosing instead to spend their limited time together in happiness. And they did, until the morning that Lulu Livingstone died in Henry McGlinchy's arms, barely two months after they had finally met, and eighty years after Henry had first pledged his love.

When he was done with his story, all of us, Henry, Bastian, and I, had lumps in our throats and tears in our eyes. Finally, after a few moments of reverential silence, this ornery old man took off his crumpled hat, held it to his heart, and spoke.

"Love," he said, "has the longest arms." And then he walked downtown.

My tears turned to sobs. Heavy, heaving, heaping sobs. I wish I could say it was because I was so moved by this man and the certainty with which he pursued this pure, devoted love, but I'd be lying.

Henry and Lulu made me start thinking about my grandmother Gladdie and Moe, her beau from the nursing home where she spent the last year of her life. They too met and fell in love in their nineties after a lifetime spent with someone else. Were they fortunate enough to find true love twice? Or were Henry and Lulu, Gladdie and Moe, passing the decades with someone merely good enough before they found the brief but true love they were always meant to have? I'll never know the answer. Even if I had been brave enough to ask Moe, he died less than six months after my grandmother. Both Gladdie and Moe are buried next to their spouses, separated for eternity.

Love may have the longest arms, but it can still fall short of an embrace. So I wasn't crying for Henry and Lulu. I was crying for Marcus and me.

And that's when I decided to fuck Bastian.

"I want to go to your place," I said, wondering if Bastian could read my real message.

"Let's go now," Bastian said in a tone that let me know he knew exactly what I had in mind.

Despite the sidewalk-scorching heat, we ran the ten blocks to his apartment, lugging our beach chairs and camcorder and TELL US A STORY board the whole way. When we first took off, I felt reckless and romantic. *I'm going to fuck Bastian! I'm going to fuck Bastian!* But sprinting past mountains of wilting garbage and hurdling curdled rain puddles did little to enhance the mood. By the time we trudged up the five stifling flights to his front door we were both dripping in a manner that is sexy in the movies, but rank in real life. Bastian's shirt was translucent with sweat, sticking to clumps of chest hair in a way that was more vile than virile. And he smelled . . . meaty.

I don't think I presented such an olfactory offense to Bastian, however, as he practically attacked me as soon as we shut the door behind us. I instinctively swerved away.

"I'm sorry!" we both said.

"I just feel so . . . gross right now," I said as I stretched out the front of my T-shirt to fan myself. "Can I use your bathroom to, you know, freshen up?"

"Of course! No problems!" These were the words he spoke, but his contracted center frontralis said otherwise.

As I made my way to the bathroom, I noted that Bastian's apartment was not unlike other grad students' apartments: dark, cramped, and crammed with thick academic books. I noticed that there were framed photos throughout, but I made a concerted effort not to take a closer look. His wife and kids were visiting family back home in Spain. I needed to revert to my dream scenario in which they didn't exist anymore and I didn't want photographic evidence to the contrary.

I slipped inside the bathroom, turned on the tap, and splashed cold water on my face and neck and what would be called my décolletage if I had any. I examined my face in the mirror. I looked greener than usual, the effect of fluorescent lighting and nausea. The longer I stood in that bathroom, the less I was sure that I ever wanted to come out.

"Would you like some chilled wine?" Bastian shouted.

Wine is such a *mature* drink. Bastian would never offer me a Frogfucker.

"Sure!" I called back.

But I wasn't sure of anything. I sat down on the toilet and made up one deal-breaking absurdity after another. *If I were meant to fuck Bastian, why would I have nasty stubble on my legs? Why would he have one of these horrible fuzzy toilet-bowl covers that give me that ick feeling? Why would I have had garlic knots for lunch?*

"Bella," he said, right outside the door. "I'm waiting for you . . ."

And then I saw it. My sign. The one that told me what I already knew: Dexy was right. I'm not the type who can sleep with married men.

If I were really meant to fuck Bastian, why would his two-year-old's rubber ducky be perched in plain sight on the edge of this grimy, soap-scummy bathtub?

NO! NO! NO! Seeing that indisputable sign of his real life, I knew that the fantasy of fucking Bastian would be far better than the reality. All summer I had succeeded in stripping him of any real identity other than the foreign lothario porno stereotype I'd first created for him. But Bastian wasn't just an oversexed, misunderstood man who needed me to emancipate him from his loveless marriage. He was an actual person. Except I had no idea who that person was because I never bothered to find out.

"Lo siento mucho!" was all I could say as I pushed past him and out the door.

the thirtieth

I stuck my key in the mailbox lock and twisted until it clicked. I reached in and picked up the black-and-white postcard inside. On it, a couple crashed into a passionate embrace. My mouth went mothbally, my stomach spun, and sour sweat arose from my fevered skin. My brain buzzed with bits and pieces of poetry: *soul disease heavenly happenstance rare creation furious flutter hummingbird heart hello hello . . .*

And intuitively, I knew the word that would be written in his hand before I actually read it. The word that would tell me why I can't let go. The word that made me discover the bittersweet truth about our relationship for the very first time:

With Marcus, I'm clinging to what might have been. And not what was.

junior winter
december 2004

December 15th

Dear Marcus,

LOVE.

All semester you had me wondering, waiting, watching the mailbox. Could you have chosen a more compelling word? What better way to keep me wanting more?

I WISH OUR LOVE...

You wish our LOVE *what?* What would the next word be? What would the next postcard bring? Oh, sweet mystery. It was the perfect cliffhanger, but I wouldn't expect anything less from you.

That said, I feel obliged to express my disappointment over the holiday message I received today: WAS. So now I've got: I WISH OUR LOVE WAS. This pretty much puts me where LOVE left me four months ago.

Which is nowhere at all.

Are you losing your touch?

How long do you plan on sending these postcards anyway? Months? Years? How long will this go on?

And what makes you think that I'll still be waiting for the answer?

Respectfully,

J.

the twentieth

There is only one thing worse than walking in on two people having sex.

Walking in on two people having sex and having those two people be YOUR PARENTS.

Even more harrowing is walking in on your parents when they don't even have the decency to be doing it in some totally boring position but one that is way more porno than parental and on the couch in the living room instead of under the sheets, in their bed, in their room, in the dark, where sex among the dimply of butt and bald of head belongs.

The only response to such a sight?

"AIIIIIIIIIIIIIIIIIIIIIIIIIIIIIIIIIIIEEEEEEEEEEEEEEEEEEE!"

And the slam of the front door.

I stood on the front steps and contemplated my next move. Should I stare into the sun until my retinas sizzle? Or play dead in a snowbank and wait for the crows to pluck out my eyeballs? I could always stab myself in the corneas with an icicle hanging from the portico . . .

Of course, these solutions weren't solutions at all. I could destroy my vision, but I could never blind my mind's eye. The memory of what I had just seen (and heard! *shudder!*) would

surely stay with me until the day I died. Oh yes. Let's just by-
pass the obvious, Freudian ways in which it would show up
unannounced—BAM!—and ruin all my future sexual activities.
It will most certainly pop up when it's most unexpected and inappropriate, like when I'm contemplating the long-term impact of
right-wing appointments to the Supreme Court, just to remind
me that it—BAM!—is still here. Years might go by, and I might be
on the verge of not even remembering that I had been witness to
such horror and—BAM!—the memory will surely come back in
all its shame.

Then I had a thought: Maybe I was at the wrong house!

I'm still getting used to my parents' condo on the bay in the
appropriately named Bayside section of Pineville. Yes, Pineville.
You would think that with all this talk about following one's
dreams, it might have led my mother further afield. But no, it
brought her just five minutes away from their old house in
Pineville, albeit in a decidedly higher tax bracket because many
Manhattan commuters are buying in this area, one of the last un-
derdeveloped waterfronts in the state.

They bought something called the Belize Royale model,
which I thought was just about the most ridiculous sounding
thing ever, especially when I found out that the only thing that
makes it different from the regular old Belize model is an extra
half bath (which prompted my dad and me to joke about "taking a Royale," which my mother did not think was at all funny).
The inside looks exactly like every other condo I've ever been in:
white walls, hardwood floors, stainless steel appliances. Everything so new and so . . . cold. Obviously, I have another reason
for not getting too excited about the place: I associate it with
the education my parents aren't paying for. That Jacuzzi tub?

Six credits! Those marble countertops? Nine credits! The vaulted ceiling upgrade? Twelve credits!

From the outside you can't tell the difference between a Royale and a non-Royale because association rules dictate that each two-story town house must look exactly like every other unit: a boxy, two-story structure with gray vinyl siding, white shutters, and a red brick front porch. So it was entirely possible that I'd gotten confused and had walked in on some other geriatrics getting their freak on. It wasn't my parents after all! Whew!

I had all but convinced myself of this less nauseating reality when my mother came to the door in her robe, my father following close behind in a T-shirt and sweats.

"Jessie, honey," she said, her voice straining for wholesome normalcy. "You came home early."

And I was afraid to open my mouth, aware of how close I was to projectile vomiting on them. It was the most uncomfortable moment in my life, and any reader of the journal knows that this is saying quite a lot. Leave it to my mother to amp up the awkwardness to a whole new intolerable level.

"If we had known, we would have sped things up . . ."

"*Moooooom.*" My bowels bellowed inside me. "Don't say another word about it."

"Since we moved in here it's been like a second honeymoon!"

"But you've lived here since September!"

She sighed and brought her hand to her chest in a swoon. "I know."

My knees buckled. I liked it so much better when I thought my parents were headed for divorce. "Dad! Make her stop! She's killing me!"

My dad couldn't look me in the eyes. "It's obvious that Jessie is upset . . ."

"Upset? She should be happy!"

"I'm clinically dead," I whimpered.

"You should be happy that you have parents who are not only still married, but still have a healthy and robust sex life."

"*Helen . . .*"

"I'm a corpse," I said, staggering across their gleaming floors to the guest room. "I can't hear you anymore."

As if my relationship with my parents wasn't already on shaky ground. Without their money, I took the maximum twenty-two credits last semester in the hopes that I'll be able graduate a semester early and save myself about $15,000 in loans. On top of this death wish of a class schedule, I worked two jobs. One was in the psychology department, cataloging narratives for the Storytelling Project, which means I was paid to watch the tapes and enter a brief description into a database, i.e.,

- **Name:** JESSICA D.
- **Sex:** FEMALE
- **Race:** CAUCASIAN
- **D.O.B.:** 1/19/1984
- **Occupation:** COLLEGE STUDENT
- **Story category:** SEX
- **Synopsis:** WALKED IN ON MIDDLE-AGED PARENTS ENGAGED IN SEXUAL INTERCOURSE AND DROPPED DEAD

This was a difficult job because I was constantly reminded of Bastian, who, thankfully, returned to his wife and kids in Spain.

So the only awkward moments I suffered were inside my own head. Which was plenty enough.

The other job was at the I Scream!, a frozen confectionery near campus. I have to keep this a secret from my family because Wally D's Sweet Treat Shoppe hasn't opened up a branch in Morningside Heights and working for a rival franchise would be considered an unforgivable betrayal. It was a logical choice though, what with a summer's worth of boardwalk experience in the industry. If the economy doesn't improve and I am unemployable after graduation, I've always got my peerless scooping skills to fall back on. And as G-Money knows, custard and donuts are fail-safe.

So I've got *that* going for me.

And to think I survived this deadly workload, only to be murdered by the sight of my parents' bare asses, a tragedy that gives a whole new meaning to the word *assassination.*

the twenty-fifth

Christmas sucked. It *suuuuuuucked*. And it's not even over yet, which means that there are still a few hours left in which my parents can explore the limits of suckiness.

First, the presents. Now, before you go off on how spoiled I am and how I should be grateful that my parents buy me presents at all, let it be known that I did not want any gifts. My parents (meaning, really, my mother) bought me presents because they (meaning she) never listen to me. I told my parents that all I wanted was money for next semester's textbooks. When my mother refused ("Christmas gifts do not come in envelopes! They come in beautifully wrapped boxes! Don't you have any sense of tradition?"), I sent her a wish list from cheapbooks.com. This morning I found out she summarily ignored that in favor of J.Crew's entire winter catalog.

The moment of ironic truth came when, after opening box after bookless box, I reached in my Christmas stocking and pulled out . . . an envelope! I thought maybe, maybe, maybe it would contain a check, which would, if not quite *restore* my faith in my mother—because that would imply that there was once faith to begin with—at least make me more optimistic about the future of our historically rocky relationship.

But no, it was not a check. It was a gift certificate to a spa.

"For a mother-daughter day of pampering!"

My hands were shaking with . . . shock. Rage. Malnutrition. Poverty.

"Not even a thank-you?" she asked.

"For what?" I asked, my voice quivering. "For something I didn't ask for? For something I don't want?"

"How could *anyone* not want a trip to a spa?"

"A day of beauty is so unnecessary in my financial situation! Did you know that I've recycled cans to afford the luxury of ordering something that isn't on the McDonald's Dollar Menu? Did you know that I've survived on nothing but ice cream and bagels for weeks at a time?"

"I thought . . ." my mom began.

"These gifts cost waaaaay more than the textbooks would have! For the cost of a day of beauty, you can feed a starving college student for a whole semester. So this wasn't about not wanting to spend money. This is about teaching me a life lesson through beauty treatments and Fair Isle sweaters! Well, guess what? The only thing I've learned here is that you know less about me now than you ever did, which is something I never thought was even possible!"

"Jessie . . ." my dad began. But I ignored him and kept going.

"You do this all the time! You have this annoying habit of doing things behind my back, like clearing out my room or buying this new house. And when I don't act all grateful for this thing I never wanted or asked for, you turn around and play the martyr saying, 'But I did it all for yoooooooooouuuuuuuu—'"

"Enough!" my dad barked. My mom's face was in her hands.

She has a fiftysomething's hands. There's very little you can do to take years, let alone decades, off your hands.

"I've had enough too," I said, and I stomped upstairs to the guest room that my mother has staged in a style that she describes as "city-country," which reminds me of Shania Twain every time she says it, which is a lot. I flopped onto the dusky rose coverlet covering the white-painted brass daybed, gazing up at the lights twinkling on the wrought-iron chandelier. I thought about Martha Stewart's daughter and how, at that moment, I was jealous of her. I daydreamed about a world in which my mother was incarcerated and it was a very peaceful place.

A few minutes into my reverie, I heard a knock at the door. It was my dad.

"Can I talk to you?"

"Sure," I said. Though I couldn't imagine what he had to tell me. We've never been very communicative, but we hadn't exchanged a word since the assassination attempt.

He ducked under the chandelier and looked helplessly around the room for somewhere to sit. All the furniture was so tastefully distressed that I couldn't blame him for doubting whether it would support his lanky frame. I scooted to one side of the daybed and he sat down on the other.

"You've really upset your mother."

"I know. But can you see how she has upset me?"

He sighed, took off his glasses, and rubbed his head. "I told her to buy the books."

"You did?"

"I did."

"Thanks for trying, Dad," I said. "Really."

"Do you know what she said?"

"That Christmas gifts come in boxes?"

"No," he said. "She said that you've been working so hard at school that you deserve some R&R."

I sunk into the velvet.

"But doesn't she see that one day of pampering won't do squat to relieve the stress of buying books? Or food?"

"No, she doesn't," my dad said matter-of-factly. "Your mother didn't go to college, and she doesn't understand what you're taking on."

"But I've tried to tell her!"

"She's tough to get through to these days. Menopause is making her crazy."

And then he went on to say that my mother is going through wild hormonal swings that are making her very difficult to live with.

"She's almost as moody as *you* were in high school."

And instead of being insulted, I felt a touch of pride. My dad's comment not only implied that I had matured since then, but that he had noticed the change.

"I worked my way through college . . ." my dad began. And just when I was expecting another life lesson about the school of hard knocks, my dad handed me a check for $250. "I know how hard it is. I'm proud of you. And so is your mother, even if she shows it in strange ways. I hope this helps."

"It does, Dad," I said, tearing up. "It really does."

And before I even got the impulse to hug him, he was up off the daybed, but not before cracking his head on the chandelier.

"I hate this damn thing," he muttered.

Getting that check depressed me more than not having it at all. Because when my dad walked out, he left a lonesome void that no one else would fill. I was surprised by how much I wanted him to stay and talk to me about his college life that I know nothing about. It's so strange how you can spend so much time with the people responsible for your very existence, yet know so little about them. Then again, how much do we ever know about anyone? Why should our parents be any exception?

No wonder suicides spike around the holidays. I've never felt more alone in my life. There's no one around to commiserate with, which has made this holiday even more dismal than usual.

Bethany and G-Money aren't here. Now that Marin is getting older, they've decided to perpetuate the Santa myth at their own home. This is the first time they haven't so much as stopped by on Christmas Day, and I don't think it's any coincidence that Bethany chose this year to start a new tradition. As much as she's supposedly supportive about their decision to "live for themselves," she has not adjusted well to the change of address. I don't think it hit her until she saw 12 Forest Drive all packed up and empty.

"It's like the end of my childhood," she said wistfully. Which is weird, because you'd think that being a wife and mother would have done it already. I said as much to her.

"Here's a secret, Jessie," she said, leaning in. "You get older, but you don't ever feel grown up."

"You don't feel grown up?" I asked.

"I feel more tired," she said as she popped up to chase after Marin before she raced into the street. "People confuse the two."

My grandmother Gladdie isn't here because she's dead. I frequently think of her, but especially around the holidays. I wonder what she would think about how I'm spending her inheritance. Spending my life.

Bridget isn't here because she doesn't live across the street anymore. But Bridget is just the latest example (Hope, and yes, Marcus . . .) of how location, location, location is not only the number one rule of real estate, but of relationships as well. Was it only a year ago that we said we'd *always* be friends, because it seemed unfathomable that we'd ever *not* live right across the street from each other? You would think that we would have seen a lot of each other since her transfer to NYU, but we haven't. It's incredible how localized one's life can become in a city with arguably the best mass transit in the world. There's life below Fourteenth Street (where she and Percy are) and there's life well above (where I am). And though it's only a subway ride away, it's a ride that we both (apparently) have been too lazy to make. I can only imagine that Bridget and Percy are enjoying the benefits of cohabitation after spending so much time away from each other. See? Location, location, location.

Another part of it, I think, was that I don't like the idea of trying to replace Dexy with Bridget. I feel like I'm always trying to substitute one lost best friend for another, like I tried to replace Jane with Dexy. They're all just stand-ins for Hope, really, who is just so happy and well-adjusted at school that I've felt no need to intrude. She doesn't need my negative influence on her very positive life, and she must agree because we're *both* showing a mutual disregard of the Totally Guilt-Free Guidelines for Keeping in Touch.

I miss her. And yet I'm relieved that she doesn't miss me.

the thirty-first

I t seemed inappropriate to worry about returning my Christmas gifts when the tsunami has caused inconceivable suffering for hundreds of thousands of people half a world away. But it's been more than a week now, and I've accepted that life in Pineville—such as it is—goes on and so should I. I wasn't alone in my thinking because the mall was packed, especially for New Year's Eve. Apparently, Americans turn to retail therapy for the answers to all their questions concerning the frailty of human existence.

This, of course, caused some inconveniences. Well, one inconvenience, really. An inconvenience by the name of Sara.

"Omigod! We're both *quote* total losers *unquote*!" she said, cornering me outside J.Crew.

"Uh, yeah. With all the stuff going on in the world right now, I'm just too sad to go out this year . . ."

Sara guffawed. She's like a set of Bose speakers. Incredible volume in a very small package. "Omigod! I'm *totally* kidding. I'm *totally* partying tonight!"

"Uh," I replied.

"I had a *quote* wardrobe malfunction *unquote* and had to buy a new dress," she explained, holding a bag from Armani Exchange.

"Uh."

"I mean, what kind of loser stays in on New Year's Eve?" Then she gasped in mock apology. "No offense."

"Oh, none taken," I said, thick with sarcasm.

"Omigod! I heard that some guy killed himself over you," she whispered with pretend concern. "You must be totally devastated. But kind of flattered too."

"He didn't kill himself," I said. "He had an undetected congenital heart defect. And I'm not devastated. Or flattered."

She girlishly pointed her toes inward, no easy feat as she was wearing a pair of those furry boots responsible for making fashion victims look like Muppets from the knees down.

"I heard that when they looked on his laptop, they found all these love letters to you that he never sent . . ."

This was true, but not something I liked to think about then, or write about now. I'd never read them myself, but they were posted on the facebook. They were all about loving and longing for a liberal girl, even though everything she believed in was wrong. And though she went unnamed, I knew. I *knew*. And somehow Sara knew too. But I was too tired of this conversation to find out how.

"He didn't kill himself," I repeated, but softer. "There was a hole in his heart."

As soon as I said it, I could hear Dexy's voice filling in the rest of the sentence with that early nineties song:

There's a hole in my heart that can only be filled by you . . .

It was almost as if Sara heard it too.

"Omigod! He died of a broken heart!" she screeched. "A BROKEN HEART!"

I'd had enough of this conversation. As I said, Mini Dub

is not someone I like to think about. This is why he often shows up in my dreams. Research has proven that the more you try *not* to think about a particular person, the more likely that person will show up in your dreams. (Don't try to outsmart your subconscious by intentionally thinking about that person before you go to sleep because it doesn't work. He'll show up anyway. At least that's how it is with me. Perhaps you're not as mind-fucked as I am.) This explains why William and Marcus often show up together. They're like characters in one of those bad buddy cop movies. You know, total opposites who have nothing in common and are forced to partner up to fight for a common cause. In this case, to torment me in my sleep.

The dreams themselves are not at all interesting. It's all textbook Psych 101 dream symbolism: flying, teeth falling out, bathtub water turning into grape jelly. Mini Dub always offers unsolicited, obvious advice like:

"You should leave that to the birds."

Or:

"You should have flossed."

Or:

"You should get some peanut butter."

In all of them, William does the talking and Marcus just stands there not saying anything, just shaking his head with an expression on his face that I can't quite figure out. I was thinking about all this when Sara's braying brought me back to the waking world.

"I heard that he had all these pictures of you . . ."

"Well, *I* heard you flunked out of school."

Sara's neck jerked into her chest. "That's just a vicious rumor," she huffed with the indignation of someone who only likes to be on the giving end of said viciousness. "I'm taking a voluntary leave of absence to explore *quote* business opportunities *unquote*."

"*I* heard you're managing one of your dad's shops."

"It's *my* shop," she sniffed. "He gave it to me." Then she glanced at the Tank watch glinting on her wrist. "Omigod! I have to go!"

"So soon?" I asked sweetly.

"You can totally come to the party if you want to. Scotty will probably be there because he's so hard-core. Maybe Len and Manda, if they can stop *not* bang-a-langin' long enough to grace us with their presence, you know . . ."

And as Sara blathered on, giving me directions and cell phone numbers and whatnot, I thought about how many times I've had this exact same conversation with her, only with different details. Because that's the thing about Sara. No matter how much we clearly dislike each other, she will always dig for and dish out gossip about our Pineville High classmates. Sara is who she is. She's annoying, but at least she's true to her annoyingness. I can always count on it, which is a strange sort of comfort in a world that can be so unapologetically random.

But that doesn't mean I have to like it.

"I gotta go," I said.

"Where?" she asked. "Where do you have to go?"

"I don't know," I replied. "But I don't have to stay here."

And by that, I didn't just mean in front of Sara, outside J.Crew. I didn't have to stay in Pineville, or my parents' house, for that matter. Neither was my home anymore. I'm not sure I can call New York home either, but it certainly seemed more appealing. Besides, my room and board was paid for—I might as well maximize money already spent.

Still, I wasn't totally convinced until I got home. That's when I saw the postcard on top of the pile of mail on the kitchen table. My mother was not pleased.

"I thought you two were over," she said.

"We are," I said in a near whisper. "We are."

"Then why is he still sending you mail?" she asked.

"I don't know," I replied.

"And what is this supposed to mean, anyway?" she said, handing it over.

I looked up at my mother. Her face was frozen into a middle-aged mask of a woman I didn't recognize.

"Jessie?"

I didn't even look at the picture, focusing instead on the message. The final word. The one that will put an end to this madness. As I requested.

And that's when I knew for sure I had to get out of Pineville.

Dear Marcus,

"RIGHT."

You must have sent today's postcard immediately, in response to my letter.

I WISH OUR LOVE WAS RIGHT.

But it wasn't. Our LOVE was all wrong.

Or maybe, according to the wisdom of Barry Manilow:

"We had the right love at the wrong time…"

Barry Manilow was crooning these very words as I held this final postcard in my hands. As I'm sure you remember, Barry Manilow was on the Cadillac 8-track the night of our first and infamous lip nip so many years ago. Barry Manilow drifted through the ceiling at Silver Meadows when you consoled me about my breakup with Len, which made possible everything that followed, including today. Barry Manilow poured out of the tent when we bumped into Sierra, a flesh-and-blood notch in your bedpost, and I realized that your promiscuous past troubled me after all.

What does this all mean?

According to Jung, synchronicity is an unpredictable moment of meaningful coincidence. More than that, he believed it to be a paranormal phenomenon that reveals the miraculous connections between the subjective and objective worlds:

"A dream dance, a sleep trance, a shared romance…"—The Police

Freud thought Jung was full of shit. (He would have thought Sting was too.)

I'm siding with Freud. Humans find meaningfulness where none exists because we want to create a sense of order in this chaotic universe. It's called apophenia. (And it's also the reason people believe in God.) Barry Manilow sang in the background during four distinct Marcus Moments. But what about all the times he didn't? It's much easier to forget about those.

Of course, it was a nice touch, making sure I got it tonight, on New Year's Eve, a date that's been so significant for us. You did your research too, sending it to my parents' new address, a house you've never seen, yet somehow known to you. This proves my point. Your postcard is too calculated to be the result of synchronistic Truth with a capital T.

And so, I'm refusing to read too much into the fact that of all the singers in all the world, it was Barry Manilow playing at the exact moment I read your final word. After all, Barry Manilow has *always* been the soundtrack my mom cleans the house to, which is admittedly rare these days since she has hired a service to do most of the dirty work. But it makes perfect sense that my mom was listening to *Ultimate Manilow* on New Year's Eve as she took the vacuum in her own manicured hands to remove every invisible dust mote in preparation for the first party in her new home.

Barry Manilow crooning about lost lovers meeting up again someday, somewhere down the road only proves that my mother has suck-ass taste in music. It does not provide adequate evidence of the oneness of the universe. It does not mean our destinies are transcendentally intertwined. I am so sure that I've decided to write this letter to break it to you.

I too wish our love was right. But it wasn't. Not at all.

Regrettably wrong,
Jessica

junior winter
january 2005

the second

I was expecting Wallach, my residence hall, to be deserted. But while the campus isn't exactly teeming with students, I *have* found company with a coterie of holiday refugees.

Wallach is quite a comedown after two years of luxurious living in Furnald. It's one of the oldest dorms on campus and looks every minute of its age, with paint-over-paint-over-paint-over-paint jobs and industrial carpeting in that vague grayish-brownish hue designed to hide all manners of filth. Wallach is one half of Hartley-Wallach, twin buildings comprising the so-called Living and Learning Center, a program meant to "integrate academic life with residential life and create a distinct society of scholars within the larger campus community." (Or so it says in the brochure.) I've lived here for a semester, and as far as I can tell the only unifying trait among all inhabitants of the Living and Learning Center is that we all didn't want to risk getting an even shittier room through the housing lottery.

Each room in these suites is depressingly cold, boxy, and utilitarian, facts that no amount of ironic artwork (e.g., a black-and-white poster of a beefcakey hunk cradling a kitten in one steroidal arm and a newborn baby in the other) can overcome.

The only exception is the ground-floor lounge, with its high ceilings, marble fireplace, and shiny grand piano. The lounge became the de facto social center for winter break malcontents like me, for whom even Wallach was better than home.

One was Tanu, who I was friendly with as a first year, but kind of fell off with when she moved to East Campus as a sophomore, which is only, like, a quarter mile away but you know, location, location, location. I might have made the effort, but she got way more entertainment value out of our friendship than I did. As a biophysics major, devoted Claymate, and writer of *7th Heaven* fanfic, Tanu is someone I've long considered to be the human equivalent to unbuttered toast. Square, dry, and bland.

Another was this guy named Josh, whom I've nicknamed ALF because I swear he crash landed from Melmac.

Then there's Kazuko. When I showed up yesterday, she was reading a graphic novel, idly kicking her chunky-heeled, silver-buckled Mary Janes over the arm of the couch. I sort of recognized her, but there's a surprising number of Asian-girl goths who wear petticoats and carry parasols, so I couldn't be sure. Tanu and ALF were both into their iPods, and Kazuko looked the most interesting, so I surprised myself by boldly making an introduction.

"Hey, I'm Jessica," I said.

"Ohhhh, I know you," Kazuko said. "You're the girlfriend of that guy who died."

First, it struck me as funny how the term "girlfriend" is only used on this campus when the "boyfriend" half of the coupling is, in fact, a corpse. Then I remembered where I'd seen Kazuko before: She broke the news on the sidewalk that afternoon.

"I'm not," I said. "I mean, I wasn't."

"You're talking about that guy who died?" asked ALF, jumping right into the conversation. "How'd it happen?"

Everyone at Columbia refers to William as "that guy who died," and not only those who were there that day. I assume it will continue until some new guy (or girl) dies on campus in a mysterious way.

"Tanu knew him, too!" I said, hoping to redirect the questioning.

"Yes," Tanu replied sheepishly. "But not as well as *you*."

"They ruled out suicide, right?" resumed Kazuko.

"And drugs," said a drowsy male voice coming through the front doors.

It was Kieran, who was in my Music Hum class last semester. He's two years younger than I am, a first year who still possesses that obnoxiously brainy hubris people develop when they have been told by every teacher since kindergarten that they're the smartest student ever ever ever. It will fade after another semester or two of impassive, unimpressed silence from his professors. He's one of those shaggy-haired, sideburned emos who owes a great debt to Conor Oberst as the champion for man-children with ink on their hands and poetry in their heavy, heavy hearts. Hailing from the lush lawns of Greenwich, Connecticut, Kieran is a philosophy major who smokes a ton of weed, which is a pretty redundant description. ("Is the existence of this bong a matter of faith? [*Long, bubbly hit.*] Or can it be proven?")

Kieran has this adorable baby face, with pinchable apple cheeks and long, dark eyelashes that you often see on toddlers but rarely on grown men. But any physical attractiveness is totally undone by his conceited need to namecheck Descartes and Devendra Banhart when rhapsodizing about disillusion and dissolution, sense and nonsense. And yet, I usually see him surrounded by those sullen argyle girls who are burdened by the mass of their messenger bags almost as much as by the ontological weight of the world.

In short, Kieran puts the "ewww" in cute.

"William had a congenital heart defect . . ." I said.

"Yeah," said ALF. "He was a Republican. He had no heart."

Everyone laughed but me. I was shocked by the impropriety of his comment, which passes for political discourse at Columbia, one of the last dig-in-our-heels liberal strongholds our nation has left. Mini Dub and I had our differences, but he didn't deserve to die so young, regardless of his sociopolitical leanings.

Kieran noticed my silence. He put his pen-splattered hand on my shoulder.

"I want to apologize on Josh's behalf," he said. "That was thoughtless of him to say, and it was even more thoughtless of us to laugh. Sometimes, like Rousseau, I hate the very human inclination toward insensitivity."

Now this, *this* made me laugh. My laughter made everyone else laugh even harder. Everyone, that is, except Kieran.

"She's on to you, assclown," ALF said.

And Kieran silently thumbed the white plug in his ear.

Despite their differences in appearance and personality, ALF and Kieran are good friends. I know this because we all just hung around the dorm, bullshitting and drinking beer for the rest of the night. We didn't even bother trying to hide our alcoholic indiscretions because if there's an RA around, no one seems to know who it is. It's pretty lawless.

I know from the Storytelling Project that people are inclined to reveal intimate details to people they barely know because it somehow feels more anonymous, and therefore safer, than talking to a friend or family member. It's the same principle that keeps psychotherapists in business. So it didn't take long before we got around to talking about the circumstances that brought us back to campus, instead of staying at home with our respective families. We all insisted that we had the worst parents, the worst hometown, the worst reason for being here.

"We are all in the winter of our discontent," Kieran said.

"Shut up, assclown," ALF said.

Of course, it turned into a competition, as most conversations here do.

Tanu is here because she told her parents over Christmas dinner that she hates biophysics—she wants to be an urban studies major. Her parents already have medical school funds earning interest in a 529 plan and did not take this very well.

"They said, 'We're not paying thirty grand a year for you not to be a doctor!'"

"And what did you say?" I asked.

"Bye-bye!"

I was impressed.

Kazuko is here because her parents sent a check for a plane ticket to Portland and she spent it elsewhere.

"What did you buy?" asked Tanu.

She thrust out her leg. "These shoes," she said.

"And?"

"That's it."

"You don't feel guilty?" I asked.

"If you met my parents, you wouldn't be asking me that," she said flatly.

ALF is here because he crashed into the Tanners' backyard and can't repair his spaceship.

"Why are you here, Jessica?" Kieran hesitated. "Jessica *Darling*, right?"

"Uh, right." I was surprised that he even knew my last name—no one introduces themselves by first and last names—let alone remembered it from when our professor publicly posted our grades.

"Jessica Darling," he repeated.

I rolled my eyes. "I know. The porn star . . ."

"Ah, yes!" ALF piped in. "I love your work."

"I wasn't thinking that," Kieran spat, his irritation directed at ALF. "I was thinking *nomen et omen*. Names are prophetic. And about how yours—Darling—might have affected you."

Before I could say anything about "Notso," my family nickname, Kazuko snorted.

"*Nomen et omen*. My parents would disagree with that."

"Why?" Kieran asked.

"Because Kazuko means 'pleasant child,'" she said with a mischievous smile.

"Mine means 'body,'" Tanu interjected.

"Wow, that's so eerie," ALF said. "Because . . . *you have a body*."

And we all laughed.

"Go ahead and mock me," Kieran said before returning his attention to me. "So do you prefer Jessica or Jess or something else?" Being unfailingly polite is all part of the dreamo gambit.

"Well, at school I'm known as J. Just as long as you don't call me Jessie, which is what my parents call me," I said. "I don't really have a preference between J or Jess or Jessica, though—" I stopped short.

"What?"

"Well, uh, the only person who consistently called me Jessica was, uh . . ."

"Your ex-boyfriend," Kieran said.

I nodded. Oh, dreamo boy. So attuned to the details.

"The dead one?" Kazuko asked.

Kieran threw her a look. "He wasn't her boyfriend."

"Right, this was another guy. A real ex-boyfriend."

"Is *he* the reason you're here?" Kieran asked.

I sipped my beer before answering. "Indirectly," I said.

"What do you mean 'indirectly'?" ALF demanded.

"By indirectly I mean, 'not directly.'"

"Which means *Jessica* doesn't feel like sharing," Kieran said. "And we should respect that."

"Respek," ALF said Ali G–style, knuckles out. We bumped fists. ALF is funny.

"There *is* a more direct reason why I'm here though," I said.

"Do tell!" Tanu begged, always too eager to hear one of my stories.

"I walked in on my parents doing it doggy style."

And then the room exploded with a shrieky freak-out.

"You win!" Tanu exclaimed. "Nothing could be worse than that!"

"I'm pretty sure that's true, but we haven't heard Kieran's reason for being here," I said, looking his way.

"Oh, go ahead and tell them," urged ALF.

Kieran was staring into the nonworking fireplace, a faraway look in his eyes.

"Ladies, get ready to weep and then drop your panties," said ALF. "As opposed to the reverse order, which is usually how it happens with me."

Kieran didn't respond.

ALF snapped his claws in front of Kieran's face.

Kieran slowly returned to the rest of the room.

"I'm here because my parents are yachting around the Caribbean. And I'm an only child. And I'm not friends with any of my friends from high school anymore, if we were ever really friends at all. And there's only so much weed you can smoke by yourself. So."

"There's more," I said.

"What?"

"There's more than what you're telling us."

"And how do you know?"

"I read faces," I said.

"Really?" Tanu asked. "Like a palm reader?"

"Well, yeah. But with faces. And I'm not a charlatan."

And before I could say "microexpressions," Kieran revealed the whole truth.

"I was supposed to go to Vail with my girlfriend. Only she isn't my girlfriend anymore. Which is painful because I'm still in love. Or in limerence. I'm not sure it matters. Our bond was illusory, but this pain is real. I hurt."

In my mind, I could hear Dexy butchering REM.

Everybody hurts . . . everybody cries . . .

I smiled sadly, thinking about my friend. She's not coming back for spring semester, as I'd hoped. Maybe next fall. While I'm sad because I miss her, I know it's better that she stays home until she's ready. This city can break the best of us.

Kieran thought I was reacting to his story. He rubbed his dry, bloodshot eyes.

"It still hurts," he repeated more softly for impact.

It worked. Upon hearing Kieran's confession the females in the room sighed.

Except me. I looked him in the eyes and told him what I thought of his sob story.

"I still win."

the fifth

To avoid a negative bank balance, I tried picking up a few hours at I Scream! But there's little demand for frozen nourishment in the dead of winter, even less when 90 percent of the university population is still on break. This includes my adviser for the Storytelling Project, which is why it's on hiatus until the start of the spring semester. So I've got lots of time, but no money for spending it.

Since it's too cold and wet to wander aimlessly around the streets, I've been spending a lot of time with my fellow refugees.

"You know what sucks?" I asked the group assembled in the lounge.

No one responded because they were all in iPod isolation. I'm fascinated by group iPoding. It's social, yet solipsistic at the same time.

I wildly waved my arms to get their attention. Kieran kept his plugs in place and didn't look up from his paperback copy of *Empire*. Tanu, Kazuko, and ALF pulled theirs out at the same time.

"I didn't hear you," they all said.

"You know what sucks?" I asked again.

"A toothless hooker," suggested ALF without missing a beat.

It's only been a few days, but ALF's constant quipping is already getting diminishing returns.

"Good guess," I said. "But the correct answer is sperm banks."

Tanu, Kazuko, and ALF all said, "Oooooooooooooooh." As if it were obvious.

Then I went on to tell them how I'm so poor that I've seriously considered selling my ova for cash, but that it's a really painful, time-consuming proposition.

"Men can just jack off at a sperm bank and make easy money," I said.

"Biology is destiny," opined Kazuko, a women's studies major.

Kieran sighed heavily to signal for attention. "It's not the bank itself that you have a problem with, but the method for donation." His plugs were still in his ears.

"I thought you were plugged in," I said.

"I only appeared to be plugged in," he said. "It's all part of the grand illusion we call reality."

"Oh, shut up," I said with my most withering glance.

"So," ALF said, returning to the subject. "You hate cock."

"I am *not* a cock hater," I said. "I love cock. I looooooooooove it."

I was being intentionally crude, mostly to see how Kieran would react. He didn't. It's very difficult to get any kind of reaction out of someone so blunted.

ALF stood up and pantomimed unzipping his pants. "Well, there's only one way to prove that . . ."

The rest of his sentence was drowned out by the sound of screams.

Later that evening, when I was making a box of off-off-brand rice and beans for dinner, I heard a knock at the door to the suite.

I nearly jumped out of my Chucks, as I had been used to complete solitude on the sixth floor. I looked through the peephole and was surprised to see Kieran there, having come all the way up from the second floor. I don't know how I didn't hear him coming, because he always wears flip-flops (even in subfreezing temps) that smack the floor with each step. Standing face-to-face in the doorway, I noted that he's only an inch or so taller than I am, and thin enough that we could probably wear the same pair of jeans.

"What are you doing here?" I said, leading him to the tiny kitchen.

"I had to ask," he said. "Is your family that bad off that you'd consider selling your eggs?"

"Oh no," I said, stirring the mix into the boiling water. "My parents are firmly upper middle class. I'm the only one that's poor."

And then I told him all about how they're teaching me a life lesson through poverty.

"Let me give you some money."

I blinked at him. One. Two. Three times.

"You're kidding, right?"

"No."

"I can't take your money," I said. "I barely know you. And besides, that would be like prostitution or something."

"Only if we sleep together," he said.

"Which isn't going to happen."

"Right," he said. "Because you hate cock."

"No, I loooooooooove it in general. Just not yours specifically."

He laughed. Kieran has a high, raspy chuckle that always ends with a "Whoo boy, that was a good one"–type whistle. It's a surprisingly lighthearted laugh for someone so . . . *heavy*.

"Seriously, I want to give you some money. You'd be helping me out."

"How so?"

"According to Plato, it's impossible to be both good and rich at the same time. So you would be doing me a favor."

I grumbled under my breath and the pot boiled over. Water on the range top sizzled and hissed.

"What?"

"You didn't need to invoke Plato, you know. You could have just as easily used any train-wreck socialite to make the same point."

"I am such a pretentious, ambitionless ass," he said, dropping his head in shame.

"Pretentious, ambitionless ass*clown*," I corrected.

I clanged the lid back on the pot to draw attention away from the smile that had slipped across my face with the stealth of a bank robber in broad daylight.

"I'm not taking your money," I said seriously. "But I will take some salsa, if you've got it."

"I don't," he said.

"Then you," I said, "are useless to me."

And then I patted his head like he was one of those skeletal puppies pictured on those fundraising cans placed next to cash registers.

I touched him like I didn't want to catch something. Something serious.

the seventh

was sitting on my bed, listening to The Cure and shuffling Marcus's postcards into alternative messages:

- I WISH OUR RIGHT WAS LOVE
- LOVE I WISH WAS OUR RIGHT
- I LOVE OUR WISH WAS RIGHT
- RIGHT OUR LOVE WAS I WISH

. . . when Kieran knocked on my door. I had gotten into the habit of propping the suite door open to encourage visits from my fellow refugees. The only one who'd taken me up on it was Kieran, so I knew it was him even before I heard his familiar flip-flopping shuffle. I stashed the postcards under my pillow and grabbed a *National Enquirer* from the stack on my desk.

"Hey," he said, sulking and slinking into the room. "It's darker than Plato's cave in here."

Wallach's rooms are all inadequately lit with weak, humming bulbs that give everyone a sickly complexion. But I don't think that's why he said it.

"I hope you name-checked Plato as a joke," I said.

"I do have a sense of humor. Though it's hard to come by these days because I'm so sad about my girlfriend. My *ex*-girlfriend. Yeah. My ex . . ." His voice trailed off and his eyes took on that wandering look. "Are you still sad about your boyfriend?"

"Oh no," I answered, ignoring the postcards under the pillowcase that said otherwise. "Being here has been very cathartic. It's kind of like a monastic retreat, complete with solitude, poverty, and chastity."

"And knowledge," he said, holding up the *National Enquirer*. He glanced at the cover, graced by Loni Anderson and Burt Reynolds. "This is from 1988." He riffled through the stack. "These are all from the eighties."

"I buy them from a homeless guy on 103rd Street for a quarter. It's my one indulgence."

"Why would you read about gossip that's almost older than we are?" he asked, skimming through an issue that devoted four pages to Delta Burke's weight troubles. "About has-beens and never-weres who have no relevance in today's society? Isn't it depressing?"

"Actually, it's not," I said. "I take great comfort in these old pages. The skyrocketing fame, the scandalous falls from grace. None of it matters anymore."

"But doesn't that just remind you of the futility of life?"

"Are you for real? Wait, don't answer that. That's only the worst question one can possibly ask a philosophy major."

"I won't refute that," he said.

"Thank you," I replied. "Anyway, these magazines remind me that everything is fleeting, the good stuff *and* the bad stuff. And no one is immune. Not Roseanne then, not Lindsay Lohan now, and not me. And that helps me take things less seriously. At least that's my goal. I can't say it's totally kicked in yet."

"It makes you think of the temporality of human existence," he said. "But in a good way."

"Right."

He was standing in a shifty way that indicated that he wasn't sure whether he should have a seat or show himself to the door. I gestured toward my desk chair and he promptly sat himself in it.

"You should teach a course about this," he said. "Get it added to the core curriculum."

"Everyone should hope to be as enlightened as I am."

And then it got quiet and Robert Smith's plaintive wail filled the room.

"*Go on, go on just walk away . . .*"

"I can't believe you listen to The Cure," he said. "Where's your ankh?"

"Oh, I'm sorry," I mocked. "Where's your Emily the Strange T-shirt?" I thrust my finger toward his birdcagey chest. "Oh *there* it is, you emo boy, you."

His eyes narrowed. "I am not emo."

"Oh give it up," I said. "No one *admits* to being emo, but emo is still out there. *Someone* has to be emo. And that person is you."

"I am not emo."

I was clearly getting to him and it brought me much pleasure. I leapt up, got him in a choke hold, ripped off his wool cap, and knuckled a noogie right into his skull. We're practically the same size, and his reflexes have been delayed by so many blunts, so it really wasn't all that difficult.

"Say it! Say 'I'm sensitive emo boy'! *SAY IT!!!*"

"Never! I'll never say it!" He broke free, fled to the corner of my room, and cowered in the corner behind a pile of dirty laundry.

He whimpered. "I . . . feel . . . so . . ."

"Emo?" I suggested.

"Violated . . ."

And there was a moment . . .

("Without you . . . Without you . . .")

. . . before we both started laughing our asses off. It was all so dumb. "Anyway, talk to me in twenty years and we'll see if anyone is still listening to Death Cab for Cutie, okay?"

"Twenty years?" he asked. He took out his combination cell/camera/Palm and tapped away. "It's a date."

And then we both settled into the pillows and thumbed through *National Enquirers* and spoke when we had something to say and were quiet when we didn't and he hardly annoyed me at all. And it was so nice that I forgot about the postcards. For a while, anyway.

Without you . . . Without you . . .

the eighth

I just woke up from a classic anxiety dream in which I'm supposed to be taking a very important math class over this winter break, the kind that covers whole chalkboards in formulas and sines and cosines and daunting stuff like that, a class I need to pass in order to graduate but that is only available during this two-week vacation period. In my dream, I sign up for this class, but never show up because I'm too busy hanging out with the Winter of Our Discontents. And when I suddenly realize that I'm supposed to be in the mathematics building with the rest of my classmates, huddled over our final exam in this subject I know nothing about, I start running around the Living and Learning Center screaming, "My life is over! My life is over!"

And then Kieran shrugs and asks, "How do you know your life exists at all?"

And then I stop running and screaming and say, "Shut up, assclown."

And that's when I woke up.

the ninth

Take note: This is how bad things happen.

Yesterday, I got a call from Bridget.

"We're back!" she said.

I didn't know they were gone.

"We spent the holidays with Percy's extended family in Chicago," she explained. "But we're back in New York now, and we called your mom and she said you're in the city too, so we should hang out."

And so that's how Percy and Bridget joined the Winter of Our Discontents. It's only been nine days, but it seems like we haven't left Wallach in years. And it's the first time any outsiders have entered our little world, so they were treated like exotic explorers from distant shores.

"You're a metropolitan studies major at NYU? What's the program like?? Do you think I should transfer???"

"I love your coat! Where did you get it? You got it downtown, didn't you? Oh, the shopping is so much better down there. Tell me about it, please? Please?"

"Take the last two shots of Ketel One. We'll take the Brita-filtered Vladimir."

And so on.

In honor of our special guests, ALF had dragged a TV and a PlayStation into the usually low-tech lounge. He and Percy got along famously over Grand Theft Auto, as guys often do. And Tanu and Kazuko had a slightly delayed, but enthusiastic recognition of Bridget from her short career as the model-actress Bridge Milhouse.

"You're the Hum-V girl!" they screamed. "The one from 'Bitch (Y U B Trippin?)'!"

Bridget instinctively grabbed for her ponytail to start chewing—as she always does whenever anyone mentions her one and only professional acting credit as one of the video girls for the already-forgotten *baaaaaad* boy band Hum-V—but the phantom hair wasn't there anymore. Recently, she was stopped on the street by a rep from a new striving-to-be upscale salon who offered her a free cut in exchange for her work as a hair model. Her choppy mess of a new 'do is not altogether different from my botched SuperCut of yesteryear, and yet she looks more stunning than ever. If she were anyone else, I'd hate her.

"Can you believe we were both Hummers in high school?" Tanu cackled.

"How embarrassing!" Kazuko cried.

Bridget's perfect complexion turned red and splotchy. "Not as embarrassing as, like, actually going out with one . . ."

Only after Tanu and Kazuko had exhausted all their questions about what the Hum-V demi-himbos were really, *really* like did they agree to run out to Rite Aid to get a ten dollar case of whatever lite beer was on special. Bridget and I finally had a moment to ourselves.

"So, let me guess," Bridget said, gesturing toward Kieran. He hadn't said much all night and was, at that moment, sitting at the piano, gently hitting the same somber, low note, over and over again. "He's the one you're going to sleep with."

"Oh, stop," I said.

"You totally are!" she said.

"And why is that? We haven't even talked since you arrived."

"I know," she said, eyeing him again. He had now drifted away from the piano and was watching Percy and ALF score coke, pick up hookers, and run over innocent bystanders in their alternate lawless universe. He looked bored. "It's, like, a very obvious not talking."

As is often the case with Bridget, I hated to admit that she was right. But she was. Kieran and I had barely said more than "hey" since our *National Enquirer* afternoon. Our relationship was very bipolar. (And I don't think Dexy would be offended if I described it as such, which I probably will when I share this story with her on the phone.)

"He's exactly like Marcus," she continued. "Only shorter."

I nearly fell over. "He's nothing like Marcus!"

"Yuh-huh," she insisted, exaggerating the affirmation. "He's *exactly* like Marcus."

"No one is *exactly* like anyone else," I said. "Not even the Olsen twins."

"Well—duh!—they're fraternal."

"I was only trying to make a point how no one is exactly like anyone else," I said, trying to steer the conversation away from NYU's most famous coeds and back to me, me, me.

"I know," Bridget said, grabbing the back of her naked neck. "And I was only trying to point out how Marcus and Kieran are like, of the same . . ." She paused, trying to find the right word. "Archetype."

"Wow, NYU has made you really smart."

"You know it's true but you don't want to admit it," she said, ignoring my gentle teasing. "They've got the same stonah lovah man thing going for them."

On cue, Kieran flip-flopped over to us.

"You look like you're having an intense conversation," he said.

"With this hair? Not possible," Bridget said, running her hands through her platinum locks. "Do you think I should get it dyed black so I'm taken seriously?"

I loved seeing Bridget like this. She had ditched acting altogether and was studying art and public policy. She's particularly interested in the development of theater and music programs for kids who, like she did, have nothing but an empty house to return to after school every day. She had gained so much confidence in her intelligence at NYU that she could now mock the whole dumb blonde stereotype. It made me wonder what my mother, and to a lesser degree my sister, would be like now if they had ever allowed themselves to have even a vaguely intellectual thought.

"So Kieran, do you have a girlfriend?" Bridget was a little drunk.

Kieran coughed, looked away, and rubbed his eyes before answering. You don't need to know a damn thing about microexpressions to interpret his desire to avoid the question.

"We just broke up," he said with a ragged edge to his voice.

"What a shame," Bridget cooed, looking at me instead of him. "Why did you break up?"

"I'm not sure," he said, his eyes drifting away. "Maybe because she's still in high school and I'm here. I'm not the one who did the breaking."

"You're the one who's broken!" Bridget said brightly.

Kieran and I waited for her to explain why such a sad statement would bring such glee.

"You're just like Jess!"

"Okay, enough about breakups," I said, cutting her off before she said anything more incriminating about my past with Marcus. "Let's talk about what a thrilling example you and Percy are setting for monogamy."

"I love him," she said, gazing at him adoringly. "So I don't sleep with anyone else. He loves me, so he doesn't sleep with anyone else. It's not too difficult."

Sometimes Bridget and Percy's love for each other can be so . . . annoying.

"But what about a year from now, five years from now, ten years from now?"

"Jess doesn't believe in marriage," Bridget said, slightly off topic.

"You don't?" Kieran asked.

"Nope," I said. "All marriages are ill-fated. The biology is boring, but humans just aren't hardwired to be with one person our whole lives."

"You don't believe in love—" Bridget began.

"I think my girlfriend and I were in limerence, not love," Kieran cut in.

Bridget grabbed her hair again. "Like, hello? Duh! Explain!"

"Limerence is that euphoric, almost obsessive feeling you get when you can't stand to be away from someone. It usually occurs when you first meet," he said. "But in some relationships it can last for years. It's rare, though."

"So limerence is mostly about lust," Bridget said. "Love is deeper."

"But how deep is it really?" I asked. "When most relationships go bust?"

"Oh, not this again," Bridget groaned.

"So you think people should just jump from person to person, from limerent state to limerent state," Kieran said with an amused lilt to his voice.

"I didn't say that," I replied, a bit boozy myself, and woozy with words.

"Then what *are* you saying?"

"Do you really think that people are capable of loving only *one* person?" I asked.

"One," Bridget answered softly, almost reverentially. "If you're lucky."

I barely considered this before pressing on, dismissing her loyalty for Percy as an anomaly, a glorious exception to the disappointing rules of romance.

"Well, I think it's possible to love someone and still be curious about someone else. And I think you should be able to act on that impulse with impunity. But in our society, where monogamy rules despite all the evidence that it doesn't work, a person is demonized for wanting to break from that traditional model of relationships. I think you can love someone, truly love someone, and still be drawn to someone else. Enough to want to kiss that other person, just to see what it would be like. Or maybe to help confirm that what you've got is better than what else is out there. Because isn't the desire alone a form of betrayal? So what further harm does it do to put those thoughts into action? Ideally, you would be able just to go back to the person you love after you've kissed that other person and discovered it wasn't as interesting as you thought it would be, which I would imagine would be the case most of the time. And in the event that it *is* unexpectedly amazing, isn't it better to have experienced that moment of bliss rather than imagine what it *could* have been like?"

I stopped talking because it was all getting too personal. Bridget's mouth was pinched shut. Kieran's hinted at a smile.

"J wants to be a swinger," ALF said, apparently having eavesdropped on my diatribe.

"She's very polyamorous," Percy said, slapping him on his furry back. Percy was ALF's new best friend.

"You should move to Japan, where hardly any women want to marry," suggested Kazuko, setting down a brown bag full of beer. "But I don't think they're having much sex either."

"And we all know how much J loves cock," ALF joked.

"I was being hypothetical!" I shouted over the laughter. Then I downed the rest of my nasty plastic jug vodka.

"Let's play a game!" Tanu suddenly proposed, much to my relief.

"POKER!" shouted ALF and Percy simultaneously, which delighted them both to no end.

"I'm so sick of Hold'em," Kazuko said, referring to the tournaments that have become a significant part of social life on campus. "Let's play a *girl* game."

ALF and Percy looked at each other for a split second before responding, again, in unison. "STRIP POKER!"

"Forget it," replied all the women in the room.

"Beirut?" suggested ALF.

Kazuko yawned, then addressed the ladies. "You'd think these boys would've gotten beer pong out of their system in high school."

"How about Shut Up and Drink?!" ALF suggested.

"How do you play that?" Bridget asked.

"You shuffle a deck of cards. You take one off the top. If you can read what it is, you do a shot."

"I don't get it," Bridget said.

"You keep taking cards and doing shots until you can't read the card anymore."

"Or until you die of alcohol poisoning," Percy added.

"Or that," ALF concurred.

"Let's play Truth or Dare!" Bridget offered.

Her suggestion was met with a chorus of excited *oooooohs*. Self-conscious regression is very popular among otherwise sophisticated college types. Nowhere is adultescence more popular than in Manhattan, where everyone's got some degree of 9/11 PTSD. This goes double when cheap alcohol is involved.

But I had another idea. A better idea. The best of all.

"Why don't we just cut to the chase and play Spin the Bottle?"

"What do you mean, 'cut to the chase'?" Bridget asked.

"Well, Truth or Dare is really all about kissing," I said.

"Go on," Percy said.

"Don't pretend you don't know what I'm talking about."

"We don't know what you're talking about," the room said simultaneously (or at least it seemed so at the time).

"Okay. You start off with non-kissing-related truths or dares. Like, 'Have you ever run outside naked?' Or, 'I dare you to run outside naked.' But that's just so you don't seem too eager. Because all everyone is really thinking about is kissing. As in, 'Who in the room do you want to kiss?' Or, 'I dare you to kiss so-and-so.' It always goes that way. Always! So why don't we just skip over the preliminaries and play Spin the Bottle, which is all about kissing."

The room was silent.

"She's right, you know," Percy said.

"She really is," Bridget said.

And then the room got quiet again and my body buzzed with anticipation.

"Well," Kieran said.

He picked up an unopened bottle from the bag and pointed it in my direction. He flip-flopped toward me, framed my cheeks with his hands, and gave me a delicate kiss on the lips.

"How was that?" he asked, his lips lingering on mine, tickling me with his words.

It was a kiss that left me wanting more. But that's not what I told him.

"There was one thing I forgot to mention about Truth or Dare and kissing," I said, still pressed against him.

"And what's that?"

I pulled away so I could whisper in his ear. "It's really about *fucking*."

He reared back in astonishment before saying, "That's . . . so . . ."

"What?"

"True."

I can't say I have any clue what the rest of the room was doing during this exchange, because I wasn't paying attention. I can only suspect that they were doing what I would have done in the same situation, which is make silent, immature, "OH MY GOD!" hand gestures behind our backs because I knew what was going to happen next—SEX!!!—just as Bridget had predicted. This automatically put us in an embarrassing situation because when everyone knows you're rushing off to hit it, there's a certain pressure to make it really hot because you already know that they will ask you for details the morning after, something they feel at liberty to do since you so publicly made your coital intentions known.

But this sex was not hot.

Oh no, it was not.

I'll spare you the inelegant in-the-act details. But here's a watershed moment:

Kieran slipped off his boxers.

"Oh my God!"

"What?"

"I've never seen one before!"

"You've never seen a *penis* before?"

"Not one that looks like . . . like . . . a pig in a blanket!"

"It's uncircumcised."

"I know that. I just wasn't expecting to see one."

"Why?"

"Because that's so . . . European. And you're, well . . . from *Connecticut*."

"Do you want to get a closer look?"

"Uh, not really. Can we just get under the covers now?"

"Okay."

"And turn out the lights."

"Okay. Do you want a blindfold, too?"

"Uh, no. Just a condom, thank you."

This exchange pretty much set the tone for what would follow, which can be best described as the clumsy rearrangement of unfamiliar limbs and the execution of signature moves (the shocker!!!) that would only work with partners who were far, far away from the mattress on which they were being performed. And it got worse.

In the moments after the act, when his penis was retreating back into its fleshy burrow like a groundhog, Kieran started talking and wouldn't stop.

"I just gained at least forty-odd sex partners in about ten minutes," he said.

It was more like two minutes, but that wasn't worth quibbling over when the statement as a whole was so ludicrous. "How so?"

"Well, I just had sex with you. And you've mentioned that your ex-boyfriend had sex with forty-something girls before you."

To this day, I still don't know the actual number. But for storytelling purposes, I'd landed on "forty-something." An outrageous but not totally outlandish number.

"And they say that when you have sex, you are having sex with every person your partner has ever had sex with, which is kind of a beautiful concept, when you think about it, all of these people bonded through what Socrates referred to in the *Phaedrus* as the blind, unreasonable eros . . ."

"Is this your idea of pillow talk?" I asked, my neck muscles strained with incredulity.

"I'm sorry," he said. "I'm out of practice. I haven't had sex with someone new in more than two years. Usually my girlfriend and I would hurry up and get dressed so I could get her home before her curfew."

"Well, that doesn't apply here, now does it?"

"We could just roll over and fall asleep," he suggested.

"I think that's a very good idea," I said, turning away from him. Should I have expected any better? I've only really known

Kieran for a week, and I'm not sure I even like him very much, yet I had sex with him. I've become the type of person who has sex with someone she's only known for a week. When did I become this person? Casual sex isn't unusual for most college students, but I've never been most college students and sex has never been casual for me.

I think that final postcard fucked me up. (Ha. In more ways than one.)

the tenth

This afternoon Kieran came knocking on my door.

"We owe it to ourselves to try again," he said.

"No offense," I said, waving him away with a *National Enquirer* with Vanna White on the cover, "but why would anyone want to relive what happened yesterday?"

And then he launched into his argument, about how the sex was so awkward and so bad because we were still thinking about our exes when we did it. And the only way we would ever stop thinking about our exes during sex is to have more sex.

"Besides," he said. "What else is there to do?"

I looked down and out my window. Faces on the sidewalks were obscured by umbrellas, hats, and hoods. I could tell from their hunched-over hurrying that no one was happy to be outside, dodging the icy rain plunging down like minidaggers from the sky. There was nothing interesting on TV. I'd read all my *National Enquirers*. My internet access was inexplicably hosed.

He had a point. And hadn't Dexy prescribed the same remedy?

So we went for round two.

And three.

And four.

And I'm happy to report that it *was* better, and not only

because it couldn't have been any worse. I guess we're getting used to each other, which kind of makes an argument for monogamy. Or serial monogamy at least.

The way I see it, Kieran and I are helping each other. It's only practical for me to get out of this love limbo—this pur*guy*tory, so to speak—I'm in right now. There's no point in pining over Marcus. My relationship with him was bound to meet its end, and not only because his newfound New Ageyness would always be at odds with my innate nihilism. No, it was doomed because every relationship ends. The only notable exception is the one you happen to be in when you die, in which case it only ends for the lonely soul left behind. You, on the other hand, are unaware that it's over because you're very conveniently dead. This isn't pessimistic, but pragmatic.

So it makes sense to move on, bringing myself one guy closer to, not the One, but the One I'm With When I Die. Kieran is the perfect candidate for the job—attractive enough that hooking up will be fun, but youngish and annoying enough that I won't try to turn him into the One. Likewise, I'm that girl for him. It's really quite simple. To be even more sensible about it, I'm only going to let this last as long as winter break. When it's over, we're over.

Done.

the eleventh

Kieran's annoyances are becoming, well, if not less annoying, then something else . . .

Arousing?

One minute we're fighting, the next we're fucking. Psychologically speaking, arousal is arousal is arousal. But I never knew how true that was until Kieran.

the twelfth

We're *really* getting the hang of this now. It's almost a shame that it, like all romance, is doomed.

the thirteenth

ust stick to the plan: Break over, break up. Period.

the fourteenth

The unthinkable is happening:
I'm falling for an assclown.

the fifteenth

Marcus who?

junior summer
june 2005

Kieran:

"Nomen et omen" was the first of many things you said that annoyed me. But perhaps there's truth to this aphorism after all. If only I had looked up the definition of your name sooner, I could have been warned about the "small" and "dark" nature of your heart. Because I waited until it was already too late, here are...

SOME THINGS I'VE ALWAYS WANTED TO TELL YOU

1. Wearing AXE deodorant body spray is *not* funny in an ironic, postmodern kind of way.

2. Ditto listening to the Grateful Dead every single time you smoke up, or shouting, "We're fuckin' to 'Truckin'! We're fuckin' to 'Truckin'!"

3. And don't even get me started on your obsession with *I Love the '90s.* Guess what? We *all* fucking love the nineties because we are *all* complete narcissists when it comes to the commercialization of pop cultural nostalgia and we *all* want to think that our own appreciation of "our" decade supersedes everyone else's so just GET OVER your need to prove that you know more than anyone about Furbies and Soul Asylum and *Beverly Hills 90210.*

4. I never minded your problem with premature ejaculation. In fact, I appreciated that sex was over before it ever really began. Intercourse didn't interfere with my studies, which enabled me to make the dean's list.

5. You play your heartache like a party trick, don't you? You've been damaged in some profound, important way. You need to be helped. Fixed. Made whole again. And as a result of your deep, deep suffering you can't be blamed for the pain you inflict on fools like me who make the mistake of trying to be your savior. We are *both* victims here, so you *can't* be the bad guy. Oh no, not a sensitive soul like you, who waxes poetic about "feeling" but is, in fact, too much of a selfish little boy to be capable of feeling anything real at all. As someone who knows the difference between love as an amusing abstraction and genuine love, I can only feel pity. And that's because I never cared enough about you to hate you.

Respectlessly,

J.

the first

Kieran cheated on me.

And I'll be homeless next fall.

I'm not sure which is worse.

Like too many couples in Manhattan, I think I'd be willing to shack up with someone I despised if the apartment had a doorman and adequate afternoon sunlight. The small but furnished off-campus-but-not-too-far-off-campus one-bedroom sublet that Kieran and I agreed to share this summer and next year had both the doorman and the sun, plus a ridiculously low rent (thanks to his parents' generous housing subsidy), so neither of us had any reason to enroll in the university lottery. This is the same apartment that he will now share with his ex-girlfriend, now his re-girlfriend, who just turned eighteen and will be attending Barnard next September. They reconciled during her campus interview in late January and continued reconciling on the weekends, on the sly, while I was working two jobs to pay for the twenty-two credits I was taking. I'd only seen Re-girlfriend in pictures on his laptop, but I was never intimidated by her plain-faced, dishwater-tressed ordinariness. What *should* have bothered me was Kieran's unwillingness to drag every last pixel into his desktop trash can.

"You were gone all the time," he whined when I questioned him about the black thong I found in the folds of his unwashed sheets. I'm aware that this is just so cliché. So excruciatingly un-creative and cliché it made me want to take a long, slow drag on a tailpipe. "I missed you, and you weren't around so . . ."

"So it's *my* fault you fucked your ex-girlfriend!" I screeched loud enough for everyone in Morningside Heights to hear.

"According to your take on monogamy, I was just fulfilling my human instincts. Don't blame me. Blame the traditional model of relationships." His face was the picture of newborn baby guile-lessness. The only thing missing was his mommy's teat in his wanting mouth. It's this put-on innocence that has allowed him to get away with such bratty, self-absorbed behavior his entire life. All I could do was shut up and storm out because I was afraid of saying something equally stupid that would somehow come back to haunt me in the future.

So ended my relationship with Kieran. The relationship I never would've had if I'd stuck to my first impression. I have long acknowledged that my first impressions are always for shit, so I figured I was safe. But no. This time I was right all along. He really was a pompous, pretentious assclown who used the oh-so-sensitive trappings of emo to mask his sadism. I was *so* right when I told Bridget that he was nothing, *nothing* like Marcus. Marcus never hurt me on purpose.

With no boyfriend and, more significantly, nowhere to stay in the city, I'm back in Pineville with my parents. This is appro-priate punishment for a semester-long lapse in judgment. I am trying very hard to look on the positive side of things. For ex-ample, I was grateful that when I opened the door to my parents' condo, they weren't bumping elderly uglies on the couch. That was good.

I guess another good thing is that I've got a job here that actually pays better than anything I could get in the city. I've been working for ACCEPT!, the Accelerated College Coaching and Educational Preparedness Tutorial! ACCEPT!'s motto: *You Are Your Application.*

The awkwardly named strip mall institution conducts a series of get-into-college classes during the school year, followed by a longer get-into-college camp in the summer. Test prep, AP class counseling, campus tours, mock admission interviews— none of this is unusual in this übercompetitive college market. But ACCEPT! doesn't leave *anything* to chance. For example, a skill that high schoolers should have mastered in first grade— Perfecting Your Penmanship!—is part of the curriculum now that handwritten essays count for one-third of the new SAT. Every lesson is intended to give an edge to those who are already considered the best and the brightest. And at almost $3,000 per session, the richest. Five years ago, Pineville was too blue-collar (okay, white trash) for ACCEPT! to set up shop around here. But times have changed, and Pineville is—however improbably— becoming a bedroom community for new-money families from Manhattan who are buying up all the waterfront property. So my mom was right, the new house is an investment that will make me very wealthy thirty years from now—*if* I survive that long on the streets.

I'm still in training, but in five days I start working with a small group who signed up for the pre-summer minisession. This is the three-week-long after-school pre-summer-session session for those who want a jump start on their jump start. In other words, the most neurotic nutcases of all.

My teaching credentials? I got into Columbia. I am who they want to be. Of course, they'd demand a refund if they had a clue as to who I really am.

the sixth

I walked purposefully into the university-style classroom and headed for one of the stadium seats facing the immaculate dry-erase board. Then I noticed that three front-and-center spots were already occupied by students with open laptops at the ready.

I'd forgotten that *I* was the teacher here. Oops.

Could it also be so easy to forget what it was like to be sixteen or seventeen, at the top of one's class, with stellar standardized test scores and a transcript maxed out on athletic, academic, and philanthropic activities?

Apparently so. Otherwise, my students wouldn't annoy me so goddamn much.

"If you didn't take the new SAT, how do we know how smart you are on the 2400 scale?" asked Will. Number one in his class. Captain of the forensics team. Champion hurdler. AIDS activist. Wants Harvard.

"Were you a National Merit Scholar?" asked Geoff. Has already earned twelve college credits. Scholastic Poetry Award winner. Founded school's archery team. Taught English in Kenya. Wants Harvard.

"Why didn't you go to Harvard?" asked Maddie. Intel Science Talent Search semifinalist. Classically trained pianist. Varsity tennis player. Volunteers at a homeless shelter. Wants . . . you guessed it . . . Harvard.

These kiddies need to unclench.

And this is coming from someone who has been grinding her teeth down to the nubby nerve endings for years. The only students enrolled in ACCEPT! are those who, at least back in my day, would've been the only ones who didn't need it. And yet they—or more likely their parents—are convinced that none of it is enough. Their paranoia is contagious, which is why "college preparedness training" is one of the fastest-growing sectors in education.

"Colleges rely on standardized tests to help them weed through twenty thousand applications," said Will. "If you're not at the top, you get tossed."

"There are eleven in my class who have GPAs over 4.0," said Maddie. "I need something that will help me stand out in a district where *everyone* has something that makes them stand out."

"Students who wouldn't have gone to college twenty-five years ago do now," said Geoff. "Which puts the Ivy League at an even greater premium."

Christ. The kiddies almost had me convinced that Columbia would retroactively revoke my acceptance. I never thought I would be thankful for coming from a high school where most students went to community college or not at all. All my get-into-college stress came from within. If I had gotten external pressure from my fellow classmates, my noggin would have imploded in a quick but powerful puff of brain cells and smoke. *Pffffffft!*

When I think back to that time, I was certain, just like these kiddies (even though they are only four, maybe five years younger than I am, they are still children) are certain, that my college choice would have an irrevocable effect on THE REST OF MY LIFE. And so, nearly every decision I made was with one question in mind: Will this look good on my college application? And once I made my tortured decision to apply to Columbia, it was Columbia or nothing. Success or failure. Live or die. It was all very dramatic and important in the way that all things are dramatic and important when you're in high school and never will be again. And now that I'm entering my last year of college in a homeless, boyfriendless, clueless (as to what I want to do after graduation) state, I think it's safe to argue that I might have been better off if I'd had my heart set on somewhere else. Or at the very least, equally bad off.

But these kiddies need to relax because they've already got it made. They were born into a fancy-schmancy suburban advantage in what is already the most privileged place on the planet. The gift of hereditary meritocracy practically guarantees that whether they excel in life has less to do with what they do than what life they were born into. For that advantage alone, they will always lead very charmed lives.

This reminds me of one of many arguments I had with Kieran, this one about the concept of free will. He believed that all men are responsible for creating their own fate. I told him that I agreed to a point.

"Some are freer than others," I said, slipping out of my Chucks.

"We're all free to exercise our autonomy," he said, pulling his T-shirt over his head.

"What about the tens of thousands of babies who were wiped out in the tsunami? Or the comparable number who die every single month from totally curable diseases like malaria? How can you tell me that they have free will?" I said, unbuttoning my jeans.

"They can choose how they wish to perceive their reality," he said, unzipping his pants.

"They're *babies!*" I shouted, unhooking my bra.

"They're *human beings!*" he shouted back, sliding on a condom.

"You're an assclown," I said, stepping out of my skivvies.

(I'm not proud to say that arguments like this fueled the hate fucks that were the cornerstone of our sham of an ex-relationship.)

Later, when we were finished and Kieran was asleep, I lay awake and thought about my brother, Matthew, who died when he was only two weeks old. What free will did he have?

It's Matthew, and, more recently, William, who remind me how lucky I am to simply exist. Though I might have trouble remembering that next semester when I'm bunking on a bench in Riverside Park with a crackhead named Shifty-Eyed Pete.

the eleventh

was startled out of my slumber this morning by the sights and sounds of my mother waving an unidentified object in my face.

"Jessie. Jessie! JESSIE! *JESSIE!!!*" my mother yelled with escalating urgency.

Despite a long history of her needlessly waking me up in this manner, I instinctively sprang out of the sheets, ready to make an emergency evacuation in my underwear. "Holy shit! What's wrong?! Is everyone okay?!"

"Phone for you," she said sweetly.

I fainted into the goose down duvet. "You've got to be kidding me," I said. "I know I don't get many phone calls, but do we really need all the drama?"

"She said it was of crucial importance," my mom said, handing over the cordless. Her eyes shone with excitement. She lives for this ridiculousness. She really does. I am a big disappointment in this arena because I keep my melodrama to myself.

"Who is it?" I asked.

My mother gave a thoughtful pause. "I don't know."

I pressed the phone to my ear. "Hello?"

"Omigod!!"

I waved at my mother to let her know that her presence was no longer required. She pouted before descending the stairs.

"Sara?"

"Omigod! Who else would it be?"

Uh. I could name about a bazillion people I would expect on the line instead of her. I cannot remember the last time Sara called me. Definitely not in this millennium. I'm pretty sure Ricky Martin was still livin' *la vida loca* at the top of the pop charts. *That's* how long it's been. Considering how his career is faring these days, I would have been less surprised if Señor "Shake Your Bon Bon" himself had called to say, "*Hola.*"

"Have you heard?" she shouted into the phone. I could barely make out what she was saying. It was like talking to a faulty squawk box.

"I'm sure I haven't heard or you wouldn't be calling me," I said as I scraped the polish off my toenails for amusement. "Let's end the suspense."

"Len and Manda broke up!" she shouted.

I took a deep breath and exhaled loudly and deeply, trying to extend the sigh as long as I could. Then I inhaled and did it again. That's how bored I was by this conversation.

"Len and I were over three years ago. Why would I care about this?" I was about to hang up.

"Manda cheated on him!" she shouted.

"Again, none of this is surprising," I replied, flicking the red specks of nail polish onto the city-country (or was it country-city?) bed quilt. They looked like dried blood.

"MANDA CHEATED ON HIM WITH A GIRL."

"Oh, whatever," I said with a yawn. "Straight girls kiss each other all the time. It makes guys hard." I've never gone girl-on-girl for show, but I'd seen enough drunken faux-lesbian makeout sessions to speak with authority.

"Okay," she said tartly. "But how many straight girls GO DOWN ON EACH OTHER?"

If I were able to speak, I would have apologized to Sara for doubting her all these years. Because it was clear to me that the entirety of our fake friendship had existed merely to set us up for this exquisite moment.

"DID YOU HEAR ME?"

How could I not? "I'm just a little shocked is all."

Sara's voice took on that very pleased-with-herself tone I know so well. "I thought you would be. Can you believe it? Manda is a total *quote* carpet muncher *unquote*. EWWWWWWWW." If Sara is any indication, LGBTQ equality has a long way to go in this country.

According to Sara, who is rarely wrong about these types of things, Len finished his finals early, drove down to New Brunswick from Ithaca, and showed up unannounced at Manda's apartment only to find her tangled up in a sapphic 69. Now that's what I call taking women's studies to a whole new level.

"Omigod! I bet Len just wants to *die!*" Sara said gleefully.

I'll bet he does. At least I didn't walk in on Kieran and Re-girlfriend in a compromising position. (Though even that couldn't have been any worse than the infamous *coitus interruptus parentis*. Ack. I just dropped dead all over again.)

As interesting as this news was, I didn't quite understand the urgency.

"Sara, why did you call me about this?"

"Omigod! I figured you'd want to be the first to know."

Of course she would. Sara is like someone who unexpectedly

wakes up after a decade in a coma and can't get her mind unstuck from the last clear-eyed moments right before the accident. Petty Pineville High gossip is as much of her present as it is her past. I suppose it's because she feels she's got so little to look forward to. I'm so over it, which isn't surprising because I was over it while I was still in it. While my Columbia years have been anything but perfect, I still believe that one of the greatest advantages of college is that I'm officially allowed to not care about high school anymore.

"Soooooooo?" Sara was looking for something. Congratulation. Recognition. Appreciation.

"Thanks, Sara," I said.

"Omigod! You're so welcome!"

I was nice to Sara because trashing her was, for me, as much of my petty high school past as gossiping was for her. Only I've grown out of it.

the sixteenth

An excerpt from today's class lecture.

The topic was Choose (Well) or Lose! (Because AC-CEPT! would be nothing without exaggeration. Or exclamation points.) Basically, I was supposed to instruct the kiddies to "think beyond the Ivies" and find "exceptional departments in the innumerable esteemed institutions this great nation has to offer." Because college isn't a "prize in a ruthless status game." Oh no. It's an "educational journey," which should start with a student's mission to find a school that isn't necessarily the "best" but is "best for them."

This would be like Dubya successfully convincing Michael Moore to join his Cabinet. Inconceivable. But they pay me to try.

"So why didn't you apply to Harvard?" asked Will.

"Yeah?" asked Maddie.

"Were you afraid you'd get rejected?" asked Geoff.

The kiddies are convinced that anyone intelligent enough to get into Harvard should go to Harvard. So, with their Harvard aspirations, they all harbor suspicions that they're smarter than I am.

"I wanted to go to school in New York," I said.

"Aren't you concerned about terrorism?" asked Maddie.

"I was worried about it before I applied," I said. "But I'm not anymore."

"Aren't you worried about dying?" asked Geoff.

"Well, I'm worried about dying in general, sure," I said. "But I'm not worried about dying from a terrorist attack."

"Even in New York?" asked Will.

"Even in New York," I said. "It's all about perceived versus actual risk."

"Huh?" they all asked.

"The things we fear most are often those that are least likely to happen," I said. "Like, the odds of being killed in a terrorist attack is 1 in 9.2 million."

They all murmured in doubt.

"You," I said, pointing to Will. "You drove here in the MINI Cooper your parents bought for your seventeenth birthday, right?"

"Yeah."

"Well, the odds of dying in a car accident are 1 in 18,000.

"You," I said, turning to Maddie. "You fake and bake, right?"

"Sure."

"The odds of getting skin cancer are 1 in 200."

"I'm not getting skin cancer," she said.

"Fine. Whatever. Have faith in your disease-resistant melanin," I said, pursing my lips like a priss. "I'm just trying to make a point."

They all grumbled.

"Do you know that last September, a city-sized asteroid missed our planet by a distance only four times that of Earth to the moon? In galactic terms, that's nothing!" I pinched my thumb and forefinger together to illustrate. "Nothing! Life as we know it! Over in an instant!"

They were all slyly but not shyly texting one another about my mental instability.

"All I'm saying is that you can't hide from certain death, so you shouldn't hide from uncertain life." It sounded profound as I said it. But hindsight is not as kind. I deserved the inevitable backlash.

"Why do we need to know this?" asked Geoff. "Teach the test!"

"The test." This, of course, is the SAT I, the be-all and end-all of standardized tests designed to assess verbal, math, and, most recently, writing skills. Despite UCLA's best efforts to devalue its importance, it is still *the* key factor in separating the Ivy League get-ins and did-nots.

"Yes," whined Will and Maddie. "Teach the test!"

And it became a chant. "Teach the test! Teach the test!"

These damn kiddies never appreciate a valuable life lesson when they hear one.

I said earlier that I'm just so over high school. I would venture to guess that this is one of the reasons I'm having trouble empathizing with the kiddies' angst. Another reason I'm having trouble is because I don't like people very much. (The Storytelling Project did little to change that.)

In choosing to be a psychology major, I decided to learn for the joy of learning for the first time in my life. I'd always been fascinated by human nature. What makes us act the way we do? Why do we make the same mistakes over and over? But I guess my interest is purely theoretical. I'm a psychology major who has no desire to work with people. This was poor planning on my part, I suppose. My parents definitely think so. But choosing passion over practicality seemed so honorable when I was a first-year student and graduation seemed so very, very far away . . .

But now, a semester away from unemployment, I realize how much better off those engineering students really are. Sure, they're boring conversationalists who make you want to run screaming because every story begins, "The other day? In the lab?" But people become a whole helluva lot more interesting when they're pulling down six figures, don't they? If I'm going to drag my friends out to my cardboard box, the pressure's on to provide some pretty goddamned sparkling conversation once they get there. And even with all my noble knowledge for knowledge's sake, I'm not sure I can.

At the very least, I'll be able to burn my diploma to keep me warm.

the nineteenth

Just in case you've been wondering why I haven't written about my social life, it's because I don't have one. This has not gone unnoticed by my parents. And when I say my parents I really mean my mother.

"So, Jessie, when are we going to meet this boyfriend of yours?" she asked yesterday.

Did I mention that I haven't told my parents about my breakup?

"Uh, never," I said.

"What do you mean never? We were so looking forward to making his acquaintance!"

I'd made the mistake of telling my mom that Kieran went to prep school in Greenwich, Connecticut. That was all she needed to hear. The cachet of that particular zip code more than made up for the fact that he was a philosophy major, which topped even psychology on the list of slacker liberal artsy majors. I'm sure she'd been thinking that if I married right, and by "right" I really mean rich, my ambitionless major would no longer be a problem because ambition is something I'd have no need for. (*See* Darling, Bethany.)

"What happened?" she asked.

"You really don't want to know," I said.

"I do!" she cried. "I really do!"

"You only think you do," I said.

She took my hand and led me to the couch of ill repute. I let go and opted for the ottoman.

"We don't talk anymore, Jessie," she said. "I want to hear what happened."

I sighed. "He got back together with his ex-girlfriend," I said. "Only he did so without the courtesy of breaking up with me before he did it."

"He cheated on you?!"

"Yeah," I said with a flat detachment that I was surprised to hear coming out of my mouth. Telling my mother about Kieran's indiscretion somehow made it unimportant.

She reached over and clutched me to her silken bosom. "My poor baby!"

It was all very dramatic.

Remember that spa gift certificate my mom got me last Christmas? After my mother released me from her clutches, she got on the phone to redeem it as soon as possible. You know, because nothing is better for heartache than a deep pore-cleansing facial.

"Good news!" my mom chirped. "A bride called off her wedding!"

"Uh . . . hooray?"

"I know!" my mom cheered, oblivious to my sarcasm. "She had to cancel the day of beauty for her bridal party, so there was a wide-open block of services available for all three of us tomorrow! A Darling Day of Pampering!"

"Whee."

I wasn't entirely enthusiastic about the idea. I don't have anything against pampering per se, it was just the principle of the
thing. I couldn't help but think of how much more useful that
money would be to me next semester. I'm not sure how much my
fellow homeless will appreciate my glowing complexion when
we're scavenging for moldy pizza crusts out of a dumpster.

But truth be told, the day started off pretty swell. The
Ahhhh . . . Spa was located on a pristine stretch of beach in
Oceanhead, the most chichi town on the Jersey Shore. The
whole place was all feng shuied to promote a sense of relaxation
and rejuvenation. Natural light filtered through floor-to-ceiling
art glass windows. Towering columns were sheathed in translucent fabrics that danced in the gentle ocean breeze. A cascad-
ing river stone waterfall gurgled like a newborn babe. The air
was spiked with citrus and mint, but not overpoweringly so, as if
this was what we were always meant to respirate.

Bethany and Mom were less awed than I was because they
have made numerous sojourns to day spas. As a spa virgin, I was
easily impressed. And intimidated. Because as we entered the
changing room, I quickly discovered that the rules of the outside world did not apply. And I realized this because my mother
and Bethany did not hesitate to get totally naked in front of me,
which sort of freaked me out, and not just because seeing my
mom au naturel reminded me of the last (and only) time I'd seen
her in that state, which was when she and my dad were doing the
dirty-bird special on the couch.

Ack.

Look, I am not a prude. I have undressed and dressed in front
of total strangers in the locker room at Columbia countless times
with little thought. There's anonymity in numbers. (Though it

was a bit awkward when I bumped into one of my teaching assistants coming out of the shower and I saw that her hotly debated rack was indeed of the saline variety, and that she'd waxed her pubes into a star shape, which reminded me of the creative topiary at the gates of Disneyland. You know, plants unnaturally pruned until they look like Mickey Mouse and the like. From that point on, whenever I saw that TA, I could only think "Tits/Ass.") But something about seeing my mom and my sister naked was just weird and I wanted it to end quickly.

I was still standing there fully clothed while my mother and Bethany were stripped down to skin. And I figured, okay, it will be over soon. They'll put their robes on and I won't have to aggressively avert my eyes so I can't see that my sister has nipples that look like pink Good & Plenties. (Probably from all the breastfeeding.) Or that my mom has stretch marks running up and down her thighs like the streaks left behind on recently cleaned glass. (Probably from decades of yo-yo dieting.) But then they launched into a conversation. And not a modest one either. A wildly gesticulating, have-no-shame gabfest.

"Bethany, did you talk to the people at Maurice Villency about that gorgeous sectional?" She threw her arms toward the exposed beams in the ceiling for unnecessary emphasis.

"Not yet. I want to replace all the draperies first," she said with a gratuitous sweep of her arms.

The word *draperies* brought to mind the pubic crudity about drapes matching the carpet and I was more acked out than ever.

I slipped off my own clothes and hastily put on my robe, hoping to set a modest example. I had just cinched the terry cloth tie when the spa attendant came into the room. She, like every other female employee at the Ahhhh . . . Spa, was overly made up in that "natural way" that dictates that no woman should ever, ever leave her house without applying six different shades of brown eye shadow. She was impeccably groomed, almost to a fault, from her flat-ironed hair to her French-pedicured feet.

"Jessica? Is there a Jessica here?" She had a vaguely British accent that I wasn't entirely convinced was real.

I lifted a finger. "That's me."

"Kayan is ready for you."

"Kayan?" I asked, sort of panicky. "Is that a man or a woman?"

"A man." The attendant blinded me with the whites of her teeth.

"Is that a problem?" asked my mom.

"Oh, no," I said, adopting an airy tone. "Not at all."

Honestly, I was a little freaked about the idea of a man giving me a massage. I haven't been touched by the opposite sex for a few months and I wasn't sure how my body would react to any tactile stimulation. But when I saw Kayan in the flesh, I nearly fainted.

He was one of the most stunning men I'd ever seen. Well over six feet tall, with flawless mahogany skin stretched shiny and taut over muscles that you usually only get to see on the starting blocks of the hundred-meter final at the Olympics. He was totally not my type. And yet just looking at his huge hands and knowing they were soon going to be all over my oiled-up, naked body, well . . . Whoa.

"Jessica?" It was the creamiest voice I've ever heard.

"Uh," I said.

"This way," Kayan said, leading me to a candlelit room. "Is this your first time?"

"Uh, yes," I said.

He offered a generous smile. "Relax," he said. "I'll make it easy for you."

"Okay," I gulped.

As I lay under the sheet and put my face through the padded toilet seat thingy, I started to think about how odd it must be to rub naked people for a living. Even though it isn't sexual, it's still pretty intimate. And I'm a clean, fairly attractive woman, but I imagine that not all of Kayan's clients are so inoffensive to the senses.

"How's that feel?" he asked as he spread his hands over the small of my back.

"Good," I murmured. "It feels good."

And it did. Kayan knew what he was doing. I tried to let my mind wander as effortlessly as his fingertips skimmed my skin, but I couldn't do it. I kept thinking about how weird it was that this total stranger was touching me in places that have gone untouched and unexplored all summer. Not *there*, mind you, but near enough to remind me that it will probably be a very, very long time before anyone touches me *there* again.

As Kayan deftly kneaded his knuckles into my hamstrings, my thoughts drifted to porn. But not in a sexy way. In a clinical way. I was thinking that maybe the indifference that Kayan feels toward his job is similar to that of those who fuck for a living.

Over the course of our sham of an ex-relationship, Kieran and I watched several XXX titles starring the Jessica Darling who isn't me. It was more out of curiosity than kink. At least for me. And I guess I didn't want Kieran to think I was repressed. I was surprised by how quickly I went from novice to critic. Like,

I got totally irritated when a film got bogged down by a bad plot. I was like, "Shut up about the nymphomaniac aliens from outer space and just get it on already!"

Sex. Is there anything that starts out more miraculous then turns so mundane? Before you do it, sex is this mysterious thing that's just out there . . . waiting. You know you're going to do it someday. But when? And with who? And what will it feel like? OOOOOOOOOOOOOOOOOH. And then you do it and those questions are answered and even if it's good, even if it's really, *really* good, you discover that maybe all the time and energy you spent obsessing about your virginity might have been better spent contemplating something else. Like low-emissions fuel sources.

I put off having sex because I wanted it to be with the right person. I thought this person was Marcus. And he was. At the time. But he isn't now. Which suggests that I probably could have done it with someone else just as easily and ended up *exactly* where I am now. Alone. With a total stranger touching me only because my mother has paid him to.

This is what I was thinking when Kayan hit a spot in my lower back that triggered a hip-to-toe charley horse.

"AIIIIIIIIIIIIIIIIIIIIIIIIIIIIIIIIIIIIIIIIIEEEEEEEEEEEEEEEEE!"

My lower body clenched tighter, as if it were ready to rumble.

"Relax . . ." Kayan urged in a soothing voice. "Relax . . ."

"AIIIIIIIIIIIIIIIIIIIIIIIIIIIIIIIIIIIIIIIIIIIIEEEEEEEEEEEEEEEEE!"

Kayan spent the rest of the time trying to squeeze cramps out of my lower half. The more he kneaded and pleaded with my flesh, the more it resisted.

"OOOOOOOOOOOOOOOOOOOHHHHHHHHHHHH-HHHHH MYYYYYYYYYYYYYYYYYYYYYYYYYYYYYYYYYYYY

YYYYYYYYY GOOOOOOOOOOOOOOOOOOOOOOOO OOOOOOOOOOOD."

If I had the power to appreciate humor at the time, I would have laughed. Because my cries sounded just like I was having an orgasm, which, not so incidentally, can also make my toes curl. There is a fine line between pleasure and pain. This is the best explanation I can come up with to explain why Kieran and I stayed together as long as we did.

"You're not taking good care of yourself," Kayan said before leaving the treatment room. "You should schedule monthly appointments."

"Sure," I said, wincing as I put my foot on the floor. "Do you take food stamps?"

After fifty-five minutes, I limped out of the treatment room physically and emotionally exhausted.

My sister was already stretched out on a chaise longue in her plush robe, holding a glass of cucumber water.

"So," she said, in between sips. "What are you going to do about your living situation next semester?"

I flopped down in the chair next to her and closed my eyes.

"Well, I applied for campus housing, but I'm so late that I'm not very optimistic," I said. "I've got a plan, though. The dorm policies at NYU and Columbia are pretty much the same. I can be an overnight guest for five days every thirty days. So I just need to migrate from room to room, friend to friend, six times a month."

"That's no way to live!"

"It will be fine. Percy and Bridget have already agreed to let me crash with them if I have to. And these girls Tanu and Kazuko will take me in too. I'll be better off than that guy who slept in the NYU library all semester."

"Why don't you stay with us?"

"Maybe Lifetime will make a movie about me," I continued, intentionally dodging her question.

"Jessie, stay with us," she said, staying the course.

I inhaled deeply. "The commute from Brooklyn to 116th Street every day would kill me," I said. "It's bad enough from Washington Square."

"Then let me give you some money," she said.

Flashback: Kieran making the same offer. I felt like someone had dropped a bowling ball off the top of the Empire State Building and it landed right in the pit of my gut.

"I feel weird taking your money because . . ." My voice trailed off.

"Why?"

I yanked at the tie to my robe.

"Why, Jessie?"

I breathed in deeply from my diaphragm, like I used to during my brief experimentation with yoga.

"Because it's not really your money."

"What do you mean?"

"Well, it's really Grant's money . . ."

Bethany slammed the glass down on the table with a clang.

"If that's how you really see me," she hissed. "Then you *shouldn't* take it!"

"Bethany . . ." I began.

Then my sister put a lavender-scented mask over her eyes and stopped talking to me for the rest of the afternoon. This went totally unnoticed by my mother, who had put her treatment time to good use by compiling a list of eligible bachelors she could set me up with.

Only I would end a Darling Day of Pampering more wound up than when I started.

the twenty-eighth

The last time I spoke to someone in university housing about my plight, I was advised to call back at the end of the month. So I did. And it turns out that I am totally and completely screwed.

"Well, I can't promise you anything," the anonymous woman said, "but we might be able to offer you a walk-through double in Wein. With a first-year student as a roommate."

I laughed heartily at her joke. I stopped when I realized that I was the only one cracking up.

"Wait," I said in between chuckles. "You weren't serious, were you?"

"I've got no time for jokes."

"Wein? WEIN? Wein is—pardon my language, but it's the only appropriate description—the shittiest shithole on campus. And I didn't live with a first-year even when I *was* a first-year! What makes you think I'd want to live with one now?"

"You should have participated in the lottery with the rest of the rising seniors," she said curtly. "If this becomes available, you should take it because it might be the only vacancy."

I don't think it's possible for them to have come up with a less desirable living arrangement. A sleeping bag under the scaffolding on Broadway and 125th is looking better and better.

"So?" she asked.

"I'll be in touch," I said noncommittally before hanging up.

So let's just say that I was in a pretty foul mood when I showed up for work. Today's topic: Work Hard! Play Hard! Live Easy! The idea was that if you struck the right balance between academics and social activities, you'll be carefree. I wasn't up to the task and it showed.

Oh, did it show.

"You need to take this job more seriously," warned Geoff.

"Our future is in your hands," Will said.

"Now I know why you didn't get into Harvard," said Maddie. "No work ethic."

And that's when I kind of lost it.

"I was like you once," I said. "And you know what?"

"What?" they all asked.

"I wish that someone had told me what I'm about to tell you."

They all inched forward until they were literally on the edges of their seats.

"None of this matters."

"What?!"

"NONE OF THIS MATTERS." I pounded my fist on Geoff's desk for emphasis, making him yelp in surprise. "You can get into an Ivy League school and earn a 4.0 GPA while you're there and get all the right jobs and internships and résumé builders and still be a complete and total fuckup."

My three charges gasped, which should have stopped me. But it didn't.

"You can still do everything right, and yet have no clue what you want to do with your life because none of the jobs your major has prepared you for seem at all appealing. And so your only logical choice is graduate school, which means you're faced with four or six or eight more years of education that you're not financially prepared to pay for because you can't even afford to pay rent and will have to live in a cardboard box because your ex-boyfriend started fucking his ex-girlfriend while you were out working two jobs to pay for the education that you severely doubt will ever pay you back because you picked a major that is largely useless unless you attend four or six or eight more years of school."

Their faces had all turned whiter than the dry-erase board. I had a feeling it wasn't because I was now repeating myself, which I had taught them was a major no-no in personal statements. Taking my own advice, I returned to my original point.

"Your parents and teachers and authority figures all tell you that if you follow the rules, if you work hard, if you behave, you will be rewarded. Maybe with fame. Maybe with fortune. And if you really, really want it bad enough and work hard enough, maybe both. This is the holy grail of American mythology. But the real world doesn't work that way, kiddies. Because there are chronic fuckups who are still wildly successful at whatever they do. And there are smart, hardworking people who just can't get a break or, worse, who squander their gifts and never, ever amount to anything special. And even worse than that, there are people who work their asses off throughout their young lives, achieve their goals by getting into a top-notch Ivy League school, and *then drop dead at twenty years old from an undiagnosed heart condition!!!*"

And just like that, it shattered: the defensive infrastructure holding up the stony façade I'd put up after William's death. After nearly a year without tears, I was keening more wildly than Dexy ever had, and right in front of the kiddies.

"There are no guarantees of success in this world, not even for those whose lives are as charmed as yours. So have fun now! Do it! Put down the books! Have sex! Drink too much beer! Do something stupid while you're still young enough to chalk it up to blissful ignorance!"

I got right in their young, fresh, *horrified* faces.

"Go out and live! Live! *Live before it's too late!*"

I got fired, of course.

June 30th

Dear Mom and Dad,

First, I want to thank you again for your willingness to waive rent this summer. That's big of you, considering none of us expected me to be here. I hope you understand that I'm trying to do the best that I can under these difficult circumstances. Mom, as you know, a heartbreak is not so easily mended. And this unexpected parting of ways, coupled with my recent employment problems, has made 2005 a summer to forget.

That said, I would greatly appreciate it if you would please refrain from nagging me about losing my job with ACCEPT! I'm even less thrilled with the prospect of working at Wally D's than you are, but everyone else has already made their hires for the summer season. Time is money and I don't have enough of either to waste in a fruitless search for more meaningful employment, as Mom puts it.

I will be the perfect guest. Quiet, neat, and easily missed. In return, I hope that you will extend me the courtesy of honoring my request.

Your daughter,
Jessie

junior summer
july 2005

the fourth

I sn't that where all the good blow comes from?"

This inquiry was directed to the lower right of my crotch, via my coworker Sully.

"What?" I asked, tearing open a carton of wafer cones.

"Columbia," he said again, gesturing to the crest on my gym shorts. "That's where coke comes from, right?"

This was strange enough to make me stop dead in my tracks, a dangerous move on a night where even a momentary pause could incite corpulent civil disobedience.

"STOP BLABBING, GIRLY GIRL, AND MAKE MY CONE!"

"GIMME MY CONE!"

"CONE! CONE! CONE!"

The Fourth of July is always one of the most insane nights of the year on the boardwalk. So I hadn't stopped running from customer to customer and cone to cone since I put on my Wally D's T-shirt. I'm on the 6:00 p.m. to 3:00 a.m. shift, which means I deal with every conceivable type of benny, from the cranky families who've got sand stuck in the crotch pockets of their swimsuits, to my carefree peers perpetually transitioning from hungover to drunk again, to the pervy lurkers who wait until five minutes before closing to satisfy their hankering for something cool and sweet and mortally high in calories. For the privilege of working this most dangerous of shifts, G-Money pays me an extra buck an hour, bringing my hourly wage to a whopping $6.15 plus whatever tips people stick in the jar by the register. (College fund, it says, which is so close to the truth that it almost makes me weep.) I'm a bazillionaire in cigarette butts, fossilized gum, and tokens for Winning Wally's Arcade. If I save up on the last, I might accrue enough points for the fake vomit I've been eyeing in the display case. *Sweet*.

Sully's face is as flat and ugly as a bug on a windshield. He's paid for all the grunt work, like fixing the busted custard machines or lugging stuff up from basement storage. He's not supposed to linger too long behind the counter where he can frighten the customers. Sully is lucky he's got a job at all. A bunch of studies just proved that being beautiful literally pays off: There's a direct correlation between how attractive people are and their hireability. Did somebody cure cancer and AIDS when I wasn't looking? I mean, how much money was spent on that research? Duh. Duh. Duh.

"That's Co-lom-bi-a the country," I corrected, using an annoyingly precise Spanish pronunciation that put heavy emphasis on the o's. "This is Columbia the school."

His face got even squashier, as it always does when he doesn't understand something, which is often. He's a few rows short of the long bus.

"Hunnuh? Columbia? Never heard of it."

This is what an Ivy League education means on the boardwalk. Absolutely nothing.

Fortunately, I didn't have any more time to mull over the

significance of this or anything else for that matter, which is one of the greatest advantages of my current employment situation.

OTHER ADVANTAGES OF MY CURRENT EMPLOYMENT SITUATION

1. . . .

Okay. Make that the only advantage of my current employment situation. But the fact that I was even capable of finding one thing is a great leap for me, as my current employment situation is one that is fraught with great psychological peril. I mean, this is the same exact job I was working five summers ago, and I hated it then. Of course, the only difference is that now *I'm* the old-timer the snide high school girls mock for having nowhere else to go.

See? If I had time to think about this, I'd probably get depressed.

the eleventh

I covered a day shift when someone called in sick today, a reward for being so dang good with the clientele. Perhaps my psychology degree is coming in handy after all. If I keep it up, I will be the most overeducated custard-slinger in the history of hydrogenated fats.

It was a perfect-ten tanning day and the water was calm and clear, so the beach was packed. I knew the boardwalk would be relatively dead until the sun went down and had brought along some reading material to kill time. It was a truly stellar issue of *Star* magazine too, devoting no fewer than eight pages to celebrities with cellulite. This is all part of my master plan of not thinking all summer.

I was studying the nooks and crannies of Donatella Versace's thighs when I heard a familiar voice.

"Um. Hey. Jess."

I looked up to see Len standing before me. He had the decrepit appearance of someone who had died and was buried without a coffin, then dug up again. Unlike Kieran, who exaggerated his postbreakup devastation to better advance his rebound relationship (i.e., me), Len was clearly in very sorry shape indeed.

"Oh, hey," I replied. Then with more compassionate emphasis. "*Hey.*"

"I know. Um. That you know. You don't have to pretend you don't. Um. Know."

"Oh," I said. "Okay. So." I wasn't sure what to say. "What are you doing this summer?"

"EMT," he said. "Saving people's. Um. Lives."

He laughed quickly, maniacally. Then silenced himself.

"I was sorry to hear about what happened," I said.

"Were you?" he asked, drifting past the colorful tubs of custard in the case.

"Of course I was," I said. "Why wouldn't I be?"

"I just. Um. Thought that you might be. Um. Happy." He paused in front of vanilla bean.

"Happy?" I asked. "Why?" I knew what he was getting at, but I wanted to hear him say it.

"Because of. Um. How we broke up."

I opened the freezer and dug into the tub. "Len, it was ages ago," I said. "Besides, two more guys dumped me after you. I've gotten used to it."

He silently watched as I worked the scoop through the custard.

"I'll never get used to this," he said morosely.

"Sprinkles?"

"Do? I? Want sprinkles?" As if this were a question he were incapable of answering, along the lines of, "What happens to us after we die?" or "What is the meaning of life?"

"Live a little, Len," I said, expertly rolling the cone through the chocolate sprinkles before handing it over.

Len inspected it as if he were an alien who had never encountered something so puzzling. So *cold*. He took an apprehensive lick, and sprinkles tumbled to the floor. The chilly sweetness spread over his tongue. He grinned like a kid.

"It's good," he said.

"I know," I replied.

"Thanks, Jess," he replied, before turning around and walking away. I couldn't see his face but I just knew that he was still smiling, even after he was out of sight.

the fifteenth

One of my high school coworkers (Clueless Crew version 2.0) who can't be trusted to work at night told me that some "totally sketchy dude" keeps coming around looking for me. I needed more specifics.

"Sketchy how?"

"He looked like he hadn't taken a shower for, like, ever," she said in between the pops and cracks of her gum. "Cute though, if you like the dirty type."

"Plain white T-shirt?" I asked. A feeble question, that. Marcus could have given them up long, long ago.

"Cornell T-shirt," she replied.

Len.

Apparently, he came back to the stand the day after his first appearance, and the days after that. But I was always working the night shift so I kept missing him. Finally, last night, he figured out that he should come after dark.

"Hey!" he yelled over the roar of the crowd.

"Hey!" I yelled back. "Too busy to talk. Call me!"

Ever the reliable one, he called me at home the next morning.

"I. Um. Forgot to pay."

"Pay for what?"

"The. Um. Cone."

I laughed. "It was a freebie, Len. No need."

"Oh. Thanks," he said. "It was. Um. Really good."

"We take deep pride in our products and customer service at Wally D's Sweet Treat Shoppe."

"It's a very. Um. Smart business model," he replied.

"Right," I said, sensing he had more to say. "Is that the only reason you called?"

"No," he said.

And then he took the next half hour to ask me if I felt like joining him for coffee or engaging in some other outing, which would be completely platonic because he is still wounded and is in no shape to enter into an emotional relationship with anyone right now. I tried very hard not to laugh at his earnestness.

"Sure, Len," I said.

And so, that's how I ended up going out with Len tonight.

My mom caught me getting ready to go out, a primping ritual that consists of taking my hair out of its topknot and shaking it out until my scalp doesn't hurt anymore.

"Do you have a date tonight? It's about time you got back out there."

"Actually no," I said. "I'm going out with Len Levy. Remember him?"

"Len Levy? The Len Levy who broke up with you to date a lesbian?"

"He didn't know she was a lesbian at the time, Mom, but yes. The same."

She pondered this for a moment. "You know," she said, tapping her fingernail on the Restoration Hardware catalog. "I *always* liked Len."

"I know, Mom, I know."

"Is he still premed at Cornell?"

It is one of life's inexplicable ironies that my mother is more invested in Len's Ivy League education than my own. "Uh . . . I have no idea," I said.

"How can you be going out with him tonight and not even know his major?"

Again, this was of strange importance for someone who had never had a college major. Thankfully, the doorbell rang before I pointed this out to her. My mom scurried to greet him.

"Len!" she gushed. "So lovely to see you! Come in! Come in!"

Len had showered since the last time I saw him. He looked clean *and* clean-cut in a sky blue Le TIGRE polo and pressed khaki shorts. Through the glass in his wire-rimmed specs, I could see that the whites of his eyes were still pink with sadness, which somehow only enhanced the intensity of his green eyes.

"No really, Mom, we have to get going if we're going to . . . uh . . . catch our movie," I said, glancing at my watch. "But before we do, Len, would you please tell my mother what your major is?"

He turned to my mother and said, "Biological sciences."

"And what is your GPA?" I asked.

"3.95."

"And what do you want to do after you graduate?" I asked.

"Apply to medical schools."

"Which ones?"

"Weill Medical College of Cornell University. Yale." Then he darted a look at me before saying, "Columbia."

"And what do you foresee as your specialty?" I asked.

"Cardiology."

I looked at my mom. "Anything else?"

My mother had rolled up the Restoration Hardware catalog so tightly that she could have used it as a weapon.

"I'll arrange for him to send you his MCAT scores when they arrive," I called out before she could answer, ushering Len out the door.

"So. Um. We're seeing a movie?"

"No," I said. "We're getting something cheap to eat. *Cheap* being the operative word there."

"Helga's?"

Helga's. I hadn't been to Helga's since the last time I saw Len, which was when I'd gone there with Percy after saying goodbye to Marcus . . . what? Two summers ago?

"Helga's," I said, slipping into the passenger side of the Saturn. He's been driving the same car since we dated in high school, and though the new car smell had faded, it still looked fresh off the lot.

We didn't say much on the ride over, choosing to fill the silence with the CD player. I could have guessed the three CDs in random rotation: *In Utero* (Nirvana); *Vs.* (Pearl Jam); *Rubber Soul* (The Beatles). John Lennon sang about an irresistible girl, one he should have known better than to fall for:

"She's the kind of girl you want so much it makes you sorry / Still you don't regret a single day . . ."

I thought it might be like pouring salt on Len's open wounds. For his sake, I talked over the words.

"Do you still play?" I asked.

"Play what?" Len asked, keeping his eyes on the bumper precisely three seconds in front of us, as is recommended in Driver's Ed for cars traveling at 30 mph.

"Guitar."

His Heineken eyes bulged in surprise. "Oh. Um. Guitar. Right," he said. "I almost forgot I used to do that. No."

"No?" I asked. "Why not?"

"School," he said simply.

I didn't respond.

"Do you still write?" he asked.

Eddie Vedder sang: "*I seem to recognize your face / Haunting, familiar yet can't seem to place it . . .*"

"No," I replied.

"Why not?"

I laughed quietly to myself. "School," I lied.

Len tapped the steering wheel with the palm of his hand as if to say, *Well, there you have it,* without actually having to say it.

"That's too bad about your guitar," I said. "You were really good."

"So were you," he said. "Um. At writing. You know."

"Yeah," I said. "I guess."

"It wasn't as much fun. Um. Once I stopped collaborating with Flu," he said. Marcus's nickname. His face broke out in crimson panic. "Oh! Um! Sorry."

"It's okay," I assured him. "You can say his name. I'm over it."

"Really?"

"Yeah, Len," I said. "I am."

"That's good," he sighed as he pulled into Helga's parking lot. "Because I don't feel like I'll ever . . . Um . . ."

Eddie moaned, "*Hearts and thoughts they fade . . . fade away . . .*" And Len failed to finish his sentence, as if he interpreted these lyrics as a command.

With all the things that had changed over the years, Helga's was as refreshingly dingy as ever. We requested a booth way, way in the back. We ordered coffee. We sat quietly, without really looking at each other. I decided to break the silence.

"I went on Accutane, just like you," I said, immediately recognizing that this was, perhaps, the most inane conversation starter ever. Why remind him of his—of *our*—zitty history now that our complexions were clear?

"You *did*?" Len asked. "Why would you do that?" He seemed truly baffled, and curious to hear if there was a non-acne-related reason why someone might go on this particular drug.

"Cysts," I said, hoping my curt response would close the topic I had stupidly opened in the first place.

"Oh?" he replied skeptically. But that was all he said, and I was grateful.

"So," I tried again. "I'm thinking that you might be able to help me out."

"How so?" he asked.

"Well, as the first of a string of guys to drop me," I said. "Maybe you can give me some insight as to why I'm so dumpable."

He took off his glasses and rubbed his eyes, as if this gesture might somehow improve his hearing.

"Um. What?"

"Kieran, my sham of an ex-boyfriend from school, said I was too much woman," I said. "I think that's only a problem when you're too much *annoying* woman."

"I never thought you were. Um. Annoying."

"Then what's wrong with me?" I asked.

"Nothing's wrong with you," he said. "It was *us* that was the problem. As I can only assume it was with you and. Um. Kieran."

"And Marcus?"

He let that line of questioning drop and offered another. "Have you. Um. Heard from him lately?"

"Not since last Christmas," I said.

"Me either," he said.

We both took long slugs of coffee. I resisted the urge to ask him about the nature of his correspondence with Marcus and what it had revealed, mostly because I knew that anything Len could tell me wouldn't make one bit of difference.

Instead I asked, "What did you see in Manda anyway?"

"I think. Um. That I appreciated that she was willing to change for me."

I groaned. "That's so Freudian, Len."

"I don't know much. Um. Freud."

"He theorized that we don't fall in love with an actual person, but with a projection of our own desires. By changing, Manda became less of herself and more like you."

"Maybe," he said in an offhand way that let me know that he wasn't a fan of undergraduate psychobabble. It put me in my place, that's for sure. But I wasn't offended because sometimes I need that.

More coffee.

"Remember when you asked why you might be so. Um. Dumpable?"

"It was only about a minute ago, Len."

"Um. Right." He seemed embarrassed by the error. "I can only speak for myself here. But. Um. I think I knew that you wouldn't change for me. Um. I don't think you would change for *anyone*. It's like what makes you *you* is unassailable."

"And that's been working so well for me," I deadpanned.

"Not changing who you are isn't a bad thing . . ."

"If my romantic history is any indication, it can't be a *good* thing."

Len drained his cup in lieu of a response.

"So you're really. Um. Over Marcus?" he asked after a few seconds of silence.

"Really," I said. I enjoyed being able to say it like I meant it.

"Do you still think about him? Because I still think about Manda all the time."

I contemplated the question. Do I think about Marcus?

The honest answer is that I try not to. But making a conscious decision not to think about someone is, by definition, thinking about them. Not to mention those studies I've mentioned that suggest the more energy you spend trying to forget about someone, the more likely it is that the person will pop up in your dreams.

Recently, my dreams all relive real moments from my past. Me buzzed at the West End in my Barnard T-shirt. Me sweating on the corner of 110th and Amsterdam. Me sparring in my dorm room. Me serving a custard cone on the boardwalk. Only instead of Mini Dub, instead of Bastian, instead of Kieran, instead of Len is Marcus, Marcus, Marcus, Marcus. And he never says a word.

"Jess?"

I'd forgotten that Len was waiting for an answer, one that would bring him peace of mind.

"I don't think about him at all."

And Len heaved a sigh of relief, confident that one day he too would forget the person who was the source of so much pleasure and pain.

As the evening wore on, I couldn't help but think about how mature this was for me and Len to talk over coffee at Helga's. Len was my first real ex (Scotty doesn't count—it was, after all, eighth grade), and one of only three guys who have seen me practically, if not totally, naked, even though it was a very, very long time ago and the cutaneous landscape has changed a bit. Still, I thought it was a really grown-up thing. It wasn't weird at all. Though I suppose it might be different if Len and I had done it. I wonder if I would feel as comfortable sitting across from Kieran. Or Marcus. I doubt I'll ever know.

Tonight, I was okay with that conclusion.

As we returned to Len's car, he said, "Um, Jess?"

"Yes?"

"I never thought you had bad skin," he said. "I always thought you looked . . ." He shyly looked down at his keys instead of at me. "Radiant."

And I told him that was the nicest thing anyone has said to me in a very long time.

The rest of the ride home was filled with more music than conversation. And that, too was okay. Kurt's words seemed to express exactly how I was feeling as I rode alongside Len.

I think I'm dumb . . . Or maybe just happy.

the twenty-fourth

For a Sunday night, it was pretty dead. So I got off work early enough to call Len and ask him to meet me at Helga's. It had become a sort of routine, hanging out on the nights he had off from saving people's lives and the nights I had off doing the opposite via junk food. With Bridget and Percy off in LA visiting her dad, I really don't have anyone else here to spend time with. So I'm grateful for his company, even if we've strayed little from our usual dialogue. I want to think that I've helped Len feel less alone in his pain. But I should have been tipped off to the contrary when he made a surprising request tonight.

"How about. Um. I meet you at. Um. AJ's?"

"AJ's?" I asked. "Are you sure?"

"Yeah," he said. "Let's live a little."

This was an unusual turn of events. First, because Len doesn't drink. And second, because AJ's is the darkest, dankest, least-inviting drinking establishment on the boardwalk. It repels bennies, and therefore is most appealing to locals and semilocals like me. AJ's only concession to any sort of décor is the hundreds of plastic potted plants hanging from the ceiling, all ashen with decades of cigarette-smoky dust. At AJ's, only two varieties of music are played: Crosby, Stills & Nash, and Crosby, Stills, Nash

& Young. I'd told Len that I'd always wanted to get a drink there for kicks, but never had anyone to go with me and I didn't want to go alone because that's the first sign of alcoholism. And while that will give me something to talk about with the street-corner winos with whom I'll be keeping company after I graduate, there's no need to get an early start on my addiction.

When I got there, Len already had a half-empty cup of beer in front of him. I decided not to make a big deal about this un-characteristic libation. I ordered whatever they had on tap. I got Budweiser, served in plastic. *Klassy.*

"I have something to tell you," he said.

Usually that precedes something that I don't want to hear. But I was open-minded.

"Go on," I said.

Len swallowed his beer, then looked straight ahead at his re-flection in the Miller Lite mirror across the bar. "I don't want to be a doctor."

"I don't want to be a shrink!"

We toasted each other, our plastic cups making more of a crunch than a clink.

"Why don't you want to be a doctor?" I asked.

"It turns out that I'm not very good with people," he said with a shrug.

"Me either! What do you think you'll do after graduation?"

He shook his head slowly, somberly. "I have no idea."

"Me either!"

"You sound very happy about your uncertain future," he said, his eyebrows crumpling.

"Oh, I'm totally freaked out," I said in a blithe tone that un-dermined the message. "But it's comforting to know that I'm not alone in my cluelessness. At least you've got an extra semester to figure it out. I'll be unemployed and homeless come January."

"That's unfortunate," he said.

"It is," I said.

We swiveled back and forth on our bar stools for a few seconds.

"What happened to us?" Len asked, staring into his cup. "We were Most Likely to Succeed. Now we're both a mess."

"Yes we are," I said. There was a fingerprint smudge on the left lens of his glasses that in his younger, more-together days, he would have rubbed off immediately with a small, square piece of felt that he kept in his back pocket for such a purpose. But this Len just ignored it, or didn't notice it at all, which was also very unlike him.

He wiped his mouth with the back of his hand. "Actually, we're messes. Plural. We're our own separate messes."

"Hey, Len, you're not stuttering," I pointed out. "Did you notice that?"

"Actually, yes, I did notice that. People stammer less when they're drunk. It's a counterintuitive but common phenomenon studied by linguists."

"I bet it's because drinking helps you let your guard down," I said. "You're not as self-conscious about what you say. You just say it."

"That's probably it," he said.

"Probably," I agreed.

He leaned in very close to my face, like he was about to say something. But he didn't. I could smell his hot, yeasty breath. Normally, this would gross me out. But there was something about seeing Len so obviously drunk and disheveled that was not unappealing. He was still very geek cute.

"Len, can I ask you a personal question?"

"Sure," he said, laying his hands flat out on the bar in front of him.

"Are you still a virgin?"

I tried to keep my eyes in my head when he nodded in the affirmative, making his glasses slip yet again.

"You did everything but . . ."

"Everything but."

"Wow."

"Wow," he replied, underwhelmed.

At the far end of the bar, a man and a woman with many tattoos and few teeth flirted with each other.

"You one dirty mufucka!" The woman cackled.

"Naw," shouted the man. "You tha dirty mufucka!"

"That's nice," Len said wistfully. "They're a nice couple." He was so earnest it hurt.

"If it makes you feel any better, Len, I don't think Manda is really a lesbian."

"They sure looked like lesbians to me when I walked in on them—" He paused mid-profanity. "What do lesbians call what they do, anyway?"

"They call it fucking," I said.

"*Ooooooooooooooooooooooooh.*" Len was quietly moaning into the foam in his cup. He was falling apart again. After sprucing himself up for the past few outings, he was reverting back to sketchy.

"I didn't want to do this," I said, swirling the beer around in my cup. "I've been saving this story, but you obviously need to hear it tonight."

And then, I put my personal mortification aside and began a tale that I hoped would convince him that walking in on your girlfriend having lesbian sex is not the worst thing in the world.

"Did I ever tell you about the time I walked in on my parents . . . ?"

This is what friends do.

Not long after, I drove Len home. He sunk into the passenger seat with his eyes closed, and I thought he was passed out. Quite frankly, I had no idea how I was going to drag his drunk ass into his house without his overbearing mom finding out and accusing me of leading him into a life of debauchery. As we pulled in front of his Colonial, a Beatles song came on that snapped him out of his stupor. He had lent me *Revolver* a few weeks back and had insisted I listen to it.

"This is the song!" he said, swaying back and forth. "It's so true! When you love someone, you need them all the time . . ."

"*I will be there and everywhere,*" sang the cutest Beatle. "*Here, there and everywhere . . .*"

I know this promise is meant to be a positive thing. A show of devotion. But what happens when such omnipresence outlasts the actual love? What happens then?

You end up like Len. And me.

the thirty-first

So much for a mature, grown-up relationship.

"I've been thinking," Len said as he finished off a beer. AJ's was our new standard. It is important, though perhaps unnecessary, to explain that Len is a lightweight. One beer and he's already silly.

"About what?"

"We should fuck," he said very seriously.

Budweiser splooshed out of my nostrils.

"But not in the lesbian way," he clarified, as if that would make it any less hilarious.

I was still choking.

"I'm sorry," he said. "That was wrong."

"No, it wasn't the wrongness that got me," I said in between slurpy gasps for air. "It's just that it was probably the funniest thing you've ever said."

"I was trying to be rakish and sexy."

"I know," I replied, pushing his glasses up on his nose. "That's why it was funny."

"We should make love?" he asked, one eyebrow raised high enough to almost touch the spider plant hanging above our heads.

That made me laugh even harder.

"I'm sorry you find my come-ons so hilarious," he said, starting to giggle a bit himself. Len actually giggled, when he did laugh, which wasn't often. Maybe it's *because* of the giggle.

A very unmasculine giggle that, juxtaposed with all this sexy talk, just about made me pee my pants.

"You've been a virgin for so long. Why give it all up now?"

He studied his empty cup for a moment.

"Why not?" he finally said. "Why not have a summer fling? I've never had a summer fling. I think my life has been deficient in fling."

This also made me laugh. I stopped only when I realized how deadly serious Len was about this.

"Look Len, I know you *think* you want to do it with me. I almost fell into the same trap last summer with this guy." I stopped to make an important correction. "Actually, he was a man. A totally grown-up man. And foreign."

Len nodded his head, impressed.

"Anyway, there was this man I really thought I wanted to have sex with. And we got really close to doing it, but I stopped myself when I realized that the reality of sex with him would never, ever live up to the fantasy I built up in my mind all summer long. So I resisted the urge and avoided what probably would have been an awkward embarrassment."

"So you didn't do it," Len said.

"Nope."

"And look how much better off you are now." He smacked his lips together with self-satisfaction.

"Hm." My abstinence argument was soundly trumped. I didn't know what else to say.

For a few seconds we just sat side by side and totally still on our swivel stools. And I don't know if it was Crosby, Stills, Nash, Young, or all of the above, but their harmonies swiftly rose above the bar chatter and lifted my heavy, hardened heart.

"Carry on, love is coming . . . Love is coming to us all . . ."

And yet, this does not adequately explain why I ended up de-virginizing Len Levy on the crusty couch in the basement storage room of Wally D's Sweet Treat Shoppe.

July 31st

Dear Len,

I'm sorry. It should have been with someone else. You deserved better than me.

Sincerely,
Jessica

junior summer
august 2005

the third

The news of yet another imbroglio broke in my bedroom. And as always, Bridget was beside herself.

"YOU DEVIRGINIZED LEN!!!"

I muffled her mouth. "My parents are downstairs!"

"Oh, come on," she said, freeing herself from my grasp. "Your mother would be thrilled. She'd probably throw, like, a huge party."

This was both unfortunate and true. It would be an elaborate theme party. With blown-up condoms for balloons and a cock-shaped ice-cream cake.

"So," she said, a naughty gleam in her eye. "Was it any good?"

Was it any good?

This was a question I'd been trying to answer since it happened. I'd never been the more experienced one, so I kind of took over and did most of the work. Len came quickly, which is a fairly reliable indicator of a job well done. And I *almost* got off on the whole dominant woman-on-top power trip . . .

Bridget interpreted my silence as a no.

"Well, it doesn't matter whether it was good or not because he's going to remember you for, like, the rest of his life," she said.

When I didn't respond, she repeated once more with feeling.

"For the rest of his life."

"I get it."

"It's just like, so *deep*," she said. "Because he waited so long."

"But it all seems like such a waste, doesn't it? To wait so long, and then just do it with someone who doesn't love him. He could have done *that* four years ago."

It was all so sad. So meaningless. Not just the devirginization, but everything.

Life.

This isn't a startling insight. It's something I've recognized for quite some time, and can usually will myself to ignore. But after I dropped off Len the other night, there was a car with a Betty Boop decorative license plate cover in front of me at a stoplight. I thought about the type of person who would go out of her way to shop for a Betty Boop decorative license plate cover, and why this person would consider it necessary to express herself through said license plate cover. After contemplating these questions in the span of a red-light-turned-green, I felt like crashing my car into the nearest telephone pole in despair.

Because it's not just the decorative license plate covers, it's also the designer checks you can special order because you think the cats-in-a-basket motif makes an important statement about your personal identity that the plain bank-issued checks simply cannot. And it's the one-of-a-kind sneakers you can custom design on an obscure Italian website, or the generic ones at Target, for that matter. It's Dexy's wigs. My mom's frozen, Botoxed face. Bethany's Prada diaper bag. Mini Dub's face piercings. Bastian's ponytail. Kazuko's Harajuku getups. Tyra Braun's ladylike guise.

And it's more than things and appearances. It's Kieran's

"sensitivity." Bridget and Percy's case for monogamy. Jane's choice of boyfriend. Tanu's devotion to Clay Aiken. Hy's and Paul's and Taryn's dedication to righting the world's wrongs. ALF's snappy comebacks. Sara's gossip. Manda's gaycation. Scotty's alpha-maleness. My dad's obsessive bike rides. G-Money's quest for capital. Hope's facebook profile. My ramblings in this journal.

And it used to be Len's virginity.

Jane was right about one thing: Marcus's T-shirts *were* a shtick. But so is *everything* we do when we exercise the free will that Kieran held so dear. And we're *all* guilty. We convince ourselves that these choices declare WHO WE ARE to the world, and we hope that others—or just one person—will see these on-the-surface signs and somehow, suddenly understand WHO WE ARE down to the depths of our souls. But the cruel reality is that these choices serve a different purpose altogether. They act as cheery distractions from the only tragic Truth-with-a-capital-T that matters:

We all die alone.

I'm in a very bad place, indeed.

"So have you talked to him yet?" Bridget asked.

"No," I said, neglecting to mention the note I'd hastily composed and dropped in the mailbox. "I think we're officially avoiding each other."

Bridget brightened. "Well, that's good news. How bad would it be if he, like, fell in love with you because of this?"

I acknowledged that it would be pretty bad.

"So I have to ask," Bridget began. "When are you going to try to get, like, a normal boyfriend?"

My spine stiffened. "What are you talking about?"

"Do you think it's any coincidence that all the guys you have been interested in or involved with since Marcus are those who are, like, so obviously wrong for you? It's like you want to doom the relationship before it even begins."

Usually Bridget's analyses are dead-on. It's one of the more frustrating aspects of our friendship. But this time I had to disagree.

"You're wrong," I said.

"You know I'm right!" she said leaping up to her own defense.

"You're *partly* right," I said. "I did choose guys who are obviously wrong for me. But it wasn't a self-defeating thing. That would be too simple."

"Okay, then why?"

"I think," I said uncertainly, still trying to get a firm hold on the idea squirming restlessly inside my brain. "I was trying to recreate the same love-hate thing I had with Marcus."

"But you were still with him when you hooked up with the dead guy . . ."

"I know," I said, flinching at William's memory. "Maybe I needed to see if what I had with Marcus was unique, or only *felt* unique because of my limited experience with the opposite sex."

Bridget's eyes lit up brighter than the Manhattan skyline. "Now *that's* an interesting theory," she said. "What's your conclusion after gaining more experience?"

In the instant between one heartbeat and the next, I summed up my post-Marcus men as follows:

- *William:* I didn't want to have sex with him, but I almost did.
- *Bastian:* I wanted to have sex with him, and I almost did.

- *Kieran:* I didn't want to have sex with him, but I did anyway.
- *Len:* I wanted to have sex with him, and I did.

The result of all the above? I'm unsatisfied as ever, sexually and emotionally.

"Your conclusion?" Bridget asked again.

My conclusion was that I had no choice other than to suffocate myself with my three-hundred-thread-count pillowcase.

the seventh

I had asked Len to meet me for coffee this morning to make things right between us. But as soon as I saw him, my embarrassment blazed as hot as the couch burns still smoldering on my kneecaps.

"Oh God," I whimpered, resting my head on the table. "This is even more awkward than I thought it would be."

"Really? I don't. Um. Feel awkward."

I kept my face pressed into the connect-the-dots on the place mat. I felt his hand resting gently on the back of my head. No surprise: zero sexual charge.

"It's really okay, Jess," he said, patting my hair. "Um. I appreciated your note."

I looked up warily. "You're welcome? I guess?"

"I know what you. Um. Meant by it," he explained. "But your apology wasn't necessary."

"Well, it's just that . . ." I trailed off, then started again. "It should have been more special or something. It should have been with someone . . . significant."

"Whaddaya want?" growled Viola, our small, surly, octogenarian waitress.

What did I want? A job. A clue. A love.

"Two coffees," Len answered for me.

Coffee would do for now, I guess.

"Jess," Len said, reaching out to touch my hand. Again, nothing. "We have been a part of each other's lives in one way or another since we were in elementary school. So I don't think you could ever be classified as insignificant. Um. Especially now."

"But . . ." I began.

"I don't regret it," he said. "Neither should. Um. You."

And then Viola shuffled over to fill our mugs. I waited until she was gone before I spoke.

"I think I regret everything I've done for the past three years," I said. "I used to think that I wouldn't change anything from my past, because doing so would inevitably affect who I am now. But considering my current state, I'm thinking it might not be a bad idea to go back in time to fix things."

Len sat up straight in the booth. "Time travel sounds like the stuff of science fiction," he began. "But there is reason to believe that it is possible. According to the equations of Albert Einstein's general theory of relativity, there is nothing in the laws of physics that unequivocally rules out time travel. Putting it into practice is another matter as it involves the manipulation of black holes, which is something that can't be supported by current technology."

He slurped his coffee, as if to fuel the speed of his thoughts.

"I'm not an expert in quantum theory or relativity, but I know enough to say for certain that time travel will not be a reality in this century. That would seem to indicate that I would never be able to take advantage of this incredible leap in technology. Then again, with human life-spans being extended as they are, it is not at all inconceivable that I could live to be a hundred and twenty years old or more, which, in turn, could put me in a position to use any time travel device that is developed. But I'm not pinning my hopes on it, that's for certain."

I could tell Len was excited by these ideas because he was talking with more than his mouth. He was putting his whole face and body into it. He wasn't drunk, and yet he wasn't stuttering either.

"To me, the most interesting theory about time travel concerns the idea of a 'multiverse' instead of a universe. As the term implies, this interpretation of quantum theory says that there is more than one reality, all of which exist at the same time, but without any interaction or interference with each other. Every object—and people are considered objects—is faced with choices, and the world splits to allow the object to take every possibility that is offered, thus creating an infinite number of parallel worlds that are as real as the one in which we exist, each world representing a different set of results for a different set of choices." He gulped another mouthful of coffee. "Here's the *truly* mind-bending part: There is a completely different world for *each and every outcome to each and every decision that is made in life.* This means decisions both big and small. For example, there is a world in which I decided to wear a black T-shirt this morning instead of the blue one I'm wearing right now. Or even more mind-bending: There is a world in which I don't exist because my parents married other people."

"Kind of like *Back to the Future*," I added dumbly.

"Exactly," he said to my surprise. "The possibilities are as limitless."

As Len continued to talk, it was clear that the interest he lacked in the very practical field of medicine was more than made up for by a passion for the very theoretical realm of cosmology. Maybe he'll end up in research. Or academia. He'll make good on the yearbook prediction. I know it.

Later, as we headed back to our separate cars, I had one more question for Len.

"Did you tell your mother about . . . you know . . . *it?*"

I would die if his mother knew about what had happened. I don't mean that metaphorically either. I would literally, physically, die. And that's because Len's mother would hunt me down and kill me because she has always hated my guts because she felt I was leading her pure, innocent son astray, which I guess I kind of did. So I guess her loathing wasn't so misplaced, now was it?

Len giggled. "If I've learned anything in the past three years," he said, "it's that the less my mother knows, the better."

Well, at least he's learned something. That's one more thing than me. According to those theories, I shouldn't worry too much about my idiocy. There's no need for me to go back in time and change any of my past mistakes because in one of my alternative worlds I've made all the decisions that add up to bliss. I'll try to take whatever comfort I can in knowing that somewhere, some version of me is getting it right. It's unfortunate, however, that *this* Jessica Darling isn't in *that* perfect part of the multiverse.

the sixteenth

Today I was sitting on the bench closest to the Shoppe during my break, ignoring the itch of an impending sunburn and watching the bennies walk by.

The world never stops changing, and yet, like Helga's, the Seaside Heights boardwalk remains remarkably the same. The pungent, greasy-sweet aroma of zeppoles and sausage and pepper subs. The ZERO TO HORNY IN SIX BEERS T-shirts. The competing *bump-bump-bump* bass lines throbbing from every stand, all demanding your aural attention. The miraculous proliferation of paranormal experts who will always see love and riches when they look at the lines of your palm. The regurgitative whirl of the Himalaya, the vomitous swoop of the Buccaneer, the pukey plunge of the Tower of Fear. All of it, unchanging. Year after year after year . . .

And then, without any specific trigger, I remembered: Matthew would have been twenty-five today.

My parents' doleful behavior usually marks this impossible-to-ignore occasion. But they seemed totally normal this morning as I left for work, my mom chattering on the phone about paint chips while my dad cursed at unsatisfactory scores in the sports section. I wasn't in Pineville on the last anniversary, which is probably why I had almost forgotten the significance of the date. So maybe, in a similar way, moving into the new house has created a physical and emotional distance from the tragedy for my parents. Of course, I'd never ask.

I used to think that it was unhealthy for my parents not to be up front about Matthew. As their daughter, wasn't I *entitled* to find out about the dead brother I never knew? I didn't respect my parents' need for privacy simply because they were *my parents*, two people who couldn't possibly have inner lives as expansive and messy as my own. Of course, now I know better. We're *all* affected by life's random outbreaks of beauty and brutality. I now defend everyone's right to keep the most moving memories sacred.

"So you're really smart, huh?" Sully asked, interrupting these thoughts as he plunked himself down beside me on the bench.

"Oh, I don't know." I wasn't being modest. I was being honest.

"You gotta be real smart to get into Columbia," he said. "Boss told me so."

"Well, that's what they want us to believe," I said.

"See, me?" he said, tapping his oversized, misshapen head. "I ain't too bright upstairs."

He wasn't sad about it or anything. He was merely stating the facts.

"So when you're off doin' your smarty-pants job next summer, come back and visit ol' Sully."

"I may not get *any* job, let alone a smarty-pants job."

He snorted. "You go to Columbia," he said. "You'll get some kinda job if you come outta a school like that. It don't have to be a perfect job, but it will be better than this, I bet ya. You got your whole life ahead of you."

Then Sully got up and lumbered back to Wally D's, where he will work every summer until he dies.

I rose off the bench, kicked off my flip-flops, and sprinted onto the beach. I ran and ran and ran across the sand and straight into the cold crash of the breaking waves. I must have looked crazy to those bennies, splashing and whooping in my Wally D's uniform, but I didn't care. The ocean was rough and it knocked me around and made me feel dizzy and reckless and *alive*.

I thought to myself, Why didn't I do this all summer?

I will die someday. No duh. Nothing can change that, so I might as well fill my life with whatever joys it has to offer. What difference does it make if a spontaneous ocean dive or a Betty Boop decorative license plate cover only temporarily diverts attention from the morbid Truth? Isn't that better than the alternative?

I need to be more in the moment, like when I was wet and wild in the waves. Being in the moment—right now!—equals freedom. It can't be scrutinized, analyzed, rhapsodized, mythologized. It can't be desecrated, debated, prognosticated. Right now can only be *lived*. Isn't this the same message I tried to get across to the kiddies in the lecture that got me fired? Isn't this the same advice Gladdie gave me right before she died?

Why is it that the most fundamental life lesson—LIVE!—is the one I continually forget to put into practice?

the twenty-seventh

Today was G-Money and Bethany's fifth-anniversary party. Their actual anniversary was more than two months ago but—to shamelessly borrow from his biggest rival—it was always time to make the donuts. Held at the spectacular beaux arts Palm House at the Brooklyn Botanic Garden, the party was replete with white-gloved service, an audiovisual tribute to their love, and a five-tiered cake made exclusively out of crullers and chocolate custard that had Marin zoom, zoom, zooming. It was a gala affair, the kind that used to be thrown for unions lasting ten times as long, back when golden anniversaries weren't as unlikely as they are now.

On a more cynical day, I'd be merciless about this. But not today.

Of course, I wasn't looking forward to this soiree. But the usual antisocial reasons were compounded by the fact that I hadn't spoken to my sister since the Ahhhh . . . Spa and that her silence had everything to do with me being so bitchy about the very love for her husband that I was here to so publicly celebrate. To make things even worse, I had also been harangued into being a spotlight participant in one of the evening's cheesier spectacles: the Not-So-Newlywed Game.

"No," I said when my mother told me yesterday that I was going to be the MC. "Let Sara do it instead. She loves the lime-light."

Sara was bound to be at the party. The D'Abruzzi/Darling-Doczylkowski families would be linked for as long as there is a consumer demand for twenty-four-hour access to conveniently packaged fats and sugars.

"You're the only one we call Notso! How will it look if some-one else hosts the Not-So-Newlywed Game?"

"It's not named after me, it's just a coincidence," I said. "Call it the Oldiewed Game instead."

"Anyone who's ever been on a cruise will know that it's sup-posed to be called the Not-So-Newlywed Game!" she exclaimed. "You just can't go changing names willy-nilly. It's just not right! *Not right at all!*"

This is the closest my mother has ever come to civil unrest. If she could carry a picket sign, it would say NOT-SO-NEWLYWED OR NOTHING! But if this game is my mother's Betty Boop decora-tive license plate cover, so be it. I gave up and gave in, figuring my participation might help smooth things over with my sister. However, until my unwanted moment at the mic, I stayed out of the way on the fringes of the party, playing babysitter to Marin.

"What's the story, morning glory?" I asked her.

"I hate this stupid dress," she said, avoiding our usual joke and jutting out her lower lip like a diving board over the dimple in her chin.

The dress was a pink flowery confection complete with a flouncy crinoline. It wasn't inherently awful, not like those lacy headbands that new parents put on baby girls until they've grown enough hair not to be mistaken for boys. Indeed, it was a lovely dress, one that surely cost more than the contents of my entire wardrobe. But on Marin, it just looked all wrong. And she felt wrong in it. She usually zipped around the room from person to person and thing to thing. Marin has a true love for life and people. To see her slumping in her chair was just too depressing. But I didn't want her to feel any worse than she already did.

"It's a pretty dress, Marin."

She rolled her eyes like a pro. "Did Mommy tell *you* what to wear today?"

Wow. She's a real smartass.

"Not today." I kneeled next to her. "But your mommy once made me wear a dress that I didn't want to wear."

"Really?" she asked, sounding mildly interested. "When?"

"When she and your daddy got married," I said.

"Five years ago," she added, proud to know this fact.

"Yes," I said. "And it was waaaaaaay uglier than this one. It was long and yellow and it made me look like a banana."

This made her giggle.

"That's right," I continued. "I'm lucky I didn't get dragged off by a gorilla!"

She thought this was positively hysterical. And when I started making *EEE-EEE-OOO-OOO-AHH-AHH-AHH* ape noises, she just about bust her little gut. Kids are so damn easy some-times.

"But you know what, Marin? Even though I was wearing this ugly dress, I didn't let it ruin my day. I danced and had a lot of fun."

But this last part of my speech was unnecessary. Marin was

already out of the chair at this point, bopping up and down to the band's very unhip version of "Hey Ya!"

"Let's go, Auntie J! Let's go!"

Hm. Maybe I'm good with people after all, because the two of us took over the dance floor with sweaty, ass-shaking abandon. I felt pure, un-self-conscious joy, just as I had when I was wild and wet in the waves. The moment felt elastic, as if I could stretch my happiness beyond this particular moment in space and time . . .

That is, until I felt someone grab my shoulder.

"Omigod! Jess!"

It was Sara . . . with Scotty and his huge head trailing behind her.

"What are you two doing here together?" I asked, putting my hands in the air, and waving them like I just didn't care, as the band had directed.

"You don't know?" She tugged Scotty's arm. "We've been hanging out for a while now."

It's ironic that she didn't use her *quote-unquote* catch-phrase around the words *hanging out*, considering how it's the commitment-phobic euphemism for any vague relationship consisting of drunken, semiregular hookups. Scotty had the confused look of a time traveler who had just beamed five hundred years into the future but couldn't remember how he had gotten there.

"Wow," I said, rolling my shoulders in time with the music. "You make a perfect couple." I was telling the ugly truth.

"I know!" she shouted. "Omigod! I heard about you and . . ."

"Not now, Sara!" I said, twirling away from her. "Not ever!"

"You and Len!" she shouted, ignoring my order. "You—"

"No! No! No!" Marin screeched as she stomped on Sara's foot. "Go away!"

"That's my girl!" I shouted as I hoisted Marin up and swung her around.

"Brat!" Sara seethed as she hobbled off the floor. I swear I saw a smile on Scotty's face as he followed her.

I could have danced all day with Marin. But my mother had other ideas.

"It's time for the Not-So-Newlywed Game!" my mother trilled, taking me by the arm.

"Now?" I asked.

"Yes, now," she replied, handing over the question cards. "Let's get the game show on the road!"

Four sets of chairs were dragged onto the dance floor. Couple #1: The Doczylkowskis (junior). Couple #2: The Doczylkowskis (senior). Couple #3: The Darlings (my parents). Couple #4: The D'Abruzzis (Sara's dad and stepmom).

"Uh, hi everyone," I murmured into the microphone.

"Speak up!" my mom shouted.

"I'm Bethany's sister, Jessica," I said, slightly louder, but without much gusto. "Your host for the Not-So-Newlywed Game."

Okay. You've seen *The Newlywed Game*—husbands go into seclusion, wives answer questions, answers are revealed, references to whoopee are made, points are earned, hilarity ensues—there's no need to go into elaborate logistical detail.

Questions included:

1. What was the first record/CD your wife ever bought?

2. Who was your husband's first celebrity crush?

And the ever popular, and in this case, nauseating:

3. Where was the wildest place you ever made whoopee?

To my shock, both my parents and my sister and G-Money knew *everything* about each other. G-Money knew that Bethany purchased *We Are the World* when she was in fifth grade. My mom knew that my dad was hot for Ann-Margret. They all knew their most outlandish whoopee-making locations, but for the sake of my gastrointestinal tract I'd prefer not recounting them here thankyouverymuch.

To end the dubious suspense, they got every question right, and ended up tied for first place with a hundred points. (The Doczylkowskis [senior] scored fifty. And the D'Abruzzis—a third marriage for husband and a first for wife—earned a meager ten points.)

Without a sudden death question, I declared them all winners. The contestants and the crowd were delighted. And as they all congratulated one another, I realized that I will never get what keeps couples like my parents and my sister and G-Money together. As an outsider, I can only see the bitterness. The bickering. The boredom. But on the inside, there's obviously an understanding between them, and only them. Which is how it should be. I've judged other couples and thought, God, I'd never, ever want a relationship like that. But that's a good thing, isn't it? I shouldn't want a relationship like anyone else's because it's so uniquely theirs.

Sometimes my revelations are so basic. Epissanies.

I was thinking about this when I was approached by this attractive, clean-cut guy in a tan, one-button linen jacket, a

pink-and-white-striped shirt, and dark jeans. It was a very deliberate outfit, and he looked like the type who is most comfortable on a sailboat or ski slope. Jaunty. He had the innate swagger
of someone who's got the world hanging from his scrotum, so I
assumed he would walk right past me.

"Jessica Darling!" He hugged me by way of a slap on the back.
"How the hell are you?"

I was caught off guard by his enthusiastic greeting. "Uh. Yeah,
it's me," I said. *But who are you?*

I reeled back from the embrace so I could look into this person's eyes, trying to make a connection. Someone from school?
Someone I interviewed during the Storytelling Project? Someone
I've served at I SCREAM! or the Sweet Shoppe? I am very bad
at putting people in context. Like, if I've only seen you in class, I
will totally not recognize you if I see you on the subway. This is
why a lot of people might think I'm a bitch. (Uh, besides the fact
that I often display some very bitchy tendencies.)

"You don't know who I am, do you?" he asked.

"Uh . . . Sure I do!"

"The best man's little bro . . ."

Once he said it, I felt like an ass for not making an instant
connection. He looked exactly the same, only with lines fanning
out from his eyes, and more pronounced grooves dug deep into
his cheeks.

"Cal!" I gasped. "Wow! I haven't seen you since . . ."

"Since I tried to have sex with you on the golf course during
your sister's wedding reception," he said candidly.

"Right," I said, not embarrassed by this declaration.

"I imagine you haven't given me much thought over the past
five years," he said.

This was true.

"But I've thought a lot about you," he continued. "It was a dick move and you called me on it. No girl had ever done that before. I learned a lot from that night, and I never treated a girl like an object again . . ."

After Cal returned to his preppy, peppy girlfriend across the room, I thought of what Paul Parlipiano said to me at that Beautiful People Against Bush party last summer. *We hardly know each other, and yet have made a big difference in each other's lives.* With Paul, the feeling was mutual. But I hadn't quite considered that maybe I'd affected someone deeply, but never knew it. It made me wonder if there was anyone else out there who thought of me as a driving force behind their self-actualization.

"You did a *genius* job with the game," Bethany said, breaking my thoughts.

Marin agreed. "Genius, Auntie J!"

"Thanks," I said. "Bethany . . ." I sucked in a lungful of air. "I've been wanting to talk to you all night . . ."

She waved her hands in front of me to stop but I kept going.

"No, please. You were kind enough to offer help and I selfishly . . ."

I hadn't intended for that to be the end of my apology. But Bethany's tackle-hug stopped me.

"I don't need to hear any more!" Tears skimmed her cheeks.

"Are you sure? Because . . ."

"I'm sure!"

When we declinched, I braced myself for the next part of my impromptu speech.

"So . . ." I fiddled with the satin ribbon on my skirt. "I was wondering . . ."

"Yes!"

"Yes!" mimicked Marin.

"Yes . . . what?" I asked.

"Yes, you can live with us!" Bethany wrapped her arms around me again. Only this time Marin joined in, clasping my lower legs.

"How did you know I was going to ask . . . ?"

"I know because sisters know things."

Even sisters who have as little in common as we do.

"Oh!" I overheard my mom burble. "Look at them!"

"Our girls!" my dad exclaimed.

"Our girls!" she repeated. "I'm so proud of them!"

At first I didn't get what was making my parents so misty. But then I looked down at Marin clinging to my calf and thought about how proud I was of the cool little kid she was becoming. And she's just my niece—I can't even imagine what it would be like if she were my own daughter. Seeing my parents so weepy with love and admiration, it wasn't so hard to believe that, despite it all, they really do have my best interests at heart. Unfortunately, they've never been very good at understanding what those interests are. I can't really blame them for that though, because I barely understand them myself.

But I'd like to think I'm getting better at it.

the thirty-first

was shocked to find an email from one Professor Samuel MacDougall in my mailbox. Since becoming a finalist for the National Book Award for *Acting Out,* he's been highly sought after by universities. And even if I had known he'd been hired by Columbia, I would have never expected him to remember a little high school kiddie he taught four summers ago, let alone go out of his way to contact me. His letter of recommendation was a big reason I got in here, but I was sure that he'd written dozens, if not hundreds, of such letters over the years.

But it's not every day that one gets an invitation from an author the *New York Times* describes as "a gay Dave Eggers . . . only smarter, funnier . . . and better." So I took the train from Bethany's place in Brooklyn up to 116th Street, found his office, and knocked cautiously on the door, having no idea what this visionary could possibly want with me.

He enthusiastically swung open the door.

"Hi! It's been a long time!" I said.

"'I don't think of the past,'" he said. "'The only thing that matters is the everlasting present.' W. Somerset Maugham."

"The everlasting present," I repeated, somewhat freaked out

that one of his trademark aphorisms so eerily summarized what I've been thinking lately. Synchronicity? Or bullshit?

"Come in, come in," he said warmly, before I had a chance to decide.

I edged my way through the tiny, cramped office. On the fourth floor, it had a small muck-covered window that opened to the brick face of another building.

"You have to win a Pulitzer to get a view around here," he said.

I laughed, not sure if he was kidding.

"So!" he said, clapping his hands together. "What have you been up to? Writing-wise?"

I decided to confess.

"I didn't major in English or take a single writing class besides L&R freshman year. I didn't join the newspaper because it seemed too intense and competitive and I hated my summer internship at *True* magazine and I barely had the energy to write the occasional letter to my best friend, though more often I'd write to my boyfriend, which turned out to be a colossal waste of ink since he stopped being my boyfriend long ago . . ."

"What's your major?" he interrupted.

"Psychology."

"Psychology?!" he blurted in disbelief. "*You* want to help sort out other people's mental health problems?"

I was not offended by this. "Honestly?" I asked, taking a furtive look around before I whispered the truth. "No! I don't!"

"Then what do you want to do after graduation?"

I shifted uneasily in my seat. "I'm still . . . uh . . . kind of figuring that one out . . ."

He grabbed at his curls. "Then why did you major in psychology?"

"I didn't really consider a career when picking a major," I said. "I wanted to learn about what makes people do the crazy things we do."

He leaned back in his chair and said, "Tch."

"You can say that again," I replied. (He didn't.)

I didn't want to waste any more of this important man's time. I was just about to get up to leave when he suddenly snapped to attention.

"What about your journal?"

"My journal?"

"Yes," he said. "Do you still keep a journal?"

"Uh . . . yeah." And I pulled this very tattered, black-and-white-speckled composition notebook out of my bag. Until he said it, I'd forgotten all about everything I'd documented in here, because I don't really think of this as serious writing.

"May I take a look?"

Mac had read another journal of mine, the one I was keeping when I was seventeen years old and attending SPECIAL. It was my journal, not anything I'd written for class, that had convinced him I had promise. (A promise I have, heretofore, unfulfilled.) But I didn't want him perusing my private thoughts this time around. These moments are my own. Fortunately, I had a substitute—I handed over a few loose pages that I'd stuffed in the back of the notebook and never bothered to remove.

"Read this instead."

"Persuasions: A Cheesy Slice of New Jersey in the Heart of Manhattan," he read. He cocked an eyebrow in bemusement. "I thought you said you hadn't written anything this year."

I shrugged sheepishly and didn't correct him. I'd written that piece two years ago.

For the next eternity or so, he read. He gasped. He moaned. He winced. Every few seconds, he'd mutter a phrase that I'd hardly remembered living, let alone writing about.

"'Homemade Bikini Contest.'"

"'Telekinetic titty-flexing.'"

"'No cushion for the pushin'.'"

And he laughed. And laughed. Oh, how he laughed at me. While I slowly died.

He put the pages down. "'I write entirely to find out what I'm thinking,'" he began. "'What I'm looking at, what I see and what it means. What I want and what I fear.' Joan Didion."

"Uh-huh."

"And I think," he said, tapping his fingers on his desk, "that if you do it well, you give others the opportunity to do the same."

"Uh . . . Sure."

"You would benefit from a more disciplined approach to your craft. You should take my advanced creative nonfiction class."

"But I don't have a writing portfolio!" I protested.

He waved the essay in the air. "This is the only portfolio I need to read, Ms. Darling."

"But I haven't taken any of the prerequisites."

"I can see to it that you get in, regardless of prerequisites."

"But . . ."

"You have the eye of a reporter and the heart of a novelist," he said. "But you have much to learn, Ms. Darling. I'll make sure that you don't throw away your gifts."

For someone like Mac to believe so deeply in my potential, well, it nearly made me weep with gratitude. Even now, I don't think he has a clue just how much his words have done for me. Mac instilled hope in me, and not only that I won't end up a

tragic waste of potential, but hope in general, which is something I've been sorely lacking for a long, long time. (In more
ways than one.)

"What are your thoughts?"

"My thoughts?" I replied, before I even realized what I was
saying. "My thoughts create my world."

Mac sat up in his seat. He scrunched his curls with his hands,
perplexed. "Who said that?"

I told him the truth.

"Oh, just someone I used to know," I said, stroking the naked
skin on my middle finger.

graduation
december 2005

Dear Hope,

No, I don't think it's strange that I was the first person you called when you lost your virginity to a person I didn't even know you were dating because we haven't talked or corresponded for almost a year and a half.

Do you think it's strange that the day you called, I was thinking about writing you again? I was thinking about writing you again because I bumped into an old friend who once mistook me for her best friend. Her name was Jane and you never met her and I intentionally never told you about her because I felt like I was cheating on you with her.

Jane and I resembled each other, shared clothes, had similar likes and dislikes, blahblahblah. Our friendship seemed so obvious that I tried to overlook how she was always judging me and trying to make me feel bad about anything she didn't approve of. The biggest one of these things was Marcus, and it was her exhilaration over our breakup that led to the demise of our friendship. This was an ironic turn of events because I reserved my own opinion about her asshole boyfriend for fear that it would have a similar outcome.

When I saw her today in the elevator, my first reaction was, "Oh my God, this is awkward." In three years we had somehow managed to avoid each other. But now, on one of my last days on campus, here we were together, trapped in an enclosed space for the interminable time it would take the creaky campus elevator to drop ten stories.

"Did you get back together with Marcus?" she asked.

"No," I replied.

She smiled. "See? I told you so."

And I could have let it go. But I didn't.

"Are you still with Jake?"

She frowned. "No," she said as the door finally opened. "He ended up being a total asshole."

"I didn't tell you so," I replied. "But I should have."

And I quickened my pace before I could get stuck inside the inevitable excruciating pause.

I realize now that our friendship didn't end because of Marcus or Jake. It ended because we weren't very good friends to each other. Period.

After Jane, I got to know a girl named Dexy, who was nothing like Jane or me. She was an exuberant spirit who made everything fun. If anyone, she reminded me of you, only without most of your depth or artistry. I never thought that we would be anything more than hangout, superficial friends. That is, until she had a nervous breakdown and never came back to school. I miss her more than I ever would have expected. But my reunion with you—the one that's happening between us right now with these very words—makes me hopeful that Dexy will return to my life when she's ready.

And then there's Bridget, who has been a part of my life since diapers, and whose positive presence I continually forget to appreciate until she's gone. But she too always comes back, and always when I can best benefit from her blond wisdom.

You, Hope, have always been a good friend to me. The best. I'm afraid I can't say the same, though I sincerely believed that removing myself from your life—not writing, not calling—was in your best interest. You've been so content these past three years and I've been...a mess. I didn't want to be responsible for fucking with your bliss, especially when it's so hard to come by in this world. Thank you for reminding me of a profound truth about all devoted relationships, be they romantic or platonic: We love each other because of our flaws, not in spite of them. They make us who we are.

I was terrified that I had ignored our friendship to the point of no return. I'm ecstatic to hear that such an end point doesn't exist. I'm glad you're back in my life, though in truth, you were never really gone. I can't wait to see you and begin our adventure. There's no one else I'd rather sit next to in a car for days and days on end.

Synchronically yours,
J.

the twentieth

December graduation is nothing if not anticlimactic. What a far cry from my high school graduation with all its pomp and circumstance and my big salutatorian speech about not wanting to change any of my crappy high school experiences because they all contributed to the content creature standing before them, the one boldly proclaiming that I was happy being me, yes me. Ha. It's easier to think you know it all when you don't know *anything* at all.

Ah, the beauty of being eighteen.

I have the option to walk in June, but I'll probably skip it. I can't afford the cap and gown anyway. To make up for the lack of ceremony, my friends splurged on a champagne brunch send-off. It was quite touching, actually. A very mixed crowd was in attendance, one that reflected the randomness of my three and a half years at Columbia University. Dexy shocked the hell out of me by showing up in full Catholic schoolgirl regalia, perhaps as a nod to the end of my education (or more likely because it made her look really hot). Tanu, Kazuko, and even ALF were there, representing the Winter of Our Discontents. Percy and Bridget were there, representing my Pineville roots. Paul and Hy were there, representing people I didn't know cared. Bethany and Marin came, representing blood love. Even Mac came, representing what I hope is my promising future.

I egotistically insisted that no one could be depressed about my departure. We joked about how I'm unemployed a full six months ahead of my classmates. Maybe I'll contact one of Mac's editor friends and beg him for a lower-than-entry-level job that will make my turn at *True* seem like the literary high life. Maybe I'll throw financial caution to the wind and apply to journalism school, or I'll miraculously develop a sense of empathy for my fellow man and get a PhD in psychology. Perhaps I'll be more practical and enroll in a correspondence school for gun repair. Whatever I decide to do, Mac assures me that I made the right decision in devoting myself to the study of the mind instead of the almighty dollar. After all, college life is so short—even shorter for me—and professional life is sooooo long.

"'This is not the end, not even the beginning of the end,'" Mac said, raising his glass. "'But perhaps it is the end of the beginning.'"

I leapt out of my chair. "Churchill!" I bellowed, blowing everyone's hair back. "Winston Churchill! I did it! I got one! I rock!"

I high-fived everyone at the table and they all indulged me by cracking up.

It seemed fitting that this was the first time I'd actually known the original source of one of Mac's quotations, because it was exactly what I needed to hear. Sure, my future is uncertain. But isn't it always? So I figured, Why worry about it right now, when I've got champagne fizzing in my glass and friends at my side?

We spent the morning happily. Hy promised Bridget a private screening of *Bubblegum Bimbos* to prove that she had done a great service in not casting the ex-actress formerly known as Bridge

Milhouse in the meta-role of Gidget Popovich because the movie really, *really* blew. ALF and Percy made plans to get together for gaming. Kazuko admired Dexy's outfit—very Goth Loli—and Dexy reciprocated with her admiration of Kazuko's cameo brooch—was it vintage or a convincing copy? Tanu asked Bethany if she would be willing to be interviewed for her thesis, titled "The 'Yummy' Effect: How the 'Hip' Urban Parent Paradigm Defines the Character of a Community." Paul leaned in, almost forehead to forehead with Mac, and grumbled about the religious right's latest efforts to "out" SpongeBob SquarePants. And Marin counted from one to ten *en español* as taught to her by her part-time nanny—otherwise known as yours truly—for everyone and no one at once.

And I—Jessica Darling!—was the silent heart giving life to these connections.

My optimism didn't fade until I got on the bus to Pineville. After so much social activity, I craved solitude, and on this bus I was never going to be alone. My duffel smacked the shoulders of row after row of aisle-sitters and I had trouble finding two side-by-side empty seats. I planned to sprawl across the first unoccupied spot and feign a narcoleptic sleep attack so no one would sit next to me. But it looked like I wasn't going to find the solitude I sought, so I searched for a passenger so absorbed in a book that any chitchat would be a nuisance. I thought I'd found her in the form of an after-school-with-milk-and-cookies mom midway through a paperback copy of *The Five People You Meet in Heaven*.

I ungracefully hurled my bags into the overhead and slumped into the orange vinyl seat. I reached into my pocket for my package of tissues, but only found cardboard covered in the plastic Kleenex wrapper. I resigned myself to sniffling for the trip back to New Jersey. I was sleeve-wiping tears and mucus from my face when my neighbor put *The Five People* . . . down on her lap.

"Are you a student?" she asked in a familiar New Yawk accent. I nodded and tried to remember which bag carried my iPod. She then asked me what school I attended. I inhaled as deeply as I could before answering.

"Oh!" she bubbled. "Great school."

I was extremely disappointed in her. She wasn't what I expected. Before I could plug myself into iPod isolation, she asked another question.

"So," she sang. "What year are you?"

"Actually, I just graduated," I said.

"You did? In December?"

"Yeah," I said.

Her eyes widened with this revelation. "So that's why you're so teary-eyed." She unconsciously ran her thumb along the pages she had yet to read. I hunched up my shoulders in a halfhearted shrug.

"Don't be sad," she said, gently but firmly enough not to go ignored. "The people who really matter, you'll see them again."

I looked past her profile and out the window. I needed to leave. I was tired of staring at the same concrete.

the twenty-first

Perhaps inspired by Hope's infectious spirit of adventure, I'm making a more concerted effort to bust my ruts, one rut at a time. And so, when Bridget called to say she had some big news, I suggested that we meet not at my house, or hers, or Helga's Diner, but Cool Beanery, a tiny, homey coffee and tea shop in downtown Pineville that I've never patronized because I've got an aversion to suburban java joints that try too hard to be hip and Manhattanlike. And you know, I'll be damned if they didn't serve up a bracingly nutty cup of black coffee. It will be a more than adequate hangout when I'm in town (which I'm sure will be more often than I'd like to admit).

Anyway, the dramatic change in setting was appropriate. Bridget broke her dazzling news before she even sat or shrugged off her coat, one of those heinous quilted numbers that look more like a sleeping bag than an article of clothing. But not even the ugly coat could dim her glow.

"Percy and I are getting married!" she squealed, stripping off her left-hand glove and shoving a diamond solitaire up my nostril.

And then I initiated what must have been the most girly girl display of my life, complete with hop-hugging, cheer-clapping, and teeth-shattering shrieks of joy.

"Not until June 2007," Bridget giggled, answering my unasked question. "After we both graduate. Can you believe it?"

"I can!" I gushed right back. "But I can't! It's so weird!"

"I know!" she bubbled, still bopping up and down. "I know!"

And then she told me the whole story. How Percy bought tickets for a local high school performance of *Our Town*. It was a very deliberate choice, as they had been cast in that same play when she was a junior and he was a sophomore in high school, and it was during rehearsals for said production that they had started their showmance. When Bridget wasn't looking, he slipped a piece of paper in the playbill, like those often inserted when the understudy is playing the lead role for the evening. Only on this paper, Percy had printed Bridget's headshot, underneath which was typed: *And tonight, and for the rest of her life, the role of Mrs. Percy Floyd will be played by Bridget Milhokovich.*

And when she read it she was, like, "Huh?" until Percy knelt down in the aisle and presented her with a velvet ring box containing the Floyd family engagement ring, passed down from none other than Grandma Floyd herself for the occasion.

It was a great story. And I could imagine Bridget telling it again and again. For generations and generations to come.

"Look, I know it's, like, eighteen months away, and you're not, like, into marriage and everything but, like . . ."

"What?"

"I would be so honored if you'd be my maid of honor," she said.

It kind of reminded me of a few years back when Marin was getting christened and Bethany asked me to be her godmother. I told her I couldn't do it because I was an atheist and it would be totally hypocritical for me to stand up there and pretend that I would raise Marin as a child of God.

But this time I said yes before I let my mind get the better of my heart.

I'm not saying that this news has totally transformed my notion of marriage. It makes no sense for them to get engaged so young, especially when they've got more than a year of school left. It makes no sense at all. But I just am so happy for Bridget and Percy that I want their commitment to make perfect sense. I want to believe in forever and destiny and, most of all, love.

They make me believe in love.

the twenty-fifth

I n my younger days, I would have begun this entry with a string of exclamation points. But I'm too old for that sort of thing now.

Unfortunately, now that I'm stripped of this youthful shorthand, I'm finding it impossible to express what I'm feeling.

Oh, fuck it.

!!

There's only one event that could make me so willing to regress. And that's what happened on this holy holiday:

The one-man phenomenon called Marcus Flutie returned to me.

"Merry Christmas," he said when I opened the door.

He was dressed in a wool cap, jeans, a black hand-knit sweater, and his old peacoat. He looked remarkably like a lot of twenty-something guys. No shirt-jacket-and-tie-goody-goody honors uniform. No snarky days-of-the-week T-shirts. No Buddhist pajamas. No gay cowboy chaps. The outfit was refreshing because it signified absolutely nothing.

And as bizarre as it sounds after his two years of absence, the sight of him under my parents' portico, one he'd never before stood beneath, didn't seem strange at all. It felt as if all the times I had opened the door to someone else were the aberrations. This—him—was the norm. He was always supposed to be there.

"Merry Christmas?" he repeated, this time more of a question.

He was beautiful. Glowing from within, a human luminaria on my doorstep. Whatever he's been looking for all these years, he must have found it. Lucky him. But his hands jingle-jangled in his pockets, betraying a nervousness that reminded me of something rather important: I shouldn't be so happy to see him.

"In or out, Jessie!" my dad shouted from the living room.

Was I in? Or was I out?

I sprung open the coat closet, grabbed my parka, and shouted back, "I'm out!"

I could hear my mother asking, "With who?" as I slammed the door behind me.

We walked toward the Caddie, which was parked by the curb. I shook my head in disbelief. Who would have thought this fossil burner would outlast our relationship? I tugged the stubborn door handle, then slipped into the passenger side. The springs under the leather creaked under my weight. Marcus slid behind the wheel, smiling to himself as he turned the key in the ignition. As the engine sputtered to life, and hot air blasted from the dashboard, I realized that I still hadn't said a word to him.

"MERRY CHRISTMAS," I shouted over the noise from the heater. This made Marcus laugh. His was a genuine laugh, full and deep in the belly, one that sounded exactly as I had remembered. Hearing it made me laugh too, even though I wasn't sure why.

"I thought you were supposed to stay in the desert until next spring," I said.

"I decided to leave early," he replied. "I learned all I needed to learn."

"So the whole silent meditation Buddhist thing, you're over that?"

"Well, clearly," he said. "I'm talking to you, aren't I?"

"Are you?" I asked, with a little edge to my voice.

"I am," he said. I turned to the window to avoid his laserlike gaze. My parents were gawking from the front door. We were still idling in the street, and I resisted the urge to ask him to take me away.

"And you're through with being a lonely cowboy?"

You'll notice how I replaced "gay" with "lonely." I wasn't out for blood. Yet.

"I'm over it," he replied. "It was a phase. One I needed to go through to get away from my other . . ." He placed his hands on top of his head, as if to reach in and pull out the answer. "Less healthy phases."

Should I be so surprised that Marcus needed to disappear for a while so he could get his head together? Haven't I also dropped out of my own life on occasion? And others' lives—like Hope's—when I didn't feel like I could live up to what I thought she deserved as a person? As a friend?

And yet, I couldn't bring myself to be quite so forgiving.

"A phase," I said archly, wringing my cold hands together. "I never thought that Marcus Flutie would still need to go through a phase."

"Well, when you think of it, isn't *everything* a phase?" he asked.

"How so?" I asked, unwilling to let on how I'd come to a similar conclusion in his absence.

He pulled off his wool cap, then stuck his long, roughened fingers into the twisted, matted clumps coming out of his scalp. His hair was a dark, dirty red, and back to the messy tangles he had when we first met. I guessed this had less to do with fashion than it did with a lack of hair-grooming products out in the desert.

"Nothing lasts forever, so everything is a phase," he said. "Some phases are just longer than others."

As casually as possible, I flicked the palm tree deodorizer still hanging from the rearview. "So what phase are you in right now?"

"A friendship phase."

I let this sink in before responding.

"You think we can be friends?" I asked. "We've never been friends."

After a slow start, I was gaining momentum. He's come back because he wants to be friends. Well, isn't that convenient for him? Coming and going whenever and however he pleases, defining our relationship on his own terms, leaving me fucked up and confused for years . . .

I suddenly had a lot to get out of my system.

"A friend, dear Marcus, would have had the decency to officially break up with me. A friend wouldn't pull what you did with those postcards." Between the heater and the intensity of my feelings, I was boiling. "What was that all about anyway? I mean, really. If you had something to say to me, why didn't you just say it? Or write a real letter or email like a normal person would?" I had imagined giving this speech so many times that the words flew out fluidly. "Don't you think you're getting a little old for these antics? Like, it's not enough for you to take a break from our relationship, you have to go on a yearlong *silent meditation.*

And it's not enough for you to give yourself some space, you have to go to goddamn *Death Valley*. Next thing you know, you'll decide it's not enough to take a vow of celibacy, you'll have to castrate yourself with a ceremonial sword carved out of strawberry Jell-O!"

This made him laugh, even though I hadn't envisioned a humorous reaction.

"I mean it, Marcus," I snapped. "It was cute and mysterious in high school, but now, now it's just . . ."

As I floundered for the right word, Marcus filled in with one of his own.

"Sorry," he said.

"It *is* sorry," I said.

"No, *I'm* sorry," he corrected. "I am who I am and I did what I did. I hope we can be friends again, which is why I'm here now. That's all I can say."

Then he reached around and grabbed a roundish package wrapped in red tissue paper that was sitting on the floor in the back seat. He handed it over to me, and the gift sat heavy in my lap.

"Open it," he urged, a hopeful expression on his face.

After a second or two of quiet contemplation, I dug my nails into the paper. And as I removed the wrapping, I couldn't quite believe what I held in my hands. Not even after I saw the blue jumpsuited image of the Showman of Our Time in all his decoupaged glory.

"Remember?" he asked.

Yes, I remembered. How could I forget the Barry Manilow toilet seat from three summers ago? This was precisely the kind of theatrics I was just talking about! A bazillion questions bounced off my brain: Who the hell does he think he is? What gives him the right to pull this sort of stunt on me? When did he decide to do this? Where did he find it? Why did he want to give it to me now? How was I going to respond?

Because I had no idea what to say next, I blurted out what is, quite possibly, the least appropriate thing I could say.

"I slept with Len!"

Despite his Zen leanings, I guess I expected Marcus to react with some measure of surprise. But I didn't get that satisfaction.

"Good for both of you," was all he said, but it wasn't with a trace of bitterness. He said it like he meant it, and his face meant it too.

I huffed beside him in my seat. "That's all you have to say?!"

He sighed before gingerly cupping my chin with his chapped hands. "Isn't this what got us in trouble before?"

He was right. Hadn't I learned anything in two years? Or, more to the point, was this a warning sign that Marcus and I were fated to repeat the same mistakes over and over and over again?

I recoiled from his touch. I wasn't ready for this. Not at all.

"It's *exactly* what got us in trouble before."

And without another word, I yanked on the door handle and left him and the toilet seat cover in the car.

Marcus idled in the road for a few minutes before slowly pulling out and into the frigid darkness. I know this because I watched him from my unlit bedroom window. I guess I wasn't quite ready to take my eyes off him.

the twenty-sixth

Last night I was kept awake by questions:

Why Marcus?

Why did I get over Kieran so quickly? Why am I not mad for Len, who is as smart and sensitive as Kieran pretended to be? Why am I not still pining for Scotty, the first boy to kiss me? Or William, whose death promises that there will never be a cathartic resolution to what could have been? Or Bastian, who might have loved me like a real man—if only for one night? Or Cal, whom I'd all but forgotten until I saw him at the anniversary party? Why not any other man whose life has overlapped mine?

Why Marcus?

Why?

The answer to all these questions was waiting for me in the mailbox this afternoon. A postcard from the National Organization of Women. On the back, one more word.

Jessica—
NOW
—Marcus

the twenty-seventh

Not long after "right now," Marcus and I shared the most sublime sex of our lives. It was utterly transcendent and confused the senses. I tasted his sighs. I was tickled by the salt in his sweat. I saw every microscopic cell in our one united body expanding and contracting in pleasure.

"Are you happy?" he asked.

"Yes," I whispered. "Yes. Yes."

"I love hearing you say that."

"I love you."

I have only said these words to Marcus. And I almost got sad, trying to remember the last time I uttered them. But before I gave in to regret, I reached up and grabbed the leather string he was wearing around his neck. On it hung several charms—a piece of soapstone carved in the shape of a horse, a Native American arrowhead, a small silver ring. I inspected the last closely and read aloud the words I knew were etched on the outside: *My thoughts create my world.*

"How did you know that I'd take you back after all this time?" I asked, sticking my middle finger through the ring and caressing the delicate flesh at the base of his throat. "When I didn't know it myself until after I saw you?"

"I had to take that chance," he said, the words vibrating through his skin and buzzing my fingertip. "The only way our relationship would be worth having is if you knew what you were missing without it."

When he said that, I was reminded of that time I came home for Christmas break and my mom had put my most treasured possessions in storage. I remember her, then me, questioning their importance. If they were *really* that significant, I would have brought them with me to school, right? I remembered poring over these items—the "Fall" poem on its deeply creased piece of notebook paper, the mosaic portrait Hope gave me right before she moved—wondering why I had left them behind, and wondering if the relationships that these things represented would be in better shape if I hadn't. But I realize now that if I *had* brought those things with me, if I had surrounded myself with them every day, they would have gradually been downgraded to nothing special, until there was little difference between a once-cherished memory and the light switch. The only way to truly appreciate something's value is to distance yourself from it for a while.

I WISH OUR LOVE WAS RIGHT NOW.

It is. It *is*.

I kissed him until I heard the tiny hairs prickling on his belly.

"You must be a long phase for me, Marcus Flutie."

"The longest, Jessica Darling," he replied.

Yes. Love has the longest arms.

the thirty-first

Hope and I are about to embark on the most haphazard cross-country trip in history.

"Can you believe it's been six years since I moved?" Hope asks as she inspects our bag of backseat snacks. Fun-sized Baby Ruths. KC Masterpiece Baked Lay's. Sour Patch Kids.

"Yes and no," I say, rummaging through my duffel for my sunglasses. I can't start this road trip–cum–senior thesis without them. Who cares if it's December and the sun can barely be detected in the dull sky? I've always imagined embarking on a cross-country trip with sunglasses. "Sometimes, when I think about six years ago, it feels more vivid, more real than all the stuff in between."

"I totally know what you mean," she says, throwing the last of the bags into the trunk.

This trip started as a joke, as most things between us do. In one of our last phone calls before she left for France and we lost touch, Hope reminded me how she's always been fascinated by a particular road sign en route to her cousins' house.

"Can you believe there's a place called Toad Suck, Arkansas, and people actually live there?"

A paper-dodging, time-wasting Google search quickly revealed that Toad Suck was in bad company. Monkey's Eyebrow, Kentucky. Nipple, Utah. Satan's Kingdom, Massachusetts. There were just too many ridiculously named towns out there. Pennsylvania alone was host to Muff, Blue Ball, and Dick.

"I wouldn't mind telling people I'm from Hell, Missouri," I said.

"I'm feeling very Uncertain, Texas, myself," Hope replied. "But I'd like to be Yeehaw Junction, Florida."

Thus, her senior project, "Mental States: A Cross-Country Tour of My Emotions," was born. For the next month, Hope will take self-portraits next to appropriately expressive town names and use the photos in some sort of multimedia installation that she has yet to devise. She not only convinced her department head to give her class credit for the trip, but somehow got the school to subsidize most of it in some work-study agreement that only Hope could wrangle. When she asked me to ride shotgun a few weeks ago, I didn't hesitate.

"Thank you, Rhode Island School of Design!" she says now, lifting her Coke can to the sky before popping its top.

"Thank you, Mr. and Mrs. Darling, for refusing to pay my tuition and making this trip possible!" I reply in kind, actually meaning every word.

"To Virginville, Pennsylvania!" Hope whoops.

"To Virginville!"

And then a voice says, "I'm not sure you two will make it past the Virginville border patrol."

I turn to see Marcus standing in front of me, holding a red box.

"I thought you didn't want to say goodbye," I say.

"I still don't," Marcus says. "I'm not here to say goodbye. I have a going-away gift."

"You already gave me a going-away gift," I reply, gesturing toward the Barry Manilow toilet seat that we've propped on top of our bags in the backseat. Hope has deemed it our good luck traveling talisman.

"That was a coming-home gift," he explains. "This is a going-away gift." And then he hands me a raw silk box meant for holding photos. It's heavier than I had expected. I don't realize that I'm just standing there staring until he says, "Open it."

I do what I'm told. Inside are at least a dozen black-and-white-speckled composition notebooks exactly like the one I'm writing in right now.

At first, I think, How did you get my journals? But then I notice that the spaces reserved for name, school, and grade have been left blank, where on my notebooks they have all been inscribed with the start and end dates of the contents within.

I open one. These aren't my journals . . . They're *his*.

This realization makes me sink to the curb with the box between my knees.

He sits next to me and says, "I was wrong the other night in the car when I told you that I had said all I could say."

I read the first page of the journal on top. There's no date. But the first line is addressed in a very specific way: *My dear Jessica* . . .

And then pages and pages and pages of words, words, words . . . everything Marcus couldn't say to me over the past two years but wants me to know.

"You're always going to pull stuff like this, aren't you?"

"Yes."

"Even though it drives me insane."

He shrugs. "It's who I am, Jessica. It's part of my charm. You wouldn't want me any other way."

And I know he's right.

I almost can't believe I'm going to make myself vulnerable to him again. But what is love but the most extreme and exquisite form of risk perception? I know that relationships don't last. And yet, with Marcus, the risk of not being with him is much worse than any other hurt I can imagine.

Marcus's gaze is fixed on the grass. His face is partially obscured, but I can see his dented brow. And he's tapping his feet in a twitchy, arrhythmic way. And I think, I'm making Marcus Flutie nervous.

"Will you still be here when I get back?" I ask.

He looks up. The frown fades and a smile arrives in its place, one that starts at his mouth but really comes out through this eyes. It's a sincere, unsullied smile.

"I want to be."

And that's when I stand up, lean in, and kiss him. I kiss him because I know exactly what he means, as much as such knowledge is even possible between two people. Marcus *wants* to be here when I get back, but he's not promising that he will. All promises are true only until they aren't, and I appreciate his honesty.

"You've changed," I seethed right before he left me that winter, nearly two years ago. And yes, Marcus *had* changed, but that was my problem, not his. A relationship ends because you've outgrown it. It can begin again because you, as two, can fill the new shape.

I thought Marcus was going to be in my life forever. Then I thought I was wrong. Now he's back. But this time I know what's certain: Marcus will be gone again, and back again and again and again because nothing is permanent. Especially people.

Strangers become friends. Friends become lovers. Lovers become strangers. Strangers become friends once more, and over and over. Tomorrow, next week, fifty years from now, I know I'll get another one-word postcard from Marcus, because this one doesn't have a period signifying the end of the sentence.

Or the end of anything at all.

Marcus,
AND
Love, Jessica

a note from the author

Not many writers are rewarded with a reintroduction of their work to a whole new audience. Even fewer get the opportunity to address—and redress—their past mistakes.

It's fitting, actually. *Sloppy Firsts*—and the four books that follow—are all about making mistakes. As an author, it was vital to me for Jessica Darling to discover herself through trial and many, many errors. Countless readers have thanked me for creating an imperfect protagonist. Her numerous flaws, they tell me, are what make her recognizable and relatable. Fundamentally, Jessica Darling is good at heart. Yet that doesn't stop her from being snarky, self-absorbed, and—within the safe pages of her private journal—very, very judgmental.

Also very, very funny.

All five books were put out by an adult publisher, not young adult. In 2001, books for teens were still lumped together with children's titles. I knew that category was not appropriate for what I wanted to write, both in tone and content. This series was always intended for a crossover audience of older teens experiencing the daily indignities of adolescence and early adulthood, as well as nostalgic older readers who had graduated long ago. That choice provided freedom and flexibility to push boundaries in ways that would not have been possible at an imprint targeted to a younger audience.

Jessica's candid, caustic observations are written for laughs. And thankfully, her sarcastic takes on her classmates, crushes, and Y2K culture are as humorous now as they were back then. Except when they aren't. Imperfect people say and do imperfect things. And they hopefully learn from their blunders. I'm not referring to my fictional characters anymore. I'm talking about myself.

I wrote these books in real time. I was intentionally specific in the use of language and pop-cultural references (even the made-up ones) knowing they would date the series. Why? I hoped my work would ultimately serve as a sort of time capsule: *This* is what it was like for a young woman to come of age in the first decade of the new millennium. However, not all attitudes that were acceptable in 2001 should be tolerated today. And artifactual accuracy is no excuse for perpetuating potentially harmful stereotypes.

For that reason, I've worked with my team at Wednesday Books to make changes to the original text to reflect these more inclusive, diverse, and progressive times. This is a conscious decision to evolve in a manner that stays true to the spirit and integrity of the story. If we've done our jobs well, readers won't notice and certainly won't miss what we've removed.

So much has changed in the twenty years since *Sloppy Firsts* debuted. But the messiness of Jessica's journey into adulthood is timeless. She's both an outsider and an insider, wise beyond her years but exquisitely inexperienced in the ways of the world. I am so thrilled for this current generation of teens to see themselves— and others—in her story.

acknowledgments

My agent, Heather Schroder, for always telling the truth and having better judgment than I do.

My editor, Sara Goodman, for believing Jessica's story is just as relevant now as it was twenty years ago. And the Wednesday Books team—including Jennie Conway, Meghan Harrington, Alexis Neuville, Melanie Sanders, Christa Désir, Michelle Li, Devan Norman, Gail Friedman, Olga Grlic, and Kerri Resnick—for putting your great and varied talents to work in bringing this series to a new generation.

Rebecca Serle, for writing an introduction that brought me to tears.

My readers, without whom this anniversary edition wouldn't exist.

CJM, for reminding me why high school is such a rich source of material.

And finally, Christopher, still my husband and best friend, for making me laugh more days than not.

about the author

© Chiara Gold Photos

MEGAN McCAFFERTY writes fiction for tweens, teens, and teens-at-heart of all ages. The author of several novels, she's best known for *Sloppy Firsts* and several more books in the *New York Times* bestselling Jessica Darling series. Described in her first review as "Judy Blume meets Dorothy Parker" (*Wall Street Journal*), she's been trying to live up to that high standard ever since.

MODERN CLASSICS

for a new generation of Jessica Darling fans!

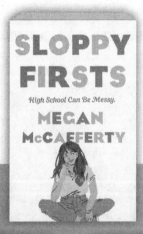

SLOPPY FIRSTS
High School Can Be Messy.
MEGAN McCAFFERTY

SECOND HELPINGS
Jessica Darling Is "So" Over Senior Year.
MEGAN McCAFFERTY

CHARMED THIRDS
New City. New Life. New Jessica.
MEGAN McCAFFERTY

FOURTH COMINGS
Jessica Darling "Thought" She Was Ready to Be an Adult.
MEGAN McCAFFERTY

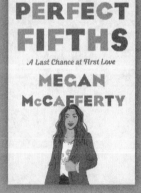

PERFECT FIFTHS
A Last Chance at First Love
MEGAN McCAFFERTY

ON SALE 11/2/21

ON SALE 1/18/22

"Judy Blume meets Dorothy Parker."
—*The Wall Street Journal*